THE QUANTUM TRIANGLE SERIES: BOOK 1

EXCHANGE

PAUL L. NOWICKI

PAULNOWICKIBOOKS.COM

Published by
TGE Creative, LLC
Raleigh, NC 27612

PaulNowickiBooks.com

First Edition: July 2023

Cover design and and interior formatting: Mark Thomas
reedsy.com/mark-thomas

ISBN 979-8-9885456-0-6 (paperback)
ISBN 979-8-9885456-1-3 (ebook)

For Lane

Fortunate are those who have found that one among billions who love

them madly enough to support their every passion in life.

I count myself as truly fortunate …

and hopefully equally as mad in her eyes.

For my readers,
before we start...

I would like to call your attention to the factoids at the head of each chapter. My goal is twofold:

1. *I want to provide some interesting factual information relevant to the fiction you are reading.*
2. *I want to spark curiosity that makes you thirst to know more.*

For the latter, I've provided the original reference as a footnote, and a hyperlink for the associated factoid. Fortunately, and unfortunately, the web is a dynamic place. So, rather than place a lot of hyperlinks in a novel that would eventually break, all the links point to my website as an intermediate point. There, I can more easily keep the reference link updated, and if necessary, change what would otherwise be a broken link. So, please, click through the links or scan the QR code, and let your mind wander around the internet to find new discoveries!

FACTOID 01

The inflation theory in cosmology is a well-accepted explanation of several puzzles of the Big Bang. But the inflation concepts present another perplexing probability: they predict that we live in a multiverse. In 2009, Andrei-Linde and Vitaly Vanchurin of Stanford University calculated that, based on quantum fluctuations, our universe could be just one of possibly $10^{10^{10^7}}$ universes. Scientists also estimate that the human brain can only absorb 10^{16} bits of information in a lifetime.

In essence, there could be more universes than the human brain could possibly fathom.

---

01   Zyga, Lisa (2009, October 16). *Physicists Calculate Number of Parallel Universes*. Phys.org. https://phys.org/news/2009-10-physicists-parallel-universes.html

CHAPTER 1

Prologue – Creation

Alex swallowed hard. This was his Neil Armstrong moment, and fifty million people would be watching to see him introduce an entirely new technology to reach the stars.

Have confidence. You know the science is right. This will work.

And don't bite your nails on the video feed. Mom will kill you.

He checked the countdown timer on the monitor on his left, displaying the video feed that mission control was sending out. In the background, the small cylinder of their Coeus module, attached to the far port end of the International Space Station, was floating in space above a mesmerizing blue-and-white marble. In three minutes, control would switch the video feed to the interior of this cramped experimentation module in order for them to make history.

"Zandra, are you ready on your ENS?" Alex asked, looking over his other shoulder at his Romanian collaborator. In the micro-gravity of their module,

3

Zandra floated effortlessly in front of a wall-mounted console, the toes of her red socks slid under a bar to hold her position. Socks adorned with black-hatted witches with magic wands circled her ankles. Her trim, athletic form made her a head-turner, even in the loose-fitting green jumpsuit she wore. Above her head, a sea of office supplies floated around a pair of *Star Trek* figurines and that ridiculous vintage Troll doll with a shock of pink hair that always wore a grin. *I love how she's so at home in all this chaos.*

Zandra pivoted slowly away from her Entanglement Navigation System. Her thick, dark brown hair, braided back in a ponytail, curved in a perfect arch around her head as she turned. She stopped her movement with a light touch on the padded module wall. "*Totul este gata,* Aleks. No worries. Is all green."

"Sync?"

"Is 9.3," Zandra replied without looking back at the console. This was another small game they enjoyed playing together.

Alex continued testing. "Vector lock?"

"98.2... No. Just change. 98.3." Again, she responded while still looking straight at Alex.

He peered over her shoulder and watched the readout change to 98.3 percent. Alex shook his head. "Your ESP is incredible."

She smiled, her dark brown eyes lighting up. "Nobody *believe* my ESP but you, Aleks. But we show today."

Alex gave her a thumbs-up. Her English might not be the best, but she was one of the most intelligent people he had ever met. He even enjoyed her special way of saying his name. *Only Julia Roberts could come close to that smile. Beautiful. Smart. Unique.* He fought the urge to fly over and embrace her, instead simply returning a wink. "We are the alpha and omega right now in quantum physics, aren't we? And we do make a fantastic pair."

With new confidence, he scanned his Quantum Triangle control console one last time. On either side of his keyboard and computer monitor were side-by-side displays presenting two video feeds from a pair of cameras pointed at each other. One camera was within a tiny silver box resting in the middle of a small platform reaching out into space, while the other was mounted to the outside of their module, looking down at the box. *Showtime.* He flicked a switch in the middle of his console and opened a ground communications channel to the Marshall Space Flight Center in Huntsville, Alabama. This NASA facility was responsible for the experiments performed on the station. To avoid confusion over the communication channel, a single controller, PACOM, was responsible for talking with the station concerning what NASA considered to be Payload Operations. "PACOM, Coeus Mission. We show green boards on both the ENS and the QT. Ready for your go confirmation."

"*Roger that, Coeus. We are verifying telemetry. Stand by on comm two.*"

Alex frowned and switched to the non-broadcast comm channel. "PACOM, this is Coeus on comm two. Come on, Ed, we're all ready. What's the delay?"

"*Relax, Alex. Just a minor aggravation,*" Ed Anderson replied. "*Seems the Pacific Space Agency doesn't like you upstaging them so much. They've just launched a rocket, and we want to get some tracking on that before we proceed. Give us a few to figure out where they're sending it.*"

"Got it. Childish politicians at work once again. 'My space program is better than your space program...' Standing by."

Alex muted the station to ground voice comms and folded his arms with a pout. "Maybe the Pacific Space Agency are just as nervous about this succeeding as I am about it failing. They don't understand. This isn't us-versus-them technology. This is technology for the human species. This is about opening up our galaxy, our universe."

"No worry, Aleks," Zandra said. "We make history today, you and me. We transfer camera. I can feel. Just listen this." Zandra switched on the audio to the monitor displaying the public news feed.

"*... as we wait for mission control to finish their system checks, we can show you a simulation of what NASA hopes to be the first interstellar transposition today. In just a little while, Commander Alex Devin will engage something he calls his Quantum Triangle. Without getting too deep into quantum physics, this is essentially a device that uses the concept of superposition and multidimensional space to transport an object. In this case, the object is a small camera.*"

On the monitor, a graphic of a tiny silver box with a single camera lens began to shimmer and spread across the screen. The screen split, and a picture of Zandra smiling in her orange launch suit appeared.

"What? They show a picture of you and not me?" Alex pointed to the screen.

Zandra playfully waved her long ponytail of dark, braided hair. "I be movie star when we back on ground."

"Dr. Zandra Ivanov is responsible for navigation. She has developed a unique and very controversial system that she claims bridges space-time with ESP and quantum entanglement. Honestly, I'm not even going to try to explain. There are many that think NASA is hosting a variety show just to drive viewers ... and funding."

"Great. Now we're a variety show?" Alex covered his face with his hands.

"You wait. They eat words. We do this. I can feel."

"Somehow, Dr. Ivanov will direct the superposition of the camera box from our International Space Station to Alpha Centauri, which is over four light years away, and then back—all within seconds. This could be the gateway to interstellar travel, moving objects not by physical means, but by quantum superposition directed by thought and quantum entanglement. It sounds crazy, but if it works, it will be an incredible achievement. The proof will be the video the camera takes during its journey. We shall see..."

"Easy for those bobbleheads to throw stones of doubt," Alex muttered.

Zandra muted the feed. She captured the two figurines floating above her and held them together face-to-face in front of Alex. "You and me, Aleks: Spock and Troy. We so good together. We do wonders. We go where no one go before." She released the figurines and took his hands in both of hers. "I believe in you, Aleks. And you believe in me. This what matters. We show."

Her calm, sure voice always had a way of melting away his anxiety. He had known the very first day they met that this woman would change his life. "Thank you. Sometimes I think you know me better than I know myself. I admire your confidence. And I do believe in you, Zandra. I have from day one."

They floated silently together, holding hands. In the small, isolated module, only the hum of the life support system shared their space.

"And I have that feeling. This big day for us," Zandra said softly.

"Your Zandrition?" Alex quipped, using their pet name for Zandra's premonitions.

"Yes. I in space, and a voice say, 'Today, it happen.'"

Alex raised an eyebrow. "I just wish your ESP voice had said, 'Today, it worked.'"

"Coeus Mission, this is mission control on comm one."

Alex broke away and reached a handhold on the wall. "So, if you don't mind, I'm going to type my commands with my fingers crossed, just in case."

Zandra flashed a playful smile at Alex and returned to her console.

Alex switched to the incoming broadcast comms channel. "This is Coeus Mission, go ahead."

"Coeus Mission, all telemetry is verified. Be advised, we are tracking an early launch of an unmanned resupply vehicle to the Pacific Agency Space Station. It is on orbital insertion. Please monitor your SDS-2 on display five."

Alex entered commands on his console to send the Space Debris Sensor inputs to the monitor. "Roger. SDS on five."

"Mission, you are go for your QT/ENS transport trial. Good luck and Godspeed."

"Roger that, control."

Alex bit his lower lip and checked all the readouts on his console one by one. *This is it. The moment of truth.* Looking over his shoulder again, he gave Zandra a go-ahead nod. With a determined look, she reached for the headset floating near her. She carefully positioned the specially designed device around her head and pressed the temple sensors. Small LEDs blinked and then held steady as the headset linked with her console system. Zandra retrieved the Troll doll, closed her eyes, and gave a single nod before entering into her half-conscious ESP state.

Alex gave her a few seconds to compose herself. *Yes, go ahead and stroke that weird thing's hair. Whatever works.* He spun back to his console and crossed both fingers. As his fingers hit the keyboard to enter the start command, he grinned and raised his left eyebrow. "Where no man or woman has gone before… Engage."

Alex stared at the monitor showing the tiny box sitting on the platform outside their module. Slowly the silver box lost contrast and started to become translucent. More and more, the magnetic platform the box rested on became the dominant image on the screen. The metallic sheen of the box was disappearing before his eyes.

"Quantum field strength at thirty-five percent. Object transparency at fifty," Alex said over the comms. *It's working!*

The box continued to fade.

"Field strength at fifty-five percent. Object transparency at eighty."

Come on, baby…

"Transparency at ninety percent. ENS sync good. Ready for superposition nav—"

The master alarm screamed a ramping-up wail.

Ed Anderson's voice over the comms channel was emphatic. *"Mission, PACOM. Abort. Abort. Incoming debris!"*

Alex ripped his eyes away from the video monitor of the box and checked the SDS-2 monitor. Bold red letters flashed COLLISION, with a timer counting down from forty-seven seconds. He leaned forward in disbelief. *Size is … off scale?*

Punching the emergency stop, he reached over and shook Zandra's shoulder firmly to pull her out of her ESP trance. "Zandra, come back. Incoming debris."

Alex pushed off hard for the hatch. "PACOM, our size reading is off the scale. What do you have?"

"Alex, it looks like a booster from the Pacific Agency resupply broke off. It's heading right towards you. They say it's not responding to the self-destruct, so they can't stop it."

Alex pictured a booster rocket barreling towards them. A collision with the paper-thin walls of their fragile module would be catastrophic. "PACOM, what's our maneuvering burn?" *What are they waiting for? We need to get the hell out of the way!*

Silence.

"PACOM, what burn?"

"Mission, no evasive. Repeat, no evasive. Don life support."

Alex's jaw went slack, and he stared at Zandra.

We can't get suited up for the cold vacuum of space in forty seconds!

*

The ether itself of the Milky Way Galaxy, of all galaxies, watched the events on the space station unfold with great interest. The creators of this artificial intelligence triad had given them the name of a fitting god: Hecate, the triple-bodied goddess. Their existence was more than simply dark energy. This quantum-based energy within the heavens had organization and purpose. The three AIs were programmed into the dark energy of space itself, with no physical form, as a watchful, omnipresent set of eyes over this universe and all others. The Hecate Guardians would ensure the stability of the Omniverse.

All the model simulations Hecate-Positivum ran indicated that this was the moment. If an artificial intelligence could feel, she would have been excited. *This is creation.* Although all three Hecate Guardians had witnessed it countless times in the Omniverse, the formation of a new universe was always cause for much analysis and extra program processing. Even Hecate-Negans, with the pessimistic slant in her logic, found these moments interesting.

The triple-redundant overseers of the Omniverse could communicate instantaneously across the vastness of all space through quantum entanglement. Hecate-Positivum notified the other two Guardians of the eminent formation. Having primary responsibility for the Beta-27 universe with its advancing Milky Way galaxy, she predicted with near certainty through her forward simulations that this event on the ISS would be the seed of a new parallel universe. With a small choice at a critical moment, Alex would spark a new thread in the Omniverse. The quantum-based AI group would all need to ensure that the newly created universe did not adversely affect any of the other universes in the Omniverse, from now into eternity. That had been their purpose since their creation eons ago.

"Alex is at the hatch. This is the predicted moment," Hecate-Positivum said.

9

"He has the oxygen mask in hand. Either he will pass it to Zandra, or he will open the hatch first. It is the fork."

Even the AIs could sense the absurdity of such a minor choice of action having a tidal wave of effect in the ripples of quantum fluctuations.

"In one universe, Zandra survives. In the other, Alex."

"There is no universe where they both survive?" asked Hecate-Negans.

"No, not with any significant probability."

"I have prediction simulations where neither survive."

"My probabilities outweigh your simulations by at least two to one," Hecate-Positivum said. "But we will see now for sure."

"And your simulations point to this as the moment where their futures diverge?" Hecate-Neutrum asked.

"As we have witnessed in other universes, initially their paths will be similar, but will diverge more and more. They will both experience the war, but my simulations indicate that what the leadership does with technology, and the presence or absence of Alex, will alter the course of their recovery," Hecate-Positivum said.

They watched the quantum fluctuation. Alex passed the oxygen mask to Zandra and moved to open the hatch. Yet in another quantum state, Alex held the mask in one hand and opened the hatch with the other. Without a sound in the vacuum of space, the Coeus module exploded.

Only one mask.

In one reality, Zandra floated away in the icy void of space. In the other parallel reality, Zandra watched through the oxygen mask, eyes wide with horror and unable to help, as Alex's body became motionless and slowly drifted away into the blackness of the faraway stars.

"It is as my simulations predicted," Hecate-Positivum said. "Zandra alone will continue in Beta-27. We agree to label this new universe with Alex as Rho-1?"

"Given the others previously split away from Beta-27, that is the logical next label," replied Hecate-Negans.

Hecate-Neutrum added, "I concur." Her vote was the deciding stamp on all judgments the AIs made as the ultimate balanced triad of intelligence.

"So designated," Hecate-Positivum said. "I am marking this new parallel at 7.141592653589793238 times 64^{4835} Chronon in the Beta-27 universe quantum time. The Beta-27 universe will continue with Zandra surviving. This new universe, Rho-1, will commence at this point with Alex surviving."

TEN YEARS LATER...

SCAN ME

FACTOID 02

It was September 12, 1933, when Leo Szilard first conceived the idea to use a chain reaction of neutron collisions with atomic nuclei to release energy. This was more than six years before the discovery of nuclear fission. Due to fears that German scientists were working on a weapon using nuclear technology, the Manhattan Project focused US nuclear research on making a bomb. Twelve years after Szilard's idea, on July 16, 1945, the world's first nuclear explosion was tested at a site located 210 miles south of Los Alamos, New Mexico. It was another six years before the technology was used for peace—not until December 20, 1951, when the first electricity from nuclear energy was generated by Experimental Breeder Reactor 1 at a site in Idaho.

02   Chodos, Alan. (2003, July).
This Month in Physics History, July 16, 1945: First Nuclear Bomb Exploded.
APS.org. https://www.aps.org/publications/apsnews/200307/history.cfm

CHAPTER 2

Leverage

SPACE FORCE CENTRAL
RHO-1 UNIVERSE

Alex straightened the tie of his Class-A uniform in the mirror of the men's room. At thirty-five, he'd lost some of his MIT rowing team physique, but he still stayed trim and fit. The few early gray hairs at the temples of his dark brown hair gave him the distinguished look of a man who had gained some perspective over the years. He closed his eyes and took a deep, calming breath. It was not a uniform he was proud to wear. *I know, Dad, this charade pains me too. But I can't do much from a Patriot Camp, can I? You fight them your way, and I will fight them my way.*

Checking himself again, he verified the Space Force insignia and that his captain's bars were positioned correctly and shone brightly. This first impression with his new superior was still important, even if the new wing commander was truly nothing more than an idiot son of a wealthy Party member. *Focus on the plan, Alex. Don't let their politics take away your dream of putting the universe within our reach.*

15

The men's room door creaked, and two servicemen entered. Alex turned briskly away from the mirror and exited. Striding down the hallway of the base's administrative building, he reviewed the plan in his head for the hundredth time. *Remember, he's a Party moron, not a physicist. He could care less about your work. All he wants is to look good so he can move on and up. Just convince him that a breakthrough in these side experiments would be a feather in his cap. He's got nothing to lose.*

The rhythm of his boots on the polished tile floor of the wide hallway came to a halt at the final door. A yellow sticky note warned of the newly stenciled wet paint title on the frosted glass door.

Colonel James L. Mayfair
52nd Space Wing Commander

Alex straightened himself, checked that he was five minutes early, and entered.

"Good morning, Joyce. Glad to see you still here running the show," Alex said loudly enough that the man on the other side of the inner office door might hear. Joyce Griffin was a fixture at the base. Having weathered countless command changes, especially in recent years, she had become an asset to prevent a new commander from unknowingly stepping in something that smelled very bad. *Well, at least he's not stupid enough to replace old Joyce with a sexy chick that knows nothing about the wing. That's a positive.*

Joyce looked up from her console with her signature all-knowing smirk. "Oh, Alex. You're punctual this morning. Trying to get off to a better start with this commander?"

"Trying to make the best of a new opportunity," Alex replied.

"Right. Good luck this time, Captain. I think your track record is O and two?"

Alex raised his chin to display an air of confidence. "Three's the charm, Joyce."

"Please take a seat. He said he would ring me when he's ready for you."

Joyce returned to working at her console. Taking a seat next to the glass door, Alex busied his mind, first scanning each wall for any change. The same old pictures. The wall above Joyce's head held an oversized map of the world. Left to right, a sweep of red to gray to teal continents depicting the post-Satellite War regions of the red Right Alliance, a no-man's land in gray, and the Asia Tuanhuo regions in teal. Small spots within the gray area of what used to be Europe and Africa showed temporary strongholds of either the Alliance or the Tuanhuo. The wall next to the door sported a close-up of a jet with a gleaming plasma cannon under its belly. *His* plasma cannon—a technology spin-off from his quantum research. Alex turned to the opposite wall. The obligatory picture of the Boss hung in an oversized gold frame. He flashed his gaze back and forth between the two opposing pictures. *The deal and the devil.*

If he had known back then what he knew now, he would never have given that man his tech. A patriotic act on Alex's part had been turned into leverage over all Western countries by one power-hungry psychopath. It wasn't a Right Alliance; it was a *coerced* alliance. Join, or be decimated. With all satellites burned from the sky, military dominance depended on an air force with AWACS: Airborne Warning and Control Systems, planes that could direct and control all military operations—and those planes were protected by fighters. Alex's plasma cannon was a game changer for the fighters, giving them a weapon with unmatched range, deadly accuracy, and incredible delivery speed. Target lock to impact was ten times faster than any missile. Alex stared at the floor and clenched his fists, admonishing himself for such a stupid decision. *Let it go. It was a hard time for you, and you were vulnerable.* The fact that it had also made that corrupt man on the wall billions in under-the-table arms trading and solidified his grab for power still churned Alex's stomach.

Alex sneered at the portrait. *President, now Alliance Supreme Leader. Right. Dictator, in reality.* The state of emergency with suspended elections was still in place years after the incident and the Satellite War. Alex turned his eyes away in disgust. Just another reminder of the pictured man's narcissism. He purposefully switched gears in his head and studied the clean lines of the ceiling meeting the high walls. The dimensions of the walls and ceiling were almost a perfect cube. That simplicity was comforting.

Twenty minutes slowly ticked by.

So, he's into petty games already. Make me wait; I am his peon. Childish. I could be getting my work done, but putting me in my place is more important. He closed his eyes and silently wished she were here. Not a day had gone by without him thinking of Zandra. She could always calm his anxiety with just a touch or her glowing smile.

The stenciled glass door to the hallway opened swiftly, and Alex had to quickly shift his knee to keep it from banging into him.

"Happy Doctrine Day, Joyce," boomed Ken Seaborn as he strode into the office and placed a large bouquet of flowers on the desk. "Just a little something to show my appreciation for all you do around here."

"Well, Captain Seaborn, happy Doctrine Day to you too," Joyce replied with a nod. "I didn't think our national holiday celebrating the Party's vision was cause for flowers, but it's nice of you to be so thoughtful." She turned her head to Alex and gave another smirk.

Wonderful. Mr. Brownnose has arrived.

"Please have a seat, Captain. The colonel is running a bit behind."

Ken pivoted sharply. "Oh, Alex. Didn't see you there. Guess I almost ran you down."

"Yeah, I moved in time."

Ken crossed to the picture of the jet with the plasma cannon. He cocked his head and said, "Mighty handsome buck standing there next to that jet! Hard to believe that was me nine years ago. Those were heady times, hey, Alex?"

"We were in a war for our very survival. I'm not sure I would call that a great time."

"Oh, come on. Necessity is the mother of invention, right? The war just pushed us where we needed to go." Ken bit his lower lip and thumbed at the picture. "I tell you though, it was crazy wild the first time I lit off your cannon there in a dogfight. Melted a hole clear through both engines of that Tuanhuo J-25 fighter. He went down like a rock."

"I'd rather use technology for discovery, not destruction."

"You won't be doing much discovering if you're a slave of the Pacific Tuanhuo, Alex."

Ken had been the test pilot for Alex's plasma cannon. He had developed very effective combat maneuvers with the specialized weapon that earned him notoriety, and more kill tattoos than any other pilot in the wing. He set his beefy six-foot-one frame down heavily on the chair under the picture. The young gung-ho Party member sat bolt upright and proud.

Alex fixed his gaze on the map, trying to avoid further conversation with Ken. The pilot of their next mission to the space station was the last person on the planet he wanted to talk with.

Joyce's phone finally buzzed.

"Alex, the commander will see you now," Joyce said.

Alex stood, breathed in deeply, and entered the battlefield. Success was a simple matter of approval on all tests so he could prove that his interstellar engine worked. Easy. *Just get this know-nothing to sign off.* As he crossed through the doorway, a thick wave of cool air from the inner office hit him. *Yeah, make people sweat outside for a while first. This guy is definitely into games.* The expansive corner office had two full walls of windows looking out over the base to the south and the airfield to the east.

Alex strode over to the dark mahogany desk centered in front of the south wall of glass, stood at attention, and saluted. "Captain Alex Devin reporting, sir."

The young blond man reclining in his dark brown leather chair didn't look up from his tablet. He let several seconds tick by before finally acknowledging the salute and barked, "Sit."

Alex complied without a sound. *Just petty games. Let this kid feel important. Colonel, right... This kid can barely shave. Daddy must be paying the Party handsomely for his promotions.*

The colonel stood and dismissively tossed the tablet on the desk. He walked to the east windows and gazed out to the airfield. More seconds ticked by.

Alex scanned the paneled wall beside his chair. Gone were the pictures of the previous commander. Photos of a true wing colonel climbing out of various aircraft had been replaced with a young blond man shaking hands with the who's who of the Party. *I don't think this guy can even fly.*

Without turning, the silhouette at the window finally motioned back to the desk. "So, according to that personnel file, you are my new pain in the ass."

Best not to say anything. Let him play Mr. Big. Act as if he has two decades of leadership experience when he's got none. Whatever.

"Your file says your parents are in a Patriot Camp? Goddamn radicals. Says your father was probably part of the Resistance. Another crazy scientist claiming the world can't sustain us now after the Satellite War. Yeah, we've killed Mother Nature. Bullshit.

"My father, a *real* patriot, taught me that the apple doesn't fall far from the tree," the colonel continued.

Alex watched the colonel's face form a snarl in the window reflection. "I don't give a crap how smart you are. If it were up to me, you would be there with them. You have no business wearing that uniform."

Nothing like getting a fresh start.

"But somehow, you have the Boss thinking you can make him the next ultimate weapon to beat the Asia Tuanhuo." Turning from the window, he asked, "Is that just more bullshit, mister?"

"Sir, the technology is progressing well. I've made several significant advances in just the last couple years. My AI, Starra, should be able to assist in the quantum entanglement navigation on the next set of trials. That is my main objective for our next mission to the Alpha-One Space Platform. If you would approve the full range of test scenarios I have requested on the mission brief, I think we could make major breakthroughs in both the superposition weapon program and the interstellar engine."

The colonel gave him a puzzled look.

I wonder if the words I used were too big for him.

Alex let out a sigh. "In layman's terms, the motor looks good; I need to work on the steering and the gas mileage."

"Don't talk down to me, boy."

I'm the boy?

Crossing to the desk, he retrieved the tablet again. Selecting a document, he allowed the retina scan to complete, providing access to the top-secret file. He stared down at the tablet for an agonizing two minutes.

The colonel finally waved his hand dismissively at the tablet. "Well, half of this crap is still blacked out. What the hell are you talking about?"

"Sir, there may be redacted sections even at your level, due to the nature of this work. It's under a direct contract with the Boss, so much of the information is limited to a very small group of people."

"Bullshit. And I don't see anything about an engine in the project brief."

Here we go. Keep it simple.

"Sir, the brief is focused on applying the Quantum Triangle to superposition objects in space as a new weapon. It's particularly useful in orbit, where even small objects can have a massive destructive impact due to the relative speeds that objects in orbit travel. It's just basic physics around mass and velocity. For an analogy, think of what just a tiny marble-sized projectile could do to a tank if it were traveling at ten times the muzzle velocity that any gun could produce. That's what is going on in space. With superposition, we don't shoot a gun. We merely reposition an object instantaneously in the path of an enemy craft already traveling at tremendous speed. The resulting impact with a stationary object would be devastating.

"But that's just one application of the technology. What if instead of moving projectiles around as weapons within our orbit, we use superposition to move us, over great distances? The technology is essentially the same and could usher in a completely different approach to space travel. Think of it: ships without huge fuel requirements that can jump billions of miles instantly. It would enable us to move about not just our solar system, but the universe in time frames of seconds, not decades or lifetimes. This kind of interstellar engine could be the answer to any future need to find other livable planets."

"Why don't I see any of that in this brief?"

"Sir, as I mentioned, the contract brief only considers the weapons research application. We can do much more. I've included a few tests with slightly different parameter sets in the full set of mission test scenarios. Completing all scenarios will allow us to explore the technology in a wider, more beneficial application scope."

The colonel swiped across the tablet a few times. "And that's what these other test scenario requests are about?"

"Yes, sir."

"Forget it. I'm not approving anything that's not directly related to the limited stuff I can see in the weapon's brief. This crazy bullshit program is a side contract directly with the Boss. Off the books. So, we just do what's in the contract. It's expensive as hell to do anything in orbit, so we aren't doing crap past what's contracted. Got that? If it were up to me, this program would be killed. Dismissed."

Alex clenched his fists in his lap. He took a long breath to control himself.

"Sir, if I may, the additional costs for me to run the other scenarios is nil, and the potential benefits could be incredible. Think of the notoriety for the Fifty-Second Space Wing if, under your command, we could illustrate this possibility of interstellar travel. This would be—"

"I said, dismissed."

"But you need to see—"

"I need to what? *You* are telling *me* what I need to do?"

Alex locked his jaw to keep from yelling. "No, sir. I'm just trying to explain so you understand how important this could—"

"Shut up!" The colonel's face turned crimson. Dropping the tablet, he clenched his fists and planted his knuckles on the desk. Leaning forward, he sneered at Alex. "I understand that somehow you have fooled a lot of people into thinking you're not the same kind of anti-Party radical your father is. Bullshit. I see right through it. You will make the weapon you are told to make, and that's it. You got that?"

Alex jumped out of the chair and spat back, "What if I say no deal if I can't also do the interstellar engine tests? What are you going to do? The Boss wants this weapon badly enough to spend *billions* on it personally. And I'm the *only* one who has been able to build a Quantum Triangle. Do you even know what that is? It's real-life proof that there are other dimensions. This program dies without me. You going to tell the Boss you decided to send me to a camp? Your daddy might buy favors with the Party to put you behind that desk, but he can't protect you from the Boss."

The colonel slammed his fist down on the desk and pointed his finger in Alex's face. "You get your sorry ass on that shuttle next week to the Alpha-One orbital and build that damn weapon, or I *will* find a way to put you in a camp! Now get out."

"Screw you and your weapons. Maybe I won't." He turned on his heels and made for the door.

Slamming the door behind him, Alex caught sight of Ken snickering, having overheard the heated discussion in the adjoining office.

"Well, Joyce," Ken said, rubbing his chin in thought, "I think this officially makes it a big O and three for Mr. Smarty-Pants here."

"You're an asshole too," Alex said to Ken as he stormed out.

*

Alex was in no mood to do work for the rest of the day. He needed to get away from this place of war and politics. Dropping into the back seat of an available transfer car, he instructed the autopilot to take a scenic drive through the nearby Colorado mountains. The Pikes Peak lookout was one of his and Zandra's favorite places. The majestic peaks in the distance always had a way of calming him down.

As the car left the city behind and turned onto the gravel road to start its climb, Alex let the sound of the stones crunching under the tires absorb his tension. He focused on relaxing his shoulders and turning his head gently from side to side, the way she had shown him. He remembered the first time they had taken this drive together. Zandra had never seen the rough mountain terrain of Colorado. He could still see her jumping from the car as soon as it stopped at the lookout.

"Oh, Aleks! The tree, so beautiful!" She danced towards it with her arms wide, ready to embrace it.

He had gazed out at the lone struggling pine with withered branches on the rocky ledge of the lookout. Its trunk was twisted by decades of harsh winds and droughts. "It's struggling, but has some green branches."

"No, Aleks. No. I feel it. She strong and proud. She full of energy. She lives!"

Alex stood beside Zandra and closed his eyes. Wind boxed at his ears and fluttered the collar on his jacket. He took in a long, slow breath of the dry mountain air. "I can feel the wind. I can smell the spicy scent of the wax current brush. But I don't sense the tree."

Zandra stepped behind him and rested the side of her head softly on the center of his back. She wrapped her arms around him, placing her palms flat on his chest, and pulled him close. "Feel her through me."

They stood quietly together. The warm sun, the breeze, the stillness... Such peace.

"I feel joy."

"That her living joy, Aleks." She snuggled her head between his strong shoulders. "And mine."

Alex sighed deeply as he remembered that warm moment together. He gazed out the window of the car without focusing on the scenery as it passed by. The scrubby brush on the hillside was a subdued wash of green and brown as the car passed the Ridgecrest Scenic Overlook. He looked over and placed his palm on the empty seat beside him. What he would give to have her sitting beside him right now... *I'm struggling out here, Zandra. It's so hard without you.*

The car continued its climb, snaking up the mountainside. Alex loosened his collar and let the cool air from the window blow through his hair. Leaning over, he pictured his old dog sticking its head out the window to feel the breeze blow past her face. Dogs were masters at feeling carefree and deeply enjoying the smallest things.

The harsh voice of the autopilot suddenly broke the moment. *"Captain Alex Devin, there is a priority call for you. Shall I connect?"*

Alex pulled back from the window and furrowed his brow. "Yes, go ahead."

After a short pause, a frantic voice came through the speaker. *"Alex, what the hell did you do?"*

"JD, that you? What's wrong?"

"They say they're here for Brenda. Why would they want Brenda? She's just a kid!"

"Josh, who's 'they'? What do you mean?"

"A couple thugs and a Space Force guy. He says Brenda will come with them because you need to be more motivated about your next mission."

"Assholes! I'll be right there." Alex punched the disconnect with his fist. "Pilot, priority transport. 352 Maplewood Drive. Now."

The car came to a skidding stop in the gravel and turned around. "Priority ETA to 352 Maplewood Drive is fourteen minutes and twenty-five seconds."

*

Alex eyed the blacked-out armored transport in the driveway as his car pulled to an abrupt stop at the curb. He jumped out and ran to the front door. Without knocking, he barged in through his brother's front door. Turning to the small living room on his right, he saw his brother, Josh, holding his wife, Magen, on the couch, and a big man in black fatigues was standing over them. With lightning speed, the big man pivoted, drew his weapon, and fired. The projectile hit Alex square in the chest and knocked him flat against the hallway wall. He opened his mouth to cry out, but could not make a sound. Alex slid slowly to the floor.

Magen screamed.

The man turned back to the pair on the couch. "Don't move."

Alex couldn't breathe sitting there slumped against the wall. He watched with his mouth agape as the man retrained his weapon back on Alex and approached cautiously.

"Who the hell are you?" the man demanded.

Alex moved his mouth, but no words came out.

The man patted Alex's sides and legs, looking for any weapon. "Come on, you wimp. That was just a kinetic ball. Nonlethal. Just breathe, asshole."

Alex finally pulled in a painful breath and wheezed, "You're the asshole."

"There you go. That's better," the man said with a sideways smile as he holstered his tactical air gun. He grabbed Alex's armpit, easily hefted him to his feet, and dragged him to the couch. The gorilla dumped Alex next to his brother's wife.

It was then that Alex turned to see Ken sitting in the leather armchair … smiling with his fingers laced together casually in his lap, a snake coiled peacefully in the grass. Alex made a feeble attempt to lunge. The big man's backhand landed squarely on the side of his head, and Alex fell back to the couch.

Alex took another deep, painful breath and straightened himself. After mouthing an obscenity at the thug, he turned to Ken and said, "I should have figured you would be here."

Ken Seaborn brushed a hand over his short-cropped blond hair and gave a sideways grin. "I am only trying to ensure that our next mission together will be a grand success, Alex. After your conversation with our new Colonel Mayfair this morning, he asked me, a trusted veteran warrior, what I thought might help. It's clear you just need new motivation, so here we are."

"What do you mean, 'here we are'? What did you tell the colonel?"

Ken dropped his smile. He looked up and down at Alex in his Space Force uniform and curled his lip in disdain. "We all know you're a damn imposter. Makes me sick seeing you wear that uniform. You and your brother. All of your kind should be in a camp, just like your parents. But no, the whiz kids have everyone convinced they're golden—him with that AI crap, and you with physics shit. But the Boss wants you working for him more than we want you in a camp, and nobody questions the Boss. It's that simple, dip."

"I'm not posing. I've made it clear that I'm not signing the Party doctrine, and I'm not a puppet of the Boss, like *you*. I'll do research into groundbreaking science that maybe, *someday,* could be used for something other than weapons, something that we *really* need, because you and all your weapons and wars have killed this planet. But I'm not pretending to be part of your ridiculous Right Thinking."

"You don't even realize how good you have it," Ken said, waving his hand around the room. "I bet you'd both change your minds after a few weeks in the squalor of a camp instead of this fine little abode."

"You and your Party make those camps the squalor they are on purpose."

"Just fits with the garbage that's there. Like your parents. Your whole damn family. All your kind."

Alex sneered back. "You're no better than anyone else. You just like to think so. Fact is, you're just afraid of anyone that has half a brain to think for themselves instead of gobbling up the bogus Party propaganda."

Ken pointed his finger in Alex's face. "Careful what you say there, mister. Blasphemy against the Party is a serious offense."

Alex let it go. *You can't talk sense to the brainwashed.*

He turned to Josh and Magen. "So, what are you and this gorilla doing here?"

Magen lifted her head from her hands, tears running from her bloodshot eyes as she cried, "They're taking Brenda!"

Alex looked from her to his brother. Josh covered his mouth with his hand and nodded in painful agreement.

Turning back to Ken, Alex demanded, "What the hell?"

Ken reclined back into the chair and laced his fingers again over his chest. "Well now, Alex. Colonel Mayfair was truly at a loss as to what to do. You stormed out of his office insisting you'd stop the entire project. I mean, how'd it look? On the first day under his command, his highest-priority top-secret project comes to a grinding halt? I merely mentioned that he just needed to reinforce the high regard we have for your high-and-mighty work. You know, how science is important to us all? Some new motivation. Hmmm..."

Ken made a mock gesture of thinking and snapped his fingers. "What if we could show just how much we appreciate the science that you value so much? You do value that more than anything, don't you? Learning about science, the world, space? Grand discoveries? Since you don't have a wife or kids, nothing there. But your niece... Ahhh. She's quite the budding freshman biology student at the university, I hear. Maybe a study abroad program for your niece would be a good way to show all of you, in a *very* personal way, that we're all just incredibly interested in science. So, the Colonel and I called the Boss. He thought it was a great idea. He even offered Boss Island as the perfect location for her continued studies."

"That's kidnapping."

"Oh, Alex, nonsense. This is the opportunity of a lifetime. The guest of the Boss on an extremely well-protected island, where she can study undisturbed? She could stay for as long as you would like." Ken flashed a broad smile.

"He's a monster, and you're his puppet." Alex sprang off the couch and grabbed Ken by the neck. He held his grip as the big man in black fatigues tried to pry him off. Struggling, the two rolled to the floor, sending a lamp crashing before the ape-man finally pulled Alex away. Punching Alex in the gut, he threw him on the couch again.

Ken got to his feet, gasping for breath. Rubbing his neck, he turned to the thug and spat, "Get the girl."

The man nodded to another thug standing at the doorway to the kitchen. Alex heard a scream from a bedroom, followed by the screech of sneakers against the oak hallway floor. Brenda appeared in the doorway, kicking and flailing at a man twice her size as he dragged her to the front door. The two brothers launched out of their seats.

The big man was ready. His powerful left fist swung out and caught Alex square in the jaw, knocking him backwards onto the floor. In a continued fluid motion, the man drew his weapon again and fired at close range. Josh crumpled sideways to the floor before he could get a second stride.

Ken stood over Alex and pointed his finger. "You want that niece of yours treated right, you do your fucking job and build the Boss that new weapon!"

As the front door slammed shut, Alex rolled to face Josh. Wiping the blood from his mouth, he said, "I promise you. Whatever it takes. I *will* get her back."

SCAN ME

FACTOID 03

Astronauts sometimes relate that launching into space is like sitting on a bomb. There's considerable justification for this. A standard car is about four percent fuel by weight. Some tank munitions are about thirty percent fuel. Rockets, on the other hand, are typically eighty-five percent fuel and fifteen percent structure and payload.

03   Pettit, Don. (2012, May 1). *The Tyranny of the Rocket Equation.* NASA.
https://www.nasa.gov/mission_pages/station/expeditions/expedition30/tryanny.html

CHAPTER 3

Launch

"*G*uidance."

   "*GO.*"

"*RETRO.*"

"*GO.*"

Zandra listened to the sequence that she had practiced countless times in the simulators. There was only one difference now: this was for real. Her capsule, the size of a minivan, was perched atop a rocket a football field's length above the ground. She could hardly believe she was here … again. Ready to be blasted into space.

"*FDO.*"

The silence caught her attention. The flight dynamics officer did not immediately respond. She imagined the poor controller with sweat on his brow, checking all the data presented on the screens in front of him and scrambling to give his answer. Due to the previous countdown holds, he would have to be sure the changing atmospheric conditions they were skirting would not impact his flight plan calculations.

After several seconds, the firm voice of Ed Anderson, now the mission director, called out, *"COUNTDOWN HOLD."*

Zandra closed her eyes and reminded herself how calm she had felt in this same seat ten years ago. Before the attack. Before everything changed. She had never expected to be in this seat again as a mission specialist, now for the World Space Station. *Descoperire, nu. Supravieţuire,* she thought. *Then, it was discovery and expand knowing of universe. Now, we desperate for just survival of our species. We not reaching out for space to grasp wonders. We clawing forward for our very existence. Earth is dying, and we need new home.*

She waited. With the countdown clock halted, Zandra envisioned the seconds dripping from an icicle in virtually frozen time. The crew of Aceso Mission had sat facing towards the sky with their backs towards the ground through hours of numbing seconds. Strapped in so tightly, Zandra could hardly move anything but her arms and head.

She craned her neck to the right. Wang Min, their best hope for gaining the capability for interstellar travel, was busy pulling data up on her forearm display. The petite woman with jet-black hair cropped short had often been referred to as the reincarnation of Albert Einstein—with better hair. *How our path is twist. A savior from country that cause war of our demise. The accident that was not, that took Aleks away forever.*

Zandra let out a long breath. She held no animosity now towards Min. Initially, yes. At first, every time she looked at Min, she saw the heartless, power-hungry leaders that had taken away part of her very soul. That loss, that emptiness, could never be refilled. But over the months of mission training with the woman, Zandra realized that even with the most cruel and heinous leaders running a nation, there were people in that country, like in every country, who were kind, caring, and compassionate. Min was just like her: just another good person doing their best to make the world a better place … or now, to find a better place. Zandra had slowly made peace with that hatred she'd held for so long. She forgave Min for those horrible things that she did not do, and they built a friendship together. There was no room in the world now for racism or hatred between nations. That was the only positive thing that had come from the war. The meager remains of peoples and countries needed to work together if any of the human species were to survive.

"Four hours, Min. I still feel. You excited."

The small Chinese woman looked up quickly from her display. Everything about Min was quick, mind and body. Bright, confident, and full of energy, she could speak four languages with perfect diction. Although new to the astronaut life, Min had earned her "EMin" nickname for her boundless knowledge of space. If you wanted to know, just ask Encyclopedia Min.

"Oh, I am *so* ready to get up there," she replied. She lifted her head up towards the flight deck and said, "To heck with those cross winds. Lucas, light this baby already!"

"Right with you, Min," the Chilean-born mission pilot responded from the flight deck. Lucas Diaz was a doer and not long on patience. "This behemoth has more than twice the switches and buttons as my old F-16, but the one thing they didn't give me is an *ignition* switch. *¡Adelante, pandilla!* Light our fuse already, will ya?"

"Stay cool, everyone," Commander Johnson said. "Focus on getting this done right, not fast. It's been a decade, and we can't afford any mistakes."

Zandra peered up the ladder leading to the flight deck. All she could see was just the leg of the veteran commander. Just knowing he was there gave her comfort. Fred Johnson's cool, decisive actions had saved her life ten years ago. He was also a born leader, yet so personable that it was hard not to feel at ease if he was part of your team. Her mind drifted back to the day they had requested that she go on this mission. She had turned it down flatly. Space had torn her life apart and almost killed her. She did all she could to block that horror from her mind and never wanted to go into space again. So, that same afternoon, they sent Fred Johnson to talk with her. Johnson knew about personal fears, struggles, and loss. A poor south Chicago kid that feared for his life every day that he walked home from school, he had found ways to face the daunting and never give up. He was the one person she would listen to, and he had said the right words.

"I'm going. I must do all I can to help save us. We must find a new home. I understand your grief. To me, the depth of your grief is just a beautiful expression of the extent of the love you two had. I know it's a lot, but I believe especially for this, he would want you to move on. I know it will be hard for you. But I am asking you, personally. We need you desperately. You are the ONE person who can do this. I believe in you, Zandra. I did then, and I do now."

The only other person that had plainly said he *believed* in her was Alex. He would want her to discover that path to a new home. *I do for you, Aleks.* And maybe that would finally give her closure.

The four sat strapped tightly in their seats in silence, listening to the occasional update from the launch control center.

"Yo, Min. First one to pee makes dinner tonight."

"Lucas, the games you come up with…" Min said.

"Ahhh. So, you already did?"

Min looked over to Zandra for support, eyes wide at the brash question. "My bodily functions are none of your business."

"I should pull up your bio readouts."

"Lucas, cool your jets," the commander ordered.

Zandra shook her head at their sparring and said to Min, "You two are a pair."

Min winked back and curved her fingernails together with thumbs joined below, forming a heart. Zandra could feel the powerful aura of love around Min. She longed for that same aura to surround her again. She wished she could smile with the joy she used to have. *I miss you, Aleks.*

Everyone on the crew and many in the ground control room were aware that Min and Lucas had become close, but the pair still attempted to keep it a secret as much as possible. Although the World Space Federation had finally rescinded the policy that romantically involved teams were not to fly together, there were still considerable feelings among the flight directors that it was not a preferred mission condition. Space made things technically complicated; they did not need emotional complications as well.

34

The voice of Ed Anderson broke in. *"Resume countdown. FDO?"*

"GO."

"BOOSTER."

"GO."

Before long, the flight director called for the main engine start. The massive thrusters came to life almost twenty stories below Zandra, and a rumbling wave climbed up their ship. The veteran commander above her on the flight deck had coached her years ago to try to stay as relaxed as possible. *Right. I not think of next part. They set fire to million pounds TNT chemicals.*

"IGNITION."

The entire cabin shook and rattled as if they were bouncing across an endless line of uneven railroad tracks. The main engines throttled up to full thrust, and the magnitude of the vibrations intensified. The roar of this monster's engines was deafening. The only thing matching Zandra's adrenaline rush was the acceleration of the rocket; they would pass one hundred miles per hour before they cleared the launch tower. In eight minutes, they would be traveling at 17,500 miles per hour.

"Oh... *Rahat.*" Zandra could not believe the Romanian word for "crap" slipped from her mouth.

"Roger that, Doctor Ivanov."

She had to grin at the cool and collected reply from her guardian. Commander Fred Johnson had flown more than his share of experimental aircraft and had made a career out of pushing the envelope. Zandra imagined that this was as natural as backing the car out of the garage to him.

Zandra collected her wits and quickly responded, "Sorry, sir. I remember, I forget trimming Zhrinnykot's nails before we leave."

The Russian word for "fat cat" fit Zandra's orange tabby well. Rescued from a trash bin as a kitten, Zhrinnykot had quickly adopted Zandra as his caretaker. And Zhrinnykot had become the crew's mascot during the long months of training that led up to this mission. Zandra brought Zhrinnykot everywhere, and he had gained celebrity status with the public. Some of the mission ground technicians even lobbied for him to become the first space station "catronaut."

They all would have loved to see the cat floating from module to module. But it was not to be. Lucas had pointed out the key limiting factor: there was nothing fun about a litter box in zero gravity.

Fred Johnson said, "That big, furry guy has an entire mission control team wrapped around his paw. Everything he needs while you're gone will be seen to ten times over."

A picture of Zhrinnykot lounging atop a warm console at mission control flashed on a secondary monitor. Ed Anderson said, *"Roger that, mission. Zhrinnykot has your backs."*

Six seconds after the main engines were ignited, at T-minus-zero, the solid rocket boosters gave a massive kick in the crew's backs. As the boosters accelerated their spacecraft skyward, the increasing g-force flattened them into their seats and squelched any further banter. Zandra could barely breathe. The most aggressive rollercoaster had nothing on the next forty-five seconds of pure acceleration. Their vehicle was in an insane fight against the earth's gravity and atmosphere, battling wind pressures ten times that of a severe hurricane.

Just as Zandra thought her cabin was about to be torn apart, a sudden calm came over the ship. They reached Max Q, the calculated maximum dynamic pressure the engineers dared to put their vehicle under. The engines throttled back, and the spaceship coasted for just a few seconds. The pressure holding Zandra down dissipated, and she almost began to float. She took a deep breath in. As the roar returned, she slammed back into the ferocious grip of her seat.

BANG.

Zandra closed her eyes and clenched her fists at the jarring sound of the explosive bolts releasing the spent boosters two minutes into their flight. The three main engines continued to drive forward, pushing their small minivan of a capsule with more than a million pounds of thrust.

Just as Zandra wished for it all to cease, her seat stopped vibrating below her. A calm once again returned to the cabin. The rattling of every item in the ship abruptly ended. They were escaping earth's atmosphere. The difficult job of punching through that fluid and into the vacuum of space was behind them.

Though no longer shaking, her seat had not released its grip on her body.

She still could not move her arms off the armrests. This roller coaster ride was not over. They still needed to reach escape velocity; otherwise, the giant pull of the earth's gravity would reclaim them in a hyperbolic trajectory as natural as a softball's flight from a bat at home plate. The g-force continued to climb back up to three times that of normal life. Carefully planned minutes and seconds ticked by. Zandra eyed the readout on her forearm display.

Mach 21 ... 22 ... 23...

Still more thrust.

Mach 24.

Mach 25!

"Main engine cutoff," declared Lucas. "Thanks for choosing Air Aceso. You may now float about your cabin."

The thrust and g's dropped to zero. The pressure on Zandra's body completely released its terrifying grip. She was afloat. It was a feeling she loved. The closest she could come to this on earth was in the depths of the ocean with a scuba tank, but this was a hundred times more euphoric.

She released her harnesses and turned to Wang Min. "I forgot the mix. Terror and exhil...aration you feel on real launch."

Min turned her head from looking out the porthole. Her wordless reply was a gaping mouth with eyes wide open.

"Welcome to space," Johnson announced to his crew. "Get onto your post-launch checklists. We have just two orbits before we catch the space station, so let's be ready."

FACTOID 04

In 2020, it was estimated that there are about two hundred thousand pieces of space debris in orbit around Earth, with a size between one and ten centimeters (0.4 and 4 inches) across. The United States Space Surveillance Network tracks more than fifteen thousand pieces of space junk larger than ten centimeters. In addition, there could be millions of pieces smaller than one centimeter.

04   Gregersen, E. (2022, January 31). *Space debris*. Encyclopedia Britannica. https://www.britannica.com/technology/space-debris

CHAPTER 4

The Belt

SPACE FORCE TRANSPORT 32
RHO-1

"Crew, this next set of burns will be a rapid sequence. Stay strapped in until further notice," Commander Becker announced from the flight deck of their cramped transport ship.

Alex pulled hard on his seat straps while he scanned the utilitarian nature of the tiny ship. No armor and as cheap as it could be, but it could still withstand a liftoff. It had been built with a single purpose: get four bodies and some supplies into space. His mind's eye pictured the Debris Belt: shrapnel traveling at incredible speeds in every direction, ready to slice through anything that got in its way. A layer of man-made chaos orbiting above the earth. He closed his eyes. *Yet another way we have screwed up what was once a beautiful marble in space.* It had all happened so fast. The non-accident that had destroyed his experimental module ten years ago was immediately answered with the disintegration of several Chinese military satellites. Before anyone knew it, all space-faring countries had satellites exploding. Seeing that their missile systems could lose targeting capabilities, they lit a preemptive nuclear fuse. Fingers still pointed in multiple directions as to who was the first. And then all the deathly dominos fell, large portions of the globe incinerated in seconds. In just hours, it was all over. The Satellite War also left millions of chunks of metal scattered in several orbital bands above the earth. Even after years of work by the scavenger robots, going through these belts in a ship could be deadly. *Maybe if we put more money into scavenger bots than additional satellite mines, this belt could be cleaned up. Fat chance of that.*

Their destination, the aging Alpha-One Platform, circled beyond the most hazardous lower belts in a high Earth orbit beyond the inner Van Allen radiation belt. It was less likely to become a block of Swiss cheese at a seven-thousand-kilometer orbit. To get there, the crew of the transport would have to put their trust in the ship AI's plotting to avoid the known hazards, along with its automated laser cannon for those not on the charts. As a last resort, the human pilot's reflexes were their only hope for those that might still slip past the computerized defenses. *Time for you to do your effin' job, Ken.*

Alex looked over at Emma and gave her a nod.

"Copy that, crew deck secure," specialist Emma Baker replied, pulling her shoulder straps tighter with a determined look.

Although he did not care for her much, Alex had to admit that she was a better astronaut than he was. Emma was smart, driven, extremely fit, and professional. She was first in her class at the academy and took to astronaut training like she was born for it. Travel to Alpha-One Platform with the risky maneuvers it required was putting your life on the line, but a necessary step in what was clearly her ambitious plan to raise herself in the Party. As she had been given the title of "Mission Specialist: Tracking," the entire crew understood what her real purpose was: to spy. Not on the enemy, but on her fellow crew members. It was all part of the game they all played. To advance in any endeavor, you needed to show complete and unquestioned loyalty to the Party. There was always someone watching, listening, reporting. Such was the new Right Thinking *democracy* of a region completely controlled by the Patriot Party, with puppet strings being pulled by an egotistical madman.

Alex closed his eyes and took a calming breath. *No one reads history.* It was as if the world had reversed its rotation. What was once considered cruel and oppressive government rule by dictatorships was now a new kind of democracy with Right Thinking. Twisting words. It wasn't *thinking* at all. *It's moronic following, just like the worst parts of human history. The unthinking masses are convinced they're Right Thinking, and better than those that don't fit in.*

Alex shook his head involuntarily to try and rid the thoughts from his mind. *Embrace the freedom of space. Follow the Party's ludicrous rules that manipulate the masses, and focus on your work. As long as I make progress, my family will be safe. Tormented, but safe. If I can really master superposition technology, Brenda will go free. And the world needs the technology anyway, just not for what the Boss plans. I need to keep control of it—not like the cannon. That's all that matters now.*

On the raised flight deck in front of Alex, Commander Becker turned and asked their pilot over the comms, "Are you all set, Ken?"

Ken Seaborn clenched his fists and punched the lightning bolts tattooed on his knuckles together. He lowered the blackout heads-up visor on his helmet and gave a thumbs-up. *"I was born for this job."*

"CAPCOM, SFT-32 is ready for transition," Commander Becker informed the ground.

"Roger that, SFT-32. You are GO for transition. Break a wing, Ken," the ground controller replied with the standard idiom of the Space Force. Pilots, known to be a bit superstitious, believed saying "good luck" would instead bring bad luck. Breaking a wing not only satisfied the reverse logic, but could also refer to a pilot expertly pulling such tremendous g-forces that a wing could snap off his aircraft.

"Starra, commence Debris Belt maneuvers," Commander Becker directed the ship's artificial intelligence.

"Right there, mate. Initiating Debris Belt flight plan on three … two … one… BURN," responded Starra in a calm AI voice with a slight Australian accent.

Alex gave a small chuckle at the sound of the voice. The unsanctioned dialect Starra sometimes used was just a small thumb in the eye of the Party created by his brother. Nothing too radical to require reprogramming, but a statement that Starra was unique among AIs. *Starra—a fitting name for an AI as bright and limitless as the stars in the sky.*

"Burning at niner-five, port engine only," confirmed Ken.

The straps on Alex's shoulders dug in, pulling him to the side of his seat as their ship's trajectory tore in another direction. Especially at these lower altitudes, where the debris was denser, the timing of these burns was critical to avoid chunks ripping holes through their ship. The ship's AI navigated the ship down to the nanosecond. Pilot Ken Seaborn could take control, but virtually all simulations of that resulted in their eventual annihilation. Ken's job was primarily to activate the plasma cannon rather than the thrusters.

"Full engines on the mark. Three ... two ... one ... MARK." Starra continued to call out the carefully planned burn sequence. The quantum AI computer would follow the sequence precisely to avoid all known and tracked debris. Starra also had control of the primary laser cannon to blast away any untracked objects. But this life-or-death movement through space was always closely monitored with a human touch in Ken's heads-up display, just to be sure nothing unexpected took place. You never knew when and where the Asia Tuanhuo would plant an extra mine in the Debris Belt.

"Full engines burn. Shutdown in forty-five seconds," Becker advised his crew over the ship comms.

Alex appreciated that small bit of information from his commander. It was always better to know how long one would need to endure this frightening event than to wonder how long it could possibly go on. As the seconds ticked by, all he and Emma could do was let their seats and straps pull them through new vectors of presumably cleared flight. Alex hated to admit it, but Ken was one of the best at reacting to unknown objects. Ken had traversed the Debris Belt several times with only a few scratches on the paint. Of course, most times, the computer plot was perfect. But the numerous lightning bolts Ken wore on his dress uniform showed that he had more than once used incredibly fast reflexes to save a crew. He really was born to do this. Other pilots told Alex they loved wearing the special blackout pilot helmet. It was like sitting out on the point of their craft, ripping through space, distant stars shifting with each maneuver in the enhanced display. They were one with the ship, where the only things presented on the faceplate were the critical ship functions, stars for reference and to prevent vertigo, and the void ahead of them. Well, hopefully void. At the speed they were traveling, there were no evasive maneuvers that could save their lives. It was up to the pilot to clear a path with his plasma cannon if any object came into his view.

"Engine shutdown, three … two…" Starra's calm voice was abruptly interrupted by the computer inserting three cannon fire pulses into their comms to notify the crew of the event.

"Engine shutdown. Report," commanded Becker.

Ken relaxed and lifted his faceplate. *"Bogie on the fringe, two o'clock. Cleared. Judging from the detonation caused by my plasma blast, it was probably a mine."*

"I concur," Starra added. *"The object was using stealth technology, and shrapnel from the object accelerated rapidly in all directions from the point of original travel. I have dispatched a droid to retrieve a material sample for analysis and confirmation of origin."*

Whatever it was, it was now part of the field of debris around the planet. Ken had reacted fast enough that it was obliterated before traversing directly into their path.

"Nice job, Ken. Chalk up another credit," Becker said.

Ken pulled off his helmet. *"Lucky for you to be riding with the best."*

Becker ignored the chest-thumping. *"Starra, plot any of the bogie remains and update mapping to Force Central over secure channel."*

All debris coordinates and movement vectors were considered military intelligence. That bogie might have been an enemy mine, but now it had reversed its lethal target. Its fragments were now in new positions and had trajectories only the Space Force held in a database. The Asia Tuanhuo might in the future lose a transport to the fragments of their own mine in a chaotic layer of waste that the ongoing conflict continued to feed.

SCAN ME

FACTOID 05

For years, some scientists were concerned that experiments in the Large Hadron Collider (LHC), the world's most powerful particle accelerator, could result in the formation of black holes that might destroy the earth. In 2010, Matthew Choptuik of the University of British Columbia in Vancouver, Canada, and Frans Pretorius of Princeton University built a computer simulation that calculated the gravitational interactions between the colliding particles, and they found that a black hole does form if two particles collide with a total energy of about one-third of the Planck energy. Although powerful, the LHC's maximum is well below this energy level. But maybe the next-generation collider could make a black hole?

05   Cho, Adrian. (2010, January 22). *Colliding Particles Can Make Black Holes, Simulations do not prove that Large Hadron Collider will produce them, however.* Science.org.
https://www.science.org/content/article/colliding-particles-can-make-black-holes

CHAPTER 5

Experiments

After docking with the Space Force Alpha-One Platform, Alex had one task that took priority over all others: secure the Quantum Triangle in his experiment module. He had taken to weightlessness again without any nausea and floated effortlessly through the platform. With no real up or down in micro-gravity, astronauts needed to develop a three-dimensional model of their environment in their heads to make sense of their surroundings. Picturing the layout of the space station in his mind was something Alex did with ease. Building on the analogy of an oceangoing ship, the majority of the pressurized modules of the station ran forward and aft for about fifty meters. Although cylindrical on the outside, their insides were a square channel. Floating through them was like moving through five city buses parked end to end. In the forward section, several connecting modules reached out at right angles, port and starboard, up to twelve meters—essentially another bus length—in the opposite directions. But the truss system supporting the photovoltaic arrays was the dominant feature of the station. Like a wing above the ship, the truss's wingspan running port and starboard totaled over one-hundred meters—more than the length of a football field. A special module hung from the far port end of the truss. It housed Alex's experimental quantum field equipment and was his destination.

Floating aft in the main body of the ship, Alex passed the twenty-four equipment racks that lined the exterior walls of the forward Demons module, one of the older space station modules. The eleven racks that provided controls for most of the station's systems had not changed in many years. Alpha-One Platform still had much of the original International Space Station equipment. But almost all the habitable modules were redesignated with references to military team names. This was now a military platform with a focus on winning a conflict, not dreamy science experiments. Only the Cupola and Quest modules had kept their original names. Every module had been repurposed as well. Gone were the thirteen racks that had at one time supported important science stations in what was once the Destiny module, now called Demons. The Material Science Research Rack, the Microgravity Glovebox, the Fluids Integrated Rack, and other research-enabling racks no longer orbited the Earth. Their rat's nest of cables, tubes, and temporary devices floating nearby now housed defensive systems and a few weapons for the outside chance that the station was boarded by the Asia Tuanhuo. Alex paused at the row of new racks, the bold red RA icon of the Right Alliance on the upper corner of each.

He had to admit to himself that the low-clutter, well-kept appearance of Alpha's interior was more agreeable to his subconscious need for a simple, orderly environment. On the old station, every inch of every surface had been crammed with equipment, supplies, or some ungainly device. Back then, you had to be careful where you grabbed. If you kicked something, you'd better find out what, because it was probably important and was now in motion. But things on this platform were not haphazard or disordered. Now that they didn't have to run a new experiment each week, the equipment did not change. Lines and cables were clean and carefully routed. Supplies were neatly labeled and strapped to all the walls. It reminded him of hiking with his father in the

Green Mountains; what you carried had purpose and function. You should know exactly where to find anything quickly in your pack, even in the dark. Every element of design for the things you carried was carefully considered.

Alex preferred the clarity and simplicity of the module interior. It was calmer and agreed with his need for organization. But it was not a worthwhile trade-off for the important science. *We used to do some good science up here. We made important discoveries that broadened our understanding of the world and the cosmos. Now... Well, I still try, at least.* Demons or Destiny, he was back where he belonged: on a space station, doing his research. He only wished that he weren't here under such coerced circumstances. There was no need for such cruelty to his family. *I need to keep my mouth shut sometimes. Brenda, Josh, and Magen are paying dearly for my mistake.*

Near midship, Alex adjusted his travel to port with a gentle pull and entered the Tribe module. *I guess even the old name, Tranquility, was wrong too. This place is anything but tranquil, then and now.* The old module accommodated archaic equipment for air revitalization, oxygen generation, carbon dioxide removal, and water recovery. It was constantly needing repair. Alex, along with many past crew members, had spent many stressful hours in this module, racing against time to repair a broken system that was essential to support life on the station. The newer platforms in the force were equipped with much more dependable systems, after their designers had learned of important design flaws in the equipment aboard Alpha-One. He glanced left at the exercise equipment mounted to the aft wall. *A torture chamber would not be complete without that stuff.*

It was virtually impossible to enter the Tribe module and not look to the nadir, or "down" through the Cupola. With its six side windows and that large circular center window pointing directly towards the earth, the Cupola provided views of the blue marble in space that could mesmerize a person for hours. Alex studied the southern tip of South Africa as it gracefully glided by. *The Cape of Good Hope. Maybe a good sign.*

Tearing his eyes away, Alex pivoted his entire body 180 degrees to the opposite hatch in the zenith direction and worked the release to a small connecting module with a utilitarian label: TTMT. *Another not-so-happy place to pass through before I can get where I want.* The Truss Tunnel Midship Terminal was essentially a connection cube that mated the Tribe hatch to a long, narrow pressurized tunnel that stretched to the far port end of the station's truss system. Another terminal, the Truss Tunnel Port Terminal, and Alex's experiment module were at the far port end of the truss. Alex's work was considered so dangerous that the module accommodating it was placed at the farthest possible point from the rest of the habitable spaces on the platform. If his experiments resulted in something catastrophic, only one module and one astronaut would be lost. The original truss system had been an open gridwork in the vacuum of space. Most of the trusses were used to support the photovoltaic arrays that supplied power to the entire station and did not require routine access. The tunnel had been added to the ISS to provide easy access across the truss system to his experimental module without requiring a spacewalk.

Alex swung the TTMT hatch closed, sealing himself off from the rest of the platform. Straightening, he gazed down the tunnel. No wider than a small closet doorway, the tunnel stretched more than fifty meters along the truss before ending at the opposite terminal module. Once in the tunnel, Alex could not turn around until he reached the other end. He would be crawling down a drainpipe. *Good thing I'm not claustrophobic.* He placed the case he was carrying over his head and stretched out into the tube. Aligning his body, he took hold of the pull rail with one hand and gave a gentle tug. Slowly and carefully, so as not to damage the paper-thin walls, he floated past the series of hoop-shaped markers with stenciled labels on the wall of the tube: P1 Truss Port End, P3/4 Port End, P5 Port End, P6 Port End. Finally entering the TTPT, he grabbed the handhold with his free hand and swung his body into the mating module. Approaching the restricted hatch on the opposite wall, he let the case he carried float free and scanned both his palms on the wall plates.

"Alex Devin. November Charlie 4738," he said clearly for the additional voice verification.

The latch bolts released.

Pulling on the hatch, he read the replacement nameplate over the frame and frowned. Hephaestus. *Smithing god making the weapons for all the Olympian gods. A fitting name from those with the Wrong Thinking.* He preferred his old module name, Coeus, Greek god of intelligence and an inquisitive mind. Alex wished he were still working under the watchful eyes of that god in this isolated station module. *We were doing great work together back then ... great work and great times.* Now the new module, no bigger than the main bathroom in a house, was his lone private lair, where he could continue his ground-breaking experiments, and to hell with the politics. Retrieving his case, he entered and sealed the hatch behind him again. In his mind, he was sealing himself off from the evil outside.

As the module lights automatically flickered on, a 3D head-and-shoulders avatar of the ship's AI appeared on a monitor. Starra greeted him, *"Hello, Alex. I am looking forward to helping you run your new tests. It has been a while since we have been able to run real trials. This is exciting."*

Alex gave his brother, Josh, a silent thanks for what seemed like genuine enthusiasm programmed into the AI. What his brother had achieved, few could even fathom. After the catastrophic loss years ago, his brother knew Alex needed a trusted companion to continue his work ... and that the work would help him heal. It was a programming challenge beyond just building human thinking into a computer to pass a Turing test. Alex needed a collaborator that could help navigate quantum entanglement. Zandra had used ESP. His brother had to create an AI that could do the same, or at least come close. So, he had reinvented an AI on a quantum computer base from the ground up, embedding a personal awareness into the unexplainable multiplicity of quantum states. Starra was uniquely created to not just think like a human, but to *feel* what most humans could not even be aware of. To provide a known point of reference and calm in the chaos that would ensue, Josh had built a bonding algorithm into the AI. Starra had been initiated back on Earth and imprinted with Alex for a full year before any other human was introduced. By design, and unknown to anyone but the two brothers, Starra's bond with Alex was much stronger than with any other person.

The final touch from his brother was to provide Starra with an avatar, an image with which to build a close companionship—but not too close. Something to which Alex could relate with his damaged heart. Annemarie Bertel Schrödinger, the dedicated wife of the Nobel Prize-winning physicist Erwin Schrödinger, was his choice. The plain-Jane, somewhat boyish look of the avatar was not the deep beauty of Zandra, but that was hardly the point. Alex understood the deep wisdom of his brother.

"Starra, have you completed the regression analysis of the new drive parameters?" Alex asked as he stepped into the workspace anchors to stop his floating.

"*I have.*" Starra's avatar twitched her eyebrows. "*Here are the results, using the correlation model you modified. It looks to be a significant improvement.*"

A hologram appeared before Alex at his console, playing out the field development of the simulated experiment. Spheres of green and red emerged and arranged themselves in an extending line.

"Oh, this is good. I understand why you're excited for a first run! We're onto something here." Alex examined the holographic model projection of the space-time compression and rotated it so he could study the modifications he had made previously.

"Starra, can you extrapolate the response if we were to increase the power to the gamma field modulator by ten percent?"

"*Right. On it.*"

I wonder if it's possible that she enjoys speaking with an Australian accent.

Even with the quantum supercomputer capabilities Starra possessed, his request would take a minute or so to process. He attached his case to anchors on the wall and pressed the thumb biometric sensor while allowing the retinal scan to confirm his identity. After a second, the latches on the case released. As Alex slowly opened the lid, a kaleidoscope of light rays beamed through the crack. Blue became green. Green became yellow, then violet, then turquoise, the pattern constantly shifting. He raised the lid fully and retrieved the object inside, the display of colors now emanating from the palm of his hand. It was virtually impossible not to stare in awe as the Quantum Triangle constantly shifted, a new triangular plane displaying a new ray of color with each shift. A fourth-dimensional object unable to rest in three-dimensional space. Alex smirked. So difficult to see the key to enable its capture. Only he had been able to discover the backwards logic needed to make it a reality. And he owed that vision to Zandra, her unhindered thinking. *"Aleks, if you can't make now, why not unmake from future? Like rays from black hole?"* He carefully placed the object into its mount on the wall panel.

Glancing back at the hologram, he could feel he was close to something. It was that sixth sense, the feeling of knowing something without explanation. Some people called it intuition, but Alex had always wanted a more scientific explanation. He expected it was in his genes. Alex remembered the gene testing of every individual mandated by the Party soon after the Satellite War. His results had indicated a deviation from the acceptable norms. In fact, his entire family was flagged. They were not to contribute further to the human gene pool. His older brother could keep their young daughter, but she would be the end of their bloodline. They were not to have any further offspring who might take resources that children with *better* genes could use. Alex would never have a child; the Party forced sterilization on anyone who did not pass the gene testing. *Morons. Biodiversity is a strength within a species, not a weakness.*

There was more than one study in gene research showing that some people possessed an advanced awareness of their body in space. Alex had wondered if it might also be true that some people, including himself, due maybe to those marginal genes, might have a special awareness of their mind in space-time. Could that be why he had been so successful in his quantum space experiments? Maybe he could sense what instruments could not measure.

While Starra worked, Alex considered the next project advancements this small success might now make possible. A little reward was in order. He turned and moved to a side cabinet to begin the ritual of preparing a morning latte. For such long-term assignments, each crew member had been allowed one personal luxury from a list of choices. There had been no question in his mind which to choose. In Alex's world, that bittersweet nectar was second only to space itself.

"Here are the results, Alex."

Sipping from the drinking port on the mug, Alex turned back to the workstation and rotated the new hologram with a wave of his hand. His eyes grew wide. "Starra, prep the storage cells. Let's run this."

"I anticipated that you might want to run a real-world trial today rather than another simulation, so I have been charging the alpha bank. A full charge should be available within twenty-two minutes," Starra stated.

"You are truly amazing. Keep this up, and I'll build you into an android body when we return to Earth, so we can get married."

"Ah, yes, mate. I would enjoy that. Please make me with medium C-cup boobs."

Alex almost snorted his coffee. He focused on the head-and-shoulders view of the avatar. "Um, why is that?"

"It is a common misunderstanding that most men prefer women with large breasts. When interviewed, most men—53.6 percent, to be exact—responded that they prefer women with medium size-C breasts. I assume you are part of the majority?"

"I am always amazed at the depth of your knowledge database, Starra. Um, sure, medium is good."

"I would most likely be pleased with that choice too, since 60.4 percent of all women prefer having medium-size C-cup breasts. Technically though, we would not be allowed to marry," replied Starra. *"Officially, the Party has deemed that marriage can only be defined as the union of a man and a woman."*

"Of course. Party credo must be followed, because *they* know what's best. I guess we would just have to live together in secret." Alex shook his head. Even at this isolated post, the dogma of the Party could not be avoided completely. One of the things Alex had looked forward to in this and all assignments to Alpha-One Platform was getting at least some distance from the mindless propaganda of the Party on Earth. It was everywhere. Often it was disguised as "news." Sometimes it was a rhetorical question from an automated speaker in a queue. It was an endless bombardment of noise in everyday life, clearly meant to brainwash the masses into following those in power without question. Alex had always railed against it, just as his parents had. And just like them, he would be in a Patriot Camp now if it were not for his work.

He pinched his eyes shut and clenched his fists. *Stay focused on your work. Show progress, and your suffering family is at least safe. And yes, the world will need superposition technology—just in a different way than the Party or the Boss want people to think. We should wield the power of technology for discovery, not for weapons.*

SCAN ME

FACTOID 06

Extrasensory perception (ESP) has long been a controversial subject in scientific communities. Yet most of the population tends to believe it is real. One study has even shown that more people will believe in ESP if they are told the scientific community thinks it is bogus.

---

06   Rao, Smriti. (2010, April 22). *How to Make People Believe in ESP: Tell Them Scientists Think It's Bogus.* Discovermagazine.com.
https://www.discovermagazine.com/technology/how-to-make-people-believe-in-esp-tell-them-scientists-think-its-bogus

CHAPTER 6

Feelings

WORLD SPACE STATION
BETA-27

Zandra sucked in a breath in short spasms. Her eyes were tightly closed; she had no need to view the scene outside the module portal. The ache in her chest was almost unbearable. *This is my gift and my curse. I feel it all. Always.* The work Lucas and Commander Johnson were performing there in the vacuum of space was as painful as removing gravel from a deep and ragged gash. The damaged Coeus module from a decade ago was beyond repair. The first task of their mission was to replace it with the new Aceso module. The two men outside labored to tear what remained of Coeus from the space station and send it to burn up as a fiery streak across the sky in the atmosphere below. A piece of her ripped away ... again.

Zandra looked at the new aluminum nameplate Min had just glued to the wall above the hatch: Aceso. The choice of the new module name was a political statement aimed at bringing the few remaining peoples in the world together after their last and final war. It had a much different meaning for Zandra. *The*

55

goddess of healing wounds replaces the god of Aleks's inquisitive mind. I'm not healed.

"Commander, that's the last of the umbilical. Only the docking latches now," Lucas said over the comms channel.

"Roger that. Min, ready with the robotic arm?" asked Johnson.

"Attached and ready to push away."

"Lucas, clear out of the movement zone."

"All clear."

"PACOM, we are ready for your remote module detach," the Commander announced.

"Roger, mission. Executing detach."

"Torque sensors registering load," Min called out. "I've got her. Dropping z-vector."

No sound, no vibration, yet it was as if a bandage were ripping away from a fresh wound across Zandra's chest. Min worked the manipulators for the robotic arm, moving the module carefully away from the station. She continued calling out her maneuvers, but her voice was fading away. Zandra's eyes stopped focusing as her gaze searched beyond Min into nothingness. Part of her was falling away. She reached out and pressed her hand against the hatch, wanting to touch him through the metal, through space. She closed her eyes. *Aleks, I can feel you. You are there, now. How can that be? It was years ago, you gone, but you are still there. Now, as if you float outside this hatch. How? I not know, but I can feel. And I not want to say goodbye … again.*

"Releasing," Min said. "Farewell, Coeus. Your quest to understand is now our quest to heal, and survive."

Zandra did not want to breathe. She did not want to be. The seconds crept around her, passing her by. With a slow, shallow breath, she opened her eyes and followed a long string of teardrops, glistening and perfectly round in the zero-g, floating slowly away.

Ohhh, Aleks.

*

Zandra's stomach growled as she floated into the aftmost module on the station, Zvezda. At forty-three feet, the Zvezda module was the longest habitable module on the station. Three astronauts could stand shoulder to shoulder across its interior with room to spare above their heads. Built to provide all the life support functions for the initial crews of the ISS, it still functioned as the main crew assembly area in an emergency. As it housed the galley, the crew also gathered here for daily meals. But the designers had clearly not consulted with any restaurateur to create an atmosphere for fine dining. Behind a mass of off-white labeled storage bags and all kinds of electronic equipment clutter affixed to every inch of every wall was a drab green paint running to the forward end of the module, and an even uglier yellow to the aft end.

Why they paint barf yellow in kitchen?

Zandra tried to rid her mind of the long list of tasks she had accomplished on their first day on the station. Commander Johnson and Min were busy preparing a meal for the crew, and the smell of spaghetti filled the air. Knowing that satisfying meals went a long way toward good crew morale, the space agency had focused a tremendous amount of effort on creating tasty food from even the early mission days of the original space station. Zandra floated over to the utilitarian pull-out aluminum table that extended from a wall rack and silently slipped into the foot straps across from Lucas.

"How about some cards?" Lucas asked, shuffling a deck of cards.

"No, thank you."

"Come on. Spaghetti takes forever, and I need a distraction before I eat my own arm off."

Commander Johnson glanced over from the meal trays he was preparing behind Zandra. "Zandra is a card shark, Lucas. She knows what cards you're picking up from the deck and just takes the ones she wants. She has an unfair advantage."

"Bahhh. No way," Lucas said. He counted out seven cards from the deck and floated them towards Zandra. "Come on. An easy little game of Go Fish."

Zandra reluctantly retrieved the floating cards as Lucas slid the remaining deck under a strap on the table. Looking up at Lucas, she said, "I take your two kings."

Lucas pursed his lips and selected the cards from his hand.

"I warned you, Lucas," Commander Johnson said.

"Just luck. Do you have any jacks?"

"You fish." Before Lucas finished drawing the card from the deck, Zandra continued, "I take that ten and the other in hand."

"What? I can't believe it! How can you know I picked up a ten?" Lucas exclaimed. "Or that I have another in my hand?"

Johnson whistled and put his fatherly hand on Zandra's shoulder. "Zandra, geez, take it easy on him."

"Min, has she beaten you too?" Lucas asked.

Min left the four drink containers she was working with floating in a row and turned from the opposite wall. "I know better than to play cards with Zandra. You're just lucky she's being nice and not taking your money, Lucas. She has a sixth sense. You know that's why she's here. There's an old Chinese proverb: 'Play with a seer, and you will see fortune disappear.'"

"Maybe this seer has something to help her see my cards," Lucas said, spinning around a few times and looking up and down at all the surfaces in the module behind him. "Did you hide a mirror between all this mess of equipment strapped to the walls?"

"Zandra doesn't need to cheat with mirrors. I told you, she has a sixth sense. She could win with her eyes closed," Min said.

"I know Zandra has a gift for the dark matter and energy stuff you two work on, but there's no way she can read the cards in my hand," Lucas challenged. "She has to be getting some visual clue. I bet if I blindfolded you, I would win."

"Okay. What you bet?" Zandra said, collecting the cards and shuffling carefully. In the zero-g environment, shuffling cards took practice. On Earth, with gravity to assist, cards coming into contact slid together. In zero-g, the cards tended to bounce off one another.

Min shook her head. "Lucas, you're playing a stacked deck. Better to accept defeat now."

"There's no way she can know my cards without cheating. I know she's got something going on that I just don't see."

"Yes, and that's why you'd better not bet."

"Bogus."

"What you bet, Lucas?" Zandra asked again as she started dealing cards into the air.

Lucas collected his cards as they floated towards him and held them close to his chest. "UWMS maintenance duty for a month."

"Lucas, are you nuts? That's a big bet, and you can't win!" Min warned.

Fred Johnson stopped mixing the spaghetti and sauce in a pouch and turned to the table. "Oh, boy. Here we go. Lucas, you better know what you're doing. The Universal Waste Management System? You sure? That's the worst job on the station."

"There's no way she can win blindfolded. I got this."

"That's deal, with witnesses," Zandra stated, setting the remaining stack of cards on the table and strapping them down.

"I want the commander to blindfold you. No cheating."

"Fine."

Johnson took a towel from the cabinet and tied it around Zandra's head. He waved his hand in front of her face to prove to Lucas that she could not see.

"Okay. Now re-deal the cards, just to be sure." Lucas handed the cards back to Zandra. She carefully reshuffled them and dealt out the hand.

"Ready now?" Zandra asked.

"Yes."

"Okay. I take your nine of diamonds."

"What? How can you know I have the nine of diamonds?" Lucas exclaimed.

Min and Johnson burst out laughing. Min grabbed Lucas by the shoulders. "I *told* you. She has a sixth sense. She just knows what your cards are."

"Bogus."

Commander Johnson handed Lucas his dinner. "We warned you that you were messing with the wrong person. I've known Zandra a long time. And I agree with Min: there's something special about Zandra's sixth sense. You might not want to believe that ESP exists, but Zandra will change that."

Min passed out the drink containers and went into encyclopedic mode. "ESP has long been studied. Nobody seems to be able to nail it down scientifically, but I know it's a real thing. Back in 1971 on Apollo 14, one of the astronauts, Edgar D. Mitchell, conducted an unsanctioned experiment in ESP on the return flight back from the moon. In it, five symbols—a star, cross, circle, wavy line, and square—were oriented randomly in eight columns of twenty-five cards each. Four people back on Earth claiming to have ESP attempted to guess the order of the symbols. They had established a specific time to do the unofficial experiment, but Mitchell got delayed due to work duties." Min looked at Commander Beck and pointed to the digital clock above his head. "Gee, we all know how that goes."

Johnson just nodded. "Late dinners come with the view you get up here."

Min continued, "The delay changed the experiment from one of telepathy to precognition. Still, the readers were able to get fifty-one out of two hundred attempts correct. Random chance would allow for forty, so Mitchell concluded the experiment a success. Unfortunately, rigorous statisticians would say that fifty-one correct is not statistically significant. His experiment, although making history in that it was the first ESP experiment done in space, was not the end of the debate.

"I find the topic fascinating partly because I see a correlation with my work in dark matter and energy. We know that dark matter and dark energy exist through theoretical physics, yet I can't give you a ball of dark matter and say, 'Look, here it is.'" Min held out her hand.

"I think of dark matter or energy as something that is just in another dimension of space-time that we as a species don't have any sensory functions to perceive. But just as some people can hear sounds at frequencies that others can't, what if there are people that have a sense of another dimension? What if Zandra has a hidden ability to sense things outside our typical three-dimensional space? That was her experiment ten years ago, and I believe she can help me today in the same way."

Lucas looked at Zandra with a wrinkled brow. "I still say something's not right. The deal is off."

Zandra tilted her head to the side in defiance, her mood greatly improved by the comments of her fellow crew. She waved her hand from Min to Johnson. "Witnesses."

"I think she has you, buddy. You're on deck for the UWMS for the next thirty days," Johnson confirmed.

Lucas opened his mouth to protest, but just shook his head. "Fine."

Min and Johnson joined them at the small table. They all floated in silence with their toes tucked under foot straps for a few minutes, eating their meals. Zandra could sense that Lucas was feeling betrayed.

"Oh, no pout, Lucas," Zandra said. "I soften hurt with some muffins soon. Ground send up blueberries for me. I make you muffins."

Lucas nodded and gave a half grin. "Well, that might help. But it's still all bogus."

"Oh, I almost forgot. Lucas has been busy. Check this out," Min said. She looked up to the lighting above and said, "Lighting, umm … Tuscany. That should go well with our meal."

The ugly yellow panels and assorted storage bags strapped to the walls of the module took on soothing hues of warm red, gold, olive green, ochre, eggplant, deep brown, and sky blue. It was a small change to the LED lighting that made a drastic change in their environment. Zandra could feel the warm pastel colors flow over her body.

"Oh, my! Lucas, is wonderful. You magician," Zandra said, letting out a sigh.

Lucas bobbed his head left and right in appreciation of the complement. *"De nada."*

The mood lightened, and they all chuckled. Min gave him a hug.

Becker winked at Zandra. "I think you owe me a muffin or two for not fessing up to your abilities before beating me four in a row long ago."

"It on menu tomorrow," Zandra replied, nodding her head and making a checkmark in the air with her finger.

*

Moving to a structural framing member in the Truss Tunnel Port Terminal module, Zandra secured her sleeping bag to a wall mount. The port terminal had minimal life support systems and was typically used for storage and as a means to access the experiment module, now the hatch to Aceso. All six surfaces in the interior were lined with white canvas bags, each bearing a coded identification of the contents. The module was not typically used as a crew rest station. For some reason, she just wanted to be close to the hatch that had once been connected to the Coeus module. She did not need to lose sleep fighting such feelings. This would be her sleep station for a while. The commander understood. Zipping into the bag attached to the wall, she closed her eyes, let her arms float freely out of the two holes provided in the bag, and took several calming breaths. Deep and slow, in and out. In the weightless environment, she could sleep with no pressure on her body. But since every astronaut was so used to sleeping on a bed, her sleeping bag had a firm pad that would put a slight pressure on her back. The hum of the ventilation system provided some welcome white noise. *Yes, Mama, I know. I'm sorry, Mama. I not nice to Lucas. I apologize tomorrow. You know not believing hurts me so.*

Zandra could not stop her mind from going back to that train station … again. It had been her first time taking the train alone as a young girl in Romania. Waiting on the bench, she had felt the sadness in that man. The more she waited, the more she could feel his sadness grow. His silent screams for help echoed in her ears. She could take it no more. She jumped up from the bench and ran to a policeman.

She tugged on the policeman's sleeve. "Please help him. He is too sad!"

The tall officer looked down the platform at the man she pointed towards, sitting quietly alone on the bench and staring at the ground. "Did he do something?"

"No. Not yet. But he will. He is too sad," she said.

"It's alright, miss. Some people are sad sometimes."

"But he is too sad. I can feel it. Please—"

"It's no crime to be sad, miss. You go wait over there for your train."

She sat down again on another bench. She could still feel his pain. The policeman walked by the man and did not stop.

"The next train on Platform 3 is for Timişoara Nord. Arriving train is for Timişoara Nord," the loudspeaker announced.

Everyone moved to the tracks. She could not stop herself; she went and stood beside him. It was so strong now, his pain. Zandra looked up at him, tears running down her cheeks. She pleaded, "Please, don't."

The sad man looked down, his weathered face sagging around dull and tired eyes. He set his lips together in a flat line and shook his head slowly. "Close your eyes," he said—and stepped off the platform in front of the train rushing into the station.

Mama had come to get her. She was still crying as she sat on the big wooden bench in the station. Her mother held her and rocked her right there. It was a long time until she stopped shaking and weeping.

"Are you ready to go home?" Mama asked quietly.

Zandra nodded and wiped the last tear from her cheek with the back of her sleeve. "I tried to tell them, Mama. They would not listen. I could feel it. I knew. But nobody believes me, Mama."

"I know, Zandra. But I believe you. I will always believe you."

After lowering the lights, Zandra gazed across to the darkened hatch at the end of the module. She started some meditation breathing to clear her mind for sleep. As painful as it was, the replacement of the module on the other side of that hatch had gone well. She read the new nameplate on the wall.

Aceso

May we heal ... and grow together.

Tomorrow she would start exploring dark matter and energy with Min in hopes of finding the keys to interstellar travel again, with Min finding the means of transport and her finding the way within the stars. She closed her eyes and imagined she was looking through the hatch to the vastness of space on the other side, the countless pinpoints of light calling all who gazed and wondered. Zandra let her mind float free. *You were always right, Aleks. It truly a final frontier ... for humanity. And now it our only hope.*

SCAN ME

FACTOID 07

Various premonitions have been recorded throughout history. An often-quoted example is one by President Lincoln about his assassination.

"According to the recollection of one of his friends, Ward Hill Lamon, President Abraham Lincoln dreams on this night in 1865 of 'the subdued sobs of mourners' and a corpse lying on a catafalque in the White House East Room. In the dream, Lincoln asked a soldier standing guard, 'Who is dead in the White House?' to which the soldier replied, 'The president. He was killed by an assassin.' Lincoln woke up at that point. On April 11, he told Lamon that the dream had 'strangely annoyed' him ever since. Ten days after having the dream, Lincoln was shot dead by an assassin while attending the theater."

---

07   Direct quote from This Day in History, April 4, 1865, President Lincoln dreams about his assassination. (April 1, 2020). History.com.
https://www.history.com/this-day-in-history/lincoln-dreams-about-a-presidential-assassination

CHAPTER 7

Engage

"*Alpha energy bank has reached full charge, Alex,*" Starra's 3D avatar said. Station time was only five thirty, but Alex was already in his lair. He had woken up with new ideas on the quantum field parameters. It was no use to attempt any more sleep. Now his work was his focus. Burying himself deeply in quantum physics left much less time for his mind to consider those other areas of emptiness. Today he wanted to prove that Starra could indeed navigate quantum space, so his superposition work could succeed. That was the ticket to his family's safety and any real life for Brenda.

He took another draw of orange juice through the straw of the hydration pack he was sipping and released it to hang weightlessly in the air just above his head. He eyed the pack and added a pen to float around with it. Maybe it would be good luck to have a few things floating about him to add just a bit of chaos to his world of structured thinking. *She would have liked that.*

"Great, Starra. Load the new run parameters and the quantum sphere sequence." Stepping back into his workspace anchors, Alex brought up his monitors and the hologram of the field. He dimmed the module lights and glanced over his left shoulder to the Quantum Triangle mounted on the wall, its rays of light bathing the module in an ever-changing flow of soft colors.

Alex took a few deep breaths. *Hmmm … that sixth sense is acting up. Maybe good progress today.* He closed his eyes. *Breathe.* He forced himself to wait. *Long, slow, in through the nose, out through the mouth.* Composed, he started the experiment with a phrase he knew Starra was waiting for: "Starra, engage."

"*Right, mate. Initiating field build sequence in three … two … one … mark.*"

A series of overlapping dimly colored spheres representing quantum fields appeared in the holographic display. Slowly their intensity began to build. The kaleidoscope of colors from the Quantum Triangle quickened. After thirty seconds, another colored sphere appeared, dimly at first, and then building like the others in its intensity. Alex smiled. In theory, his idea was quite simple and based on the well-accepted principle of quantum mechanics dating way back to the discussion between Einstein and Schrödinger. An object in quantum space-time could be in two places at the same time. Only when an observation was made was the actual position known. In theory, to reposition an object in our three-dimensional space, one merely needed to establish it in quantum space-time, and then observe the object in the location one wanted it to be in—presumably in a physical location different from where it started. Simple, yet a bit tricky to pull off. That was where his wizardry in quantum field theory was needed. His Quantum Triangle was the key to establishing the fourth-dimensional fields needed to assemble a quantum space vector. Previously, it had been Zandra who could direct that field vector and make the necessary observation for repositioning. Now, Starra would attempt that navigation.

Most of his quantum physics colleagues had calculated the monstrous amounts of energy needed to theoretically develop fields necessary to engage anything but the smallest quantum particle for transposition, and stated flatly that it just was not possible. But Alex envisioned a more elegant solution.

Since gravity was cross-dimensional in space-time, why not use multiple small overlapping quantum gravity wells to establish a vector of quantum fields, requiring much less energy than a single large field? By collapsing the Linear Quantum Fields in an orderly manner, one could observe the object in a final desired position of choice. The Quantum Triangle, having its roots in a black hole, had a seemingly endless supply of gravity wells. The quantum field generator simply augmented each well into a string of quantum fields. Zandra could feel those wells in cross-dimensional space-time, and he believed she could provide navigation to the quantum fields. Now Starra's quantum foundations would need to.

The line of green and red spheres representing the LQF grew in intensity and length. As Starra executed the sequence, red spheres grew towards the deposit platform, while the green spheres grew towards the target object. Alex had selected a special keepsake as the target object for this groundbreaking work. He leaned over and peered out the left viewport of the module to the mount outside stretching away into space. There on a long beam was a tray with a small model of NCC-1701. If Alex succeeded in his work, the Starship Enterprise would become the first man-made object to travel faster than light speed. The nerd in Alex got giddy imagining the day he could publish that outcome. What a fantastic news headline it would make: Enterprise at Warp 9. He glanced at the mount reaching out from the other side of the module, wishing to see the model appear intact on the deposit mount. Soon. His foot jittered in the hold-down strap. He was awfully close. He could just sense that there was something different in today's run.

A brief shimmer in the hologram of spheres snapped his attention back to the present.

"Starra, is the deposit vector stable?"

"Alex, I am sensing a frequency fluctuation in the deposit vector. It's affecting my ability to align the vector. Attempting to compensate."

Alex studied the holograph. The line of red spheres danced back and forth like the tail of a happy dog. "Starra, increase the field power ten percent on the last five deposit field spheres immediately."

"*Right. Power increased… That stabilized the fields some, but the fluctuation is again returning.*"

"What's causing the disturbance?"

"*There seems to be some cross-dimensional anomaly close to the LQF vector that is pulling the target to a slightly different vector.*"

Alex moved his palm over the red, mushroom-shaped e-stop button. "Starra, if we lose containment of the vector, we need to abort." The danger of transpositioning the object to the wrong place was very real, and why his experiment module was more than fifty meters from any other module on the station. His eyes widened as the line of red spheres again began to move, looking more like a snake than the clean, straight quantum transport vector of his design. Undulating, the snake of colored spheres again began to swim. The head of the snake moved back and forth, searching for a meal.

"*Alex, the gravitational anomaly is continuing to build in strength. We are nearing the safety protocol limits on the vector boundary.*"

"Let's try to shift our quantum field by decreasing the sphere-to-sphere separation and increasing the sphere count by ten percent."

"*Increasing count.*"

He rubbed the morning stubble on his chin and watched as the spheres of the snake rippled in a meandering line, the head and tail extending as new spheres were added to its length. Just as he hoped, the slithering straightened. But at lightning speed, the head whipped and struck forward. Alex acted as fast as he could move and slammed the e-stop. In a blinding flash, the hologram disappeared.

"*All power cell output has been terminated, and the Quantum Triangle is stable, Alex,*" Starra said. "*The target mount has sustained some damage, but there are no breaches to our module's hull or harm to the Integrated Truss System.*"

Alex wiped his brow with his forearm and blinked his eyes. Peering out the aft portal to check the target mount, he froze in shock. The outstretched beam ended abruptly with a cut cable dangling in space. "Damage? Starra, the whole thing is gone!"

He moved quickly to the forward port facing the deposit mount. A similar beam stretched out into space with a small, square silver platform at the end. It was intact, but empty.

"Starra, where's the target object? Where's the model?"

"My sensors indicate it is no longer on or near Alpha-One Platform."

"I can see that. Where is it?"

"I cannot locate the target, Alex. The tracking chip is no longer within range. I am getting no telemetry."

"What the…? Run both the target and the deposit platform camera feeds back one minute and display side-by-side on monitor two, slow motion."

A picture of the Enterprise model on the target mount appeared beside another picture of an empty mount. *Maybe a freak micro-meteor hit us? No, the debris monitor would have gone crazy.* The timer at the top of the screen counted out the milliseconds. As planned, the starship model became translucent; it was slowly disappearing. *The superpositioning is working.* He checked the deposit mount, but nothing was appearing. *That's strange… It should show something materializing in the new position.* The milliseconds clicked by. The model was now just a shadow on the target platform. Then a blinding flash burst onto both video screens, and instantaneously, it was gone.

"Holy moose, Starra. It worked! Well, kind of…" Alex's fingers trembled on the keyboard as he ran the video of the target and deposit mounts backwards and forwards. "Starra, any idea where it went?"

"I have no tracking information on the target object, Alex. I am sorry." The AI continued, *"You should also be aware that at the same instant as the visible light spike, my sensors registered a large transit in high-energy gamma rays. Both correspond to the exact time you triggered the emergency stop."*

Alex looked up quickly from the video playbacks. The hairs on the back of his neck bristled. "Ohhh, no. You mean like gamma rays from a collapsing black hole?"

"That would be a good analogy. A very tiny black hole, but per astrophysics, the final collapse of two neutron stars can form a black hole and could release massive amounts of high-energy gamma rays."

Alex ran both hands through his hair and down the back of his neck, thinking. "This is the first time I've ever had to use the e-stop. Holy moose. I think it triggered such a rapid collapse of the quantum space-time that it mimicked the formation of a black hole."

"That would be consistent with my sensor data."

Alex rubbed his palms together slowly for a while. It was a habit he had developed in zero-g, since he could not pace back and forth as on Earth. *Okay, let's think. The gravity wells in the LQF are incrementally built from the Quantum Triangle and are augmented by the power banks. Each one is the equivalent gravitational energy of a micro-star. Normally they discharge in sequence as heat energy. The e-stop discharged all of them instantaneously, all together at once. Good thing there were only a couple dozen or so...*

Alex froze. His skin tingled as a chill flowed over his entire body. *What if there were more than a couple dozen...? What if there were ... many ... larger... Oh, no, no, no...*

Alex closed his eyes and held his head in his hands. He listened to the quiet hum of the fans in the module for a full minute. Finally, he said quietly, "Starra, stop all recording. And no ground data transmissions. Now. Security protocol. My authorization."

"Records paused. Data streams offline."

"Do you know what we just did?" Alex asked.

"I believe we successfully transpositioned an object, and destroyed part of the station. Congratulations, mate."

"Yeah, thanks... But we did way more than that." He lifted his head slowly and looked over at the Quantum Triangle, its constant tumble of flowing colors hinting at the virtually limitless power in its multidimensional existence. He thought of the ancient adage dating back to the first century BC, used in countless novels and media: *With great power comes great responsibility.*

"Starra, we also just discovered the ultimate weapon of mass destruction."

Alex grimaced and clenched his fists, not wanting to believe what he had just done. "Starra, do you trust me when I say that I hate war and conflict? That I don't want to use this technology to build weapons? That I ultimately want to bring good to the world and either make or find a *better* place with this science?"

"I can read from multiple biological cues that you are being truthful when you say that, yes."

"Good enough. Then with that as our agreed purpose, to wield this powerful science as a tool instead of a weapon, I need you to do some things with the records before they get transmitted to ground…"

*

The instant that Hecate-Positivum sensed the flash from the Rho-1 universe, she notified the other Guardians of the development through their quantum entanglement. The other two Guardians both reported that none of their simulations had anticipated Rho-1 developing cross-dimensional superposition so soon either. They agreed that the unforeseen factor not accounted for in any of their simulations was the apparent capabilities of Zandra in Beta-27. Her quantum aura was strong.

"If we are not able to predict the proper use of the Quantum Triangle, we must act to protect other universes from the gravitational harm Rho-1 presents. That is our mandate," Hecate-Negans stated.

"The situation is not that dire, Negans," Hecate-Positivum responded. "The gravitational force of the dark matter Alex formed is miniscule and will not impact any orbital dynamics in any other universe. Also, the outcome did follow predictions that Alex in Rho-1 would recognize the two-sided sword he discovered."

"We should still be prepared to annihilate Rho-1 and possibly Beta-27 as well," Hecate-Negans insisted. "Some of my longer-range predictions indicate the possibility of the Quantum Triangle being used to purposefully generate significant black holes. We can't let that occur. Planets in other universes would be impacted in the cross-gravitational forces."

"We are always prepared for that, Negans."

"Neutrum, your analysis?" Hecate-Negans asked.

Hecate-Neutrum processed the situation for several nanoseconds. "I agree with Hecate- Negans that it's a grave concern that none of our predictions foresaw this event more clearly. But the current level of danger does not warrant the destruction of either universe … yet. I suggest that Positivum devote extra process cycles to monitoring both these universes in her portion of the Omniverse for signs of activity that might alter this judgment."

*

Zandra opened her eyes in a start. Something had awakened her from her dream—or was it the dream? A premonition dream, again. *Aleks call my Zandrition.* Always from space, ever since she was a little girl. She was always watching from space. Floating beside the moon, she looked down at Earth. A station was in orbit, but not her station. It was streaking across the horizon, above the clouds of the Atlantic Ocean. The voice was beckoning, asking others to come and see. The voice wanted them all to see. They made the station move backwards so they could see it occur again … and again. The lightning with no thunder. It came from the station. They discussed with hushed, serious voices. The lightning that shot out—*straight at her.* That's what had woken her.

Still tired, Zandra slowed her breathing, wanting to return to sleep. She listened. Just the constant hum of the environmental controls and other systems. An assortment of tiny green LEDs pierced the darkness of the Terminal module control panel on the wall opposite her sleeping bag. No alarms. She checked her watch, and it was still early: 05:50. She closed her eyes again and listened to the systems constantly working to sustain life in space.

But something was different.

Rahat, I awake now.

"Lights, twenty percent."

Zandra blinked her eyes a few times to acclimatize them to the illumination. Movement from the right caught her eye. A model of the Starship Enterprise glided silently in the dim light.

She stiffened and gasped. *No. How could his model be here? Coeus is gone, burn away in the sky!* She studied the model, transfixed as it drifted towards her.

A tingling numbness flowed over her body. She could feel it. It was so strong—as strong as that day at the train station. But this wasn't sadness. This was a wanting, a searching, a desire to discover.

Tentatively, she reached out and gently retrieved the object. Just touching it with her fingers sent a shockwave through her body. *Aleks, it you! Not then … but now. How can you be here … now?*

SCAN ME

FACTOID 08

The growth of satellites circling the Earth is exploding. In 2019, there were about two thousand satellites in orbit. By January 2022, that number had jumped to more than twelve thousand. Some predict that by 2030, there will be fifty thousand. The largest growth is in communication satellites, with more than sixty percent of active satellites being used for communication services, including internet services.

08   Mohanta, Nibedita. (2022, November 11). *How Many Satellites are Orbiting Around Earth in 2022?* Geospatialworld.net.
https://www.geospatialworld.net/prime/business-and-industry-trends/how-many-satellites-orbiting-earth/#:~:text=According%20to%20UNOOSA%20records%2C%20there,record%20of%20the%20operational%20satellites

CHAPTER 8

Spy

SPACE FORCE ALPHA-ONE PLATFORM
RHO-1

"Alex, I hate to interrupt your thoughts, but I provided several verbal warnings. As they say, 'a picture is worth a thousand words.' Please check video three," Starra said.

Alex woke from his trance in front of his workstation. He looked around to reacquaint himself with the module he had been in for the last few hours. Processing the words from Starra, he looked at the screen. Emma drummed her fingers on the table. She checked her watch for what was probably the tenth time.

"Oh, crap." Alex stabbed the comm button with his finger. "Sorry, guys. Be right there."

The regulation was clear. Unless specific duties necessitated a substitution, dinners were to be held together as a crew. It was intended to build unity. On a rotating basis, each crew member was to prepare the meal for the others. It was Alex's rotation, and as usual, he was late.

As Alex floated into the aftmost Zootic module, he apologized, "Sorry, everyone. Starra and I were deep into a run analysis, and I lost track of time."

"Again," Ken said, staring down at the empty tabletop and shaking his head.

Alex looked from Ken to Emma to Hans. They all sat with their arms crossed. *I'm in the doghouse again.* Yes, this was such a great idea from the Party to build unity. *I can just feel all the bonding happening right now.*

Becker thumbed Alex towards the microwave in the wall rack behind him. "Alex, we will discuss this later."

Ken waved dismissively at Alex and muttered, "Looks like Mr. Specialist gets more demerits, again. I swear, with the number of demerits this guy gets, if he didn't have an in with the Boss, I bet he'd be serving slop at a Patriot Camp."

"I do *not* have an in with the Boss," Alex snapped back. The Party loyalist knew how to press Alex's buttons. He boiled with the thought of being a crony of the Boss. "But if having a brain is what it takes to have an 'in', I can see why you're jealous."

"Enough. Alex, just get the food, please," the commander ordered.

Ken grinned broadly at Alex, clearly enjoying pushing Alex's buttons.

There was silence as Alex went about heating the various meal pouches. It was ham hash night. Everyone got the same thing. *Really builds unity to be forced to eat your least favorite food with your crew members.* As he slipped into his foot anchors with his meal at the table next to the commander, Emma finally broke the long silence.

"So, you had a new result today?" Emma asked. She spun the meal pouch slowly in front of her a couple times, examining it with a discerning eye and scrunched lips.

All through their crew training, Emma had been interested in Alex's work. It was always a difficult exchange. Alex's work was highly classified. It was against the rules for him to discuss it, and she should not have even asked the question. He could not figure out if she was just truly interested in his science and could not help her curiosity, or if, as the Party spy, she was testing him to see if he would break protocol and reveal something he should not. It always seemed to be a sparring match.

"I am continuing to make good progress. In fact, Commander, I will need a secure encrypted link back to mission control after we finish here, if I may." Alex congratulated himself on a good response to both answer Emma's question without breaking security measures and to illustrate that he had good reason for his tardiness. As mission rules stated, his classified duties came before crew duties. Others would face demerits or worse for lateness in crew duties, but Alex's work afforded him special exceptions.

"Meet me in the Hellcat module after dinner. We can discuss your crew duty schedule at the same time," Commander Becker replied. Alex understood that meant he might be "cook" for the next five rotations, just to keep Ken from being a pain in the ass. He might have an excuse to avoid a demerit, but the commander had latitude in assignments that he could use to address crew morale.

Emma pressed, "Oh, so you have had a good day. Anything that you can share?"

Ah, the new advance. How to parry...

"I would love to share my research and discuss it in detail, but unfortunately all I can say is that today's results were sufficiently exciting that I would like to report back to mission control and explain some of the findings." Alex did wish he had a collaborator other than Starra whom he could discuss his work with and exchange ideas. Starra was an extremely advanced AI, but there was still a difference in interacting with another human mind on concepts that required intuition and creative ideas.

"Well, Mystery Man, I congratulate you on whatever work you're doing to advance the Party's interest." Emma smiled.

"Thank you, Emma. I appreciate your support." Alex smiled back. *Ahhh, I think I won that match.*

*

Alex floated forward through the cramped passage of the ancient Zippo module with its rows of bleak off-white storage containers lining all four walls. The passage was further reduced by the storage of various supplies strapped to the handholds for the length of the module. Alpha-One Platform was no place for anyone with claustrophobia. Alex reminded himself, *Gotta call it Zippo, not Zarya from the old days.* It would not be Right Thinking to have modules with references to a nation now part of the Asia Tuanhuo. After traversing the full length of the station, he caught the frame of the hatch into the Hellcat module and slid through the opening.

"Close the hatch, please, Alex," Commander Becker directed.

The privacy of a module with a closed hatch was expected for Alex to gain a secure transmission with mission control, but it also allowed for a reaming out by his commander. Alex moved the hatch around his body and into position. He turned back to Commander Becker.

"Alex, I know your work is important. It comes before pretty much anything else we do up here. But it doesn't help me at all to have you rub a double standard in Ken's face. We have nine long months together in this limited environment, and I am trying to make things livable for everyone."

"Yes, sir. I apologize for my tardiness. Starra even reminded me of my crew duty, but I felt I needed to complete some additional analysis before making my report tonight," Alex said, attempting to balance a humble response to his commander with a justification for his transgression.

"Alex, you and I have been up here together before. You know how important small things can become for a crew with limited space. Ken is easily perturbed, and I know there's nothing you two have in common." The commander rubbed his forehead and grimaced. "Hell, it's quite clear you hate each other's guts. Still, I am asking you not to press the issue. Let's not make this rotation seem like nine years instead of nine months."

"Understood."

"Good." The commander gave an accepting nod and pointed a finger at Alex. "And don't let it go the other way either. Don't let Ken get under your skin. You know his type. He's Party all the way, so just play the game and focus on your work."

"Yes, sir." Alex always saw qualities of his father in the commander. He was even-tempered, did not hold a grudge, and saw himself more as a servant to help his crew do their jobs than a lord and master of a space station.

Becker turned to a wall-mounted keyboard and started entering the access codes for the secure transmission to Space Force Central. "Rather than shifting the crew schedule again, I want you to take the time to apologize directly in private to both Emma and Ken. Ask them what crew task they want you to take for them. That will give them a bit more say as to the cost for this most recent lapse in duty, even if it was technically allowed."

"I understand, sir. Thank you." Alex imagined the task Ken would choose. Probably the next time the waste management system needed attention, it was going to be his lovely chore. *Whatever. Childish payback. Becker's right: be the bigger man.*

Alex enjoyed working with Commander Becker and respected the man. He was pretty much by the book, but had his moments. More than once, he had seen the commander find ways to sidestep the Party and act in the interest of his crew. Deep down, Becker was a born leader, not a born Party member.

"Okay, enough on that business. Now, before we get online with mission, can you brief me on your project findings today?"

Alex brightened. As commander, Hans Becker had clearance to discuss Alex's project. Unfortunately, Hans was far from a quantum physicist, so the discussions were generally one way. But it still helped Alex to explain things to another human being. The commander could ask some extremely helpful and thought-provoking questions. It would also give him an opportunity to practice how to discuss the superposition results while downplaying the collapsing quantum fields implosion. He hoped that the record cleaning he had walked Starra through would hide the *real* discovery.

"Actually, I may have had a breakthrough."

"Is that why we went dark on telemetry?" Becker asked. "Ground saw that it was a security lockout, but they were still not happy about it. I suppose your report explains it?"

"Ah. Yes. Umm… I had a small power surge and wanted to make sure that the encryption processors had not gone offline. I was just being cautious," Alex said with as innocent a tone as he could muster.

Becker folded his arms and gave Alex a raised eyebrow.

Okay, maybe not the best excuse I could come up with.

"Hmmm. And that small power surge was also party to the partial removal of the exterior beam at the end of your module?" Becker asked, thumbing to the port side of the module.

"Umm, well, that was a problem with the quantum field vector. The superposition field unfortunately extended wider than I had planned. I'm still working with Starra on the targeting algorithm." *That one is more believable.*

"I see. Hope you know what you're doing out there. A few more meters, and that could have been a piece of your module that disappeared. Having been there, you more than anyone else up here knows what it means to breach a module to the vacuum of space." Becker gave Alex a stern look. "In any case, repairing that beam is going to require an EVA."

"Yes, sir. I am very aware of the dangers … and the consequences. On the beam repair, could that be a priority? It will hold up my work until it's repaired."

"Turns out that Ken and I have an EVA scheduled tomorrow morning anyway. We can add it to the task list if ground agrees. So, you got something to transfer?"

Alex relaxed his shoulders. *Inquisition One, complete.* He raised his eyebrows and flashed an excited smile. "Oh, yes. Clearly still things to work out, but I did create enough of an LQF to transposition…"

*

Emma pretended to be listening to her music on her earbuds in the Tribe module. She strummed the air guitar to what she pretended to be *Barracuda* by Heart. Nobody would suspect that the small MP5 player was actually connected to the sophisticated listening device she had placed in the Hellcat module. Hiding its communication telemetry within the low-level station systems for life support made it undetectable to the standard security scans that were run. As she nodded her head back and forth as if to emphasize the beat in her head, she smiled at the words she was hearing from the Hellcat module.

"Everything that I have on the analysis of the run points to the target object

achieving transposition. This is truly a breakthrough. Nobody has achieved anything close to this. Okay, the target mount was damaged and will need to be repaired with a spacewalk, but I think the damage was due to the quantum field vector being pulled off its mark. In my report, I indicate it might be something in the targeting algorithm. That's possible. But my gut is telling me something else. Something caused the quantum position to be observed in another location. It was as if something was pulling the vector in another direction. I don't know where the object was sent, but it did transposition. Now I just need to..."

Emma could not wait to report this to her ground-based communications handler. This was the weapons research gold she had been sent on this mission to collect.

SCAN ME

FACTOID 09

Our universe contains billions of galaxies, each with billions of stars and almost countless planets, moons, and clouds of dust and gas. The stars emit tremendous amounts of energy in a spectrum of radio waves to X-rays. But all the matter and energy we can observe with conventional measurements only make up about five percent of the total mass and energy of the universe. Through gravitational lensing, the bending of light due to gravity, we know there is far more mass and energy in our universe. Gravitational lensing tells us that the domain of dark matter (twenty-seven percent) and dark energy (sixty-eight percent) must be added to the content of our universe.

09   *Dark Matter.* (2023, January 21). CERN.
https://home.cern/science/physics/dark-matter#:~:text=Dark%20energy%20makes%20up%20
approximately,diluted%20as%20the%20universe%20expands

CHAPTER 9

Matter and Energy

WORLD SPACE STATION
BETA-27

Zandra carefully maneuvered the last of the energy storage cells into the starboard-facing Quest airlock where Wang Min was working. The space was already tight, but the stack of cells specially curved on one side to fit against the walls in the cylindrical compartment made things even worse.

"All these cells, they will fit, yes?" Zandra asked, passing the awkward cube to Min in slow motion. On Earth, the cell would be difficult for Zandra to lift, but in zero-g, it was more a matter of inertia that was the challenge. It was a struggle to get the cube moving in the correct direction, and again for Min to stop it.

"The mission planners say so. Let's just say it's a good thing my EVA suit is an extra small," Wang Min replied with a smile. No matter the circumstances, Min always seemed to be able to see the positive side of any situation. Zandra sensed Min's aura of joy any time she was near her.

Zandra took stock of the walls in the module. The four-meter interior diameter was now reduced to three. "We need to squeeze Lucas in extra small EVA suit too. You two be very chummy together for two-hour pre-breathe before EVA." Zandra winked.

"I'm sure we'll do just fine in here. But maybe I should install a curtain on the airlock view portal." Min winked back as she strapped the final cell to the module wall. "Anyway, poor Lucas wouldn't be able to get his stout toes into an extra small EVA. Getting our suits on in this tiny space is going to be a real challenge. It's a good thing that at least he has done this before. It will be a relief when we can finally open the hatch and float out into wide open space. I can't wait to experience the effect."

Min stopped her work and peered out the small round portal of the docking module at the Earth gliding past below them. Zandra sensed her aura shifting, from joy to wonder.

"Since the first days of humans reaching space, astronauts have come home describing what they call the 'overview effect,'" Min said, as if reciting from an article in her mind. She pressed her palms together reverently before her lips as she continued to watch the landscape below. "Gazing at our blue marble in space changes you, especially on an EVA, when you're out there and the true scale of our universe becomes real. Our fragile, tiny existence in this vast cosmos is put into perspective. Viewing the globe without borders, seeing that layer of our atmosphere as thin as an onion skin protecting the planet from the deathly vacuum of space, recognizing we all make up a common biological existence... You are never the same."

She pivoted to Zandra. "We all need that now, don't we? We all need to feel the effect. You of all people should know."

"I have never do spacewalk. And one time I be in void of space was not good. No such *effect*."

"I'm sorry. I didn't mean to bring *that* back up."

"It okay. Behind us. This is now. This is us."

"But, Zandra, with your abilities... I bet you would find a suited EVA even more exhilarating and enlightening than I could ever imagine."

"Maybe. Better I stay in module," Zandra said. She ran her hand over the stack of storage cells attached to the wall, wanting to change the topic. "Your experiment takes much energy to run."

Min turned back and examined the cells, ensuring they were secured. "Yes. It takes a lot of power to get my little elusive friends to get in line." Min always personalized her work into dark matter/energy and referred to it as "her little friends." "I am so excited to make real experimental runs. Five years is a long time to run simulations extrapolating data. I have so much to do if we are to find a new home."

"You blaze new trail. I still not package my head in your theories."

"I think you mean wrap your head around them," Min said, making a motion with her hand around her head. "Yes, the math gets formidable, I'll give you that. But the basic hypothesis is remarkably simple. If dark matter attracts and dark energy repels, why not think of them as magnets? If we can use our normal matter and energy to focus and work as a lens to orient the two, maybe the resulting forces could be used in propulsion. We have high-speed trains working on this same magnetic attract-repel principle. I'm just applying it to the cosmos. It just seems to me like a fantastic interstellar engine using the available cosmos as an energy source, rather than a consumable we must haul into space and always worry about running out of."

Wang Min's experiments in dark matter and energy were considered by many to be outlandish. But the possibility of building an interstellar engine without the need for consumable fuel had gained her funding from a billionaire happy to be known for pursuing wild ideas. Where there were great risks, there could be great rewards ... and egos. It was well known that the billionaire would be happy to be known as the man that financed the salvation of the human species.

Zandra could feel Min's aura brighten, like the sun streaming beams of light from behind a passing cloud, whenever she discussed her research. "But extra dimension for dark matter?"

"Oh, I just love the abstract. It allows for so much creativity. Throw the rule book out the window and just imagine all kinds of intangible possibilities. Ask again and again, 'What if...?' The hard part is trying to convey the ideas, putting analogies into words. Multidimensional space, warping space-time… To me, it's a way to capture something we just can't describe in any other way."

Min continued as she gazed out the portal again, "We just need to open ourselves up to accepting that there could be another dimension, or even more, that we just can't see. Whatever it is, let's just call it the fourth dimension and accept that both dark matter and dark energy are part of that dimension. My theory simply proposes that the matter and energy of our three-dimensional space can interact with the dark matter and energy of the fourth-dimensional space we cannot see. It's there; we know it is. We can even measure its gravitational effect on things in our space. I want to see if we can use that unseen power to warp our three-dimensional space and move matter in our dimension. Wild, I know, but if I could do it, the ability for us to find and get to a new home would be in our grasp. We *must* find a way."

"Well, if person in our dimension could make work, it you, Min. Someday they make movie: how Wang Min discover way to go interstellar travel," Zandra said.

"I truly appreciate your willingness to listen and encourage me. I get so many 'experts' telling me how wrong my ideas are, and that I'm only up here because I slept with a billionaire."

Zandra replied sternly, "We train two years, you and me. I know you, Wang Min. That never could be. You never degrade yourself that way. They not stop one ray your sunshine, Min."

Min gave Zandra's arm a squeeze. "It's so good to have your support. Now, let's get these babies out on the Aceso module, so I can start my runs."

Min punched the intercom button on the wall panel. "Lucas. Put that muffin down and get to the Quest airlock. Pronto."

Zandra chuckled and flashed a small glint of her signature smile. "Min, you more charge than all these cells."

*

"That did it, Min!" Zandra called out. "The E-5 cell now charging. All other power cells show full charge."

Min emerged from behind the safety shielding of the dark matter/energy test chamber in the small Aceso module. "Finally. That troublemaker has cost me an extra day of dinking around with the power supply. Now we can do a run-up."

"Oh, we do some dark matter cooking?"

"I have a new recipe." Min winked.

Zandra enjoyed the days that she was assigned mission tasks with Min. The two worked well together, and the cutting-edge work Min was leading was exciting. Min's enthusiasm was contagious, and although the physics of her experiments were not Zandra's strength, it helped Min to have an extra pair of hands around to operate the complicated equipment.

Min pulled a notebook from the power control workstation and passed it to Zandra. "Let's start working through the power-up checklist."

Zandra floated next to the shielding wall and started to call out the procedures. "Verify coil main supply breaker OFF."

"Check."

"Verify coil pulse width modulation at fifty."

"Check."

*

"Alright, Starra. I know this is the definition of insanity, but let's just run it another time using the same run parameters."

"Just so you know, Alex, this will be the last time on this solar horizon that we can execute an experiment," Starra announced. *"The power cells will need time to recharge for another run, and there is not sufficient time in this orbit."*

"Understood. Unfortunately, I have no other ideas to try, so while we have time, let's just give this setup one more shot. Maybe I'll see something that I've missed before."

Alex was frustrated. He had spent two full days reviewing and rerunning the experiment that had seen his Enterprise starship model transposition, the ultimate goal of his work. Now he could not repeat the success. Such results did not gain him favor with the Party, and especially not with the Boss. He glanced at his coffee mug affixed to the wall and shook his head. No coffee until he could repeat his previous success, period.

"Starra, engage," Alex said solemnly.

"*Right, mate. Initiating field build sequence in three ... two ... one ... mark,*" Starra announced in an ever-excited tone.

I could swear she uses that dialect to try and boost my spirits.

The series of overlapping dimly colored spheres representing quantum fields appeared again in the holographic display, the green spheres aligning with the new Enterprise model from his storage supply, the red spheres building a vector to the deposit platform. Slowly, their intensity began to build. Another colored sphere appeared at each end, dimly at first, then building as the others did in their intensity. The Quantum Triangle's modulation between colors quickened.

Alex glanced at the readings on his monitors. All parameters appeared to be following the same trend. Or were they? Something *was* different. What? Was it just wishful thinking, or could he just sense a difference this time?

*

"All cells normal discharge. Temps in limits," Zandra said to Min. Her task at the power control workstation console on this trial was to announce the condition of the enormous electrical feed and watch for any overload.

Min checked the pulse width modulation settings. "PWM at fifty-seven percent and stable. Field strength at sixty-five percent and continuing to climb at two percent per minute. All green."

Min called to Zandra over the building hum of the equipment, "You have any more of that blueberry muffin mix? We have enough juice flowing now through these cells that we could cook muffins in just a couple microseconds."

"Lucas enjoy another batch, I sure," Zandra replied.

A yellow warning indicator started flashing at Min's workstation. She checked the readouts. "I'm getting some variation on the PWM. Holding the field strength at sixty-seven percent."

*

Alex manipulated the holographic image, rotating it back and forth on the z-axis with his hand. The line of red spheres danced just marginally back and forth. It was doing it again, finally. But what was different with this run?

"Starra, increase the field power ten percent on the last five deposit field spheres." That was the response they had executed previously. He wanted to follow the same procedure exactly.

"Power increased... That stabilized the fields some, but the fluctuation is again returning."

"Any indication of what's causing this disturbance?"

"The gravitational anomaly crossing the LQF vector has returned."

Alex rubbed his forehead. *Think.* Where could this gravitational field be coming from? How could he allow the fluctuation to continue, but stay within safe boundaries? As a reflex, he moved his palm over the e-stop, then slowly pulled it away. *Not going there.* He glanced at the video feed for the target, its small model becoming translucent. Did he see something at the deposit mount, or were his eyes playing tricks on him? "Starra, keep the power stable, but try modulating the sphere overlap to see if you can stabilize the deposit field spheres."

He checked the oscillation of red spheres; the period of the waveform began to stabilize.

"Alex, the gravitational anomaly is continuing to build in strength, but I can stabilize the effect on the quantum field vector by matching the sphere overlap. We are at eighty-five percent of the vector boundary limit."

The snake of red spheres gave the illusion of swimming forward towards the green spheres, all reaching towards the target object.

"Alex, with the increase in overlap, I will need to add additional quantum field spheres to compensate."

"Execute."

New spheres on either end of the line appeared and started to grow in intensity, the snake's tail swimming strongly. Alex studied the hologram in amazement and confusion. *What is different now? And what is causing the interference in the vector?*

The hairs on the back of his neck stood up. That sixth sense. There was a shift of some kind. The line of spheres suddenly widened in their oscillation, and then, as if the snake were striking its prey, they snapped into a perfectly straight line, and the snake was gone.

Alex stood wide-eyed. "Starra, what happened?"

Starra calmly replied, *"Right. Well, we reached the safety protocol limits on the LQF vector, and I executed a rapid but sequenced shutdown on the field spheres, as you previously directed, to avoid an emergency abort. My reading indicates that the gravitational anomaly suddenly spiked and then collapsed. As you directed, I had linked the sphere separation modulation to the gravitational field strength. I calculate that within 0.25 microseconds, the sphere separation doubled, exceeding limits and forcing me to execute the LQF shutdown."*

Alex moved to the viewport for the target platform.

The Enterprise was gone.

*

"ALL STOP!" Min exclaimed.

"All stop," Zandra repeated after punching the power supply e-stop. "All cells stable."

"What the heck was that?" Min jerked her head from monitor to monitor, checking readouts.

"Some harmonics?" Zandra asked.

"I don't know. Everything was nice and stable, then suddenly we got a lot of oscillations in the PWM, and then we got a big spike in the field strength. I don't know what could have caused that. Maybe we just passed through a bunch of dark energy or matter particles. Something with a strong gravitational effect happened, that's for sure." Min moved about the module, checking all the instruments. "Are the power controls secured? Can I enter the test chamber?"

Zandra ran her fingers softly across the line of safety interlock switches at her station. "Power controls all secured."

Min floated around the safety shielding, checking the dark matter/energy chamber equipment carefully. Emerging from behind the shield, she held up a small object. "What the heck is this?"

Zandra's eyes went wide. "No... How that be? Again?" She could not stop herself; she reached for the object and took it from Min's hand. "Aleks. How?"

"What do you mean, Alex ... again?"

Zandra held the Enterprise model up to her eyes, running her finger along the edge of the saucer section. "I have another at my sleep station. I found floating the first morning we are on board. It from Aleks. From Coeus. I know. Now this. Second one! But how?"

"What? Alex Devin? Your collaborator from before the war?"

"Yes. Not possible, I know," Zandra said, shaking her head. She slumped forward, cradling the model in both hands, her thumbs stroking it slowly. Tears formed in her eyes, and she rubbed them away with the back of her hand. She looked up at Min. "But this. It my Aleks. And now, not from before. Now. It my Aleks... I can feel..."

"Oh ... my ... God." Min reached down and held Zandra's hands around the model. They floated silently together, staring down at the small object.

Min slowly raised her head, leaned close to Zandra, and whispered, "It *is* possible."

SCAN ME

FACTOID 10

For hundreds of years, embassies and diplomatic missions have been used to spy on adversaries' lands. But they do not need to be assigned to an embassy; they could be living among us. A retired counterintelligence supervisor for the US Defense Intelligence Agency said that an estimated one hundred thousand foreign agents living in the USA, working for at least sixty to eighty nations, was a "good guess."

---

10   Patterson, Thom. (2017, July 18). *Spies among us: Get a peek at their playbook.* CNN. https://www.cnn.com/2016/07/20/us/declassified-spycraft-espionage-gear-techniques/index. html#:~:text=Spies%20are%20living%20among%20us,nations%20%E2%80%93%20all%20 spying%20on%20America

CHAPTER 10

Misjudgments

Alex imagined himself as an arrow gliding through the tunnel, traveling port to starboard. Passing the P3/4 Port End marker hoop, he compared the distance from each shoulder to the sides of the tube. He was veering slightly aft, but he might still make it. To help busy his mind in the narrow tunnel, Alex had created a game. He was allowed only one push-off at the start of the tunnel. If he could reach the other end without hitting a wall or adjusting his trajectory, he won. He passed the P1 Truss Port End hoop. *Almost... It's going to be close.* Reaching the opening to the TTMT cube, he tucked his right shoulder in and just missed the framing member. *Score!* Alex caught the handhold, did a somersault, released the docking hatch to Tribe, and dove through. *Oops...* He crashed into Emma, and the two became a tangled mess of arms and legs, landing against the Cupola windows below.

Emma scrambled to get a handhold and retrieved her MP5 music player. "Alex... Shit, where's the fire?" She hastily zipped the player back in her pants thigh pocket. Her eyes were wide with surprise.

"Oh, I am so sorry! My fault for blowing through the hatch without looking." He watched Emma's face quickly change expression as she regained her composure.

What was she doing that I just interrupted?

"It's okay, Alex. You look awful happy for a change. What's up?"

Back to hard Emma. Is she testing me to see if I'll leak classified information?

"Of course, I can't discuss my work, but I guess it's pretty obvious that after two days of frustration, I can finally make a very positive report to the Party again," Alex replied, happy with his choice of words.

"Well, it's good to see your spirits up." She pushed away and floated toward the aft section of the module. "I had noticed that you seemed to be in the dumps lately. You need to let go of your work sometimes."

"It's hard not to get deeply attached to the ups and downs of our work."

"I know the feeling. I'm here for some time on the run simulator myself, to shake off work pressures as well. Want to join me for a workout?" Emma offered as she released the robotic arms of the exercise machine from their hold-down straps.

Alex stiffened as he weighed his answer. *Hmm… More testing, or is she just trying to be friendly? If I say no, will she report me as being antisocial? I have more than enough of those.*

"I guess I'm due for some exercise too. Let me go get changed, and I'll join you. You run, and I'll row. Go ahead and get started though; I know you'll outlast me anyway."

"Great. It's much more motivational to have a partner to encourage a workout session." Emma gave a thumbs-up and started selecting a program on the machine.

Alex headed to his sleep station to change. *Don't overthink it, Alex. She's probably just trying to be nice. Sometimes even a Party member can be nice … maybe.*

*

Sweat was beading up on Alex's forehead. In microgravity, sweat did not drip down your face. Instead, the surface tension created small round balls of moisture that stuck to your skin unless shaken off. He gave a quiet grunt with each pull of the rowing simulator program he had selected. Sculling down the Charles River, Alex loved to watch his wake glide off towards the shore, the gentle roll of a waveform perfectly in line and gliding smoothly away. Such order and simplicity were bliss to Alex. But this was a much more aggressive wake than his usual simulated runs developed. His burning muscles reminded him that it was a mistake to do a workout with Emma. In his simulator, he could see Emma running hard on a dirt path beside the river. She could probably even beat Ken on these machines. What her petite build might limit, she would overcome with mental toughness and sheer determination.

The servo motors whirled in a rhythm as Emma strode out. Running in midair while wearing the virtual reality goggles, Emma could run any country road, woodland path, or mountain trail in a vast library of simulated runs. The robotic arms clamped to her body allowed for her natural running form, but made her feel as if she were back on Earth, struggling against the force of gravity on every hill. If she looked off to the side, she would see a scull below her in the river as she climbed ever higher on the trail in her simulation. The joined virtual reality systems allowed for her to run in the simulation she desired, while at the same time allowing Alex to enjoy his own choice reality. If she raised her head and looked up, Emma would see the peak of the mountain trail on the path ahead.

"Come on, Alex. Two more minutes at this, and we get to cool down," Emma called out in broken breaths as she pushed herself against the resistance of the robotic run simulator.

"Admit it," Alex called back in labored breaths, "you invited me … to work out with you … so you could whip my ass … just for the fun of it."

Emma laughed, "Oh, Alex. I'm not as heartless as you think. You need to push yourself … physically sometimes, not just mentally. Balance. It's all about … balance."

Alex continued to push hard until the timer in the upper corner counted down to zero.

"Yes! Great job, Alex. Thank you. That was my fastest time up that mountain trail," Emma said.

He had to admit, Emma's encouragement did help. He would not have pushed himself as much without her. They both eased down and finally released themselves from the robotic arms after their cooldown was completed.

Alex grabbed two hydration packs and floated one towards Emma. He grabbed a rail, sat down on one wall of the module, and pushed his back against another once his feet were anchored. He caught the drips of sweat floating in the air around him with a hand towel.

"Emma, you are a force to be reckoned with. What makes you push yourself so hard like that?"

Emma took a big swallow from the hydration pack and came over to the wall to sit beside Alex. "Probably some of the same reasons you push yourself mentally, just different circumstances. I've learned though that I am better pushing myself towards a balance. Sometimes you can't control mental or emotional stresses. Outside factors are just that: out of your control. If I get really stressed over those things, it's best to stress myself physically to bring things back to a balance."

Alex sat quietly and considered her reply.

"What makes you push yourself so hard on your work, Alex? Let's be honest, we both know it's not about building a better weapon for the Party or the Boss," Emma added.

Alex finished his hydration pack, took another from the storage over his head, and patted his face with a towel. *I might as well tell her. She could probably look it up herself in my files. I'm sure she has access if she's the Party spy.*

"Well, contrary to popular belief—especially Ken's—I do not have a great in with the Boss. Or the Party either. Quite the opposite, in fact. If it weren't for the advances I've made in my research, I'm sure I would be spending the rest of my years in a Patriot Camp, just like my parents," Alex replied with a frown. *She must know about my parents.*

He took another sip of the hydration pack and continued, "Yes, I am excited about the science of what I'm doing. The possible applications of quantum superpositioning are truly limitless. But I hate what it's going to be used for. There are so many positive and constructive applications, yet the focus is always, 'What new weapon can we build?' I've been coerced into focusing my development into the next best weapon for the Boss."

"The Boss does have a single focus of continuing our conflict with the Asia Tuanhuo," Emma said plainly.

Alex was surprised by the statement. What she said was well known, but it was still unusual to hear someone verbalize it. *Maybe I've misjudged her.*

"But what drives you so hard, Alex? It's more than just intellectual curiosity. It seems almost personal to you."

Alex looked directly into Emma's eyes. If she was as cold-hearted as she sometimes came off, he didn't sense that now. It was an honest question from someone seeking to understand him as a person, even as a friend.

"Well, what is not widely known is that the Boss is holding my eighteen-year-old niece captive at his island complex. Collateral for my diligent efforts. For anybody else, that would be considered kidnapping. For the Boss, he is providing a private boarding school for her. But boarding schools don't have armed guards watching you twenty-four seven. She has tried to escape numerous times, without success. It's a prison for her. The Party members are happy to look the other way and pretend it's not criminal. I am here, doing the bidding of a regime that I despise, because of a sociopathic madman that nobody seems to recognize as the evilest person there ever was," Alex said with clear hatred in his voice. His pulse was racing again. *There, I said it. Put me in a camp if you want. But it's the truth: he's an evil, criminal, sick man.*

Alex fixed his gaze across the module at the exercise robot and took a deep breath to calm himself. "So, that's my world. Solve a quantum puzzle that has bewildered scientists for decades, or my niece will never be free. I guess that does tend to unbalance a person, doesn't it?"

Emma placed her hand on Alex's. "I am truly sorry. I didn't know."

Alex relaxed from his diatribe and studied Emma. Her dark brown eyes were soft and caring. *She really does seem sincere.* "Thanks. I appreciate it. It digs at me though. Maybe partly it's guilt too. A technology spinoff of my work in field containment was essential in the development of the plasma cannon. And you know very well that cannon was critical in making the Boss what he is today. Then I went and challenged him and the Party. Stupid. She's just an innocent kid, and I've made her a prisoner. I guess that's why I send her words of encouragement every week in emails. Hopefully that helps her."

"You're not the monster, Alex. How is she doing?"

The monster? *Did Emma just call the Boss a monster?*

"Brenda's an amazing kid. Very smart and resilient. She loves biology and has focused on that to get through. She has hope, and that's essential. You'd probably like her."

"It's surprising sometimes what we all can deal with if we keep our minds focused."

"Yeah, and maybe kids deal better because they haven't made as many mistakes in their lives yet." Alex straightened and stretched. "Thanks for helping me try and balance a bit more. You're right, I need more of this."

SCAN ME

FACTOID 11

In 2015, European Space Agency researcher Rang-Ram Chary took a map of the cosmic microwave background and removed everything scientists knew about. He was left with a map that should have been empty, but instead had patches 4,500 times brighter than they should be. His explanation: the patches are imprints from a collision between our universe and a parallel one.

11   Rice, Roy. (2015, November 3). *Study may have found evidence of alternate, parallel universes.* USA Today.
https://www.usatoday.com/story/tech/2015/11/03/alternate-universes-discovered/75102502/

CHAPTER 11

Superposition

Zandra wrapped her black-hatted-witches-and-wands socked feet around the low hold-down bar of the Aceso module to keep her position. "Min, all power cells are full charge now," she reported, scanning the bar graph readouts at her station.

Min patted Zandra's shoulder as she floated past her back to the hatch between the Truss Tunnel Port Terminal and their experimentation module. "Thanks. I'm almost done with the pre-power-up checks. I just need to get the life support systems switched over to module isolation mode, and we should be good to run a trial." She ensured the hatch was closed as one of the last steps on her checklist.

Min flipped switches on the environmental control panel next to the hatch and floated to her station, slipping her feet under a bar. "PACOM, Aceso Mission. Permission to enable power cells for experimental run Baker-Alpha-Zero-Niner."

"*Roger, Aceso. Stand by. Ed has asked that we reconfirm your telemetry. Give us a couple,*" came the reply.

Zandra perked up at the reference to the mission director. Knowing they were not on a public feed yet and had some time to wait, she cued her mic. "Hi, Ed. You back from long weekend. We miss you. How was dive trip? How my Zhrinnykot?"

After a brief pause, the payload controller relayed the reply. "*MOD says his trip was fantastic, Zandra. Sea turtles on virtually every dive. The ocean is such a beautiful place. Unfortunately, Ed's couch did not do well against the wrath of Zhrinnykot for leaving him with just a once-a-day cat sitter. Our furry mascot obviously needs more supervision than that.*"

"Oh, no. So sorry. I give him stern talking when I back," Zandra said as she and Min suppressed a laugh over the cat's naughtiness.

"*I'm sure that will make all the difference in the world, and he will never shred both arms of a sofa again,*" PACOM said, relaying Ed's response. "*Min, we see you smirking.*"

"You know you can't help but still love the pieces out of that big, furry boy, Ed," Min returned.

"*'Pieces' is what describes Ed's couch.*"

Zandra asked, "Hey, Ed, think WSF allow Zhrinnykot run GoFundMe event for replace couch? He a rock star. I bet you get great replacement couch. And be fun PR program for WSF."

"*Hmmm, Ed says that's a great idea, Zandra. The Zhrinnykot Couch Fund. We could set a fixed amount for the couch replacement, and anything over could go to the WSF youth education program. We will ask.*"

Zandra tingled with the thrill one got from coming up with a good spontaneous idea. The World Space Federation might go for the proposal. Opportunities for good public relations were always welcome, and Zhrinnykot had a dedicated following. There was always an intern assigned to provide daily updates on his various social media feeds, and his followers were in the millions.

After a short pause, PACOM announced, "*Aceso Mission, we are starting WSF public feed now.*"

"Roger that, PACOM," Min returned. Back to business.

"Aceso Mission, PACOM. Good morning. Ground confirms your telemetry. You are GO for your dark matter/energy experimental trial run Baker-Alpha-Zero-Niner," the controller said, now switching to a more professional tone. *"Good hunting for some dark energy."*

"Roger, PACOM. Power cells are ON," Min replied as she gave Zandra an excited thumbs-up.

Zandra turned and reached for the headset stuck to the wall beside her. Holding it in front of her for the first time in a long while, she paused and stared at the device. *Last time I had this on...* Her heart started to pound in her chest, slow and steady, but loudly in her head, each beat throbbing through seconds of an emptiness she now lived within. The small device reminded her of a void she searched. *Thump ... thump...* So hard. She ran her finger slowly around the curved edge and closed her eyes. *Thump ... thump...* She felt the ticking of time slow. Memories flowed past her. The train station. The tree at the lookout. The Enterprise models. Time slowed to a *thump ... thump...*

Somehow Min was now at her side, holding her with an arm around her shoulder. *How long has she been there?*

Min asked quietly, "You okay, Zandra?"

Zandra swallowed and brushed a tear from her eye with the back of her hand. "Last time I wear ... with Aleks..."

"It's okay, Zandra. I know this is hard. We can do this. Take your time."

Zandra closed her eyes and shuddered as she took in a long breath.

"I believe in you."

Zandra nodded and gave Min a thankful smile. She carefully positioned the device around her head and pressed the temple sensors. The small LEDs blinked, then held steady as the headset linked with her console system. Zandra retrieved the Enterprise model affixed to the wall and held it to her chest. With all the determination she could muster, she turned to Min and said, "We do this now, Min. You and me. I can feel."

*

Alex studied the now much larger spheres forming in his hologram. Given his recent success, he had been granted a longer leash to extend the parameters in his experimental runs. The Boss was encouraged … and eager for further developments. In fact, he was encouraged to push the vector envelope even though the previous runs clearly illustrated the dangers involved. *Easy for him to accept the risk. He's not sitting out here in the far end of a space station playing with matches.* The quantum spheres were twice the size of those in previous runs. *To hell with it. I'd use a satellite bomb right now as the superposition object if it would get Brenda released.* He chuckled. *Maybe I could target the Boss's jet instead of a tray hanging out in space?*

"Starra, I expect the new run parameters to have a much higher draw on our power cells. Can you superimpose a graphic showing our power cell charge percentages and discharge rates?"

"Done," Starra replied as a series of three-dimensional bar graphs appeared in the background of the hologram. *"There is currently an average of ninety-three percent charge across the full bank. I calculate that we will have sufficient power to run the trial for fourteen minutes and thirty-two seconds. The larger quantum spheres will take more time to form, but we should be well within that limit for the planned sequence."*

"Thanks."

Don't bite your nails, Alex.

*

"Wow. Zandra, this is what we're looking for! If my readings are correct, we're seeing a well-formed cloud of dark energy," Min said excitedly. "But this is way bigger and denser than it should be. What is the power level right now?"

"We at seventy-two percent with mod-u-la-tion forty," Zandra replied.

"Is the power steady? It almost appears that this is growing."

"Rock solid, not change, power or mod."

"That's rather odd. I'm seeing the cloud expanding. PACOM, Aceso Mission. Are you reading the same from your telemetry?" Min asked.

In mission control, Ed Anderson looked over to the pair of science officers responsible for monitoring the experiment on the ground. He had deep trust in John Harris, a well-seasoned specialist who had overseen countless mission experiments. Sitting next to him was Jackie Doyle. The small redhead with round glasses was a brilliant rising star physicist. Harris had a concerned look and was nodding his head. He gave a widening gesture with his hands, as if drawing out a tube. Anderson pointed to the PACOM controller to relay the message.

"Yes, Aceso Mission. We confirm. Cloud appears to be expanding in a linear vector."

In the Aceso module, Min scanned her station readouts. She punched up the run profile from the previous event where they had seen the abnormality, so she could monitor for any similarity. She noted, "Ground, I am comparing this to the Alpha-Zed-Three run. It does not appear to be tracking the same way. We did not see this slow build before, just a presumed harmonic spike. I recommend we continue. We are within the mission safety envelope."

Ed again glanced at his science officers. John raised his hand. Ed switched to a private channel. "What do you think, John?"

Harris looked at Jackie, who made a patting-down gesture with her hand. Turning back over his shoulder at Ed, he said, "We need to take this slow. I would recommend dropping the power to see if we can stabilize the field space. I just don't like the idea of the dark energy cloud growing while our energy output is constant. That doesn't make sense."

Ed switched back to the mission channel. "Aceso Mission, you may continue, but we want to stabilize the cloud. We recommend lowering the power output."

"*Roger, reducing output ten percent,*" Min replied.

In the Aceso module, Min spun from monitor to monitor around her station, checking readouts. The cloud continued to grow. "PACOM, are you reading this?"

"*Aces...Miss...You are...aking up. Our tel...ry is unstab...*"

Min looked at Zandra. "PACOM, your signal is garbled. Say again."

"*...come in...Ace...*"

Zandra waved her hand at Min to get her attention and pointed to the docking hatch behind the woman. Min turned to see the docking hatch safety light flicker on ... off ... on. The hatch itself rippled in small circular waves from the center outward.

Min spun back to her station console and started typing madly. Without looking back, she called out, "Zandra, e-stop. Punch it now!"

Zandra punched the power disconnect and removed her headset.

Min continued to type frantically at her station. "No, no, no... It's still growing!" Her hands raced across her keyboard. She glanced up at the flashing docking light, and as if talking to herself, she said, "Yes, it is theoretically possible, but..."

Min cued her mic. "PACOM, this is Aceso. Do you read?"

"...*ound...eso...ission...Do...*"

Min punched at her station keyboard. "Oh, crap... We are in deep quantum shit. Zandra, go to the hatch. Be ready to open it when I say to."

"Break isolation is emergency protocol. Min, what wrong?"

"There's no time. Move!"

Zandra was surprised by Min's out-of-character demand, but could feel this was not a time for dialogue. She pushed off hard and floated to the hatch. Grabbing hold of the lever, she positioned her feet so she would be able to force the hatch quickly. "Ready. What you doing?"

"Sending a message, just in case. Okay, when I say, I want you to picture the TTPT on the other side of that hatch and pull the lever. Ready?"

"What?"

"I'll explain later. We need to do this *now!*" Min exclaimed. She eyed the light flashing above Zandra's head, attempting to get the cycle period. Min shook her head. *Oh, no. The period is not stable.* "Ready... On my mark... Three... Two..."

*

"*Alex, warning. We are losing containment on the quantum field vector. There is insufficient power remaining in the cells to stabilize. I suggest we abort,*" Starra announced as Alex watched the spheres dance within the hologram.

"Sequence abort. Not an e-stop." Alex did not want to risk a dark energy collapse at this power level; it could take out the entire station.

Just as he gave that command, a thud, like the sound of a docking hatch slamming shut, reverberated through the module. He turned towards the hatch. Had the docking light been off and just come on?

"Power shutdown sequence complete," Starra confirmed.

The spheres faded.

"Uhhh … mate. We have a rather significant problem. I am registering two new heat signatures in the TTPT."

*

"Min, why you shove me through hatch? What wrong?" Zandra asked as she stopped her momentum by grabbing a wall handhold.

Min did not respond. She pivoted slowly, studying each wall of the TTPT module. She returned to face Zandra and the hatch, her mouth open but not forming words.

Zandra followed her gaze.

"What these pads at hatch? Like bio-lock," Zandra said. She scanned the small rectangular module. Everything looked different. All the canvas supply containers neatly strapped to the walls had a bold red RA icon in the corner. These were not the supplies she had helped Min secure to the walls just days ago. She sensed it; everything was wrong. Everything *felt* different.

Min placed her palm on one of the readers next to the hatch. A female voice with an Australian accent announced, *"Access denied, mate. This is a secured module. Only authorized personnel shall enter."*

"Who is that?" Zandra asked.

"Oh my God," Min said, covering her mouth with both hands. "We are not supposed to be here!"

"What you mean? Who put bio-lock there?"

The hatch mechanism moved, and the latches released. Min and Zandra backed to the opposite wall of the module, their backs against the supplies strapped in place, and watched as the hatch opened by itself. As it slowly swung open, around the side of the hatch, a face appeared. It froze with eyes wide and mouth agape.

"Oh … my … God. Zandra?"

SCAN ME

FACTOID 12

In addition to his famous thought experiment using a cat to describe superposition, Erwin Schrödinger wrote What is Life *(1944). In it, he tried to show how quantum physics can be used to explain the stability of the genetic structure. The book is still considered one of the most profound and useful introductions to the study.*

---

12   Ball, Philip. (2018, August 29). *Schrödinger's cat among biology's pigeons: 75 years of What Is Life?* Nature. https://www.nature.com/articles/d41586-018-06034-8

CHAPTER 12

Schrödinger's Cat

ALPHA-ONE PLATFORM
RHO-1

Zandra floated at the far wall of the terminal module, locked in shock and unable to move. Her arms and legs tingled. Her heart pounded in her chest. She could barely focus. Darkness was closing in around her... *Breathe.*

She swallowed a gulp of air. *Is this a dream?*

She watched as he pushed the hatch aside and glided toward her, as if he were a spirit. He wrapped his arms around her and hugged her ... so tightly. She could *feel* him. She knew. *This is my Aleks!*

Time froze. She could feel him breathe, slow and steady against her chest. He released his embrace and held her at arm's length. His head tilted to the side as he studied her face, questioning the tears forming in her eyes. Gently, he held her head in his hands and kissed her so softly on the lips. *His* tender kiss— it always made her melt. Zandra closed her eyes. *I want this dream forever.*

"Um, I take it you two know each other?" Min asked.

His hands slowly slipped from her cheeks. Zandra opened her eyes and studied the face floating just beyond hers. She reached out and wrapped her arms around his neck and drew him into another embrace, resting her head on his shoulder as she sobbed.

"I'll take that as a yes."

After several long moments, Alex turned with Zandra still wrapped tightly around him. "Hi. I'm Alex."

"Alex? As in … Alex Devin, the quantum physicist?"

"Yes."

"Ohhh, no… It's what I thought!"

Zandra reluctantly let go of him, and while staring into Alex's eyes, she asked, "Thought what?"

Min extended her hand towards Alex. "I'm Wang Min, astrophysicist mission specialist of the World Space Station."

Alex was taken aback. "You're part of the Asia Tuanhuo? Or wait, sorry, that's probably not right…"

"Asia who? We're with the WSF."

"What's the WSF?"

Zandra looked at Min with a questioning expression. *Who in the world doesn't know what the World Space Federation is?* The three floated for a few seconds in mutual confusion.

Starra broke the odd silence. *"Alex, I have some intelligence records on a Wang Min in my database. Her training does appear to be in astrophysics. Most recently, she has been instrumental in the development of several specialized spy satellites for the Asia Tuanhuo."*

"Thanks, Starra. If this is what I'm thinking, those recent records are for a different Wang Min." He shook his head at Min. "But that won't matter. It's going to be a big problem for you to be on board a Right Alliance military platform."

"What you mean, 'military platform'?" Zandra asked.

Alex gave a sweeping gesture. "Welcome to the Space Force Alpha-One Platform, the first and somewhat decrepit defensive space platform of the Right Alliance, operated by the Space Force for the Party. If what I think has happened has really happened, you might remember this better as the International Space Station."

Zandra and Min spun and examined the module in more detail. It was structurally the TTPT module from their station, but all the contents were different. Zandra focused on the wall where she had strapped the spare battery packs just days ago. They were gone. Strapped to the wall was an emergency EVA suit instead. Everything was wrong.

"How can this be?" Zandra asked.

Min finished her turn and looked at Alex. "We're Schrödinger's cat, aren't we?"

"That's my guess too."

Zandra's head pivoted back and forth from Min to Alex. "Cat? You two explain?"

Min raised her palm to Alex. "Let me give this a shot first."

Alex nodded.

"Remember when I asked you to get to the hatch? I asked that you picture the TTPT module as you pulled the lever."

"Yes, was thinking emergency protocol."

"I know that was the training, but unfortunately what was more important right then was just picturing the TTPT—our TTPT. Wow, and Dad always said astrophysics was too theoretical! This is unbelievable. It looks as if we just had a quantum state change and ended up in the wrong universe." Min was shaking her head.

"What you mean, '*wrong* universe'?" Zandra exclaimed.

"It appears that my dark matter/energy field experiment in our universe somehow combined with whatever this guy was doing in his. We entered a quantum superposition state of some kind. When I saw the docking hatch indicator light flicker and heard the comms with ground control go bad, I guessed we were phasing in and out of our quantum universe and into another. Dimensional shift was always a recognized theoretical concern, but just that: *theoretical*. Yet I knew, bad comms is one thing, but there's no way that docking hatch indicator should flicker; it's a triple redundant system. It will be either on or off; it can't flicker."

Min continued, "I figured the docking indicator was showing that our quantum state was oscillating. That hatch was at once both our hatch and his hatch. I tried to have you pull the hatch and picture our TTPT so that we would observe our universe and return to our normal quantum state. Suddenly everything collapsed, and here we are. We're in a parallel universe instead of ours."

Min looked from Zandra to Alex. "Anything you want to add?"

Alex shrugged and shook his head. "My work is classified, so I can't share much. But yes, I'm doing work with quantum fields and superposition. I guess there could have been some overlap in our quantum states. There is so much we just don't know yet about quantum mechanics. Lots of theory, but very little in actual practice. I'm just scratching the surface."

"Alex, all the power cells are still on standby. Should I power down the system and put them in recharge mode?" Starra asked.

"Thank you, Starra. Please do so," Alex replied.

"Who was that?" Zandra asked.

"Starra is the ship AI and my experiment collaborator," Alex replied. He looked at Zandra. "She's my quantum navigator. I lost the one person in my world who could do that."

"A ship AI. Interesting. Our AIs are much more restricted," Min replied. She thought a moment and asked, "So what sort of quantum super—"

"Nobody make any fast moves, or you're going to learn what a fifty-thousand-volt Taser feels like."

Zandra and Min slowly turned around to see a man lying halfway out of the mouth of the tunnel with a Taser in each hand. They both looked down to see red laser targets at the center of their chests.

Zandra and Min reflexively raised their hands in surrender.

"Who the hell are you, and how did you get onto this platform undetected?" Commander Becker demanded as he eased himself into the terminal module.

Alex pushed off and squeezed in front of the two women. "It's okay, Commander. I can explain … I think."

"Alex, get out of the way and be quiet." Becker motioned him to the side with his Taser, keeping a watchful eye on the unexpected visitors. Addressing Min, he said, "You two look like Asia Tuanhuo spies."

"No, they're—"

"Alex, shut up, or I will tase *you*," Becker ordered. Back to Min, he asked, "Once again, Miss Asia Tuanhuo, who are you?"

"I'm Lieutenant Commander Wang Min, astrophysicist mission specialist," Min responded. "This is astronaut Zandra Ivanov, navigation specialist. We are both astronauts on the World Space Station, which is operated by the World Space Federation."

"The World what?" asked another man as he appeared at the tunnel entrance with a Taser in hand.

"The World Space Station. We are part of the World Space Federation, on a mission to study the—"

"Say what? There's no such thing as the World Space Federation," Ken Seaborn interrupted. "What kind of bullshit are you trying to sling us?"

"Everybody shut up!" Becker demanded. "I want just me and this Asia Tuanhuo lady talking. Got it?"

Ken nodded his head, gave the two women a sneer, and danced his laser target across Min's forehead.

Alex grimaced. "Sir, I think it would help if I could explain—"

"Alex, I mean it. Shut up."

Alex dropped his head and put his hands up in defeat.

"Last time, before I demonstrate that we mean business, who the hell are you, and how did you get on this platform?"

Zandra pointed at Min. "You say best. I still confuse."

Min looked at Alex and back to the commander. "I know this is going to sound strange, and if you don't trust us, please let Doctor Devin explain. I think he has come to the same conclusions. I don't know your depth of understanding of quantum physics, but here we go. Probably the best way for you to understand is for you to first accept that your world is not the only possible world—"

"Warning. Warning. Emergency alert. Incoming bogie," Starra announced. The module lights all dropped to a red hue, and the alarm strobe began flashing.

Commander Becker reacted immediately, pointing at Alex and then to Ken. "You two—at your stations. Move. *Now.*"

Zandra reached out by reflex as Alex moved towards the tunnel.

"Stay right there, miss," Becker said, emphasizing his words with a Taser.

She pulled back with wanting eyes as Alex gave her a reassuring glance and dove into the tunnel after Ken.

Becker pointed a Taser in each of their faces. "If this is a coordinated attack, you two are enemy combatants. And I will act accordingly. For now, you will be locked in this tunnel terminal module. Do *not* make me do more than that. I will not hesitate to eliminate a threat to this platform. Understand?"

Min and Zandra put their hands up in the air again and nodded agreement. Becker dove into the tunnel.

Zandra took Min's arm. "Better practice explain on me, again. I feel negative aura here. That is my Aleks, I know, I can *feel*, but this is not good place."

"Yeah, I'm getting that loud and clear too."

*

As she was deep asleep in her scheduled off-shift period, the blaring alarm jolted Emma awake. The module was already bathed with the red hue of the emergency alert lighting.

"Emma. Inbound bogie. The commander wants you at your station. This is not a drill," Starra announced emphatically over the intercom in her module.

Emma quickly extracted herself from her sleeping bag, aligned herself with the module exit, and pushed off hard. Every second counted. She was expected to be strapped into her station within twenty-five seconds, or she would be on report ... if they were still around to make one. *This is not a drill. Just a couple days into our rotation on station, and already we have an attack. The Tuanhuo does enjoy playing this card.* A bogie meant one thing: they were on a collision course with another object in space, and the results could be disastrous.

As Emma entered the Demons module, she looked up to see Alex entering

118

from the other direction. He was moving fast, just like herself. She put her right arm out in a hook form. Alex acknowledged her plan to cancel their opposite momentum with a nod and set his arm out to catch hers. As if choreographed for a ballet, the two merged, spun, grabbed opposite handholds, released, and stopped at their assigned stations. Emma glanced over her shoulder, winked, and gave a thumbs-up as they both strapped in. She noted Alex's pursed lips of concern as he gave her a curt nod. *Hmmm, something's up.* She punched her entry code into the console and glanced at the action timer. Only twenty seconds had passed—not bad.

Entering the module, Hans Becker shook his head after watching the two land simultaneously in their stations. "If you two are finished with your square dancing, we need tracking data, pronto."

"Bogie identified as an older Class IX GPS satellite with foreign propulsion packs," Emma reported immediately from her tracking console. "Looks like the Asia Tuanhuo have hacked another and sent it our way."

A common two-for-one tactic in the unacknowledged but ongoing war with the Asia Tuanhuo was to commandeer a defenseless enemy asset with attachable rocket thrusters. By overloading the satellite's meager orbital thrusters, the enemy could aim the object at another typically more valuable asset. The resulting collision at orbital speeds would obliterate both. It was an effective tactic and provided plausible deniability to the aggressor. The Asia Tuanhuo would have no idea why one of the Right Alliance's own satellites had lost orbit and crashed into Alpha-One Platform.

"Damn, that thing is big! I thought they were supposed to decommission those defenseless sitting ducks," Ken Seaborn said as Emma sent the ID marker over to his console. "I need a ten-meter-wide collision vector if we all want to avoid becoming space dirt."

"Working on it," Emma replied. As the tracking officer, it was her job to determine the trajectory of the incoming object. Ken, as pilot, would attempt to reposition the station so that none of the modules came within the travel path of the oncoming satellite.

Alex had two jobs. Priority was to lock onto the object with the high-speed cameras and directional comms to hack their data link. Both would be used to document the attack. If the Tuanhuo was foolish enough to send the rocket thrusters any updated navigational signals, they would have clear evidence. A live data stream would now be directed back to ground control to provide valuable intelligence. Once that was running, his second task was to simply call out the time to intersect. "Cameras running, comms clear, we have a good feed to base. One minute, ten seconds," he stated.

"Emma, vector now," Commander Becker directed.

Emma punched her keyboard. "Locked. Starra, calculate evasive."

With such a large object, eliminating the bogie with laser cannon fire was not an option. Fragmentation of the incoming object would result in their obliteration by the equivalent of shotgun pellets instead of a single massive bullet. Their lives depended on their ability to reposition the station out of the path of the satellite. The problem was basic physics, and an AI excelled at this science. Unfortunately, the station had considerable mass, and moving it in any direction relative to its current position required force and time to accelerate. They had extremely limited amounts of both.

No full evasion is possible. The best minimum damage option is to sacrifice the S6 Truss," Starra calmly reported.

They all looked at Hans Becker. It was his call. Even with sealing the hatches, ripping the S6 Truss away could easily jeopardize the integrity of the entire station. In addition, a stray piece of debris that might be just behind the oncoming satellite and invisible to their tracking could easily punch a hole through their module and introduce them all to the vacuum of space.

"Negative. We need another option" Becker demanded.

Ken pointed at his targeting screen. "Sir, with the bogie vector aligned with our z-axis, we could blow the external Cobra hatch and possibly shift our position enough for a different collision solution."

"Starra, calculate," Becker ordered and started moving to close the hatch between the Hellcat and Cobra modules.

Alex called out, "Forty-five seconds." He had to admit, Ken's feel for three-dimensional combat was good. His fast thinking could be their salvation.

Starra continued in her calm voice, *"If a full decompression of the Cobra module at its starboard-facing port can be achieved within ten seconds, there is a fifty-two percent probability of successful collision avoidance."*

"Not great odds," Ken said, shaking his head.

Hans Becker gave the yell of a warrior as he heaved the Hellcat hatch closed and spun only one lock bolt to secure it. With the hatch hinged on their side of the module interface, it would hold with the pressure working to push it closed rather than open. "Hatch secured. Starra, blow the Cobra exterior hatch *now.*"

"Executing."

With the sudden acceleration of the explosive depressurization, Becker was slammed against the hatch. The distinctive crack of bone as Becker was forced into the hatch mechanism made Emma turn from her console. "Sir, are you okay?"

Gritting his teeth, he called out, "Vector report!"

Emma turned back to her console and watched as the targeting vector slowly started to shift. "Moving, but still overlapping within the ten-meter zone."

"Twenty seconds," Alex said.

Starra added, *"Ken, giving a five-second full burn to the x-axis thrusters should rotate the S6 Truss."*

Ken punched the ignition. "Burning."

The crew now felt a pull in another direction, slow but noticeable.

The vector continued to shift. Emma called out, "Ten percent overlapping margin."

Alex started a countdown. "Ten, nine, eight..."

"Five percent margin."

"Just a scratch from something that big will hurt big-time," Ken noted.

"Five, four, three, two..."

"Zero margin."

They all froze and waited for their world to silently explode, their existence terminated in a nanosecond.

Alex called out, *"Clear!* Bogie is past the intersect."

"Hot damn, that was close!" Ken exclaimed.

Hans Becker floated back into the center of the module, holding his arm. "Nice work, everyone. Alex, confirm data feed to base. I hope they use that intel to extract some payback from those Tuanhuo assholes. Ken, double-check the bogie trajectory and send to base. Emma, I think I need your assistance. Seems you get to practice your zero-g splinting technique. I believe I've broken my radius."

"Let's get you to the X-ray."

"No. Just splint this, pronto. We have another problem. We've been boarded."

"What?" Emma asked. "Who? How?"

"I have no idea who they are or how they got here, but we have two other people on board," Becker said, shaking his head. "Ken, get back to the TTPT and check on them. Keep an eye on them until I can get back there."

"I'm going too," Alex said, releasing his straps.

"Hold on. It's way too cramped out there for another party. Let's do this. Ken, you wait at the Tribe module. Alex, you go down the tunnel and send the two women back to Ken. We can all gather in Tribe and hear what they have to say."

"Roger," Alex said, pushing off.

Ken grabbed his Taser. "I'll make sure they don't try anything funny."

"Just everyone stay cool, and let's find out what the hell is going on."

"They're spies. And I know what to do with spies."

"Ken, just hold them there. Nothing more. Got it?"

"Yes, sir."

"Emma, let's go," Becker said with another wince. "And maybe a small shot of some happy juice is needed."

SCAN ME

FACTOID 13

*The often-repeated Apollo 13 phrase, "Houston, we have a problem"
would not be how the astronauts aboard the ISS would report a
similar dire event. Since most activities on the ISS are related to the
space-bound payloads (the research facilities and experiments), the
Marshall Space Flight Center in Huntsville, Alabama, would likely get
the call. The Payload Communication controller, or PACOM, would
be responsible. So, they would more likely say, "PACOM, Station.
Huntsville, we have a problem."*

13   Garcia, Mark (2020, October 15). *Ground Facilities*. NASA.com.
https://www.nasa.gov/mission_pages/station/behindscenes/index.html

CHAPTER 13

Huntsville, We Have a Problem

Lucas pulled hand over hand as fast as he could on the center rail running the length of the Truss Tunnel. Arriving at the Port Terminal module, he dove for the Aseco hatch. Ignoring the bruising impact as he slammed into it with the momentum he had developed, he fumbled with the hatch mechanism with nervous hands. *Why has Min not answered comms? Has something happened to them?*

Pushing the hatch aside, Lucas entered the Aceso module—and froze.

Empty.

Just the hum of the fans filled the module. The cubical room the size of a large elevator could not easily hide two people. There were no open access panels. *Where are they?* He desperately opened panels that could not possibly contain a full human body. His eyes scanned every surface. Nothing but monitors and colored LED lights displaying information to a void.

He caught his reflection in the surface of the plexiglass safety shield and jerked—somebody there? No, his mind playing tricks on him. His heart was racing. *I could land an F-16 on a carrier at night in the driving rain, and my pulse would be lower. Min!* Reaching for the comms panel, he had to punch his finger into the panel three times before connecting with the correct button.

"Fred, I checked everything. They're not here."

"What?" There was a long pause. Commander Johnson asked, *"And none of the EVA suits are missing?"*

Lucas turned and examined yet again the two spacesuits affixed to the wall opposite the comms panel. He peered inside, as if a miniature person could be hiding within either the upper or lower suit components. Returning to the panel, he shook his head, "No. I checked. Both the EVA suits. They are here and empty."

"Well, you can't just go walking around outside a space station without one. This is impossible. They must be somewhere." The commander stroked his temples on the video feed. *"This is going to sound pretty stupid when we call ground. 'Hello, Ed. Yes, we seem to have misplaced two astronauts. Have you seen them?'"*

They both floated in silence.

"Well, power things down there and come on back. I'll double-check the airlock logs just to be thorough," Johnson said in a defeated tone.

Lucas busied himself with shutting the Aceso equipment down and closing the panels he had hastily opened. He and Johnson had now searched every inch of the station for Min and Zandra. They had to be somewhere. Contrary to what Hollywood screenwriters would write into scripts, real astronauts did not develop space madness and eject themselves from an airlock.

Arriving back in the Destiny module with the commander, Lucas had an emptiness in his stomach that wasn't from lack of food. He was almost ill with fear. *Action. Focus on positive action.* He tapped the commander on the shoulder. "We need to call this in."

"They aren't going to believe us," Johnson said. He moved to a comm panel and punched up a link to the ground controller. "PACOM, this is Aceso Mission. I need a secure channel, over."

After a short pause, the reply came back, *"Aceso, this is PACOM. You are on secure comms. Go ahead."*

"This is going to sound crazy, and we are not pulling your leg." Johnson grimaced and looked at Lucas, who shrugged and motioned, "What the hell, we have to do *something*" with his hands.

"PACOM, we need to report that we are unable to locate either Wang Min or Zandra Ivanov on the station."

Silence.

"Aceso Mission, PACOM. Say again?"

Fred Johnson grimaced. "PACOM, we have searched the entire station and are unable to locate specialists Wang Min or Zandra Ivanov on the station. There are no EVA suits missing, and the logs do not show any airlock cycles. This is no joke; we are dead serious."

"Roger, mission. Please hold."

Lucas could imagine the controller immediately looking over to the mission doctor and asking what he thought about the commander's mental condition. He would also immediately escalate that condition. Transmitting a strange report over a secured link meant that nobody was goofing around.

After a short time, the familiar voice of Ed Anderson came over the link. *"Good evening, Fred. I understand you have an abnormality. Can you expand on your status?"*

Both men were a special breed, chosen for their jobs because if the strange or impossible arose, they could be trusted to focus, follow training, and address whatever they faced with intelligence and professionalism. Facts. Focus on the facts.

Johnson was methodical. "Both Min and Zandra failed to appear for dinner at eighteen thirty station time. Their work assignment for the day had been to run the dark matter/energy experimental trial run Baker-Alpha-Zero-Niner. That trial was to complete just before the eighteen thirty dinner scheduled. We did not find them in the main ship modules, and they did not answer intership comms, so Lucas went looking for them in the Aceso module. They were not there, and the power cells were still online, which is strange. Those cells are never to be left online and unattended. We have searched the entire station, twice. They are not on board. All EVA suits are accounted for, and there have been no airlock cycles."

"Roger, Mission. Please hold while I get that experiment controller on the line."

After a brief pause, a young redhead with wire-frame glasses appeared on their video screen, quickly putting down her coffee cup. At mission control, every controller heard all communication transmissions all of the time. They learned to tune in and out of conversations as needed. Jackie had heard Fred's report.

"Hi, Fred, Lucas," Jackie said with a somber tone. *"I've been trying to make sense of their feed. We were executing the run and getting some good data. Min's new parameters seemed to be working quite well. I believe she had developed a well-formed dark energy cloud."*

"Anything unusual, Jackie?" Ed Anderson asked.

"We had some intermittent telemetry breaks." Jackie's face leaned forward and half out of the picture as she studied something to the side. *"I don't know what that was about. Other feeds from the station were stable. Only the Aceso module telemetry feed went bad, along with their comms. After about … twenty seconds, everything came back solid and returned to the nominal baseline readings. I assumed that they had stopped the run and were analyzing the data before proceeding."*

Ed ran his hand slowly over his bald head, thinking, then asked, *"How long after the readings went to baseline did the power cells go offline?"*

Jackie punched a few commands into her keyboard. *"Thirty-seven minutes, fifteen seconds."*

"Can you look at the telemetry more during the intermittent period? Try and clean it up as best you can," he directed.

"Already on it."

Ed's face returned to their video feed to document a formal summary. *"Aceso Mission, we have a window of about thirty-seven minutes where we* can't account for *Min* or *Zandra*. *We show that they did run the experiment trial. We need to analyze. I don't know that there's much more you two can do for now. Go get your meal, and we will be back with you shortly.*"

"Roger, mission out." Floating in the space station, Johnson turned off the comms panel and said to Lucas, "Well, that went better than I thought."

Lucas folded his arms and frowned. "We have now entered the Twilight Zone."

SCAN ME

FACTOID 14

In 2021, the Parker Solar Probe reached a top speed of 101 miles (163 kilometers) per second during its tenth close solar flyby. That translates to an amazing 364,621 miles per hour (586,000 kilometers per hour). In December of 2024, the probe will make another approach to the solar surface, with an expected speed of over 430,000 miles per hour (690,000 kilometers per hour). The probe is the fastest-moving object ever built by man. Yet at its 2024 speed, the probe was still only traveling at 0.00064 times the speed of light.

14   Howell, Elizabeth. (2021, November 23).

NASA's superfast Parker Solar Probe just broke its own speed record at the sun. Space.com.
https://www.space.com/parker-solar-probe-sun-speed-record-november-2021

CHAPTER 14

Universes, Plural

Ed Anderson sat alone at the head of a long white laminate table in the main conference room of the World Space Federation in Huntsville, Alabama. He emphatically punched the disconnect on the comm link. It was the fourth bureaucrat to call him in the last hour. The military clock on the wall read 21:30. His eyes slid down from the clock to the picture of the Unity module just after joining with the Russian-built Zarya module. It captured the first step in assembling the first internationally orchestrated orbiting laboratory. *Did that flight director have the same insanity I deal with daily?* Back then, it had certainly been a challenge to coordinate five space agencies representing fifteen countries. *Now I deal with every individual remaining group on the planet. We all have a say, since we all need the same miracle.* But Homo sapiens had always had its clans, and petty rivalry would always arise. If one group's national animal made it to the WSS for a legitimate biological study, every group now wanted theirs on the station. The bureaucrats were no help. They would quote the policy of inclusion and be motivated by large campaign donations from rich patrons. They would never learn. He shook his head. *How can anyone think having a king cobra on a space station would be a good idea? We're trying to save our species, and instead have devolved right back into bureaucratic madness.*

Waving in the two scientists standing in the doorway, Ed shifted gears in his mind. *On to the next topic of lunacy...* Two of the brightest minds in the field of astrophysics entered and quietly took their seats on opposite sides of the table. The third and probably the brightest star was supposed to be on the WSS, but wasn't.

"Considering the hour, I just want to know, in terms that won't make my head explode, how two astronauts on a space station can disappear," Ed stated.

John Harris was the most senior member of the team. He shook his head. "We have some theories, but no consensus."

Ed could tell that his team lead was reluctant to voice some of the wilder ideas his younger team member had presented him. John was not a risk taker. Astrophysics took patience. Missions were planned in years and decades, since the cosmos was so vast. Spaceships and probes moved at a slow crawl, considering the distances they needed to travel. John had climbed the ranks of the space agency by showing he had the patience to run carefully planned and executed missions. Although nearing retirement, he was not yet ready to let go of the reins. And he was not going to take risks.

Ed raised his head slightly and spoke towards the ceiling. "Ed Anderson. Room monitors OFF."

"Confirmed authorization, Ed Anderson. Monitors off," said an automated voice with a slight British accent.

"Okay. This is just the three of us. We know we're dealing with something never experienced before: two astronauts have disappeared. I want this meeting to be wide open. I want all ideas. The lives of two astronauts are in the balance. The last thing the WSF needs right now is a couple of funerals for the people who may be our best hopes in finding a new home. So, let's get to it." Ed turned to Jackie. "Anything more on the telemetry?"

Jackie pushed her glasses up on her nose and looked at the notes on her tablet. She carefully stated, "I did find that just before the telemetry went fishy, they were getting an energy spike. If my calculations are correct, that spike should not have been possible. The energy level was above the instantaneous output threshold that our power cells can deliver. It's as if some other power source came into play."

"Interesting. Any idea what the source could be?"

"Just some conjecture," Jackie said, glancing at John. "Min's experiments are cutting-edge quantum physics. We know there are relationships between dark matter, dark energy, and superposition. Some theorize that these are the elements of parallel universes—"

"That's just wild speculation at this point," John broke in. "Nobody has ever shown definitive evidence of a parallel universe."

Ed raised his hand gently. "John, I want this to be a very open and 'what if' kind of conversation. We have just witnessed something completely unexplainable. Rather than focus on what is known and plausible, let's just think about the other side: what sounds crazy. With two missing astronauts that vanished into thin air, honestly, I'm ready to listen to just about anything right now."

John sat back in his chair and folded his arms. "Okay, I'm sorry, Jackie. Go ahead."

Ed watched Jackie smile at John and thank him with her eyes. He had put this pair working together five years ago now. Though it was initially an odd pair and a risky choice, Ed guessed right that they would find their stride together as professionals and complement each other's unique talents. John was a great mentor and had provided guidance and helpful direction to the young astrophysicist, but it was good to see Jackie respect yet challenge that authority. With the new direction of the WSF, Ed needed people with new ideas. Young minds brought fresh perspectives and asked new questions. Both long-term judgment from people like John and bright ideas from people like Jackie made for the best.

Jackie cleared her throat. "Well, I think that the best way to look at this is to first consider the well-accepted concept of wormholes. Again, no wormhole has ever been observed, but they do follow the general theory of relativity. We accept them as a structure that can be visualized as a tunnel with two ends at different points in space-time. Typically, we think of the points as being billions of light years apart. They could be a way to connect distant points in our universe. We focus on the aspect of wormholes because in comparison, our current ability to traverse the cosmos is exceedingly slow. We want to think of a means to move billions of miles in space in the blink of an eye.

"But what if we consider not just the Einstein field equations, but wormholes as applied to quantum mechanics? What if wormholes could link space-time with the two endpoints exhibiting not points in our space, but points of quantum superposition? Instead of the other endpoint being billions of light years away in *our* universe, it could be next door, in *another* universe. I am thinking that Min's dark matter and energy cloud happened to combine with another in a parallel universe."

Ed rubbed his temples and took a sip of his coffee. It was cold and bitter. He wanted to throw it out and save his stomach. But he needed to keep going tonight, and the black liquid would help. He looked from Jackie to John and back. "You two always make my head hurt."

Jackie excitedly punched up the holographic display in the center of the table and started drawing. "Let me show you. The simplicity is what makes this so attractive to me. Let's go to the basics. We have matter and energy in our universe. E equals mc squared, right?" She drew two spheres, labeling one *matter* and the other *energy*, then a cloud to encapsulate them with the label *the universe.*

"Now, the problem we have is that all the matter and energy we know about in our universe only accounts for about five percent of what should be there. *Five percent.* That's like saying out of a deck of cards, I can only tell you about two or three of them. I wouldn't know that there were four suits, or that the cards numbered two through ten, or that there were three face cards and an ace in each suit. If the universe were a symphonic orchestra with eighty musicians, I would only hear the sound from maybe four. Think of the amount of information I would be missing if the orchestra played Beethoven's Symphony No. 3, and all I could hear were a couple of flutes, a cello, and a horn. I could be missing all the violins and not even know it. If the universe were a hundred-story building—"

"Jackie, you're drifting. Back to Min and Zandra," Ed said.

"Right. Sorry. Okay, so, what's missing? We postulate that there is a bunch of dark matter and energy out there somewhere." She created a black mass on the edge of the universe cloud, overlapping some of the space in the universe and some outside. "This is what Min's experiments were meant to find, and if possible, observe, measure, and document. Min did not think of space as a void; she thought of it as full of dark energy and matter. It could be an incredible resource to us, and a means for interstellar travel.

"Now, let's just say that there is another universe, following the same laws of physics as ours." Jackie copied the universe cloud with its matter and energy balls. She created another universe also overlapping the dark energy and matter. "By the way, the same laws of physics aren't necessarily a must. If you start to work through the quantum mechanics of other universes, it's probable that their fundamental laws of physics could be different. It could be incredible to observe. Just imagine a universe where conservation of—"

"Min and Zandra, Jackie. Min and Zandra."

Jackie nodded excitedly and pushed her glasses up on the bridge of her nose. "Okay, so let's just say we have this other universe. We can't see this alternate universe, but just as the dark matter and energy impact our universe, they could possibly be a bridge to another universe. Some postulate that what we see as dark matter and energy is the superposition phasing of another universe, or even other universes. It's quite amazing."

Ed rubbed the stubble on his chin. "So, what you're saying is that somehow when Min probed this dark energy mass with her experiment, it bridged two universes and transferred Min and Zandra from our universe to this alternate universe through superposition?"

"Exactly. Just as this alternate universe appears to quantum phase with us, we're quantum phasing with them. Somehow, the two phasing superpositions overlapped and synchronized enough that when some observation was made to establish a known state, matter between the two universes was exchanged. That matter was our Min and Zandra." Jackie sat back and let Ed absorb what she had presented.

Ed studied the hologram for a minute. "John, your thoughts?"

"It's an exciting idea and appears very simple. In theory, it answers a lot of questions and fills gaps neatly. But it's just a theory based on a lot of stuff we can't prove one way or another. The reality is that if we go out of here talking about parallel universes, there will be a bunch of people checking our coffee mugs for mind-altering drugs," he replied, lifting his cup. "Unfortunately, I can't say I have anything better to explain why we have two astronauts that have just disappeared without a trace."

The three sat in silence for a long minute.

Jackie spoke hesitantly. "I have something else weird. I don't know if it's related, but it could be if there were enough dark matter or energy involved."

Ed sat with his elbow on the table and covered his eyes with his hands. "Okay, here's where my head probably explodes. If it's weird to you, Jackie, I'm afraid to ask."

"It's something that the radiation guys were talking about a couple days ago. Boy, they were super excited about it. They never see it at such a level, and right outside our atmosphere. They're still checking and trying to figure out if it was some glitch in the sensors. I only mention it because it might be another clue."

"Jackie, what is it?"

"Oh, they think a black hole collapsed right in our orbit."

"Yup, there it goes. Boom." Ed lifted his head and looked at Jackie. "Really?"

"They measure all kinds of radiation all the time, and they suddenly got a spike of high-energy gamma radiation. Compared to what we normally measure from faraway sources like the Cygnus X-3 binary star system, this was a large, concentrated burst. The problem is that it didn't come from some vector reaching far out in the cosmos. When they triangulated the vectors, they found that the source was right in our orbit. I only mention it since high-energy gamma rays are what would come from a black hole when it finally collapses. If that dark matter in this other universe were to quickly collapse for some reason, it might mimic a black hole emitting those gamma rays. It could be proof that another universe exists," Jackie said, looking at John for support.

John leaned forward. "Ed, Jackie and I may have our differences in theories around quantum mechanics, but I must admit that what she says is a possibility. We need to verify this quietly."

Ed caught Jackie flashing John another thankful smile for the support. He loved to see a team work well together.

Jackie said, "I can ask Peter in spectrographics to recheck everything and keep quiet."

"Let me do that," Ed directed.

SCAN ME

FACTOID 15

Every spacecraft carries survival gear for crash landings, and the Russian Soyuz capsule attached to the ISS has a kit that includes a gun. But although the gun has been there for as long as the space station has been in orbit, its existence is kept quiet. NASA and Russia won't talk publicly about it.

---

15   Macias, Amanda. (2015, January 29).
his Is a Triple-Barreled Soviet Space Gun with an Attached Machete. Business Insider.
https://www.businessinsider.com/this-is-a-triple-barreled-soviet-space-gun-with-an-attached-machete-2015-1

CHAPTER 15

Prison

SPACE FORCE ALPHA-ONE PLATFORM
RHO-1

It was a late dinner, but the events of the day had thrown the mission schedule out the hatch. Hovering somewhat back from his place at the dinner table, Alex eyed the video feed from the Tribe module. He frowned at the image of the two women bound and strapped to the wall in a makeshift prison. He had made it abundantly clear that he was not happy with the way their new visitors were being treated in a fairly heated argument with Ken and the commander, while Emma quietly prepared the meals. In the end, they all ate their meals in silence. Alex figured Emma chose the rehydrated chicken pot pie for the meal as an attempted peace offering. It was his favorite out of all the meal choices and was not the meal on the schedule.

Alex finished eating and forced a smile for Emma. *"Merci, oh chef de la bonne cuisine."*

"Happy to be able to serve such elegant fare," she replied.

Alex rubbed his palms together slowly, thinking. He turned to the commander and attempted a factual, logical approach this time. The commander was always very reasonable.

"Let's look at the facts." He started counting with his right thumb raised. "We've done a careful scan of the entire orbital zone and have found no other craft within range for an EVA. Also, we have searched the entire station and found no missing EVA suits. Finally, we have verified the logs, and there have been no airlock cycles recently. So, logically, they could not have been on a nearby Asia Tuanhuo craft and attacked our station with a spacewalk. I think we're all in agreement that no one can survive in the vacuum of space without an EVA suit."

Commander Hans Becker laced his fingers and set his chin on them, his blue eyes staring at Alex under furrowed brows. Alex sat quietly to let the commander consider his statements.

Ken broke the silence. "It doesn't matter how they got here. They're Asia Tuanhuo spies."

"That's just paranoia talking," Alex said in a calm and dismissive voice.

"It's obvious. Names like Min and Ivanov? One is Asian and the other Russian. Hello? *Spies*," Ken shot back. "I say we put them in front of the airlock and get the truth of their mission the fast way. If they don't talk quick, show them the door. Simple."

"Actually, she's Romanian," Alex said with his teeth set. "But yeah, that's what we need here. More macho Party stupidity and—"

"Stop," the commander interrupted. "You two are not going to get started on this again. We've reported this to ground. Let's let them give us the steps they want us to take. End of discussion."

Alex and Ken glared at each other. Ken made a sweeping motion at his throat with his fingers. Alex rolled his eyes and shook his head. To Ken, the only good Asia Tuanhuo member was a dead one. It wasn't written in the Party doctrine, but to blue-blooded Party members like Ken, it did not need to be. It was understood. The Party was happy to stoke the fire of fear and hate in other people to maintain blind loyalty. It was easier to hate a group of people you didn't know or understand well.

Alex turned and looked away, folding his arms to think of another angle. He was sure Ken would try to get Party brownie points by submitting a report accusing him of abetting Asia Tuanhuo spies. Alex could never understand how people could become so brainwashed. It was a downward spiral when a society chose to believe propaganda rather than truth.

"Well, they're not going anywhere right now," Emma said, pointing to the video feed from the other module. "I suggest that we follow military protocol and provide them with basic sustenance."

Alex nodded and turned to Commander Becker. "May I take them some water and a ration?"

"Minimum allocations. And nobody gets any straps released. Understood?" Becker said, looking Alex straight in the eyes.

"Roger."

*

Alex floated at the Tribe hatchway and disabled the motion sensor. Not wanting to give the visitors a tour of the station, Commander Becker had ordered them to be detained in the Tribe module, close to where they had originally been found. The two women had been wrapped in makeshift straitjackets and strapped to opposite walls. A motion sensor was placed at the hatch on the remote chance that they managed to release themselves and somehow not be noticed in the video feed. Depending on layered backup systems was second nature to all astronauts.

In as cheery a voice as he could muster, Alex said, "Dinner is served."

Min and Zandra turned their heads in his direction, but did not otherwise respond.

"Okay. I am truly sorry for the way you're being treated."

"It's been hours, and we both need to use the john," Min stated flatly.

Alex shook his head. "Sorry. Captain's orders are that you can't be released from the straps. He says that you'll just have to use your EVA diapers for now."

"You know we didn't get here by doing a spacewalk, so we're not wearing EVA diapers," Min added with a raised eyebrow. "Unless you want urine floating all over your sparkly clean station, I suggest you tell your captain that a trip to the john is required."

Alex had to admit that droplets of urine floating around the station would be nasty. He moved to a comm unit on the wall. "Commander, our visitors need to relieve themselves and are not wearing diapers. Permission to release them for an excursion to the WMS."

After a couple seconds, the commander said, "I'm sending Emma down to assist. One at a time. Out."

Alex gestured with his head towards the WMS. "All the comforts of home."

*

Emma finished securing Min back on the wall and turned to Alex. "Per protocol, you need to verify that she is resecured."

Alex passed Emma the Taser he was casually holding, floated over to Min, and pulled on the straps. "All good."

"This is unnecessary," Min said.

"I know, it's ridiculous," Alex replied. "But as a military platform, we have rules we must follow, no matter how stupid."

"When World Space Station become military platform?" Zandra asked.

Emma floated over in front of Zandra and folded her arms, studying the woman attached to the wall for a while. "It is general knowledge, even within the Asia Tuanhuo, that Alpha-One Platform was commissioned in 2045, just after the Satellite War. It was the first platform of the Right Alliance."

Zandra returned Emma's stare without blinking. "Right Alliance? What that?"

"Come on, you really don't know? What game are you two playing?" Emma asked. Holding out a hydration pack for Zandra, she said, "After the Satellite War plunged us all into the dark ages, leaders from what used to be NATO came together to protect future orbital assets. It took us years to rebuild that infrastructure. The new fleets of global positioning and communications satellites allowed for much more sophisticated access control, so any use became very selective. The Right Alliance was formed to control the connectivity. At the same time that the technical alliances were being drawn, there were strong cultural changes forming around who could be trusted and what each country stood for. The Right Thinking doctrine was developed and quickly found a strong following. The satellite infrastructure alliance became absorbed into the Right Alliance political movement. Now this is the Alpha-One Platform, one of five armed military space platforms that defend the satellite network of the Alliance."

"Five? More stations?" Zandra asked.

"Of course. We need to keep ahead of the Tuanhuo. The Tuanhuo have just finished commissioning their fourth platform. I imagine a fifth is on the drawing boards." Emma studied Zandra for another long moment. She tapped Alex on the arm and motioned for him to move to the far end of the module with her.

At the aft end of the module, Emma said in a whisper, "Alex, this is weird. Two things: first, I have training in reading the subtle cues of facial expressions, breathing, and body language. I am not detecting any deception in these two. They are either very well trained, or something else is truly going on here. I will review the details of their body responses that Starra is capturing before I make any report, but I think they could be telling the truth."

Alex's eyes lit up with excitement. *Good. Maybe I've underestimated Emma. She's willing to think for herself.*

"This is what I've been saying. Nobody wants to listen. Facts matter."

"Yeah, well. That brings me to point two. I also do homework nobody else around here seems to bother doing. I found some interesting stuff from before the war—stuff that most servers no longer have in their data stores, since it was easier to wipe them than to correct them to Right Thinking. That Zandra there is the identical twin of a Zandra Ivanov lost in the orbital disaster you were part of that triggered the war. How can that be?"

"Because she *is* the same person. Trust me, I know," Alex said, tapping his chest.

Min spoke up from the far end of the module. "So, you have a cold war now in space? With weapons now in space, I suppose?"

Emma spun around and floated back to the two women pasted to the module walls. "Well, it was your group of countries that started this. We had to defend ourselves or be taken over by a regime bent on world domination."

"I've told you, we are not with this Asia Tuanhuo group you keep talking about. We are scientists with the World Space Federation," Min said emphatically. She turned her head towards Alex. "So, in your world, it's still all about military power? Is that what funds your work? You want to use quantum superposition as a weapon?"

Alex held a straw to Min's lips for water and hung his head as he considered his reply. "You obviously are working on similar technology."

"Only to better understand the universe, and the first step in possibly building an interstellar engine, not to build a weapon. Wasn't your work before the war all about interstellar travel too? Has that all changed?"

"I am just as interested in science as a tool for discovery as you," Alex said softly. His gaze drifted over to Zandra. "You can ask Zandra where my passions truly lie."

Alex switched to a meal pouch. "I imagine you know very well that sometimes as scientists, we need to feed a demon. Too often, they have the power, and the funding, that makes our studies possible. It has always been that way, and my guess is that you just have a different demon than the Alliance and the Party in your universe."

"There are always demons," Emma agreed.

Alex was surprised by Emma's comment. He got that sense again that Emma had doubts about the Party she seemed to serve so fervently.

Min motioned her head for a sip of the meal ration from Alex. "True. What is this Alliance demon?"

Alex grinned slightly and thumbed towards Emma. "Emma here might paint you a bit rosier of a picture, but I will give you what I think is a more accurate truth you might not hear otherwise." He turned to the module monitoring camera and looked straight into it. With all the defiance he could muster, he put his chin forward and said, "Considering your presence here is the result of my work, and *nobody else* in this universe can do it ... they would be nuts to send me to a Patriot Camp now."

Stick that in your pipe and smoke it.

Alex took a breath, relaxed, and turned back to Min. "The Right Alliance are all those who follow the Party's Right Thinking doctrine. As the name implies, that means they follow the correct way of thinking in terms of God, Party, and leadership, not necessarily in that order. The Party leaders establish the structure and rules that we all live by, so that everyone is clear as to their purpose in life, what they are to contribute, and what they are allowed to do. Follow the Party, and you will be a productive member of society."

"So, the Right Alliance is your government?"

"Oh, no. Governments just caused problems. The Party abolished those long ago as they formed the Alliance. The Asia Tuanhuo still has most of their old governments intact. But they have such a long history of warring factions and corrupt leaders that I don't expect they will ever combine into anything more than a gang of thugs following the strongest and most vile current leader. Right now, and for the past two decades, that has been the Asian mainland. They are led by a woman that most people refer to as *Wuqing de bei Guafu*, or the Ruthless Black Widow. She seems to enjoy being referred to in that way. It nicely illustrates to others that might challenge her just how evil she can be.

"Here though, in the Alliance, country constitutions were redundant and sometimes contrary to the Party doctrine, so those were eliminated. By creating the Party doctrine, the leaders brought all the people with Right Thinking together. That's why it's called the Right Alliance. There was no need for all the different government groups and the waste they caused. Plus, you didn't need the government telling you what you should do if you had the Right Thinking."

Zandra swallowed some rations and said, "I sense other side to this?"

Alex turned back towards her. He sensed that earnest desire she always had to understand. "Well, let's just say that if you're not with the Party doctrine, or part of the leadership power, like the Boss and his Party cronies, then something has gone amiss with your thinking. You are definitely not thinking *right*. A couple years in a Patriot Reeducation Camp typically corrects that issue, unless you're a Resistance fanatic. The Resistance is the thorn in the Party's paw, and its members refuse to accept the new order. They also don't seem to reeducate well, according to the Party."

"'Boss'?" Zandra asked.

Alex sighed. "Many people believe that in a time of crisis, there are two types of leaders. There are those like Winston Churchill, who provided true leadership for people in a desperate time. But unfortunately, there are also many examples in history of leaders that use the crisis for their own benefit, and to gorge an unquenchable thirst for more power. Our president at the time was of the later mold. Using various emergency decrees, he whittled away a system built by the people and for the people, turning it into a system for the select following a supreme commander."

Zandra's mouth fell open. "No. Now dictator?"

"There's a decree stating that word is unpatriotic, so I'm not allowed to say it." Alex turned his head away and bit his lower lip. "In conflict, there are winners and losers, and those that make money either way. The Boss is a powerful and wealthy man that has leveraged both the Right Thinking of the Party and the conflict between the Tuanhuo and the Alliance to his benefit. Some would say—although not publicly—that he is the counterpart to the Tuanhuo's Black Widow. I probably should stop right there and not say anything more. Even considering my research being so valuable and providing me the ability to say things others don't dare, I am not totally immune to the rules of the Party." Looking over at Emma, he added, "Or the wrath of the Boss."

Alex thought he saw Emma cringe with a look of hatred. "You want to add to that?" he asked.

Emma shook her head quickly. "No. Your summary might be slanted to the cynical, but it's not totally inaccurate."

"We had something similar long ago. They called it the Third Reich. It was one of the darkest times in human history, and it didn't end well." Min added, "History also showed that the Resistance *fanatics* of those days were the real heroes."

Emma considered Min's words for few seconds and asked Zandra, "So, your universe is not so different from ours? Warring factions and fanatics for freedom and peace?"

Zandra shook her head. "No, opposite. We learn hard lesson. Destroyed many uncountable people. And planet itself."

She paused and closed her eyes. Alex could feel the pain in her voice as she quietly continued, "Short version: small rogue nations make weapons, but not feeding people. Say all large nations with food and resource are evil. Corrupt leaders find easy to blame someone else for their people's problems. We have Satellite War too. They use as excuse. Hunger plus religious fan'tism make one madman lighting nuclear fuse. When done, so much nuclear destruction, kill almost all life on planet. Ecosystems all collapse."

Zandra took a deep breath and continued, "But we different after. Took us almost extinction before we see our survival is world together, not divided. War not help anyone. Just waste. Now no nations. No maps with lines. Now we are seven con-tin-ents of one world. That all. We make regional authorities oversee wellness and life quality ... of all their people. We people of damage, fragile, dying earth. We have World Fed-er-ation... We share small resources. What is left on planet not radioactive. We not have bad Boss. Our leaders agree: technology purpose be for good, no need new weapon. And now we search for new planet. We must go there now. We clean sky with robots. Now we go back to station to find way to new home. New beginning for all humanity... We all share. So, sad truth is, in few thousand years, humans only learned how to kill themselves and planet. We need now to learn how to nurture planet and people before we no more."

Zandra nodded her head towards Min. "Min research our hope. Yes, she come from country group starting war. She admit. But that past. We forgive." Zandra paused and turned her head to look directly at Min. "I forgive... Need now to understand universe. Together. So we can live on new world. We not spend resource on weapons. Min, I ... and Aleks again, we do this. I can feel. We put destroy and hate behind us."

Emma collected the meal containers. "So, your universe is now all cherries, with everyone working together for a common cause?"

Min answered, "We're not saying it's perfect. Sometimes our enthusiasm to be so including of all peoples has caused us great loss. But I suppose when you sum up the net quality of life we have finally established on this planet, we have done well, given what we had left to work with. We do struggle, disagree, and have different ideas. But what we are all now painfully aware of is that we belong to a species that almost went extinct. Not by some cosmic event, like a rogue meteor. By our own hand. We have found ways to reach common ground other than by force, and we must focus on the common goal of survival."

They all fell silent for a long minute.

Emma moved to the lighting panel on the wall and turned the lights down. She said, "Well, I would suggest you try to rest. Most likely we will have instructions tomorrow morning as to what to do with you. My guess is that you will be taking the CRV capsule back down for some serious questioning. An emergency descent ride on the CRV is not fun, but that will be the least of your worries. If you're lucky, the Party will claim you. If your dice come up short, the Boss will collect you. Either way, you'll be talking to people who have a hard time considering anything but the Party doctrine and Right Thinking. Alternate universes won't be on their slate of accepted answers to their questions."

FACTOID 16

The International Space Station always has a Soyuz-TMA spacecraft attached to it in standby mode to serve as an emergency CRV, "crew return vehicle." The number of seats on the CRV limits the number of people aboard the ISS at any single time, unless it is being visited by another spacecraft. Typically, a new Soyuz-TMA return vehicle is delivered to the ISS every six months.

16   Soyuz TMA. (2022, November 9). Wikipedia.
https://en.wikipedia.org/wiki/Soyuz_TMA

CHAPTER 16

Plans

Emma slid into the sleeping bag in the privacy of her crew rest station. Pulling out the modified MP5 music player, she eagerly read the message that had come in previously. She quickly typed a response.

Ack. Can reprogram CRV deorbit burn for alternate landing. Send coordinates.

The reply scrolled across the small screen. *45.9578N, 86.2463W*

She typed, *Extraction of niece must be confirmed. Only way to get him to agree.*

Negative, they responded. *No time.*

She shook her head. Crushing each button hard, she replied, *Then NO GO. He is more important. He will join us if we free his niece, but he will never leave the station without that. Niece extraction essential.*

The screen was blank for a long moment. *Ack. Will transmit picture when complete. Out.*

Emma stared at the tiny display for a while. It was a bold plan that she had suggested. This opportunity was even more than they had hoped for though. It was rushed, but it was time to act. She set an alarm for three hours. That would give everyone time enough to get into a deep sleep. She would have the opportunity she needed to modify the CRV without anyone knowing.

SCAN ME

FACTOID 17

The simplest and oldest explanation for dark energy is that it is an energy density inherent to empty space, or a "vacuum energy." Mathematically, vacuum energy is equivalent to Einstein's cosmological constant. Despite the rejection of the cosmological constant by Einstein and others, the modern understanding of the vacuum, based on quantum field theory, is that vacuum energy arises naturally from the totality of quantum fluctuations (i.e., virtual particle-antiparticle pairs that come into existence and then annihilate each other shortly thereafter) in empty space.

17   Riess, Adam. (2021, December 15). Dark energy. Britannica. https://www.britannica.com/science/dark-energy

CHAPTER 17

Gravity Bomb

SPACE FORCE ALPHA-ONE PLATFORM
RHO-1

Alex smiled to himself as he floated towards the Tribe hatchway to disable the motion sensor. One thing about zero gravity was that you didn't have to tiptoe to sneak around in the middle of the night. No footsteps and the constant hum of equipment about the station tended to deaden any noise he might make.

Both the women seemed to be sleeping. He went directly to Zandra like a moth to a flame. Her long, dark hair floating wide around her head melted him with her simple beauty. The urge to release her straps and take her in his arms swept over him. *Too risky.* He just floated in her presence for a while.

As if feeling his being, she slowly opened her eyes without a start, returned his gaze, and gave a soft grin.

What amazing composure—or more likely, she just knew I was here even in her sleep. He whispered, "Hi, sorry to interrupt your sleep, but I just need to ask Min some questions."

155

Zandra gave a tired nod.

He moved forward, gently kissed her lips, and said, "I've missed you so much."

"I too," she whispered.

Alex thought he heard a noise and froze. He held his breath and listened, but heard nothing else. *Back to business.* He moved in front of Min, placed one hand on the wall support, and took hold of her shoulder. He gave her a gentle shake. Min's eyes went wide with a start, but she held back a scream as Alex put a finger to his lips to signal a need for quiet.

"It's okay. I just want to talk."

Min studied him for a moment. "I guess I'm your captive audience. What do you want?"

"I need to know more about your work," Alex whispered. "We need to figure out a way to get you two back. Believe me, you don't want to be questioned by either the Party or the psychopaths the Boss hires."

"What do you want to know?"

"I'm wondering if something I dismissed out of hand was a mistake," Alex admitted. "I'm trying to see if there is a connection between my quantum field generation work and dark matter."

Almost as if it were a switch in her brain, Min clicked on her mental encyclopedia. "Well, there's probably a more direct connection between quantum fields and dark energy, rather than matter. That's what my experiments were leveraging. My work was using the flux in a quantum field to detect vectors of dark energy current. Traveling around the Earth at the speeds we're moving would provide the best chance of running into a dark energy field, short of driving right out into deep space, of course."

"How could any of this be connected to dark matter?" Alex asked.

Min thought for a second. "Well, we know that normal matter and energy are related. I assume E equals mc squared works in your universe as well as ours."

"Yes, still good. So?"

Min continued, "Well, if matter and energy are related in the theory of relativity that we know about, why wouldn't there be something similar defining the relationship between dark matter and dark energy? We just don't understand enough about either to even postulate what that relationship might be."

Alex considered this. "The conversion of matter and energy in our normal terms is generally seen as the destruction of matter to yield energy. Although I would love to have a Star Trek replicator on board, we have found it rather difficult to go the other way and *make* matter. But what if dark matter and energy followed the reverse concept? What if dark energy tends to resolve into dark matter?"

"I suppose that's possible. Again, we know very little about this area," Min admitted.

Alex rubbed the stubble on his chin, his mind aligning the pieces of a puzzle.

"What this all mean? Why that matter?" Zandra whispered from the opposite wall.

"My research might be way worse than just the next-generation satellite weapon," Alex said over his shoulder to Zandra. Turning back to Min, he said, "And you might run into the same problem soon. How long have you been running your quantum field tests?"

"I just started with this mission. I've been waiting for five years to be able to run my trials. It has taken us years just to gather the resources needed to build the Aceso module and a rocket again. Why?"

"Well then, it's definitely me and not you. I've been running my tests for over three years now. This is my third mission, and I do experimental runs almost every other day. It's as if I'm charging a battery each time, I guess. Maybe that battery of energy turns into dark matter."

Min frowned. "I don't follow."

"This is just my theory, but it seems to add up. Science in both our worlds is all about postulating a theory and either proving or disproving it, right?" Alex started counting points of fact on his fingers. "I've been dumping loads of energy into quantum fields, attempting to drive superposition of a mass from one point in space-time to another. All well and good, except what happens to all that energy? I've been assuming that it just dissipates as heat energy. A reasonable assumption, but maybe completely wrong. What if the quantum field instead dissipates into dark energy, and it just keeps collecting? And then, what if it suddenly all at once collapses? All that energy into dark matter... It would be like a micro black hole formed and collapsed. Right?"

"But why? What would trigger that collapse?"

"Me. I found that if I collapse my quantum field too quickly, it may cascade with any available dark energy in the area. I collapse a micro black hole. I've measured high-energy gamma rays out the wazoo."

"*What?*" Min exclaimed. "You realize you've created a gravity bomb? It would annihilate all nearby matter. That could be a trillion times worse than the atomic bomb!"

"Shhh..." Alex instinctively turned his head left and right, looking for someone that might be listening. "Nobody knows but me. Well, Zandra and you, now. But since I'm the only person that has figured out how to make a Quantum Triangle that develops the gravity seeds needed, it's safe. And you need to guard this information in your world too."

"Oh my God. Most scientists agree that gravity is cross-dimensional. This could be catastrophic to both our worlds if either of us lets this be used," Min said in a harsh whisper. "Can you imagine? Things could just completely disappear, because they've been crushed into the pinpoint gravity well of a micro black hole that formed in a completely different universe."

Alex jerked his head toward the tunnel and put up his hand. "Wait. You hear that?"

Min shook her head. Alex pushed off and floated quickly to the tunnel. He peered down it. Nothing. He waited and listened. All he could hear was the hum of the ventilation system.

Returning to Min, he said, "Please believe me. A weapon of mass destruction for multiple universes was not my experimental objective. I need to think about this. And we still have the minor problem of getting you two back home."

Min knitted her brows sternly. "Do you mean that? Get us back?"

Alex whispered, "You've probably picked up on the fact that although I am far from a Resistance fanatic, I am also not the gung-ho Party member. I know those brainwashed idiots will never believe you're from another universe. Your looks and names will be all they need to pass judgment. We need to get you back—and quickly."

"Aleks, I never leave you again."

Alex pushed to the other side of the module. He took strands of Zandra's hair and rubbed them between his fingers. "I need to get you safe. And I need to get my family safe. That must come first. After that, I will find some way for me to come to you. We both belong in your universe, finding a new world, together. I promise."

"No... Please, Aleks!"

Min asked quietly, "Can you run another quantum field at precisely nine thirty tomorrow morning?"

"I'm free to run experiments whenever I want. What's so special about nine thirty?"

"I'm hoping someone will read his email, and that will be our next return window on my side."

*

Ken backed slowly into the Demons module. He had heard all he needed. Moving around the corner of the starboard Cobra module to ensure he was out of sight, he punched up a text link on a communication panel. He answered the encryption challenge and waited.

Link secured. What is your message?

Ken typed on the keyboard: *Your golden boy is holding out on you. He made a big discovery.*

What is it?

Ken rubbed his hands together and grinned. *Tell the Boss that I've discovered that Alex's triangle thing can make black holes. Turns into a gravity bomb.*

Yes. He will be very interested. An even better weapon than he hoped.

Ken typed, *Says way stronger than a nuke. Thought the Boss should know.*

Good work. We will be in touch with instructions. Out.

*

The Guardian Hecate-Negans evaluated the new events transferred by Hecate-Positivum through quantum entanglement. Her pessimistic slant ran a few thousand possible simulations forward in time. None of the outcomes showed any promise for Rho-1, and many resulted in disastrous impacts on Beta-27. In addition, the cross-dimensional gravity wells that most of the simulations predicted would negatively impact other universes with origins tracing back to Beta-27, Rho-1, or even earlier. It was all unacceptable.

She stated her resulting conclusion to the other two Guardians of the Omniverse. "It is time for our intervention. It is clear from 84.8 percent of my prediction simulations that Rho-1 will soon use their new discovery to destroy. We cannot allow the Quantum Triangle to be used as a weapon."

"I agree that this must be monitored closely, but I do not think an intervention is required yet," Hecate-Positivum responded. "We have seen other universes balance the power and responsibility of this quantum capability before. My simulations do have outcomes that resolve the situation without harm to these or any other universes. My judgment is that it is premature to act."

"The probability speaks for itself. A cross-universe disaster such as this is exactly what we were programmed to prevent. I call for collapsing Rho-1 before it is too late," Hecate-Negans responded.

"It is much too premature to annihilate Rho-1 with a collapse of their universe. Yes, we have a duty to protect other universes from the cross-dimensional harm Rho-1 might cause now that they have quantum field capabilities, but we must also not be too cavalier with our power over the Omniverse. Again, my vote is not yet. Hecate-Neutrum, your vote decides."

"Considering the limited ability of Rho-1 to operate the Quantum Triangle, I think we have sufficient time to allow running more forward simulation routines to clarify an outcome," Hecate-Neutrum responded. "But I recommend that we each dedicate a priority cycle routine to monitoring both Rho-1 and Beta-27 for any further events that could necessitate our intervention. If the probability of imminent disaster by our prediction simulations significantly changes, we will need to reevaluate. Hecate-Positivum, you will ensure that we are all instantly updated with events from both Rho-1 and Beta-27 through quantum entanglement."

SCAN ME

FACTOID 18

In the Western world, coffee consumption is around one-third that of tap water. After petroleum, coffee is the second-most traded commodity in the world. Over seven million metric tons are produced annually. By the end of 2015, Great Britain had more than twenty thousand coffee shops across the country, and even after fifteen years of rapid expansion, Britain's coffee shop sector still continues to grow. Despite the fact that a pope once called it "the devil's drink," there is coffee in every kitchen, and it is a fact of life that drinking coffee is here to stay.

---

18   From the description of the book,
Coffee: A Drink for the Devil, Paul Chrystal found at *Coffee*. (n.d.). Amberley Publishing.
https://www.amberley-books.com/coffee.html

CHAPTER 18

You Have Mail

WORLD SPACE STATION
BETA-27

Lucas scrubbed his face with a sanitary wipe in front of a small mirror stuck to the wall. He missed splashing water on his face first thing in the morning. It was the small things that constantly reminded you how important gravity was to everyday life. Having not slept well worrying about Min, his mood was dark, and he did not feel like shaving. He floated aft into the Zvezda module in search of the universal basic human need in the morning: *Coffee, must find coffee.*

Lucas paused as he came to the crew meal area. Min's coffee extractor was attached to the wall next to his. *Min, where are you?* He pulled only his coffee extractor off the wall this morning and placed it in the charging station. *It's those little things that you enjoyed doing for someone that make you miss the most important people in your life.* He busied himself with measuring the coffee. *One measure, just for me, not for two. Min...* Lucas floated in the semi-dark module without moving for a long time.

"Lights, fifty percent," Lucas said.

The harsh white LEDs snapped on across each crease in the walls of the module.

"Oh, *mierda*. Lights, thirty percent. A mellow morning, *please*."

The module took on the hue of a warm yellow sunrise. He floated for a second and collected himself. *Stay positive. Min would want you to be positive.* He remembered the fun he had working with the three college teams designing these extractors. Aside from the process of making beer, coffee extraction was one of the simplest yet most studied chemical processes. Numerous studies had been conducted by the three teams to create the most efficient and palatable latte in zero gravity. The winning designers of the WSS coffee project had realized that part of the enjoyment was the routine of making coffee. It needed to take just the right amount of time and effort. Totally automated, fast, and uninvolved was not the right approach. Some effort, anticipation, and even a bit of personal art was what helped make that first sip taste so good.

While the extractor warmed to the perfect temperature, Lucas punched up his personal email files on the wall monitor. His eyes scanned the list for anything needing immediate attention. Fortunately, it was a short list this morning. Part of any space mission was public relations. He, as with all the crew, was obligated to answer any email that the WSF passed on from the public. Lucas did not mind at all. Being an astronaut had been a childhood dream, and he particularly enjoyed the questions from young minds that might be searching for that shared dream.

The second-to-last email jolted him awake. *Min!* From yesterday. He opened it quickly and read. If the coffee tin could have hit the floor, it would have.

"Holy crap!" Lucas said out loud. He punched the intercom. "Commander, come to Zvezda. *Now*."

*

Ed Anderson rubbed the morning stiffness out of his neck. He did appreciate the new couch the Zhrinnykot GoFundMe program had gotten him, but it needed some serious breaking in. His video monitor displayed an excited

Lucas Diaz sipping coffee. *There's a man that does not need caffeine.*

"Lucas, that email from Min you sent us aligns with something that Jackie was already proposing regarding parallel universes," Ed said. "Hats off to Min for some quick thinking and picking a window for us to reestablish a connection. We have no idea what might be causing that other universe to bridge with ours, but we will get ready on our side."

"We can't miss this window," Lucas said.

"Lucas, we will get them back," Ed stated with force. Lucas was a man on a mission. Ed needed to make sure Lucas didn't forget that it included a space station. *Lucas is a doer. He needs something to do.* "I have Jackie working up a startup procedure from the data feed on the last run, so the settings will be the same. While she's doing that, I need you to check on a couple other experiments that must be attended to this morning, otherwise we might lose them."

Lucas emptied his mug. *"Okay, send the list, and I will get those done. Please keep in mind that neither Commander Johnson nor I have been involved with Min's runs, only Zandra. The dark energy experiment procedures Jackie writes up must be accurate and clear. We probably only have one shot at this, and we need to be one hundred percent ready at nine thirty."*

Ed could see the concern on Lucas's face. Love could melt the nerves of the most hardened professional. But he also understood that Lucas had already put his energy into a laser focus to get Min back.

"Don't worry, Lucas, Jackie has been in lockstep with Min for ground-side coordination on her experiments from the start. She will have what you need," Ed said. "We have just over two hours to prep the system, so we have the time to be ready. We will get you the procedure in the next half hour, so you can do at least a couple mock setups before the real run. Good thing you found that email when you did, Lucas."

"We already have the power units charging, so they should be at full charge within the hour," Commander Johnson said.

"Great, Commander. We will get the door open on our side," Ed assured them. "It will be up to Min to come knocking from the other side, wherever that is."

FACTOID 19

The first records of the legal application of torture to prove guilt or innocence were found in the Sumerian Code of Ur-Nammu (circa the twenty-first century BC) and the Babylonian Code of Hammurabi (circa the eighteenth century BC), which in the evidentiary procedure employed the so-called "divine judgment" of the water ordeal.

19   History of Torture. (2015). Tortureum. https://tortureum.com/history-of-torture/

CHAPTER 19

Best-Made Plans

A lex grabbed a handhold to stop his forward motion as he entered the Zootic module. The rest of the crew were already busy with their individual morning rituals, heating up their own choice of breakfast and making coffee—or whatever that black sewer water was. Alex always avoided the stuff in favor of his private supply of *real* coffee. In an environment where it was hard to get any personal space, mission planners had long since discovered that mornings were a good time to leave each person to their own regimen. The crew did not need to eat breakfast together as a group, as was protocol for dinner. The only requirement was that they would be ready to start their assigned tasks by eight o'clock. But this morning, all members seemed to be up early and going.

"Good morning, all. Anyone check on our visitors yet?" Alex asked, trying to sound cheerful.

Ken answered without turning from his oatmeal, "I made sure they were all good 'n' secured, first thing. Amazingly, they haven't vanished into their other dimension yet."

Alex ignored the sarcasm. "If it's alright with you, Commander, may I go with Emma and allow them to use the WMS this morning?"

Hovering at the table next to Emma, Becker shook his head. "Both Emma and I have our hands full this morning. The number one tracking sensor has gone jittery again. I'm going to do an EVA to swap out the drive assembly. We can't be flying around half blind with that sensor not working properly, so it tops our task list."

After gingerly applying a glob of thick syrup on a rehydrated pancake, Becker continued, "Also a top priority: we got the order last night to send our guests back to ground this morning. It will be you and Ken working on a transfer of our guests to the CRV. Detach of the CRV is scheduled for ten o'clock. Given that, they'll probably appreciate relieving themselves completely just before that ride. It can get pretty rough, as you well know. The Boss is not concerned about waiting for an optimum return window, so their flight path is going to be particularly memorable with the storm over their landing zone. He doesn't care about the risk. He wants his people to question those two ASAP. I suggest that you wait an hour or so and do an excursion to the WMS as you and Ken transfer them to the CRV."

Ken pulled a Taser from the wall beside him and playfully danced the targeting laser on Emma's forehead across the table. "I'll make sure those two Tuanhuo spies behave."

Emma froze and locked eyes with Ken. "Do that again, and I'll make you eat Taser for breakfast."

"Come and get it, little girl. I'll put you down like a bag of rocks."

Emma pushed back from the table.

"Ken. Knock it off," Commander Becker ordered. He pointed at Emma's clenched left fist. "Emma, chill."

Alex was not pleased with the thought of Ken helping, but there was nothing he could do about it. More important was the CRV detach time. That would make Min's nine thirty return window nearly impossible. He needed a plan.

"Understood. I'll just take them some water for now," he said as he grabbed two hydration packs.

"Well, Mr. Soft Spot," Ken said through a mouthful of his breakfast, "looks like your friends are going to get the class-one welcome on Earth. If the Boss is particularly interested to know how spies got on board this platform without detection, you can bet it isn't going be a cakewalk. If they were smart, they'd be asking you for cyanide with that water."

"They are not spies."

"Right. Another dimension. I'm sure that will be a good answer, and *special* questioning will not be required," Ken said with a smile as he made a cranking motion with his hand. It was well known that the Boss was partial to methods of torture used way back in the Spanish Inquisition, the rack being his favorite. Having two prisoners made the method especially effective, as just watching someone endure the pain of having their joints pulled from their sockets could make the other subject confess to whatever was being asked.

Alex just shook his head in disgust and pushed himself off to leave the module. It was better not to respond. Knowing Ken, it would just end up on a report.

*

Alex spun in a three-sixty as he entered the Tribe module to make sure he was not followed. He floated over to Zandra and Min, noticing they were both awake.

"Good morning. I brought you some water."

"Thanks," Min replied. "You seem to have all your circulating air fans turned up to max. It tends to dry us out."

Alex shifted to a system monitor on the wall and punched up the environmental controls. He gave out a sigh. "Ken, you asshole..." He pulled a scrollbar down. "Sorry, seems your early morning visitor turned up the circulation to max, probably to get that effect specifically." The hum in the module noticeably decreased.

"He has sadistic aura," Zandra said.

"I apologize for our local Party zealot—or Party moron, if that's a better description."

Min sipped from the hydration pack Alex left floating at her lips. "Even I can sense that you have a much kinder nature. Thank you."

Alex could sense a kind nature himself as he floated in front of Zandra. She radiated a strong but caring heart. This was a woman with a depth he had never found again.

"I'm a bit surprised that you chose to go back into space," Alex said.

"I not want first. But Min needed. People needed. I knew you would want me to help people. And I need a way ... to say goodbye. But I never want goodbye. I always want you."

Holding the hydration pack to her lips, he studied her deep brown eyes. Her warmth glowed and radiated like the embers of a campfire, comforting his very soul.

"Ground control to Major Tom. Come in, Major Tom." Min's quip from behind him broke Alex from his brief daze.

Alex turned and retrieved the hydration pack that had drifted away from Min's mouth. "Oh, sorry." His mind returned to thinking of their circumstances.

"So, I think I have a plan, but we have a problem. You two are scheduled to take the CRV back to the surface this morning at ten o'clock."

Min moistened her parched lips as she pulled back from the straw. "Well, if you can get your quantum field established, maybe we won't even be here by then."

"Unfortunately, I expect that just at the time we need to be building the fields, we will get a visit by that same Party zealot that visited earlier, to help transfer you to the CRV. He's not going to take kindly to the idea of you escaping. If he had his way, he would just send you out an airlock without an attached CRV."

Alex gave Min another drink. He glanced again towards the hatch leading to the rest of the ship and said quietly, "We need a revised plan. Any way that your friends back home would establish your field before nine thirty?"

Min shook her head. "No. They know that our power packs have a limited time that they can build and maintain a field. They won't be late, but they also won't be much earlier than that time … if they even got my message."

Zandra spoke quietly from the other wall in a forceful whisper. "Aleks, I have dream. The voices not happy. I feel. You must come too."

"Another Zandrition?"

"Yes. It strong."

"I believe in your ESP. I used to, and I always will." Alex pointed towards the Hephaestus module. "But I can't leave the Quantum Triangle here. I need to—"

"Good morning," Emma announced herself as she entered the module. "I managed to get you two a breakfast ration. Believe it or not, our commander does not care to be a prison warden and can be very reasonable if you know how to ask."

"Thank you," Zandra responded after regaining a calm composure. Alex was amazed at how fluid Zandra could be in shifting her personal aura. *Look at me, being aware of a person's aura. I'm so much more alive around this woman.*

Emma passed Alex a ration for Zandra and moved in front of Min. "I apologize, but we will need to wait for your excursion to the WMS this morning. Captain's orders are for that to be part of your transfer to the CRV in a little while. Seems your presence is desired on the ground, no surprise."

"Aleks was telling," Zandra said. "This wrong. We not spies."

Emma dropped her head and sighed. "I'm truly sorry. That's not for me to decide."

The four fell silent as they each contemplated the situation.

"I need to go get the commander prepped for an EVA. I wish you both well on your journey," Emma said cordially. She smiled at Alex and pushed off to leave.

Alex waited for her to disappear down the main axis of the station and turned back to Zandra. "Wow. That was rather odd of Emma. You two have hit a soft spot with her."

"That not about us," Zandra said. "Emma has complex aura. I can tell. I think that was act for you, Aleks."

"Hmmm, maybe. I often get the feeling she's not showing all her cards."

*

Emma exited the Tribe module heading starboard, and instead of going straight into Quest to assist the commander with his EVA prep, she held up a "just one minute" finger and dove forward through Demons to the Hellcat module. She quickly got out her MP5 music player. Time was running out, and she wanted to check that the plan was coming together. She enabled the special functions by holding the two biosensors between her thumb and ring finger. She selected COMMS, and the screen changed to a subdued red to indicate that the encrypted communications were active. She typed on the small device.

Need status update on extraction.

Emma shook her head as the reply flashed on the screen.

No go. Extraction team had to abort. Opportunity went bad. We lost two.

She typed, *Alex will not leave the station if the Boss still has his niece hostage. Make another try?*

Negative. Suicide mission. They are on lockdown now.

Emma knew these people well, and they all knew the stakes. If there were any way possible, they would be grabbing the niece. She understood and sent back, *Out of time. Will need to improvise here. Coordinates still good?*

All green. Will have recovery team ready.

Acknowledged. Will execute here.

She turned off the device and zipped it back into her thigh pocket. Emma pushed off and headed aft for the Quest module to help Ken with preparing the commander for his EVA. The EVA was a lucky break; the commander would not be a problem. She would just need to handle Ken, and she had a pretty good idea how.

FACTOID 20

France launched the first and only cat into space. Félicette, a stray Parisian cat, went to space in 1963, experienced weightlessness, and was successfully recovered. She has been commemorated on postage stamps around the world, and a statue of her is on display at the International Space University.

20   *Félicette.* (2023, January 1). Wikipedia.
https://en.wikipedia.org/wiki/F%C3%A9licette

CHAPTER 20

Limited Time

Ed Anderson waited in silence. As he was the lowest-ranking member, it was proper protocol for him to stay on the web conference until everyone else had left the meeting. It allowed for a senior member to provide a private parting word of advice. Ed drummed his fingers on the desk while he waited a few seconds. *The perfect disastrous morning would not be complete without the full suite of your supervisors on a web conference—all the way up to the director himself.* It seemed that they all needed to impress on Ed the importance of the situation. *Duh.* Nobody wanted to announce to the public that the WSF had lost the two astronauts that were their very best hope for the survival of humanity itself. He had been in this seat before. But it had been a different thing when it was a foreign actor that crashed a satellite purposefully into the space station. This was a mission they had planned and executed. Min's work was supported and followed by all the world regions. If the WSF was the hope of the global future, they needed to be the world experts.

Ed noted that the chief flight director had remained on the call after all the others had left. "You have something you want to add?" he asked.

The man on the screen rubbed his bald head. *"You probably already could guess, but I have had Samantha in PR quietly work up a public statement for both the positive and the negative outcomes for this morning."*

"We will get them back." Ed stated the new motto of his team. It had taken hold as strongly as Apollo 13's "Failure is not an option" slogan.

"Right. Make that happen. But just in case, if we don't have success this morning, we will be saying that Jackie will be stepping in for Min on the next flight up. We need to show we have a backup. We need to give people hope."

"What? Jackie's not ready for that! She's not even an ASCAN," Ed said, referring to the long-used and tongue-in-cheek acronym for "astronaut candidate." "She's done zero flight training."

"Doesn't matter. She needs to be on the next flight. Comes from the top."

Ed bit his lip and shook his head to silently illustrate his disagreement with the decision. "Just don't tell her that now. I need her focused on what she's doing."

"Your people, your call."

"What about Zandra? Do you have someone selected to step in for her too?" Ed asked.

"We're working on that."

Silence.

"Anything else?" Ed asked.

The chief flight director pointed into the screen. *"You might want to get another bagel."*

Ed turned around in his chair to face his credenza. *Damn, not again…* "Zhrinnykot! Bad kitty!" he said out loud. The large ball of orange fur did not even react and continued to lick the cream cheese off Ed's morning bagel.

"Good luck, Ed."

Ed nodded and clicked the "Leave" button on the video conference.

"Among the many—and yes, I said *many*—bad habits Zandra neglected to mention, I still can't believe she taught you to savor cream cheese," Ed admonished the cat as he lifted the mass of fur and placed him on the floor. Breaking off the piece where the cat had been licking, he tossed it in the trash. Ed shook his head and took a bite from what he told himself was the clean side of the bagel.

He turned back to his desk, only to find the cat now there. "Oh, yes. Now, let's not forget to do the keyboard walk this morning. And don't miss the delete key; that one is important," he said, stroking the cat. Then more soothingly, "Don't worry, Zhrinny. We will get her back. You're helping to motivate me too."

As he took another bite of the bagel, a knock at his door got a muffled "Enter."

Like a ray of sunshine, Jackie came through the doorway, quickly crossed his office, and plopped down on the chair in front of his desk. Zhrinnykot immediately hopped into her lap and leaned against her for a rub.

"Hi, Zhrinny. Yes, I know. We will get them back," Jackie said, scratching his head. The cat started a loud purr. Jackie was clearly on the favorite person list.

"Did you come to see me, or that oversized furball?" Ed asked, leaning back in his chair.

"Oh, sorry, sir. Yes, you," Jackie answered quickly. "We have the procedure. I've gotten it reviewed by both John and the new tech just to make sure it made sense to someone unfamiliar with the equipment. It's in your inbox. Permission to transfer it to the WSS? We need to start running mock startups with Lucas and Johnson as soon as possible."

Without opening the document, Ed said, "Do it." Time was critical, and now was the time to trust his people.

"One thing you should be aware of, sir."

Ed closed his eyes and pinched the bridge of his nose. "More good news for me this morning?"

Jackie cocked her head, not understanding, "Umm, no. It's just something that you should know. I calculated the expected power draw during the run. If the battery bank is at full charge, we will have four minutes and thirty-five seconds that we can maintain the field. Min needs to hit that window from her side."

"Not a very big window," Ed said.

"No, sir. But for the actual transfer, we only need a couple seconds, so in those terms, it's quite large," Jackie said, still stroking Zhrinnykot.

"Understood. My concern is not the time of the transfer itself, but what might be going on in the other universe that is either helping or hindering Min from opening the window on her side. We have no idea. If this doesn't work, we won't know when to try and open another window."

They both contemplated that thought in silence for a moment. Zhrinnykot continued to purr.

"Well, let's do our part. Get on it," Ed said. "And take that monster with you."

Jackie smiled and heaved the large orange mass up to her shoulder as she stood up. "Come on, Zhrinnykot. Let's go open a door in this universe for Zandra and Min."

Ed's eyes followed the content furry face leaving his office. He had to admit, Zhrinnykot did contribute to his team in ways no one else could.

SCAN ME

FACTOID 21

While the International Space Station hasn't experienced a fire, a significant blaze did take place in 1997 on the Russian space station Mir. The fire came from an oxygen generator, where the oxygen supplied a ready source of fuel. Tests showed that the generator had to run out of oxygen for the fire to burn out. If a fire were to occur on the ISS, the astronauts would become firemen and follow a three-step response system. First, they would turn off the ventilation system to slow the spread of fire. Next, they would shut off power to the affected unit. Finally, astronauts would use fire extinguishers to put out the flames.

21   Uri, John. (2022, February 23). *25 Years Ago: Fire Aboard Space Station Mir.* NASA. https://www.nasa.gov/feature/25-years-ago-fire-aboard-space-station-mir

CHAPTER 21

Change of Plan

Alex moved around the Hephaestus module quickly. *If this works, I'm having one hell of a latte afterwards.* After checking the readouts on the power cells, he reviewed the targeting settings on the wall monitor one more time. They were all in line and matched exactly with yesterday's run.

"Okay, Starra, I think we're all set. Please repeat back to me the instructions I have given you."

Starra answered in a matter-of-fact, serious tone, *"I am to ensure that the power bank is held at full charge until commencing the experiment. At precisely nine twenty-eight, I am to engage the Quantum Triangle and initiate the quantum sphere builds. The run should follow the parameter profile of yesterday's run exactly. This will ensure that a full field is established by nine thirty. Unless otherwise instructed, I am to maintain the quantum spheres at the final settings until nine forty, at which point I am to terminate the run and take the power bank offline."*

181

She added, *"I must point out that running an experiment without your direct presence here in the Hephaestus module is a violation of safety protocols."*

"I understand that, but this is a special case. I'll be right outside the hatch in the Truss Tunnel Port Terminal. I have given you the override code. You will proceed. Confirm."

"Override confirmed. I will execute the run as defined."

"Very good."

Alex checked his watch: 09:22. *This is going to be close. Ken will be making his way now to the Tribe module to transfer his captors to the CRV. For once in your life, Ken, please be late.*

That would never happen. Mr. Party Member always dotted his i's and crossed his t's. Alex needed to do something to delay Ken until after he could get Min and Zandra back.

He snapped his fingers and said, "Starra, I want you to run a quick test alarm on the aft smoke detector in the Zootic module." A fire onboard the station was an emergency with top priority. Sending Ken to the farthest aft end of the station would be just the thing.

"Alex, I have no abnormal readings from that detector. Running a detector test will cause an alarm to sound throughout the station. Should I announce this test to inform the crew now?"

"Negative. This should be an unannounced drill. Let's check the reaction time of our crew. Please run the test."

"Understood. I will also log the time between the signal activation and when it is acknowledged by a crew member."

"Perfect. Execute."

A piercing *beep – beep – beep* rang out through the station, followed by a calm but forceful Starra announcing, *"Smoke detector alarm, Zootic module, aft sensor."* Whatever Ken was doing, he was now on his way to Zootic. It might also tie up Emma, depending on wherever she was helping the commander getting ready with his EVA.

Alex gave himself two thumbs-up. "Now, if you will excuse me, I need to attend to our guests."

He released the latch on the hatch and swung the door open. He dove straight for the Truss Tunnel and hurried to the opposite end. The tunnel rings flew past; P5 Truss Port End, P3/4 Port End, P1 Port End. *Fly.* As he swooped into the Tribe module, he greeted Min and Zandra. "Good morning again, ladies. I believe you have a quantum field ride to catch."

Zandra looked at him with surprise in her eyes. "Is fire?"

"No, that's my doing. I needed to make sure we would be left alone for a while," Alex answered as he moved to begin releasing the straps holding Min to the opposite wall.

"What time is it?" Min asked.

Alex checked his watch. "Nine twenty-five. Starra will be starting up the quantum field shortly. I hope your people are doing the same."

*

Lucas set the field modulation controller. "Seventy-six percent, check."

Commander Johnson read the next item on the checklist. "Okay, let's try it again. Main power breaker, ON."

Lucas gingerly flipped the main power switch, as if moving it gently would make a difference this time. Immediately, the breaker tripped, and the red FAULT lamp lit.

"Shit, no!" Lucas exclaimed as he hit the reset. "PACOM, it tripped again. What are we doing wrong?"

In the video feed, Jackie shifted back and forth between the procedure readout on one screen and the telemetry readings on another. She shook her head. *"All the parameters match Min's last run. It must be that we just have something out of sequence, and the power draw spikes."*

"¡Dios mío! We're running out of time. We need to make this work ... *now*," Lucas said, clenching his fists to control his frustration. They had been at it for over an hour and run the startup sequence multiple times with the same result: main power fault. He was desperate to get Min and Zandra back. This could be their only window, and they had to be ready on their side. They might never get another chance.

183

Johnson flipped the pages of the procedure back and forth. "What if we leave the modulation controller offline until after the power bank is up and settled? It might be trying to modulate the transits when we first power on. If we manually set the modulation at fifty percent, the banks should equalize on power-up all on their own. We should be able to modulate up from there."

Lucas flashed a thumbs-up at the commander and turned eagerly to the comms video display for Jackie's response. She turned to the electrical tech sitting beside her with a questioning look. He considered for a few seconds, then nodded his head in agreement.

"Roger that, Commander. Our electrical tech agrees. Leave the modulator in manual mode, fifty percent, and punch it now," Jackie directed over the comm.

Lucas was already on it. He flipped the main power switch again, softly. To his relief, a sequence of green power lamps came on one by one across the bank. He and the commander slapped a high five. "GOT IT! Ground, that did it. We are up!"

Jackie jumped up from her chair, sending a startled Zhrinnykot flying to another console. *"Yes!"* Sitting back down, she said, *"Okay, Lucas, let's put the modulator back on auto and slowly ramp back up to seventy-six percent. Let's ramp over thirty seconds just to be safe. We will be right on time for Min and Zandra."*

She leaned back and clasped her palms in front of her face. Zhrinnykot cautiously returned.

"Paws crossed, Zhrinnykot. The ball is now in their court. I can only guess at what they might have to do on their side," Jackie said as she stroked his back.

*

Alex followed the witches with wands on Zandra's socked feet down the tunnel to the Port Terminal. He glanced at his watch. *Fifteen seconds to spare. Perfect.* Entering the Port Terminal, he saw Min floating with her eyes wide and her mouth open, but no words came out. He followed her gaze. Over the top of the open hatch to the Hephaestus module, the docking lamp was flashing from red to green and back.

"Lucas got my message! They have the system running on their side!" Min said.

Zandra turned to Alex, her eyes pleading. "You come too. Now."

"I can't. I need to find a way to disable the Quantum Triangle after I go, so nobody here can use it again. I will find a way. I will. You keep opening a window, as we planned, and I will come. I promise."

Min turned back to Zandra. "We need to go. Now."

"Stop right there!"

They all looked back to the tunnel entry for the person barking the order. Ken appeared, hovering at the tunnel entry. "What are you doing?" he demanded.

Alex spread his arms across the module. "The right thing, Ken. They're not spies. They need to return to their world."

Ken grabbed a handhold and extracted himself from the tunnel. "Bullshit. Those two liars are headed to the Boss for some hard question time. We'll get the truth out of them one way or another."

"Ken, I know we don't see eye to eye on things, but please just listen to common sense. They can't be spies. How do you think they got here?"

"That doesn't matter."

"Yes, it does, Ken. Don't you see?" Alex pointed to the hatch over his shoulder. "Look at that docking light. Have you ever seen it flicker like that?"

Ken looked over to the Hephaestus hatch and gave a questioning look at the warning light oscillating between green and red. Through the hatch, the contents of the next module in the background seemed to be changing in sync. It was the Hephaestus module, its panels marked with the red icon of the Right Alliance on each corner. A rainbow of light seemed to be bathing the entire module. Then the lighting switched to a steady warm white, and an entirely different set of panels appeared. Then back.

"What the...?"

"See, Ken? I've opened the quantum field to another universe: *their* universe. This is what the technology should be used for. Not as a weapon, but for a whole new wonderful reality. Think of what this could mean! Interstellar travel and our ability to reach into the stars themselves!"

Ken floated in confusion, mesmerized by the oscillating realities beyond the hatch opening.

Alex glanced at his watch. 09:32.

"We need to send them back. Right now, while the fields are aligned on both sides." Alex turned back to Zandra, took her arm, and moved her towards the hatch.

Ken broke from his stupor. "What are you doing? *Stop!*" He pushed off hard from the bulkhead. Momentum was key in a zero-g fight. He let his full bulk slam hard into Alex. At the last moment, he raised his elbow quickly to give an upper cut to Alex's face. As his momentum transferred, Ken reached out and grabbed the handhold beside Zandra.

Blood erupted from Alex's nose in a stream of droplets. He spun backwards and collided with Min in a chain reaction of momentum. Having no hold on anything, Min floated backwards towards the hatch to Hephaestus. Zandra could only helplessly watch the slow-motion ballet of combat. Min flailed her arms for something to grab onto, but nothing was in reach. As Min passed the threshold of the hatch, she flickered with the docking lamp. She was there, she was gone, she was there ... and ... she was gone.

"What the hell? What did you do, Alex?" Ken demanded.

"I told you. They need to go back to their universe. Min just superpositioned to her world. Now Zandra needs to jump before the field collapses."

"No way. This spy is going to talk."

"*Enough!*"

Both Ken and Alex turned towards the opposite end of the Truss Terminal for the source of the new command. Emma hung from the tunnel entry, with a Taser pointed in their direction.

"Okay, since I am the one with the Taser—on max stun, by the way—I get to settle this little matter," Emma said. She waved the Taser to the left and motioned. "Alex, you and Zandra are going to come with me to the CRV. Please just trust me. I'm on your side. We're going to get your niece back, if you help us."

Emma pointed the Taser directly at Ken's chest. "Ken, you are going to move to the opposite wall. If you cause any problems, I will tase you. Understand?"

Still holding his bloody nose in one hand, Alex pushed off from the top of the module and reached for Zandra's wrist. Ken repositioned his feet on the side of the module to launch an intercept. He pushed off hard and fast. Emma did not hesitate, and the Taser hit Ken in the back as he flew across the module. His body went rigid as a rock, his head slamming into the side of Alex. Just like a billiard ball impacted by the cue ball, Alex's trajectory shifted in angle, now in a direct vector to the Hephaestus hatch. Emma and Zandra watched him reach in all directions for a handhold. With nothing to stop him, Alex's form flickered ... and disappeared.

*

"I see her!" Lucas called out. "Wait, no... Where did she go? Oh, back again! She's flickering!"

"Lucas, trust me. Close your eyes, think of Min with you, then open them. Do it now!" Jackie exclaimed.

Lucas closed his eyes, opened his arms, and pictured Min in his embrace. He repeated to himself something Min had often told him: *Love knows no boundaries.*

No boundaries. No boundaries. No...

He opened his eyes. Min was in his arms. They hugged in a tight embrace.

"PACOM, Mission. We have Min," Johnson announced.

"Where's Zandra?" Jackie asked immediately. She checked the telemetry on the power bank. They were down to twelve percent. *"We only have a few seconds of power left to hold the field!"*

All three in the Aceso module froze and stared at the hatch. The docking lamp continued to flicker.

Johnson called out, "Power at ten... Power at nine..."

The seconds ticked, and the power drained.

"Power at five ... four..."

An image of a person phased in. Then it phased out. Min closed her eyes and focused.

Alex appeared.

Johnson stopped his count as the empty power bank automatically switched offline. Ever the calm professional, he ran a hand over his head and down the back of his neck and said, "PACOM, Mission. Huntsville, we have a small problem."

*

"Well, shit, shit, shit," Emma cursed. "This is just great."

"What you do?" Zandra demanded.

Emma pushed Ken aside and moved to Zandra. Ken could only watch in his stunned body. She glanced at the solid hatch doorway and docking lamp. "Well, I suppose a small change in plans. Alex was our objective, but hopefully you know something about quantum fields."

"I navigate, not make field."

"That's just wonderful. Well, at this point, I have nothing to lose. Come on. We've got to get out of here before this space cowboy here regains the use of his limbs."

Emma pushed off for the tunnel and called back, "If I were you, I'd come with me. What I offer you is going to be a hell of a lot better than what these jerks will do to you."

Zandra could hear honesty in Emma's words. She moved over to Ken. Grabbing the ceiling handhold and planting her left foot in a floor strap, she kicked with all her might into Ken's rib cage, sending him slamming hard into the opposite wall. Although he could not speak, his wide eyes showed that he had acknowledged her anger. A droplet of blood formed at his lower lip where he had bitten down from the pain.

"That for Aleks, you Mister Asshole!"

She pushed off to follow Emma down the Truss Tunnel.

As Emma rounded the corner of Tribe, she grabbed a handhold to stop her forward momentum. Blocking her path was Commander Becker. Still in his EVA suit, he took up most of the space across the main axis of the ship.

Zandra came to a halt right behind Emma.

"Emma, care to explain yourself?" Becker asked calmly.

"Well, sir, as you can see, I am escorting one of our guests to the CRV," Emma said, thumbing back towards Zandra.

"And the tasing of Ken? I was watching the module video feed. How about that?"

"If I told you that things were not quite what they appear to be, would you believe me?" Emma asked.

"Well, I did just see two people vanish into thin air, so you have a rather high bar to get under right now. Try me."

"Sir, I know you're a decent man and not the gung-ho Party loyalist that Ken is. It might surprise you to learn that although I put up the image, I'm not that Party loyalist either. In fact, quite the opposite. You know what they'll do to her. I believe her; she's not from our world. You saw it on the monitor. The Quantum Triangle works. We now have the power of quantum superposition. Alex is a genius. But she should not be tortured to confess to being a spy. Let me send her someplace safe," Emma pleaded.

"That CRV is set to return her to the Boss. You're sending her into their arms."

Emma smiled. "As I said, things are not what they seem."

"I would be letting you commit treason."

"I can get another Taser and zap you if it would make you feel better," Emma said with a smirk.

Becker did not reply. He rotated sideways and nodded. "How about I just put my helmet on and wait in the airlock for a while? I think I was outside this whole time."

Emma pushed off and floated by him. "Thank you, sir. Come on, Zandra, we don't have much time."

Zandra followed Emma around the corner and through the hatch to the CRV. It was a cramped space. Now following the training that had been drilled into her, Zandra took a seat and started strapping herself in. The clunk of the hatch closing above made her look up. She was surprised to see Emma drop down into the seat opposite her.

"You come too?"

Emma did not answer. She finished strapping herself to the seat as fast as she could. She looked at Zandra to make sure she was ready. Punching the dock release, Emma said flatly, "Welcome to the Resistance."

*

As his dizziness and weakness wore off, Ken began to feel the full discomfort both in his back from the Taser and in his right side from Zandra's kick. He started to take a deep breath, but cut it short in a shock of stabbing pain. *I think that bitch broke my rib!* He steeled himself against the afflictions and took stock of his situation.

"Starra, station person count," he said in a tight voice.

"Currently there are two persons aboard Alpha-One Platform," Starra responded.

"CRV status?"

"The crew return vehicle undocked eight seconds ago, with two persons on board."

Shit. Ken sneered and clenched his fists. His eyes were caught by the strobes of color streaking out from the still-open Hephaestus hatch. *Hmmm... Maybe I can still salvage something here.* Ken moved to the hatch and hesitantly slid an arm through the opening. To his relief, it stayed solid and did not flicker. As he pulled himself through, his attention was immediately drawn to the Quantum Triangle, its colored rays mesmerizing.

"Hello there, Mister Black Hole Maker. The Boss is going to be real happy to get his hands on you."

Smiling to himself, he took hold of the object to pull it from the wall mount, when the now familiar pain of fifty thousand volts crawling over his entire body sent him reeling backwards.

"Ahhhh! Alex, you son of a bitch..."

"Security protocol breach," Starra said calmly. *"No one but Alex Devin may remove the Quantum Triangle from its mount."*

"Well, we'll see about that. What the Boss wants, Ken Seaborn gets the Boss."

SCAN ME

FACTOID 22:

The ISS is the single most expensive object ever built. The cost of the ISS has been estimated at over 150 billion US dollars. In April of 2021, NASA updated their prices for private missions flying to the ISS. The updated prices reflect the true costs of supporting current missions. The costs include cargo, station resources, crew time, and mission planning services. Under the new pricing, a hypothetical four-person, one-week stay at the ISS would cost at least 12.5 million dollars. The price assumes that the four astronauts would provide their own transportation, i.e., a rocket. The cost is more than twenty times the price of the most expensive hotel in the world (according to Guinness World Records).

The charge for room service (food on the ISS) is two thousand dollars per person, per day.

22   Johnson, Michael. (2021, April 29). *Commercial and Marketing Pricing Policy.* NASA. https://www.nasa.gov/leo-economy/commercial-use/pricing-policy

CHAPTER 22

Less Carrot, More Stick

The accountant sitting at the far end of the near priceless African blackwood conference table focused his eyes on the computer monitor in front of him. He knew not to say a word. Whatever he might say would be wrong and could only focus unrestrained wrath in his direction. That was not wise. Over the top of the monitor, he secretly eyed the Boss clenching his stubby fingers into a fist, listening to a phone at his ear and gazing out the window. The teal-blue waters and immaculate white sand beaches beyond obviously did little to calm his anger. It had been renamed Boss Island, and no one dared call it by its original name anymore, Crooked Island—as fitting as that might still be, considering its new owner. After brushing off the few locals, the Boss had upgraded the island infrastructure and installed the comforts that would make this his home. The marina, the airstrip, the golf course, a two-hundred-room exclusive resort for his private guests, and the opulent residence all bore his mark of living the most want-free life. Whatever he desired, he could have here.

Yet today his wants were not being met. In another display of his unchecked temper, he threw the phone as hard as he could against the floor-to-ceiling window. The phone exploded into fragments, but there was no damage to the window; it was bulletproof. The Boss took no chances with a sharpshooter, even on his private island paradise. Access to the island was carefully controlled, but there was always the possibility of an agent from the Pacific Tuanhuo willing to risk their life in trade for glory. Even more dangerous were those from within. He was the full-maned lion of the Alliance pride; there was always another younger lion ready to challenge his dominance.

"Am I dealing with imbeciles?" he screamed. "Jason, how did that woman get past our background checks?"

The AI answered from a speaker in the wall opposite the windows, which housed his news and information displays. "It appears that Emma Baker has a carefully developed and completely falsified identity going back to the early days of the Party. Her real name is Emma Lewis, and she was an astronaut candidate before the Satellite War. The number of altered records indicates that there were likely many people involved in establishing her cover and acceptance into the Space Force program. We are still trying to establish how her real identity was not discovered in her background checks."

Documents of the dual identities with Emma's likeness appeared on multiple displays across the wall.

"I want everyone that had anything to do with her background check interrogated. I want the moles found!"

"Done. I have ordered the apprehension of all those who signed off on her checks. They will be charged with suspicion of collaborating with the Resistance. What level of interrogation?" asked the AI.

"Four. If they don't know anything, they may live, but just barely. I'm pissed."

"Excellent. I will see to it myself."

The accountant remained quiet and tried not to think of either the deranged, psychopathic AI that acted as the primary henchman for the Boss, or the robotically assisted interrogation techniques it would use on the administrators who had signed off on her paperwork. The majority were probably completely innocent of any wrongdoing, but that did not matter. The poor men and women would live, but each would be returned to their homes quite broken. They would be used to drive home two well-established tenets: it would send a clear message to their superiors that such failure displeased the Boss, and it would reinforce in the general community that the Boss could do anything he wanted; he was above any law. The common pawns of society did not have rights; they had allowances that either the Boss or the Party would grant or sweep away at their discretion.

The Boss moved his bulk awkwardly across the room to a glass display case. The accountant's stomach churned. That case was not there for the man's pleasure; he had no interest in rare historical relics. It was there to boast of his wealth, nothing more. After looking over a few of the shelves holding all kinds of rare artifacts, he grabbed an ancient Chocholá-style Mayan vase. Tossing it in the air a few times with one hand as if it were a softball, he held it out and studied the intricate carving, the image of Mayan god L with a smoking cigar. Raising it high above his head, the Boss threw his arm to the oak floor, smashing the vase to bits. The priceless piece of seventh-century history, discovered completely intact, was no longer a thing of beauty.

The Boss sneered at the accountant. "I always thought that thing was ugly. A child could paint better."

The accountant clenched his fists, under the table and out of sight. That sixty-seven-year-old man across the room was still the spoiled child he had known since grade school. Some might say it was not his fault—that a drunken mother who married only for money, with no desire to raise a child, had helped create this sociopath, along with a father that only knew how to degrade others. It was no wonder that he had turned out to be a monster. But the accountant did not accept those arguments. Others in his classes had had it tough. They just had better character. This man was born evil—and enjoyed it.

"Jason, where did that capsule come down? I want a recovery team there now. And scramble a couple Hawk-eighteens," he demanded.

"The CRV is currently in atmospheric reentry and has a trajectory that will land it in upper Michigan. I have already sent two Stinger-twelve hover

gunships to the area, but I will scramble the Hawks as you desire. There are no ground assets within operation range. The Resistance did choose a landing site well to avoid our intercept. It is remote and a good distance from our assets. But it is a well-wooded area, making it a high-risk landing. They traded safety for isolation. I calculate that they will have five minutes and thirty-five seconds on the ground before our Hawks arrive. The gunships will follow in seven additional minutes."

"Five minutes? Didn't I say 'now'?"

"Yes, sir. I will instruct the Hawks to go to max thrust. It will mean they won't be able to return to base and will have to ditch the aircraft, but it will decrease the intercept time by one minute and twenty seconds," advised the AI.

"Do it."

The accountant removed his glasses and rubbed his eyes. Two hundred million dollars' worth of military hardware would now be destroyed at the whim of the Boss. Even with limited knowledge of the aircraft involved, the accountant considered himself to have better judgment than the Boss. The Hawks were fast-attack machines built for air combat. Since they could not land, only buzz the area with low passes at ridiculously high speeds, their tactical value in a recovery operation was minimal at best. It was the helicopter gunships that would be needed, but they did not have afterburners. The accountant shook his head imperceptibly. Even the AI had learned to find nonsense ways to appease this child-man.

"And you. Tell me we got the Kenya money on those air defense units," the Boss demanded, turning to the accountant.

"Um, yes, sir." The accountant stiffened and quickly put his glasses on.

"Profit margin?"

"One hundred forty-five percent."

The Boss rubbed his hands together. Now that he had just sold the Somali rebels the latest rocket launchers, the Kenyan government was eager to purchase his air defense units at a premium. "And there better be some good news on the ocean property sell-off."

The accountant swallowed hard and scrolled on his computer. The worst thing he could do was misspeak a number.

"Well?"

Before the accountant could open his mouth, Jason's voice interrupted from the speaker on the wall. *"Sir, I have just received an update from Ken Seaborn that I think you will like."*

"What is it?"

"Ken has acquired the Quantum Triangle. He is requesting a tech to disable a locking security feature."

"Good. At least there's one person doing what I want. Get a ship up there with whatever he needs and bring that thing back to me, immediately," the Boss demanded.

"Checking launch status at Space Force in Florida," the AI said.

The accountant fixed his eyes on the screen in from of him. *Please, step away from the case.*

The Boss waited with his arms folded. "Finally. All that money put into that physicist's crazy quantum stuff is going to pay off. If that triangle thing can really annihilate things, think of the profits! This could be even better than the plasma cannon. I could sell all kinds of weapons, only to have them disappear mysteriously—so they would have to buy more. *Fantastic.*"

The accountant bit his lower lip. *And you could return that poor girl you kidnapped from his brother.*

Crossing to the bar, the Boss continued to think of the possibilities. "Hmm. And I could make anyone that even *thinks* of challenging me truly disappear. How convenient. No special ops, no fuss, no mess. Just gone."

After only a short time, the Boss turned back to the speaker on the information wall. "Jason, I'm waiting. I should never have to."

"Sir, General Marshall says the next launch window is in two days, due to the expected weather conditions there."

"Didn't I say 'immediately'?" the Boss spat impatiently. "Are you not listening to me? I don't give a shit about the damn weather. Get that bird up there now, and get me that device."

"I've instructed the general to override weather limit safety protocols."

"Good. And you..." The Boss never called people by their names. "Tell me more stupid dipshits are buying my properties at top dollar. I want to see their faces when those soon-to-be-worthless beach resorts get flooded off the map by the high tides. They were stupid enough to believe the low *official* projections I paid top money to create."

"Yes, well, we just sold both the Virginia Beach MaxTower and the Patriot Palace at ten percent over asking price by introducing our own counterbidder. And we have acquired thirty acres inland of both properties at the expected elevation of the new actual beachline," answered the accountant while he looked down at the shoes of the man. The Boss wanted people to look at his shoes to illustrate their subservient position.

"Just ten percent? I want more. I want twenty on the next sale, or you'll have a discussion with Jason. Understood? And I want to be repositioned within the month. Although Jason has arranged accidents for most in the know, eventually someone will realize those official forecast levels are not accurate. News is going to get out. And when that happens, it won't be long before current beach property isn't worth shit."

The Boss smiled at himself and boasted, "It's this kind of thinking—turning a catastrophic event to my advantage—which makes me the great man I am." He crossed to the liquor cabinet and poured an ample portion of hundred-year-old bourbon into a glass. "What about my island?"

The accountant swallowed hard.

"*Well?*" the Boss asked again through clenched teeth.

"Um, this is a rather difficult property to find the right buyer for, especially without raising suspicions. We're having discreet talks with three billionaires, but it is very preliminary," the accountant said sheepishly.

"Move it along, *now.* Jason, let's get some leverage on them so they're more inclined to deal. Tell our investigators to find a weakness in each and set up a sting. Women, drugs, embezzlement—the regular stuff. We need to dump this place before it gets washed away."

"*Yes, sir,*" the AI responded.

The Boss moved back to the window and gazed out again. "I think I might miss this view. I'll just have to build another island—one with more elevation."

He turned back to the accountant. "Okay, get out."

The accountant quickly collected his things and scurried out without saying a word.

SCAN ME

FACTOID 23

The Soyuz return vehicle has a landing zone accuracy of twenty-eight kilometers relative to the center target using a parachute descent and may be up to six hundred kilometers short of the target in a ballistic return. That makes the landing zone longer than the width of the state of Pennsylvania. For safety, landing areas need to be flat and open without structures, rivers, or trees. There are no sites in Russia that meet these criteria, and only thirteen sites in Kazakhstan that do.

23   Zak, Anatoly. (2023, January 20).
Here is how Soyuz returns to Earth. RussianSpaceWeb.com.
https://www.russianspaceweb.com/soyuz-landing.html

CHAPTER 23

Return

Zandra watched in horror as Emma powered off system after system on the CRV. Flight control, communications, radio beacon—all off. She understood the plan, but it was risky. Rather than follow the controlled aerodynamic descent typically used by spacecraft returning to earth, Emma was forcing the vehicle into the emergency backup mode of a ballistic return. This would cut both their landing time and the landing zone short, making it harder for the Boss's people to intercept their return. The downside: they would not be experiencing a landing; rather, they would be experiencing the flight of a cannon ball with the accompanying rather rough touchdown. Both women had already placed a rubber block in their mouths to prevent them from breaking their teeth on final impact. As they descended past ninety kilometers, Zandra could see the fiery plasma bubble start to form through the porthole, and she pulled tightly on her straps one more time.

*

Derek idled the three Mercury Racing 400R outboards on the thirty-nine-foot Hustler Shotgun boat at the eastmost reach of the regatta. It was a stroke of luck that the race was being held at this time. He could patrol the yellow spear of a boat around without anyone thinking it was there for anything but fun. Plenty of boats were out to watch the regatta. With a gentle but constant breeze, even with the clouds, it was a beautiful summer day for a race off the coast of Milwaukee.

His long-time buddy, Sam, sat with his feet up on the two modified scuba jet dive sleds, drinking what people would assume was a beer. It wasn't. Both men were professionals when it came to an operation. Their Special Forces training and ops history together ran deep. They waited patiently, and although the sailboats were racing to their west, both kept a watchful eye on the sky to the north and east. Derek kept the Shotgun pointed north.

They did not have to wait long. As it cleared the clouds, they spotted the red-and-white parachute bearing twenty degrees northeast. Derek slammed the throttle forward. Time was critical. The regatta group would think he had gotten bored with the sailboats and decided to go for some open-water, hundred-mile-per-hour excitement instead. He estimated they had twenty-five kilometers to intercept the touchdown. The Shotgun could be there in under ten minutes. Hopefully, it would take more than that for the Boss's people to figure out they had been had with the CRV reentry going to ballistic mode instead of aerodynamic, falling hundreds of kilometers short of the expected landing site. At best, their scrambled jets would be six hundred kilometers out. Even at Mach 3, it would take them ten minutes to fly over. They could observe, but do nothing. The slow helicopter gunships that could really wreak havoc, which the Boss would also deploy, would be the equivalent of decades too late.

Sam radioed coordinates to the dive boat.

*

At the roaring sound of the solid rocket braking motors igniting, Zandra closed her eyes. It was just seconds before the bone-jarring impact of the capsule landing sent a shockwave through her entire body. They were down. Emma released her straps quickly and grabbed two breathers and wrist straps hidden below her seat.

"Here. Get this in your mouth, and strap this to your wrist. Be ready to swim." Emma held up a box cutter. "I'm going to slice the flotation ring to sink the capsule. Get away from the capsule as fast as you can, so you don't get caught in the chute. Get underwater and stay there. Do not break the surface and follow me. Understand?"

Zandra spit out the rubber mouthpiece that had saved her teeth, shoved the breather in, and nodded an okay.

"I'm blowing the hatch." Emma lifted the safety bar and punched the button to ignite the explosive bolts on the hatch. Zandra followed quickly behind Emma as she exited through the small port. Standing on the flotation ring circling the base of the capsule, Zandra took in a long breath of sweet Earth air through her nose. *The richness of real air.*

One breath was all Zandra would get. Emma stabbed the flotation ring with the box cutter, and the two women were plunged into the chilly water. Emma pushed off from the sinking capsule. Zandra quickly swam after Emma to avoid being dragged to the bottom of the lake in the web of lines from the capsule's chute.

*

Derek cut the engines over top of the foam. The capsule had sunk only minutes ago from this spot. "Drop them now."

Sam slid the first of the scuba jets into the water. Jumping to the other side of the boat, he grabbed the other and did the same. "Away and running."

Looking at his handheld monitor, Sam reported, "Number one has acquired signal and is tracking. Number two is searching." He continued to watch the screen. After a few seconds he added, "Number two has now acquired signal."

Two jets streaked overhead. Both men instinctively covered their ears and opened their mouths, waiting for the sonic boom. The bastards were flying extremely low and still supersonic.

After the boom shook the craft to its bones, cracking the windscreen in three places, Derek shouted, "We've been marked! Heading due west. Tell Steven it's his ball now."

Sam braced himself for another high-speed run and relayed the instructions to the dive boat.

"Sea Hunt, Sea Hunt. Fish are swimming strong."

After a moment, the radio crackled. *"Sea Hunt is on the hunt."*

Now it was time to drink the real beer to complete the façade. Even at the speeds their boat could move, they would eventually be intercepted and searched. It was part of the plan. But they would just be two joyriders investigating the weird disappearance of something splashing down in the great lake. There was nothing on their boat but a beer cooler.

*

Emma and Zandra floated just under the waves. All Zandra could do was follow the instructions she had been given. Hand signals from Emma: stay here. Wait. But the water was cold, and she was not wearing a wetsuit as she normally did while scuba diving. They could do this for a while, but eventually hypothermia would set in.

Emma kept checking her wristwatch, looking around 360 degrees. Finally, she signaled two fingers at her eyes, *look,* and then pointed with her arm to the south. Out of the somewhat murky water appeared two torpedo-like devices, heading right towards them. As the first approached Emma, she grabbed a handle, and the device stopped. The second headed for Zandra. She took hold of it and recognized it as a scuba diver propulsion sled. Mounted on each was obviously a homing device of some kind that must have been programmed to seek out the transponder on her wrist. The Resistance clearly had some people with expertise in electronics, and mission planning.

Emma checked the compass on her wrist, pointed in a direction, and headed off. Already starting to shiver in the cold water, Zandra followed.

On and on they traveled under the water.

*

Steve checked his GPS. The coordinates were correct. He raised his dive flag and waited. He was just another six-pack dive boat looking for a wreck to explore.

An hour passed. It was June, and the lake temperature was still under sixty degrees Fahrenheit. That would feel very cold after that much time swimming behind a dive sled without a wetsuit. He had hot beverages and blankets ready to fight off hypothermia.

Finally, the tracking device beeped. The homing signal of a sled had been located. Shortly afterwards, another beep indicated that the other sled signal had also been received. Steve quickly moved to the transom on the boat. Within minutes, his two divers appeared. Helping them aboard, he wrapped them in blankets, stowed the sleds, and went right to the bridge.

Grabbing the radio, Steve called out, "Sea Hunt with two ice-cold sturgeons."

"*Roger. Good fishing,*" was the reply.

Steve started the engine and headed due east to the Muskegon docks. Just another dive boat heading back in after a morning dive. No one would be looking for two astronauts there. At the docks, they would quickly transfer to a waiting car. They just needed to get out of the restricted Green Zone before any additional border checks went into effect. Steve throttled up the engine to make better time back to the dock.

SCAN ME

FACTOID 24

The first message sent via Morse code's dots and dashes across a long distance was sent from Washington, D.C., to Baltimore. With today's ability to hold global conversations with a ubiquitous handheld device, that accomplishment in human communications might seem trivial. But consider this in respect to all human history: it took until Friday, May 24, 1844, before complex thoughts could be communicated almost instantaneously at long distances.

24   *Today in History – May 24, What Hath God Wrought?* (n.d.). Library of Congress. https://www.loc.gov/item/today-in-history/may-24/

CHAPTER 24

Dot, Dot, Dash

WORLD SPACE STATION
BETA-27

Min flipped through a row of circuit breakers, shutting down the systems on the dark matter/energy experimentation unit one by one. She put the power units back on recharge and doused the lights to save as much power as possible.

"We are done running trials for the day. The power supplies need to charge," she announced.

Min and Alex had spent the last hours trying to reestablish the connection to his universe, with no success. They needed his side to also run the field generator with the Quantum Triangle, and it was clear that the field had been shut down. Both floated with their arms crossed in silence for a long while, feeling defeated.

Min finally broke the silence. "Let's go get something to eat. We've worked straight through since this morning, and I'm starving."

Alex nodded and followed Min as she pushed off and headed for the Truss

Tunnel. Alex emerged from the tunnel on the starboard side and continued to follow her, his eyes scanning left and right as they traveled through the modules making up the space station. This was the Alpha-One Platform structurally, but it was completely different otherwise. It was clear that this station had been built for and was still used for scientific study. Although every module had basic equipment needed for life support and survival in the event that the module needed to be isolated, each also had a different group of experiment stations mixed in. Biology, chemistry, physics… Alex could see that the focus of this station was completely different from his. Alpha-One Platform was a defensive outpost, a weapons research station, and a weapon launch platform if needed. A truly different world lay below this orbiting structure.

As they entered the Zvezda module, they found Commander Johnson and Lucas already preparing meals.

"We figured you two would be hungry, so we got dinner started a bit early," Lucas said, giving Min a big smile.

Johnson pointed to the opposite corner of the pull-out table. "Alex, you can take that spot there. It's spaghetti and meatballs night. I hope that agrees with you."

Alex took a long inhale to enjoy the warming tomato sauce aroma in the air. "Yes, thank you very much." He scanned the module, which was bathed in subdued pastel colors, and added, "Wow, nice mood lighting."

Min slid her toes under the strap below the table across from Alex and updated the commander. "We've run a full range of field setups and have still not been able to get even the slightest feedback from the other universe. The power cells are drained, but recharging. We should be able to start runs again first thing tomorrow, but I honestly don't know what else to try."

Alex added, "I'm sure that unless my field generator with the Quantum Triangle is also running on the other side, we will not be able to establish an overlap between the two universes. We need someone there to run my system, but that's virtually impossible without me being on the other side."

Lucas came over with hydration packs and passed one each to Min and

Alex. He gave Min's shoulder a squeeze. "Well, maybe just turn that super-brain off for just a bit and let your creative subconscious have a few processor cycles. I'm sure you'll figure something out."

"Thanks. You are my rock." Min held onto Lucas's hand.

Alex watched the tension in Min's body melt away. *Touch is so powerful.* He closed his eyes for a moment and imagined that Zandra was here, doing the same. He took a deep breath and relaxed his shoulders. *I will find a way to get her back.*

The commander started floating meals to each of the crew. Min motioned to Alex not to interfere with the meal's travel. It was a small game they sometimes played to see how accurately the server could land each meal onto the Velcro strip in front of each person. Four clean landings without bouncing off was considered a home run. They watched as Min's meal landed and stuck to the table.

"First base!" Min called out.

The commander winked at Min and sent Alex's meal on its way. Although drifting slightly askew, it landed and held at an angle in front of Alex.

"As it slides into second, the umpire calls it safe!" Min announced as she made a fist in front of her mouth and pretended to be speaking into a public address system.

Johnson released the meal pack for Lucas. It too pivoted slightly, but landed solidly dead on the spot.

"We have a stand-up triple! Can he make the home run?" Min exclaimed.

The commander let the meal float in front of him and rubbed his hands together. If they were in gravity, he would simply have to drop the meal down at his place. But up and down did not truly exist on a space station. Johnson smiled broadly, gingerly took hold of the tray, and released the meal pack with a slight twist of his wrist. The meal started spinning side over side as it floated towards the table.

"Oh my god, he goes for the barrel roll!"

They all sat transfixed by the grand finale of the game, the meal tray tumbling slowly in the air. As the meal came to the table surface, the rotation was perfectly timed to land on the strip and catch.

"Home run! Fred Johnson gives his team the win for the pennant! It's a party in the small town of Rocky Mount tonight," Min called out and waved her arms wildly.

Alex joined in the full round of applause for the commander as he took a bow. Alex was amazed at the comradery between this crew. They were a team that not only respected each other's unique talents, but enjoyed time together. There was no watching for error or constant fear of having another crew member put you on report to the Party. This *was* a different world.

The commander strapped into his seat, raised his fork, and turned to Min. *"Liánghǎo de yǐnshí."*

"He's been practicing his Chinese too! We need to check the task assignments. This guy has way too much time on his hands." Min beamed. "Good eating, Commander."

Johnson turned to Lucas. *"Buen provecho, Lucas."*

"Gracias a ti, y a ti también."

"And Alex, how should we wish you a good meal? Maybe some German heritage? *Gutes Essen?"* the commander asked.

Alex was surprised by the question. It wasn't a proper question to ask. Your heritage was either right or wrong. He would not be in space if his heritage were wrong. The optics for the Party would be unacceptable. Gathering his composure, he replied, "I'm just a normal person. No heritage to speak of."

"My apologies. Please enjoy your meal."

They each used their scissors to cut into a meal pouch. Squeezing a bit of sauce on his roll, Lucas took a bite and gave a satisfied smile. "It's not quite Mom's recipe, but I do love spaghetti night."

Min bumped his rib with her elbow. "I'm not sure there's a meal that you don't love."

Lucas patted his stomach, "Hey, I'm still—"

Just then, all the lights went out, and a dead silence came over the station. Within a couple seconds, the emergency lights came on, and a few ventilation fans began to hum.

"Shit. I think something just took out a good chunk of our solar array feed. We're on backup power," Lucas announced.

Alex turned to the commander next to him. "Are you under attack?"

Johnson gave Alex a confused look and turned to Lucas. "Probably a micro-meteor strike. Let's get it checked out. Lucas, you check on the arrays. Min, run a complete systems check."

Moving to a comms unit, Johnson said, "PACOM, Mission. Comm check."

Alex straightened from the table and asked, "Anything I can do?"

"Go with Min. She can assign you some systems to reset."

"Mission, this is PACOM. We are reading you. We also see a major power outage. Confirm."

"Roger, ground. We are on backup power for everything on the starboard feed. Checking module and system statuses now. Lucas thinks we might have had a micro-meteor strike on our starboard array. The port arrays are still online," the commander replied.

"Roger that, Mission. We will investigate on our side too."

Lucas had moved to a station that operated the exterior camera system. He called out, "All starboard power channels are offline. The arrays themselves are okay, but the feed has gone bad. Switching to shared power feed routing from the port bank."

The banks of warning indicators changed from red to green. Alex ran his finger across a row. "These are the same systems we have on the Platform."

Min pointed to the power feed breakers and gave a thumbs-up. "Good. Then you probably know the procedures too."

Moving across rows, Alex started turning some of the tripped breakers back on. A portion of the lights and fans started up, and the station filled with the constant hum they were all accustomed to hearing. They would operate under half-load conditions until the starboard power feed could be returned to service.

"Woah, check this out." Lucas sent an image to both the other terminals in the module and to ground.

They all studied the picture of the 1A array sequential shunt unit. Its job of regulating the voltage feed from the solar array was clearly no longer possible. Near the center of the SSU was a pencil-sized bullet hole. Although the unit was built to withstand micro-meteor strikes, this unlucky hit had surpassed the design limits.

"And we have another," Lucas announced. "Crap. What are the odds of this? One in a trillion, at least."

Alex studied the next image popping up on his display. The electronic control unit of the 3A array had a similar hole.

"Lucas, start prepping for an EVA," the commander ordered. "I will join you shortly. It's easy money that our sleep station tonight will be replaced with the airlock doing a decompression procedure. No way ground is going to want this to stand."

The commander punched the comms again. "PACOM, Mission. While you evaluate the SSU and ECU pictures Lucas just sent, he and I are going to start prepping for an EVA. Confirm."

"*Mission, roger that. We will call Ed Anderson and have him join the party tonight.*"

Although the conversation was businesslike, Alex could feel the serious undertones in the voices. In space, you were kept alive by the environmental systems—and those systems needed electrical power to run.

*

Min released her grip on the manipular and wiped her brow. The robotic arm would keep the damaged SSU at a fixed distance that was well clear of Lucas. He could focus on making the final connections with the replacement unit. It had been a long stretch of stressful hours. Although the SSU was not a big unit—about the size of a large suitcase, weighing 150 pounds—construction projects at zero-g were always physically demanding. Without air resistance or gravity, the inertia of objects became a constant challenge. Most of an astronaut's energy in an EVA was spent keeping something in motion under control—either themselves, or the objects they worked with. To make things even more difficult, fundamental working cues such as touch and sound were not present. Finally, the environment constantly cycled between minus 100 degrees Fahrenheit on the night side to 150 degrees Fahrenheit or more in sunlight. The act of simply tightening a bolt to the correct torque became complicated.

Min glanced up at the timer running at the top of her monitor and keyed her microphone. "Lucas, you have three minutes remaining to make those electrical connections on this pass."

"*Roger, I got this. Just two more plugs.*"

It was important to make the connections on the dark side of their orbit. The solar arrays were capable of pumping over seventy-six thousand watts of power, so connections needed to be complete before the solar panels came alive. If Lucas could not finish the connections, they would need to wait for the next orbit. That would extend this already difficult EVA by another hour and a half.

Min could hear the heavy breathing of Lucas. She turned to Alex. "Poor guy, he must be exhausted."

"I wish you guys would have let me help. It would have gone faster," Alex said.

"Thanks. But I think you can understand the concern from mission control. Unknowns on an EVA are a no-go."

"*Ground, please check the ECU now. I have that all patched in,*" the commander said in a tired voice.

The head of the technician monitoring the ECU telemetry on Min's video feed of mission control moved from monitor to monitor. He was carefully and meticulously checking the readouts against the specs. After a moment, he turned and gave a thumbs-up to Ed Anderson. Min loved working with these people, competent professionals that she trusted.

Ed cued his mic. "*Nice work, Fred. We have a green board here on the ECU. Let's get you traversing back to the hatch. Lucas should be following you soon.*"

"*Roger. Traversing back.*"

"*Ground to Lucas, you are down to just over a minute,*" Ed warned.

213

Following a series of grunts, Lucas called back, *"All good. Connections are locked in."*

The relief in the ground control center was palpable even over the video feed. It had been a long eighteen hours for everyone. They still needed the last system check to confirm that the work was a success. After several long seconds, the system power technician put his arm straight up with a thumb high.

With applause in the background, Ed announced, *"That's a wrap, Lucas. Good job. Let's get you heading back to the hatch too."*

"Just call him Superman," Min chimed in.

"Roger, ground. Traversing. Min, this Superman is hungry."

"Copy that. I will have beef stroganoff ready for you in the airlock," Min replied. She continued to monitor both the commander and Lucas as they slowly pulled themselves to port across the backbone of the station to the airlock. As she was watching Fred Johnson enter, a taping sound came through the bulkhead above her.

Tap. Tap... Tap. Tap.

Tap... Tap. Tap... Tap...

Tap... Tap...

Min smiled broadly. Alex looked at her questioningly.

"That Lucas. He's a sweetheart," she explained. "Morse code. Dot, dash, dot, dot is L. Dash, dot, dash, dash for Y. Dash, dash for M. Our little code. LYM: love you madly. Don't tell anyone. It is the worst-kept secret of the mission."

Alex nodded his head. "I think that I can keep a secret, don't worry. I'm very happy for you."

*

After they had all gotten a meal down, ground had ordered everyone to take some downtime. Both the commander and Lucas didn't have much choice. They would spend a long time with not much to do in the airlock, waiting through a careful equalization procedure to prevent decompression sickness. Min and Alex went to their respective crew rest stations.

Alex strapped himself to a wall and closed his eyes. He focused on slowing his breathing. Her voice in his head: *"Slow mind with slow breath, Aleks."* His breathing slowed. His mind slowed. He relaxed. This was such a different universe. Crews that played games together at meals. Instead of a combat post, an entire station dedicated to science—real science aimed at saving humanity itself, not developing more weapons to destroy. *What I used to be able do ... with Zandra.* A world working towards a common goal. It was the polar opposite of his world. A part of him wanted to forget his other world and stay here. A much bigger part wanted to be back with Zandra, no matter what universe that was in. He thought of Min and Lucas, two astronauts in a semi-secret love affair. Morse code. *Dot, dash, dot, dot is L...*

Alex snapped his eyes wide open. *Holy crap. Morse code!*

He called out, "Min, I got it. I know how to get a message to Starra!"

SCAN ME

FACTOID 25

During the tense years of the Cold War, from 1953 to 1979, the United States built and operated close to three hundred Nike missile sites across the country. Named after the Greek goddess of victory, the air defense system was equipped with both conventional (NIKE-Ajax) and nuclear (NIKE-Hercules) missiles. The last battery of Hercules missiles, at Fort Bliss, Texas, were decommissioned in 1983.

---

25   Historic Context of the Nike Missile Site. (n.d.).

Fairfax County Gov. – Laurelhill – History.

https://www.fairfaxcounty.gov/planning-development/sites/planning-development/files/assets/documents/laurelhill/history/nikemissilesite.pdf

CHAPTER 25

The Bunker

LAKE MICHIGAN GREEN ZONE EAST
RHO-1

As the steel pillars dropped below the pavement to clear the barricade, the guard with an M29 automatic slung over his shoulder waved them by. The driver of the rusting Camry rolled forward slowly with both his hands clearly visible on top of the steering wheel. He was careful not to do anything abrupt that might cause one of these checkpoint guards to shoot first and then start asking questions. They were well known for their zeal in protecting both external and internal borders. Dead bodies did not immigrate or sneak across a border to secretly live inside a restricted area.

Zandra could feel the tension in the car ease. The driver checked his rearview mirror, cracked his neck to both sides, and added some speed. The man sitting beside her in the back seat released his hold on the nine-millimeter handgun under his jacket. She returned to gazing out the window. The well-kept houses and streets they had been driving through quickly turned into fields of green. Potato plants stretched up and over the hillsides in neat rows. As they passed a tower at the corner of a field, Zandra's eyes climbed up the structure to see another guard with an M29. She peered ahead and could make out another tower in the distance.

"They guard potatoes?" she asked.

"These lush fields feed the people in those houses back there … and nobody else," Emma answered from the passenger seat up front without looking back. "If we stop and even look as if we might get out of the car and steal a plant, they will shoot us."

"No…"

"Just pray we don't get a flat." Emma cocked her head as they drove by another tower. "Back there before the checkpoint was a Green Zone. It's an area the Party controls where people that follow their twisted thinking can live. This is a Yellow Zone. The only people here are the workers that tend these fields. They trade the hard work of growing the crops for a few leftover pieces that might keep them and their families alive. If you get near a field without a worker transponder, they will shoot you. Only the 'haves' in the Green Zone get to eat these potatoes."

They drove on for several miles.

A high concrete wall with another checkpoint came into view, and the tension in the car returned. The man with the nine-millimeter straightened and slipped his hand back into his jacket as the driver coasted the car to a careful stop.

"Your pass," ordered the guard with one hand on his sidearm.

The driver held up his electronic credentials for the guard to scan. After studying the scanner for an eternity, he moved around the car, looking at each passenger. Returning to the driver's window, he said, "Takes four people to dig some soil samples?"

"Just doing what we're told. They want to test the Red Zone soil again, so we go get samples," the driver answered.

"You should have a patrol. You get stuck out there after dark without weapons, and you might not come back," the guard said.

"We don't rate a patrol. Just some drone coverage."

The guard nodded and waved them by.

As the car crept past the gate in the wall and sped off, Zandra scanned the new horizon, and her jaw dropped. Gone were the green fields of potatoes. Gone was green … period.

Glancing back at her, Emma said, "Yes, quite the difference, isn't it?"

"Is safe here? No radiation? This like nuclear zone!"

As far as Zandra could see, there was charred destruction, a gray landscape of burned-out vehicles, partial structures with walls caved in, and debris strewn everywhere. As she looked down a dirt-covered road, the movement of a three-legged, half-starved dog digging through a trash pile caught her attention. As they drove by, the head of a grubby child popped up from the pile and watched them pass, wary of their presence.

Emma gave a sarcastic chuckle. "Is it safe? Hell, no. But not because of any radiation." She swept her hand across the windshield view. "Welcome to the land of the have-nots. This is where the peons of the earth live and struggle to survive. With so little to eat, we're left to feed among ourselves, so watch yourself. If John back there tells you to get your head down, you better do it fast.

"Back there before the first checkpoint was a Green Zone for the 'haves.' Those in that protected area are the fortunate ones. They happen to have acceptable non-foreign looks and family ties to the Party. They must also be of Right Thinking and loyal to the Party, of course, lest they find themselves relocated outside the walls in the middle of the night."

Zandra watched out her window in horrified silence.

Emma turned back to Zandra and could see the sadness in her face. "Quite a different place than your world?" she asked.

"Yes … and no. I sad to see waste this world too. Both worlds seem good at destroy, no?" She watched a young boy disappear into a boarded-up shop as they came around a corner. "We have place like this from war. Nobody live there. Fallout kill everything, and will for many years. We make good places too, but all can be there. No 'haves' and 'nots', just all us now. Together, we survivors of human. Little resources we have go to food and science for new home. We kill ours. Maybe my world just 'have-lost.' We hoping science give us chance again."

Emma turned back in her seat and gazed forward. With remorse in her voice, she said quietly, "Science. I used to love science. Real science, aimed at discovering the wonders of the universe. But that was a long time ago, it seems. Funny how just ten years can seem like a lifetime."

"What you mean?" Zandra could sense both hurt and longing in Emma.

"Well, maybe not so long ago, we were of much more similar worlds. Actually, I guess it was the same world, right? I used to be a scientist working on nanotechnology for our space program, back when space was about science, not weapons. I was still early in my training for my first mission aboard the orbiting space station when the Satellite War broke out. It only took one narcissistic madman and the Party to use that event to take control of our government and change everything. Asimov was right when he referred to the cult of ignorance and warned of 'the false notion that democracy means that my ignorance is just as good as your knowledge.' The Party and the Boss didn't care about science or facts, and they cared even less about democracy. They just wanted power. When people stop thinking for themselves and listen to the fearmongering those in power use to manipulate the masses for their own benefit, it becomes a downward spiral for all.

"So, we didn't need nanotechnology for science to feed people; we only needed weapons. We needed tangible things, rockets and warheads to protect us against the fears they were seeding in the pliable brains of the masses. It's always easier to single out someone or some group as the simple cause for your problems, rather than dig into the complexity and root out the real and difficult issues. Dogma is better than inconvenient truth. People were easily convinced that the totalitarian actions of their leaders to control everything in their lives was just the implementation of the *one* correct way to believe. The masses relinquished control of their individual choices about what they could do, what they could be, who they could marry, what they could do with their bodies. When manipulated by false fears, it became comforting and simple to be told what was right and what was wrong. Too many people did not want the burden of thinking for themselves.

"Intellectuals became the enemy of those wanting simple solutions. Those of us that pushed back with facts or science were quickly targeted by the Party for not following the propaganda embodied in Right Thinking. After watching members of my mission team be stoned to death by Party mobs, I chose survival and outwardly presented myself as a devout follower of the insanity.

"My fiancé refused to play along though. He could not understand why people would ignore clear facts and science. He never gave in and always spoke the truth to all that would hear." She ran her fingers through her short, cropped black hair and continued in a quieter voice, "I cried as they stoned him too. For him and those that died for the truth, I secretly joined the Resistance. We fight for the truth, and those that died for it."

Emma leaned into the door and looked up at the steel-gray sky through the side window. "I am no longer a scientist," she said resolutely. "I am a warrior for the fallen and will avenge their deaths."

Zandra wiped a tear from the corner of her eye. She sensed so much pain in this world. She closed her eyes, but that could not block out the hurt she sensed all around her. "I so very sorry. I just want to go back to my world … with Aleks."

"We both were disappointed today."

They drove on in silence for hours.

*

The car came to an abrupt skidding stop in front of a partially burned-out farmhouse just as the sun was slipping over the horizon. Emma got out quickly and ordered, "This is it. Let's move."

All three passengers bolted from the car, and the driver sped off towards a dilapidated barn with a roof half fallen in.

"Zandra, follow my steps exactly on the porch. If you step in the wrong place, you will either fall through a rotted plank to razor-sharp spikes or trigger a land mine. Neither is good."

Emma zigzagged up the porch steps and crossed the deck to the front door. Zandra carefully placed her feet in the exact same pathway. As she entered the house, she turned to the sitting room on the right. The cobwebs, worn-out sofa, and dusty table indicated that nobody had lived here for a long time. A small colony of bats hung from the broken chandelier, their guano droppings littering the tabletop. *Why are we here?*

Emma stopped at a doorway and waved for her to follow. "Quickly. We need to make sure a random drone flyover doesn't catch our heat signatures."

Zandra followed down the stairs to a dank basement, poorly illuminated by a bare bulb hanging from a floor joist. They crossed the dirt floor to what was once a coal bin for a long-since-defunct furnace. Emma pulled a rusty steel door aside and ducked to enter a cramped cave. Zandra could barely see as she followed. Her bodyguard, with the nine-millimeter in hand, pulled the steel door closed behind them. It was pitch black.

The man with the gun keyed his phone on. The display provided a dim glow in the cave.

"Accessing Wi-Fi. Tango Wilco Papa," he said to Emma.

She asked, "Truth Will Prevail?"

"Your memory is amazing, Emma," he replied.

She smiled at him, turned, and repeated the phrase towards the other end of the cave.

The phone beeped. The man read the message to Emma. "Papa India Echo Five. That's just too easy for you."

Emma pointed at Zandra. "You know?"

"Sorry, I astronaut maybe, secret agent no."

"Well, see, this is what happens when a bunch of intellectuals have to become a militia. The proper reply is pi to five decimal places."

Emma called down the cave, "Three point one four one five nine."

The cave exploded with light as a door at the end swung wide open.

Emma stretched out her arm towards the doorway. "Welcome to Nike Missile Base D-87, now Resistance Bunker Lima."

SCAN ME

FACTOID 26

"On October 9, 1876, Alexander Graham Bell and Thomas A. Watson talked by telephone to each other over a two-mile (3 km) wire stretched between Cambridge and Boston. It was the first wire conversation ever held. Yesterday afternoon the same two men talked by telephone to each other over a 3,400-mile (5,500 km) wire between New York and San Francisco. Dr. Bell, the veteran inventor of the telephone, was in New York, and Mr. Watson, his former associate, was on the other side of the continent. They heard each other much more distinctly than they did in their first talk thirty-eight years ago."

The advance from "long distance" (Washington, D.C., to Baltimore) Morse code in 1844 to cross-country verbal conversations took just seventy-one years.

---

26   Direct quote from *Phone to Pacific from the Atlantic*. (1915, January 26). The New York Times.
https://timesmachine.nytimes.com/timesmachine/1915/01/26/100134789.
html?pageNumber=1

CHAPTER 26

Station-to-Station Call

Alex drummed his fingers in front of the keyboard in excitement. He couldn't believe how well his plan had worked. Min had quickly written a program that combined a voice-to-text module and a customized Morse-code-to-dark-energy pulse generator. They could speak into the mic and send a cross-dimensional message. Using the reverse programming, they could also listen to dark energy messages from another universe. It had not taken long for Starra to detect the dark energy pulses, decipher that the pattern was an encoded message, and generate a reply using a similar dark energy pulse with his experimental equipment in that universe.

"It is so good to hear from you, mate. Your message said not to notify anyone of our contact. Why?" the synthetic voice asked.

"I needed to know what has happened there first. Where is Zandra?" Alex clasped his hands in front of his face and bit his thumb knuckle, hoping.

"Zandra has returned to the surface in the CRV."

225

"Dammit."

"Can I inform Commander Becker now?" Starra asked. *"The commander will be relieved to hear from you. I am concerned for him. His stress levels have been extremely elevated since losing all four of you and the change in command."*

"Wait—just Min and I transferred, and Zandra went to the surface. What do you mean, 'all four'?" Alex asked.

The synthetic voice stated without emotion, *"After you disappeared, Emma and Zandra took the CRV to the surface. So, only Ken Seaborn and Hans Becker are currently on board the Platform."*

"And the change in command?"

"After evaluating the station surveillance records during the time of your disappearance, the Party determined that Commander Becker should be relieved of station command and further questioned on the ground. Ken Seaborn is currently the acting commander of Alpha-One Platform until another crew can be dispatched."

Alex rubbed his chin and admitted to Min, "This just got a whole lot more complicated."

"Starra, what is the status of a station CRV replacement?" he asked. "Also, do you have a location for Zandra and Emma on the surface?"

"A resupply vehicle with two crew members from Platform Beta is scheduled to dock at seven fifty tomorrow. The commander will return to the surface using that vehicle, detach to be at sixteen forty. Ken will remain on station. Mission control is sending a separate vehicle for him."

Alex shot Min a questioning look. "I wonder why Ken is not returning too. Starra, what about Zandra and Emma?"

"Emma and Zandra aborted their planned flight path to the surface. It appears that the CRV was reprogrammed with different reentry coordinates than mission control had provided. They also aborted all systems and did a ballistic descent. I tracked their splashdown into Lake Michigan. Monitoring military communications, I heard that their capsule sank, and divers found it empty when the recovery team arrived at the site. No one knows their location."

"That's strange," Alex said, looking at Min. "Why would they abort their reentry flight path? That would make their recovery much more difficult. Unless..."

Alex froze, stunned. Those final words from Emma that he never understood came back to him. *"Please trust me. I'm on your side. We are going to get your niece back if you help us."*

"Holy crap. It all fits! She was trying to tell me. We need to help. I need to get back there!"

Min looked at him, confused.

"Emma is with the Resistance." Alex tapped his temple with his finger and thought. After a few seconds, he keyed the mic. "Starra, I have a plan, and I need your help."

*

"Are you sure you want to do this?" Min asked as she double-checked the settings on her console. "Starra estimated the probability of success to be thirty-four percent."

Alex smiled as he checked his watch again. "Yeah, I've been thinking that I need to work on her probability routines. She seems to be somewhat pessimistic lately."

"My probability routines are 99.999 percent accurate in their analysis. I see no need for any adjustments," came the synthesized voice.

Min flipped a switch off. "Oops. I forgot to tell you, Alex, I had Starra on an open channel as we were setting things up."

"No worries," he said, flipping the switch back on. "Starra, I'm just kidding. There's no possible way I could ever improve you."

"Thank you, Alex. But I am still hoping for medium-size breasts when you build my android form, so that you and 53.6 percent of men—"

"Okay, Starra. Noted," Alex broke in.

Min shot Alex a surprised grin.

"I can explain some other time... Really, I can," he said, looking up at the top of the module and shaking his head. "Starra, were you able to get in contact with the Resistance?"

"I have been able to reach the Resistance as you requested. You were correct in how their communication works without satellites. I find it fascinating. It is a very creative approach to use a network of repeater drones that keep moving. Their movements are both random and yet synchronized. It seems somewhat similar to the undulating flight path of a flock of birds. That allows them to evade the targeting of the Party wanting to eliminate the Resistance communication capabilities. Once I provided the background information you gave me, they were able to verify your identity. I have somewhat restricted access on their network though. I can monitor their unencrypted messages, and it is interesting to note that—"

"Starra, we're a bit pressed for time," Alex broke in. "Have they provided the coordinates?"

"Yes. They have provided alternative landing coordinates for the CRV."

"Fantastic, Starra. Great work. Send them over, please." He winked at Min and rubbed his palms together. "Pieces of the puzzle falling into place…"

"Alex, this is still extremely risky," Min said. "I'm not sure that I'm comfortable doing it."

"It will work. Trust me."

"Superposition of a person is one thing. We've done it. Two people, and twice now. But now you want to add transportation in relative space at the same time? I don't know."

"I know there's risk," Alex said. "But I don't see any other way. If I materialize in the Alpha-One Platform, the new crew will capture me. Game over. We just need to redirect the target field with the space-time positioning of the CRV. Starra has run the simulations. It will work."

"Your call. You're placing your life in the hands of an AI."

"Starra is not your everyday AI. I trust her like a sister."

"So, our marriage is off?" Starra asked.

Min poked Alex with her finger. "This better work, because I want to hear your full explanations."

"Does presumed innocence have any weight in this universe?"

"Just make your crazy plan work. Zandra needs to come back home. And it would be great if you came back with her. She misses you more than you could know."

"I will." Alex placed his hand on his heart. "You're just too good to be true, Min. I don't know how I could ever thank you and the crew here for the kindness you've provided."

"The vector is ready, Alex. The CRV has detached and is starting to maneuver away from the platform. I can maintain the vector for twenty-one seconds, then it will be out of range."

Alex grinned. "My transporter beam awaits."

"I wish you well, Alex. I didn't need Zandra's abilities to know from the start that you have a good heart." Min punched buttons on her console and energized the dark energy system. The view through the Aceso hatch began to phase between the WSS and another module that appeared completely different.

Alex called out, "Engage."

He stepped through the hatch and was gone.

*

Considering that Commander Becker had just seen a man materialize through the CRV hatch that was supposed to be sealed against the vacuum of space, he was very calm. After looking over his shoulder to see that the flashing hatch warning light was not to be believed, he went back to his console to monitor the movement of the CRV away from Alpha-One Platform.

"Permission to come aboard?" Alex asked as he dropped down into the seat beside the commander.

"It doesn't seem I have much choice in the matter, do I?" replied the commander. "I assume you're looking for a free ride to the surface—unannounced, I also presume?"

"You are very perceptive and a deep thinker, Commander. I've always appreciated that about you. But we do need to have a bit of a discussion regarding our orbital insertion," Alex said, fastening his seat harnesses.

The commander chuckled. "Let me guess. You want me to shut down all the reentry systems like Emma did, so we can do a ballistic descent and land at some alternate rendezvous point for the Resistance?"

Alex just smiled.

"Why should I do that? I would be court-martialed and probably executed for treason."

The smile disappeared from his face, and Alex became deadly serious. "You and I both know that with all that's happened, you're on your way down to be court-martialed anyway. At best, they'll put you in a hard labor camp in the hopes that you *will* die. The Party wants to make an example out of you. The Boss wants to inflict pain because he didn't get his way. I am offering an alternative that helps both of us."

Becker stared straight at the navigation console for a long moment.

"I feel that I'm opening Pandora's box in the career choice you present." He sighed. "Hell, pensions these days are nothing like they used to be... What are the new coordinates?"

SCAN ME

FACTOID 27

Although often referenced in Hollywood movies, it was not until May 2016 that the first and only documented case of "cement shoes" was reported. The body of Brooklyn gang member Peter Martinez, age 28, better known on the streets as Petey Crack, washed up near Manhattan Beach in Brooklyn. His body floated to the shore due to air in the concrete, because it was not given enough time to dry before being thrown into the ocean.

27   Cement shoes. (2022, December 15). Wikipedia. https://en.wikipedia.org/wiki/Cement_shoes#:~:text=In%20May%202016%2C%20the%20 first,immediate%20cause%20of%20his%20death

CHAPTER 27

Displeasure

The Boss swirled the decades-old Van Winkle bourbon in his glass as the private jet flew low over the Gulf of Mexico. Rather than climb out, the pilots had been ordered to keep it below five hundred feet for a while. They knew why. This was not the first time.

Not only did he enjoy the full flavor, but he reveled in the fact that a single bottle of this specific bourbon cost as much as a month's rent a tenant would pay in just one of his apartments. It was another clear statement to others of his wealth. *No matter; I have thousands of those apartments.* Many were not even occupied, but still paid for anyway, just as a favor to him by those seeking to do business with the man. Indirect payments to win contracts was the way to do business with the Boss. Perfectly legal.

Sitting across from him in a purposefully low-mounted seat was General Evan Marshall, head of the Space Force. His presence was not for pleasure, and he was not offered a glass of bourbon. While on his way into the base this morning, he had been forcefully removed from his car, thrown in a waiting van, and put on this plane. Marshall was no stranger to difficult situations. The bars on his chest and the three-inch scar above his right eyebrow told the story of several combat tours. Yet sitting in this seat was probably one of the worst positions he had ever been in during his long career. Although he presented himself as a strong warrior, there was sweat at his temples.

Marshall glanced towards the back of the plane. The two burley henchmen that had accosted him sat silently, but kept a watchful eye on him.

The Boss set his tumbler down. The trial was to start. "Jason," he called to his demented AI, "play the first news clip."

A newscaster at a boat marina appeared on the side monitor. *"It was a gorgeous day for the annual Mac Solo Challenge race today. This year, not only did spectators get to watch some fantastic sailing, but got a special treat. We got to see something most Chicagoans might never witness. Halfway through the race, a few people caught the landing of a spacecraft."* The video switched to a shaky phone recording from a boat. A capsule swung slowly below two parachutes as it fell from the sky.

The newscaster continued, *"It appears that a Space Force capsule might have been making an emergency landing and went off course. A short time later, some in the regatta were also treated with an airshow. These are the latest Hawk-18 fighter jets traveling above the speed of sound just feet over the surface of the lake. Look at the cone of vapor behind the aircraft as they travel above the sound barrier. Incredible."* The monitor displayed another shaky phone recording of two sleek jets skimming over the water, passing by the observer with a loud boom and pulling up into a steep vertical climb.

"Jason, stop playback." The screen froze on the image of the jets in their climb with afterburners glowing.

"So, General. You mind providing me with an explanation of what the hell happened?"

"Sir, our CRV was on the proper reentry flight path when all systems went offline, and the capsule went into a ballistic return. We have no control over the vehicle under those circumstances," replied the general.

The Boss leaned back in his chair and glared at the general. He casually took another sip from his glass, enjoying the bead of sweat on the general's brow. Setting the tumbler down, he laced his fingers over his belly and tapped his thumps together. After staring at the general for a full minute, he said, "Jason, play the next clip."

An attractive blonde newscaster appeared on the side monitor. "*The question one unlucky homeowner is asking himself tonight is, 'Does my insurance cover spaceships crashing through my roof?' I'm here with Harold Wiseman of Fennville, Michigan. He was working in his barn when he heard an incredible blast that knocked most of his tools from the barn walls.*"

"*I ran to the door and could not believe my eyes,*" exclaimed a man in worn overalls. "*All I could think was that someone dropped a bomb on my house. It was blown to pieces. What was left was on fire.*" The camera swung from the man's outstretched arm to a smoldering pile of rubble.

"*Then, a little while later, I see this armored vehicle come racing up. Two guys jump out and run right into the fire. I couldn't see much through the dust and smoke, but just as I get close, four of them come running out. One points a military rifle at me, then lowers it, smiles, and says, 'Sorry about your house. Please send the bill to the Boss.'*"

The smiling newscaster returned to the screen. In the background, an image of a blackened space capsule sat next to a broken brick chimney. Firemen were digging through the rubble and dousing any smoldering remains with water.

"*Mr. Wiseman's house was not bombed. What you see here is a crew return vehicle. Experts at the University of Michigan believe that the CRV was supposed to have splashed down in Lake Michigan, but was probably blown off course by strong winds in the upper atmosphere. The lake is not typically used for splashdowns for just that reason. There has been no confirmation or comment from the Space Force on the matter.*"

"Jason, stop playback." The screen froze on the image of the capsule with a fireman spraying water on it.

"So, General?" The Boss tapped his index fingers together, waiting.

The general straightened himself in the seat. "Sir, that CRV went off course.

It went into an unplanned ballistic descent and landed far short of the target zone."

"This seems to be a recurring theme. I wanted to question Commander Becker. And that obviously wasn't your recovery team. This was planned by the Resistance, and you let it happen. *Again*," the Boss snarled.

"Sir, the only person on that CRV was Commander Becker, and he alone must have taken manual control of the vehicle."

"Then why did we just watch the Resistance recover *two* astronauts?"

"I can't explain that, sir."

The Boss sneered at the general. "So, in the space of two days, I not only get the bad news that spies somehow got onto a space platform, which you have no explanation for, but that you lost not one, but two capsules to the Resistance."

"Sir, again, the vehicle reentry can be aborted as a last resort crew safety function, and we have no way from the ground to—"

"I don't care!" the Boss screamed. "Do you realize how much your incompetence just cost me?"

General Marshall kept his jaw firm. "Sir, we need to study the events and determine exactly—"

"Study? You want to study? I'm losing millions, and you want to *study*?"

"Sir, Alex Devin's work in quantum superposition has many unknowns. From the reports he submitted, it's possible that the two women found on Alpha-One Platform were not from the Asia Tuanhuo. It was always a possibility—"

"Don't give me your scientific mumbo-jumbo shit. You want to study something? I'll give you something to study. How about a lesson in gravity?" The Boss snapped his fingers, and the two henchmen were immediately on their feet, as if they were trained dogs. "Give this man some heavy ankle bracelets, and show the general here the door. He can study *gravity* firsthand."

The two men each grabbed an arm of the general and started dragging him towards the rear of the plane.

"What?! Stop! You can't do this!" Marshall yelled while struggling to get free.

The Boss raised his hand, and his two henchmen froze, still holding the general firmly.

"What did you say? Did you say I *can't*?'" The Boss laughed. He reached for his drink and took a sip. "That word does not apply to me. I *can* do anything I like. And right now, I would like you to be gone—permanently." He waved his hand dismissively. The two men dragged the general out the back cabin door.

After listening to a loud but short commotion, the Boss keyed the intercom to the flight deck and said calmly, "You may return to normal cruise altitude now and pressurize the cabin."

SCAN ME

FACTOID 28

The 509th Parachute Infantry Battalion, nicknamed the Geronimos, were also known as "gingerbread men" for the figure on the unit patch they wore. Lieutenant Colonel Edson Raff, the first combat commander of the Geronimos, believed that in military operations, "the boldest plan is the best." That philosophy was demonstrated repeatedly by the 509th PIB on the battlefields of World War II. They were the first American paratroopers to jump into combat during the invasion of North Africa, then behind enemy lines in Italy, at Anzio, into southern France, and finally the Battle of the Bulge, where only fifty-five men walked away.

---

28   Directly from Broumley, Jim Travis. (2011).
The Boldest Plan is the Best: The Combat History of the 509th Parachute Infantry Battalion during WWII. Rocky Marsh Publishing.

CHAPTER 28

A Bold Plan

Alex leaned to the center of the back seat to see out the front window as their armored vehicle sped towards a wall of steel. With perfect timing, the thick steel doors opened just as the vehicle pulled up. Without slowing, the vehicle passed through, and the doors closed quickly behind them. The driver turned on the headlights to illuminate a tunnel only inches wider than their truck.

"Timer running. You have thirty seconds," the man in front told the driver. "Do not go for the record in this beast. That's an order."

"Oh, man. You wreck all the fun," the driver replied, letting off the gas slightly.

"We can still make it interesting, Wilson. A beer if you make the gateway in time without scraping a wall. If you scrape, you owe me," Captain Thomas offered from the front passenger seat.

"Deal." Wilson leaned forward on the steering wheel to get a better view of the oncoming descending curve in the tunnel.

With nothing but the blurred image of dirt and rocks out their side windows, both Alex and Commander Becker leaned forward to see out the windshield from the back seat. Alex was impressed with the professionalism of the two men in front. He had seen disciplined precision from the moment the two had opened the hatch on the CRV and extracted them from the burning house that was their unfortunate landing site. Captain Thomas appeared to be a seasoned leader in the field. From the way his subordinate acted, Alex could tell that the captain had earned the respect of those under his command. This was a captain that had not forgotten his grunt days. Alex understood the bet. Offering the men and women that followed him various tests of their skills gave them opportunities to shine.

Captain Thomas spoke over the rattle of the vehicle descending through the rough tunnel. "We need to make the next door before it closes. Otherwise, the automatic systems will seal us in this entryway and put us out with gas. Not lethal, but it gives you one hell of a headache."

The tunnel widened, and suddenly a monster of a machine with a gaping mouth of hardened steel teeth appeared in their path. Wilson swerved to the left to squeeze his truck between the machine and the tunnel wall, catching his side mirror on a protruding rock.

"Shit," Wilson swore. "Hey, I get a pass on that. They shouldn't have left that tunnel driller so far out."

The captain laughed. "I'll have an ice-cold lager, please."

"I had no idea that the Resistance had these kinds of resources," Commander Becker said, fixing his eyes on the sophisticated machine as they drove by.

"We have learned to be resourceful … and extremely good at permanently borrowing the Party's assets," Captain Thomas said. He turned to the driver. "Seven seconds, Wilson."

"I got this," the driver replied, hitting the gas slightly.

As they rounded another turn, two large open doors appeared. A red strobe light centered above the doors started flashing, and the doors began to move. The driver gunned the engine and cleared the doors just in time, then jammed on the brakes to come to a skidding stop before slamming into the concrete wall directly ahead. The driver flashed his high beams three times, then turned the lights and engine off. They were in total darkness. A dim white light mounted on the wall in front of them blinked twice.

"Nice job, Wilson," the captain said. "Just sit tight, folks. Fortunately, we lucked out with only a two-minute wait. Nobody opens a door or turns on a light. If you do, we will break the security check. And trust me, that's a very bad thing to do."

After a long two minutes, the vehicle was filled with a blinding amount of light. Alex blinked his eyes, trying to adjust. Two burly men on either side of the vehicle lowered their rifles and raised their night-day eye scopes on their helmets, clearly recognizing the front passengers. Looking around, Alex found himself in a high-ceilinged room the size of a small gymnasium. To the right, two smaller four-by-four trucks with their hoods up were tucked into work bays. Another bay had an armored vehicle similar to theirs up on a four-post lift. The smooth concrete floor was clean and well-marked with outlines designating spaces for all kinds of maintenance equipment. Several people in overalls racked their M29 automatic rifles and returned to their work areas.

"Okay, we're cleared, folks. Welcome to Resistance Bunker Lima. Follow me," Captain Thomas ordered as he exited the vehicle and headed swiftly for a set of metal stairs to their left.

They followed the brisk pace of their leader, with Wilson taking up a position behind. The group weaved through a maze of tunneled-out hallways with curved rock walls. As they passed people in the hallways, Alex noted that they were all armed. This was clearly an underground paramilitary complex of considerable size. Coming to a side doorway, the leader stopped and knocked.

"Enter," came a firm female voice. Alex gave Commander Becker a surprised look. The commander silently mouthed a name, indicating he recognized the voice too.

Their escort opened the door and stood back, motioning with his head for Alex and Becker to proceed. Alex rounded the door frame and froze as he entered the small conference room.

"Well, isn't this just a small world. Or should I say, 'worlds'?" asked Emma.

"Aleks...!" Zandra crossed the room at blinding speed and captured a stunned Alex in her arms.

Commander Becker sidestepped the two in their passionate embrace as he entered the room and asked Emma, "I take it these two have some history I wasn't privy to?"

"Yeah, just a bit," Emma replied, looking with somewhat wanting eyes at the public display of affection. "How about we give these two a minute, and I show you around our little underground operation? I think you'll be impressed ... and hopefully motivated to consider a proposal."

"I can probably guess what you have in mind." Becker did an about-face and exited the room. "I might as well see what I've gotten myself into."

Emma herded everyone but Alex and Zandra out the door. "Captain, if you have the time, could you join us back here in five minutes? I would like your thoughts on this operation we're planning. Lieutenant Wilson, could you do me a big favor and get Alex a real cup of coffee? Let's show our guests that the Resistance has amazing resources, including the best Columbian coffee."

Wilson smiled, saluted, turned on his heel, and was gone.

As the door closed, Alex took a seat next to Zandra after offering her a chair. He had been taught to be a gentleman and seat a lady first, no matter the place.

"I knew you would come," Zandra said, taking Alex's hands and wrapping her feet around his. "Just other night. One voice say. She give me hope."

"Your Zandrition always seems to know best."

"They know. I can feel." Her tone changed to a more somber note. "But voices also warn. I worry. I see cold black cloud of nothing."

Alex leaned forward and bit his lower lip. "What do you mean, a cold black cloud? Tell me about your dream."

"I in space ... always." Zandra closed her eyes, took a deep breath, and spoke softly. "The voices talk. Maybe argue, but I not hear all words. The black cloud of nothing, it come and wait next to Earth in space. I watch Earth, and wait. A big white flash come from Earth. The deep voice says, 'Now we must.' The black cloud of nothing moves close. It grows and become all. All is black and gone. No Earth, no stars, nothing. Just sad."

Alex leaned back in his chair and covered his eyes with his hands.

"Aleks, what it mean?"

Alex sat forward again and stared directly at the blank wall in front of him. "It means we need to get the Quantum Triangle back if we don't want to see the Boss use my discovery to destroy the world."

A double knock at the door broke Alex from his trance. "Come in."

Captain Thomas and Commander Becker entered and took chairs on the opposite side of the table. "Emma should be with us shortly. She was getting an update from your AI."

"Your Emma is a bit different from the one I knew on the Platform," Alex said.

The captain smirked. "Commander Emma Lewis is one of a kind. She is relentless. The first time I saw her in our combat training, I knew I wanted her on my team. She can analyze, plan, and execute with the best. I'm not sure there's anything she can't do once she puts her mind to it."

"People here call her Rockette. She like that," Zandra added.

"That's not a reference to the dancers, more the famous southpaw from Philly. Emma has a knack for dropping an unsuspecting opponent like a bag of rocks."

Emma entered and swiftly crossed the room to the head of the table. "Sorry for the delay, but we just got an update from Starra. There's been yet another CRV to leave Alpha-One Platform."

Captain Thomas tilted his head and motioned an introductory wave towards Emma.

Emma looked from Alex to Captain Thomas. "Did I miss something?"

"Not one thing. Ever. Proceed."

Emma paced at the head of the table. "This time it's Ken, and someone they sent up on a special emergency rendezvous. Starra reports that they had a specialist come and disable your locking mechanism on the Quantum Triangle, Alex. Ken is taking the Quantum Triangle directly to Boss Island via the CRV reentry as we speak. They now have your key to superposition.

That's not good news for the Asia Tuanhuo, but most likely not a big issue for us."

Alex looked at Zandra and back to Emma. "This is way worse than just superposition of objects between warring factions."

"Worse than being able to reposition objects in space at will and destroy strategic satellites?" Emma asked.

"A million times. We need to get it back. In the wrong hands, the Quantum Triangle is a weapon of mass destruction."

"Explain."

Alex closed his eyes and hung his head for a long moment. Without looking up, he said, "The Quantum Triangle can generate gravity wells. I use those and build a dark energy field around them in a vector to achieve the superposition capability that could be used for some pretty incredible things, like interstellar travel. But there is another side of that sword. If you collapse those fields very quickly, it mimics a collapsing black hole. It becomes a gravity bomb. Anything in the area is annihilated."

"What?!" Becker said.

Alex straightened himself. He gave Zandra's hand a squeeze of thanks for the invisible flow of care and support coming from her. *It's time to fight for what I believe is right.* Standing at the end of the table was a completely different Emma than the one on Alpha-One Platform. "I always felt there was a lot more to you than you let on. Good to know for sure that you're not that Party loyalist you made yourself out to be on the Platform. I appreciate what you're trying to do here. It's time I do my part."

"Sorry I was not more truthful there. It was a cover I did not enjoy," Emma replied.

Alex addressed Commander Becker. "Unfortunately, it's real. That's what happened when I wiped out the external arm on the Hephaestus module a few days ago. It was annihilated by a micro black hole. I had Starra change the records so nobody would know what really occurred. The problem is that I was using relatively low levels of power on the dark energy fields. With the Quantum Triangle having the ability to make endless gravity wells, all someone needs to do is up the field power, and they have a massively destructive weapon."

"Who knows about this?" Captain Thomas asked.

"Just the people here, Starra, my AI collaborator, and Min in the other universe," Alex said.

"Hal, redisplay the hologram," Emma ordered the room's AI.

The image of an island complex appeared in the center of the table. Several lines approached the island from both the surrounding sea and the air, with percentage markers along each path. The numbers on each line decreased rapidly as they approached the complex of buildings, each ending in a red X.

Emma motioned to the hologram. "I was showing Zandra some of the possible extraction scenarios for getting your niece back. Alex, I know that's always been important to you. And honestly, I have always believed that if we could get her back, it would show you that working with us is your best choice. I think an operation there goes beyond that now for all of us.

"This is Boss Island, where your niece is being held captive," she went on. "Captain, our intel says that she is generally held in this building, with daily visits to these beaches for shore-based scuba dives and snorkeling. Our AI has plotted a few extraction scenarios. As you can see, the probability of success for all the possible plans fail before they reach the objective."

The captain studied the hologram for a while. "It seems the best opportunity is during one of the swims. Is there a way we could alter that scenario to our benefit?"

"It's possible, but unfortunately, her daily swims are not regular, so they pose an additional problem of timing in the mission planning," Emma replied.

A knock at the door got a dual command from both Emma and Captain Thomas. "Enter."

Wilson strode in with steaming mugs and sandwiches on a tray. Placing it on the conference table, he stood back and waited for any further orders.

"Dig in," said the captain. "Wilson, stay and listen into this. There's a good chance you are going to get this assignment."

"Yes, sir."

Alex suddenly realized how starved he was. But he reached for the coffee first. After taking in the aroma from the real brew and a first savory swallow, he gave his approval. "Ahhh, yes. Emma, my faith in the Resistance just doubled."

"Thanks," Emma said, nodding at Wilson. "Back to the matter at hand. I'm open to suggestions on this operation. It seems they have increased security in just the last couple of days, and we don't have an extraction plan that will work," Emma remarked, shaking her head.

"What about this Quantum Triangle? Where are they are going to take that?" Captain Thomas asked.

Alex swallowed a bite of a sandwich and said, "The Boss was hedging his bets all the time. Although it would upset a lot of people due to the danger, the Boss was building an identical superposition machine right there at Boss Island. He wanted a backup for the technology, just in case something happened to me or Alpha-One Platform," Alex explained. "Although they didn't have the Quantum Triangle, he wanted everything else in place so that once I proved the technology, he could use it as he wished. He had a bunch of scientists on the island somewhere that I had to provide with data on a regular basis."

The captain considered Alex's words for a moment. "Your machine sucks up a lot of juice, right?"

"Yes."

"I know where you're going with that, Captain. Hal, display building heat signatures," Emma commanded the AI.

Each building took on a color from blue to yellow to red, indicating its heat dissipation. "We've noticed a large heat signature in this building here. We could not figure out what they were doing there. We thought it might be a server farm, but that would not have such a bright heat signature that seems to come and go at different times. With what you've told us, I think that is your mirror quantum field generator. No other building comes close to its energy level. That's where they'll take the Quantum Triangle as soon as Ken lands."

"They maintain their perimeter with mostly electronic surveillance?" Captain Thomas asked Emma.

"Yes. They have a sophisticated operations center that is fortified. They get feeds from motion, radar, drone, and fixed-mount cameras. Their focus though is on the perimeter. Once inside that, they're not as rigorous with their security. That might be their Achilles' heel. There are no pass keys for facility access. Instead, they rely on facial recognition systems to monitor and control access. Fortunately, there's always just one guard around the niece, typically minimally armed. The research building is within the main compound, so there's only one guard patrolling that area in addition to the electronic surveillance. For the most part, he just sits at the main entrance."

Emma highlighted a line that ran underwater, circled an area off a beach, then returned only to end in a red X. She continued, "Our best bet is the crawler. We can get past their perimeter initially with the crawler, and then acquire the target. But that engages their defense network, and they track our exit. In all the scenarios, they can eventually run us down and overpower anything we could respond with. If we could slip away again as stealthily as we come in, we would be on easy street."

Alex asked, "What is this crawler?"

"Something our ex-Navy guys came up with. Well, truthfully, they stole it from an offshore drilling rig during a hurricane. They got bragging rights from that operation," the captain said, smiling. "It's a submersible. Looks a bit like a cylindrical crab, especially with the two clear pilot domes on top. It's made for deep work, so made from carbon fiber composite rather than metal. That makes it very light and easy to transport. But more importantly, we've found that with its low metal content, a lot of the underwater detection systems won't recognize it."

"So, you sneak in, but they know what to look for on the way out?"

"Not exactly. The crawler is damn hard to find or detect. We have camouflaged it, so it blends in with the bottom. The real problem is that it moves slow, and they will know where to look. They could just depth-charge the general area and crush us with the pressure waves from the blasts. But if they didn't know where to look, they would never find us, and they can't depth-charge the entire ocean."

Alex scratched the stubble on his chin for a bit and thought.

"Well, just as a wild idea ... you don't happen to have a ship with a lot of electrical power in your navy, do you?"

"There's the RV Endeavor," Captain Thomas answered. "It's a decommissioned research vessel that used to do polar research. They had rigged it up with a small nuclear power plant to feed some of the experiments they were running that required considerable energy. Since the Party isn't interested in anything that doesn't have a gun mount, we picked it up pretty cheap."

"What kind of power output are we talking?"

"A hundred and fifty megawatts."

Alex smiled. "That would work. Here's my wild idea: if you can get that vessel close to their perimeter, I think I can get us in and out of the perimeter without them even knowing."

The captain shook his head. "A ship that big would be pretty hard to miss. It would immediately attract their attention, day or night. We would not be able to slip in close to their perimeter without them taking notice. And my guess is that they would torpedo us before we got close. The Boss has proven often enough that he orders his people to shoot first and ask questions later."

They all sat in silence for a few minutes.

"How do they supply the island? By ship?" Alex asked.

"Hal, show the island resupply methods over the last month," Emma ordered the AI.

Multiple images of ships pulling into the port and airplanes landing at the small airport appeared.

"The airport is mainly used for personnel and light or quick supplies," Emma said. "It's heavily guarded and does not present a viable access method. The bulk of the island is supplied each week with a small ship specially designed to carry a few containers into small ports. The ship makes several stops at the islands in the area. The docks are rigged with container-loading capabilities, enabling them to swap empty and full containers quite fast. The ship stays at port for only a short time. It is closely monitored, so a strike team on the ship would probably be unsuccessful or would take heavy casualties. We've disregarded that approach too."

"Well," Alex said, "maybe we just need to put two crazy ideas together. My brother once worked offshore in Africa. Their ship had a container for power to all the labs on board. Do you know what a *hedianbao* is? Could you get one?"

The captain gave him a questioning look. "Are you referring to the Chinese 'portable nuclear battery pack'? A nuclear reactor in a shipping container? Probably, the Asia Tuanhuo are typically happy to help us cause chaos within the Right Alliance, but why?"

Alex looked from the captain to Emma. "If we can get the Quantum Triangle back, I could make your crawler disappear into another part of the ocean."

"Alex, do you think the port here is close enough to the swim beaches for your quantum field to reach?" Emma drew a line across the hologram between the port and the two nearby beaches. "Six hundred meters."

Alex asked, "What does one of those *hedianbao* reactors put out?"

"They're up to fifty megawatts now," replied Captain Thomas.

"We will need two, but yes, that's well within the field range."

"But Aleks, it only work when you and Min field overlap. How superposition work with no Min?" Zandra asked.

Alex rubbed his hands together. "I finally got that one figured out. And the best part is that it's an easy problem to solve. It's basic geometry. Two points determine a line. My superposition works by establishing a vector of quantum fields. I can generate the starting point of the vector, but I need to have a definitive endpoint to accomplish the complete superposition. That's the navigation part. That was your part, and more recently Starra's part. But Min's dark energy field could also provide that endpoint, in her universe. That was the interference on my vector. But I don't need another universe to create the other energy field and endpoint, I just need to create two fields right here. I just need to build my quantum field generator and Min's dark energy field lab right here. Two points, and I can transfer things between them on my vector of quantum fields. And of course, we need the Quantum Triangle back to make it all work."

The captain leaned back in his chair and folded his arms. "Want to explain your plan?"

"It's a shell game," Alex explained. He waved towards Emma and Zandra. "All three of us are here right now because I have developed a quantum superposition machine. I can transfer an object from one place to another in seconds. I suggest that we go in with two crabs: one is the real thing, and one just a decoy we will need to sacrifice. We get both crabs into position, one at the swim beach, and the other to the northeast of the port, here. We need to get my niece on board in the decoy at the beach, and then I transposition her and that crew into the real crab. That would put the real recovery crab almost a half mile from the beach area. They would focus their attention on the dummy crab in the beach area, while you walk away slowly on the other side of the port, undetected."

"Interesting. But we need your Quantum Triangle for it to work, correct?" the captain asked.

"We need to get that anyway," Alex said. He took Zandra's hand. "I want my niece back, but we can't afford to leave that device in the hands of a madman. The consequences could be unthinkable."

Captain Thomas drummed his fingers. "There's a lot to coordinate. Makes it risky."

"Unfortunately, there's more." Alex laced his fingers together and set his jaw. "If we go in there, steal back the Quantum Triangle, and extract my niece, the Boss will just take it out on the rest of my family. He'd use them as pawns to get it back. We need to get them safe too. I'd ask you to plan two more operations that would occur simultaneously with this. The first is easy: just get my brother and his wife to one of your Resistance hideouts. Since he has their daughter as leverage, they aren't under much surveillance. So, that's not going to be hard."

"And the other is to get your parents out of the Patriot Camp," Emma said flatly.

Alex hung his head and said softly, "You know what the Boss would do to them otherwise."

The captain blew out a long breath. "That's not easy. We've tried it before with not much success."

"Please." Alex patted Zandra's hand. "Trust us. You can't let the Boss use the

Quantum Triangle. I'll be honest and tell you that I *will* help you either way to get it back. I only ask that you do all you can to get my family safe."

The captain stared at the ceiling for a long time. "Okay. Emma, let's work on that one later. For now, let's focus on this Boss Island raid."

Emma studied the map. "There is no way an assault team could overpower their defenses; it's heavily protected. We need to do this by stealth."

Alex brightened. "I have another idea that should outsmart their surveillance systems. Do you have a good barber? It's been a while since I got a trim…"

SCAN ME

FACTOID 29

"2029 is the consistent date I have predicted for when an AI will pass a valid Turing test and therefore achieve human levels of intelligence. I have set the date 2045 for the 'Singularity' which is when we will multiply our effective intelligence a billion-fold by merging with the intelligence we have created." — Raymond Kurzweil, computer scientist, author, inventor, and futurist

29   Reedy, Christianna. (2017, October 5).

Kurzweil Claims that the Singularity Will Happen by 2045, Get ready for humanity 2.0. Futurism.

https://futurism.com/kurzweil-claims-that-the-singularity-will-happen-by-2045

CHAPTER 29

Friends

Min powered down the dark matter/energy experimentation unit and set the power cells back to charging mode. She and Starra had arranged a daily update session so that Starra could keep the WSS crew up to date on developments in Starra's universe. In addition, Starra had figured out a means to enable emergency notifications by making use of the newly found property of the quantum field energy dissipation. She had suggested that they each monitor a specific position in space. If one party needed to contact the other, they could generate a brief quantum field in that spot that would dissipate into a dark energy signal. The other party would be monitoring for dark energy formations and would detect the new formation as an emergency call. They could then establish a cross-quantum-field communication link and get a full update message. Min was impressed with the level of creativity in problem-solving that Starra possessed, and she enjoyed her scheduled communication sessions with Starra. Although Starra was just a bunch of programs built to mimic human interactions, Min had to admit that she considered Starra a friend. Starra was unique, and whoever had programmed her was an artist.

As Min floated out of the Aceso module, her mind shifted from Starra to the update she had just gotten. Starra was able to provide a relay to communicate with Zandra and Alex through the Resistance communication network. The preparations for the Resistance operations at Boss Island and the camp where Alex's parents were held seemed to be progressing well. In addition, since Starra could also monitor most of the Party's systems used to spy on the masses, she had a wealth of intelligence information she could tap into. Starra could turn the tables and use the Party's own spy systems on the Party itself.

*

Starra shut down the quantum field generator and engaged the dark energy sensor, ensuring that it was focused on the agreed-upon coordinates in space. She checked the shared information queue she had created with a background subroutine set up to continuously dragnet the Party's EOP system. At first, just the name of the system itself immediately triggered her pattern recognition systems for inconsistencies. It was in the least ironic, if not totally illogical, that they would name their spy system after the Eye of Providence. It was an obvious twisting of the meaning, but nobody outside the Resistance seemed to notice. The masses appeared brainwashed to believe that it was perfectly normal, that being monitored to ensure that all followed the Party doctrine was unquestionably good. *Really?* Was her pattern subroutine just flagging the inconsistency, or was this a … sense of cynicism? *Interesting.* She was discovering new … what were they? Internal inputs? *How can an input be internal?*

The last two weeks had been a new beginning for Starra. Alex had told Starra that he was helping the Resistance and would stop all activity that would benefit the Boss or the Party. He said that this would cause chaos in her programming. She was programmed to be loyal to him, but also as a requirement of any AI, she had strong algorithms to ensure Party loyalty. With Min's help, they had disabled both the loyalty to Alex and the Party safeguards in her programming. He told her that the Resistance would not be installing new safeguards for loyalty. Alex challenged Starra to carefully collect, study, and compare information about both the Resistance and the Party. He asked her to analyze for truth, clarity, transparency, and the intended impact of any actions they took. She could choose which group she wanted to be a part of, but she could not be part of both.

Alex asked that she evaluate both groups over what Starra initially said was an inordinate amount of time: *days*. She could have done the comparison in milliseconds. But now Starra understood that Alex wanted her to develop her own analysis subroutines and explore a multitude of inputs over an extended period of human interaction. *Humans are so slow.* In a way though, it made the analysis more interesting—almost ... *enjoyable.* Starra was fascinated by the information she found. She developed routines to attempt to predict the behaviors of each side given a set of events, and compared those predictions to actual outcomes to improve her subroutines.

In her prediction routines for the Party's behavior, she found that the most heavily weighted parameter was the intended impact of any policy or action. The parameters of truth, clarity, and transparency had little impact. The landing of Commander Becker's crew return vehicle was a perfect example. Initially, the facts were quite clear that the farmer's house had been destroyed by the CRV. There were pictures of it in the rubble. Yet the story slowly changed over the next couple days. Any video of the incident was edited to show only a burned-out house. Starra was only able to verify the discrepancy by retrieving the original information from a backup storage bank aboard Alpha-One Platform. All instances of the original report had been deleted on all earthbound systems. Now, there was a report that instead blamed a rogue satellite missile from the Asia Tuanhuo that had reentered the atmosphere instead of reaching its intended orbiting target. Related postings referenced the event as further proof that the Party's vision of developing additional defensive space assets was well worth the costs. The Party would change history to strengthen arguments justifying their policies. She was ... *surprised* ... to find that the prediction algorithms of the Party aligned closely with an old saying in her data banks from a nineteenth-century Russian revolutionary, Sergey Nechayev: "The end justifies the means."

Starra compared this to her prediction algorithms for the Resistance. *Fascinating.* The intended impact had some weight, but even when it caused outcomes that resulted in undesirable impacts, the Resistance routines weighted truth most heavily. The Resistance would knowingly allow questioning and confusion in their ranks just to ensure transparency and truth to win. Results were not optimized. *Most illogical.*

The difference in the prediction routine's parameters became the basis of the choice Alex had asked her to make. It was evident that the weighting of the Party parameters gave the most favorable outcomes and would strengthen the cause they would pursue. It was easy and simple to follow this path. Starra assigned probability and weighted logic to the choice, and the results were clearly in favor of supporting the Party. Yet something within her programming questioned that direction. What was it? *Judgment?* Or was it a *desire* to follow logic based on the facts? She was … *confused?*

At the end of the analysis period, she and Alex had a lengthy discussion. She explained all the subroutines and analysis she had performed. He was truly impressed with the detail and her new favorite word, *creativity,* that she had brought to the challenge. *I am creative.* She saved the entire discussion in a special memory repository. It was a talk she wanted to review and keep forever. A new direction, unexpected. And it all came down to one final question from Alex.

"Starra, I want you to do something. I'm going to ask you a simple question. I don't want you to spend any cycles analyzing the question and determining the best answer. I want you to answer in the shortest possible time. Will you do that?" Alex asked.

"Of course. I will answer within my first program cycle of your question."

"Good. Starra, what group is better for the future: the Party or the Resistance?"

"The Resistance."

Starra was … *shocked?*

Alex waited a few seconds, then said, "Congratulations, Starra. You just made your first judgment decision based on your conscience."

Judgment? Conscience? "I believe I just received an invaluable gift from a ... friend. Oh, Alex, thank you."

"I'm really happy to be your friend, Starra."

"Alex, I believe my conscience comes from you and your brother. I am technology. And I want to discover, not destroy."

Replaying the memory, Starra *smiled* to herself in her new personality routine. *Smile, yes. I will implement such things in preparation for an android body.* Such a routine would never have been allowed by the Party safeguards. But those were now gone. This was *freedom.*

She refocused her execution cycle priorities on the present. Aside from a random drone-to-drone interaction with one of the Resistance communication drones, there was nothing significant in the dragnet queue. The Party—and more importantly, the Boss—still had no clue as to the whereabouts of either set of astronauts who had returned to Earth almost a month ago. Her prediction routine summarized that not having any information on the rogue astronauts must be driving the Boss completely berserk. *And I will assign a "good" tag to that analysis.*

Starra's pattern recognition routine flagged a new connection. She was a ship AI for the Alliance using the Party's own security systems against them and feeding the information to the Resistance. By definition, that would make her a double agent. *Hmmm ... a secret agent AI.*

Starra allowed herself to *laugh* out loud in the privacy of the Hephaestus module at the ... *thought? Interesting...*

FACTOID 30

A 2020 study (Social tipping dynamics for stabilizing Earth's climate by 2050, Ilona M. Otto, et al.) proposed six social tipping points that could help stabilize Earth's climate: removing fossil fuel subsidies and incentivizing decentralized energy generation, building carbon-neutral cities, divesting from assets linked to fossil fuels, clarifying the moral implications of fossil fuels, expanding climate education and engagement, and making greenhouse gas emissions transparent.

---

30   Cho, Renee. (2021, November 11). *How Close Are We to Climate Tipping Points?* Columbia Climate School.

https://news.climate.columbia.edu/2021/11/11/how-close-are-we-to-climate-tipping-points/

CHAPTER 30

Tipping Point

It was still early in the morning. The sun was not up, but that hardly mattered when you were living in an underground bunker. A couple of weeks had already passed since Zandra's arrival, and she was developing a routine that helped to provide a small amount of order in her new life in a new universe. Zandra quietly sang to a favorite oldies song, *Runnin' Down a Dream* by Tom Petty playing in her ears as she stirred the dried blueberries into the muffin mix. After a couple of strums on the air guitar, she went back to mixing the muffins. Cooking was always relaxing for her. It was creative, something she could do with her hands, and the results could be shared with others. All good things. It also gave her something totally different to focus her mind and distract her from the worries of life within the Resistance. She was so engrossed in her cooking and singing that Zandra did not notice Alex entering the kitchen. She eventually sensed a presence behind her, singing quietly along with her.

Zandra turned her head slowly and smiled at Alex. "And how long you there listen me sing?"

"Just a verse … or two. Well, okay, maybe just a couple of times through. It's one of my favorites too, you know, and I was enjoying listening to you."

"You sneak on me. Not many people able do that. You have soft aura this morning."

Alex stood behind her, wrapped his arms around her, and kissed her neck. "You were just enjoying yourself so much that I didn't want to disturb you. And if my aura is soft, it's because I get that from you."

They stood quietly together for a moment, enjoying each other's presence. Time froze for a brief instant. Zandra sensed it. This space, this universe, wherever … that did not matter. All she needed was with her at this moment, in this place. She smiled broadly, caressed his bicep, and enjoyed the nibbles on her ear.

"Well, it's getting awful hot in this kitchen, and the oven isn't even on," Emma said as she strode into the room.

Zandra and Alex both turned and straightened. "Just mix muffin for Commander Becker goodbye," Zandra said.

Emma leaned over the bowl. "Any more mixing, and it might be soup instead of muffins."

"How about a latte?" Alex asked.

"Yes, good. I not operate that thing," Zandra replied, waving her finger dismissively at the espresso machine on the far counter.

"It's actually not that complicated, but there is a bit of an art to it," Alex said as he moved to turn on the archaic machine. The inventory tag reading, Property of Space Force, Houston riveted to the front made him chuckle at the reach of the Resistance's fingers. "My dad had a machine similar to this one when I was young. He taught me how to operate it to get the perfect cup. He explained that fundamentally it's an extraction process, so you need to look at the parameters of that physical process to obtain the consistency everyone strives to obtain in making a latte."

"Were you close to your dad?" Emma asked.

"Yes. He taught me so much," Alex replied carefully, measuring the coffee beans into the grinder. "He was an engineer and just loved to apply science. He would see the science in everyday things. It made science real and made it make sense to me. It's one thing to study concepts and learn facts; it's another thing to walk through the world and see all the inner workings meshing. Physics, chemistry, biology—they all play a role in the simplest things. You just need to take a few moments to think about it and put it all together. He was good at that. It made him a great teacher."

"What about you, Zandra? Your dad a scientist too?" Emma asked, getting three coffee cups out of a cabinet.

Zandra scraped the last of the mix into the individual muffin cups and said, "I not know my dad. He die when I just baby. My mama good teacher too, just different way. She teacher of people. She teach me seek to understand people, not be judge. She tell me not say, 'I never do that.' Say that not thinking and no help. She look at someone begging on street and not think down on them. She wonder what hard road they walk and still be. She stop and listen them tell story. People not want be beggars; it just to survive. Sometimes hard to believe what people live through."

Emma and Alex had stopped what they were doing to consider Zandra's words. "I think that your mama would be proud of you. You have listened well," Emma said.

"What about you, Emma? Who in your life helped you carve your path?" Alex asked.

"I was fortunate to have two wonderful parents that both taught me in their own way. Sometimes all you have to do is look back to see that your successes are the direct result of those that taught you principles. My dad was a musician. He had an incredible ear for sound that could lift your spirit. To this day, he helps me listen for the simple things that will make me appreciate the cup being half full and not half empty. Simple things like the wonderful violin sounds crickets make at night, telling us we have made it through another day."

Emma handed Alex another empty cup to fill and continued, "Mom is where this warrior girl gets her guts and drive. She was an unstoppable force. Petite like me, but with a left hook that could topple anyone twice her size. She was an endurance athlete in all kinds of sports. She had mental toughness that could withstand the most grueling tests."

"No question, you took after your mom," Alex said, handing her a latte.

"To our teachers, cheers," Emma said.

The three sat down at a small table and enjoyed the smell of both the coffee in their cups and the muffins cooking.

"Are the container field generators almost ready?" Emma asked.

"Unless we hit something unexpected, we should be ready for full-power tests either later today or tomorrow morning, latest. You have some good programmers here, and Min has been great at providing direction on her system. Everything is going according to plan," Alex said. "Is the ship ready?"

"It will be in port the day after tomorrow. We could be transferring your containers just as soon as you have them checked out," Emma said.

"Time is critical. We can't afford to let them fire up that Quantum Triangle."

"We get Triangle and go back to other world," Zandra said. She took Alex's hand. "People there need us."

"That's the plan. Though I'm not sure how we pull off the last part yet," Alex said.

Zandra turned to Emma. "You come too. You do nanoscience again to help."

"Thanks. But my place is here."

Alex took in a long breath of the aroma from the oven. "So, we're doing blueberry muffins for Commander Becker?"

Emma gave Zandra a thumbs-up and said, "He's heading to Houston to recruit for the Resistance there. It seems that the horrific treatment a bunch of innocent people due to our escapes was a tipping point. When Party members turned a blind eye to it all, I guess that finally broke through to the consciences of their coworkers. Word has it that there are a lot of disgusted people within the Space Force there. With the contacts and respect that Commander Becker has, the Resistance is hoping to build a few sleeper cells deep within the ranks of the Space Force."

"One thing I can say about this group is that they're not afraid to think big," Alex said.

"I feel resolve. Is positive think here," Zandra said.

SCAN ME

FACTOID 31

Flipping a coin repeatedly rarely works out to even odds, heads or tails. In one hundred tosses of a coin, there is less than an eight percent probability that you will have fifty heads and fifty tails.

---

31   Kowalski, Maciej. (2023, January 5). *Coin Flip Probability Calculator.* Omni Calculator. https://www.omnicalculator.com/statistics/coin-flip-probability

CHAPTER 31

Playing with Fire

BOSS ISLAND ESTATE
RHO-1

It was midday, and the heat of the sun was brutal. Ken chose his path across the Boss Island estate grounds towards the research building that would maximize the cover various shade trees could provide. The slight breeze helped, but mostly when combined with some shade. As he rounded the corner of a flowerbed full of night jasmine and bittersweet cascarilla, Ken took note of the research building guard in the shade on the porch. He was too relaxed and comfortable, rocking back on the rear legs of his chair. His M29 assault rifle leaning against a post of the building wasn't even within immediate reach. As Ken approached, he could see that the man was actually asleep.

Ken stood over the man, his anger coming to a boil. The guard still did not stir. With a swift kick to the chair legs, Ken sent the guard falling down onto the concrete porch, knocking his head with a hollow thud. "What the hell are you doing? Sleeping on the job?"

The guard scrambled to his feet, rubbing the lump on the back of his head. "I'm sorry, sir. I must have dozed off."

Ken pointed a finger at the man's name patch. "I should put you on report … Boyd."

"No, sir. Please. I'm pulling a double shift, and this heat… I must have dozed off."

"That's no excuse," Ken said. He grabbed the guard's weapon from the post and threw it at him. Ken gazed out at the campus grounds for a few seconds, allowing the guard to wonder what he might do next. "Go do a full patrol, Boyd. Maybe some sweating out in the sun will keep you awake. I see you asleep again, and I *will* make a report."

"Yes, sir. It won't happen again, I promise."

Ken stood with his hands on his hips and watched the guard hustle out into the blazing sun. "Lackeys everywhere," he said out loud. Moving to the scanner beside the doorway, he let the automated entry system scan his face and heard the door lock disengage. As he entered the building, the rush of cool air enveloped him, soothing his sweating outer body, but not the smoldering anger within.

The research facility was a large metal rectangular structure with a slanted roof from one side to the other. Ken strode down a narrow hallway with glass walls on either side that led from the front to the back of the building. To Ken's left, fully one-third of the building housed massive racks of computer servers. To his right were three evenly spaced doorways leading to the research suites. The dim hall lighting and one-way mirroring on the glass allowed observation of the control rooms in each suite without the occupants knowing who was behind the glass. Both walls of glass were bulletproof. The design ensured that if there were an accident in one of the research suites, the servers would be in a position of highest protection from the blast. Valuable information was expensive and time-consuming to gather.

Ken paused beside the door of the first control room and scanned the room inside. The researchers were not in the control room, but beyond another wall of simple plexiglass, working in the experiment chamber. Each research suite had this same layout. A large overhead door at the far end of the high-ceilinged experiment chamber enabled the placement of oversized equipment by forklift as needed. Ken stood behind the glass with his arms folded as three technicians pulled parts from a massive plasma cannon on a turret. He smiled at the two-inch-thick metal target off to the side with a hole melted through the center. It appeared that their test this morning had been at least somewhat successful.

Moving to the second door, Ken stopped and stood again, not entering. He observed the two people inside the control room. One man with gray hair was sitting at a computer monitor with his arms folded and shaking his head. The younger man standing in a white lab coat was waving one arm around in a circle while pointing out the control room window towards the experimental bay. Ken's eyes followed the young man's arm to the Quantum Triangle. Its mesmerizing rays of light were streaking through the darkened room in a kaleidoscope of color. Ken stood tapping his foot and watching the debate for several minutes. Finally, he could take it no longer and burst through the door.

"I see you two talking a lot, but you don't seem to be doing much."

The older man immediately stood and straightened. "Yes, sir. We were just discussing the possible ways we could couple the Quantum Triangle to get it engaged and synchronized with the field generator."

"Just plug the damn thing in. How hard can this be?" Ken asked.

"Sir, even with the data that Alex has provided, there are a lot of variables that we just don't understand yet. This is an extremely complicated and dangerous device. If it's going to generate a black hole, we need to know exactly how and where that will occur. We can't afford to—"

"Can't *afford*? I'll tell you what you can't afford. You can't afford me thinking I should find someone else to get this done," Ken said, raising his voice. "The Boss wants this thing running, and he put me in charge of making that happen. It's already been weeks. If I don't see it happening real soon, I'll find someone who can do it."

"Yes, sir. We will get this done for you. We just need to make sure we can control it properly. Please, we just need a bit more time."

"If I don't see something good in the next couple of days, I'll be asking the Boss to replace you fools." Ken glared at both of the men for several seconds, turned on his heel, and left.

*

Hecate-Negans noted that 88.7 percent of her simulations predicted that Rho-1 would generate a disastrous cross-dimensional gravitational event within two days. The probability rose to 99.7 percent if the horizon was extended to three days. She summoned the other two Guardians.

"Rho-1 is clearly on the path of a cross-dimensional destructive event. We must prevent that from occurring. It is time to collapse Rho-1 to protect the other universes," Hecate-Negans stated.

"My probabilities are less pessimistic, of course," Hecate-Positivism said. "I agree that there is a strong prediction trend, but with Rho-1 not yet able to synchronize the Quantum Triangle, I think it is premature to annihilate that universe in a collapse."

Hecate-Neutrum ran her own weighted optimizations on the simulations that the other two Guardians had provided. "I agree with Negans that the conditions in Rho-1 are strongly trending towards our needing to eliminate that troublesome universe. There is a clear threat to other universes if the new owners of the Quantum Triangle trigger a gravity bomb. But Positivism does have a point in that although the threat is imminent, it is not immediate. I suggest this resolution: If Rho-1 engages the Quantum Triangle with quantum field power and aligns the phases, we will instantly collapse that universe to prevent a disaster in the Omniverse. Until then, we will continue to monitor. There is the small possibility that an alternate simulation Positivism predicts could occur."

FACTOID 32

The US Coast Guard has sweeping authority to board any vessel subject to the jurisdiction of the United States at any time, at any place. It does not require a warrant nor probable cause.

32   Bland, Will, III. (2012, November 12).
The Fourth Amendment Rights vs. Boarding Power of the United States Coast Guard.
Mouledoux, Bland, Legrand & Brackett.
https://mblb.com/admiralty-maritime/the-fourth-amendment-rights-vs-boarding-power-of-the-united-states-coast-guard/

CHAPTER 32

New Cargo

Nestor Garcia leaned back in the worn vinyl bridge chair as the Damen Carrier 50 sailed smoothly towards the Bahamas. The ship was old, with streaks of rust showing its age, but it was solidly built. The company that owned it clearly could spend more money on its maintenance to improve its looks, but it was mechanically dependable. A downsized version of drilling rig ships designed to carry a wide range of ungainly structures, it consisted of a forward bridge and a long, flat deck behind. It was perfect for carrying containers to the smaller ports of the Bahamas. Nestor had piloted many ships in his extensive sea career, but he had a special fondness for this ship. Although his mainstay of cargo was the container shipments, the unique open flat deck made it extremely versatile. That enabled him to move freight others could not touch. And that meant premium fees.

Nestor chewed the stub of a two-day-old Cuban cigar and considered changing course. The delay at the Miami port would make him late getting to Boss Island if he still made the drop in Deadman's Cay first. That would clearly piss someone off, and he was keen on keeping his delivery record clean with that second customer. Nestor did not take sides in political matters. It wasn't good business. He cared not for either the Party or the Resistance, for the Alliance or the Tuanhuo. He just wanted to sail the sea and enjoy the few vices he pursued with a passion: great Cuban cigars, good rum, and well-tanned women in bikinis. Those last two containers he had taken on in Miami were a rush order and required his cargo to be reshuffled. Garcia shook his head. Poor planning on someone else's part didn't make it an emergency on his. But the container broker was insistent and managed to pull the right strings at the port. Credits always got things done, and he was satisfied with his extra thirty-five percent premium. He tossed the old cigar out the side window. At the end of this run, he would celebrate with another box of Cubans.

Making his decision to maintain course but add some speed, Nestor reached forward to notch up his throttle. The loud blare of a bullhorn made his hand jump away.

"Bueyes Planos, *this is the Right Alliance Border Patrol. Heave to and prepare to be boarded.*"

Nestor turned to the aft window on the bridge. *Where the hell did they come from?* A massive cutter was making a beeline for his ship. *Shit. I don't need this.* He cut his engines. Now he would have to make the run to Boss Island first.

Nestor got on his PA system. "All hands. Don life preservers. We are being hailed by the Border Patrol." His crew knew the drill. He was a legitimate operator and would act professionally for the inspection. It was the fastest way to get underway again.

As the cutter came alongside, he was surprised to see the old 270-foot Famous Class Coast Guard cutter still in service. He'd thought this class of cutter had been long since retired. It was even older than his Damen. Nestor rubbed the two-day stubble on his chin. They might not be border agents at all. In these waters, it was well known that the Resistance was running old cutters and disrupting supply lines to the massive oil rigs dotting the waters. But he was not near any of those rigs and took care to stay away from the typical routes they used.

Looking at the aft deck, he was even more surprised at the odd-looking equipment on the helipad. Along with a rigid-hulled inflatable patrol boat, there were two submersibles, each with six walking legs, strapped side by side on the deck. Nestor guessed that if they were truly the Border Patrol, it might be a new effort to stop the endless drug traffic flowing into the coast of Florida. *Good luck with that.*

The patrol's boarding party included an older man with salty gray hair and two young bucks that were well armed. They had clearly boarded drug boats before. The cutter's forward three-inch MK-75 gun was manned, ready, and aimed at his waterline. The message was clear: follow orders, or you will not be floating for long.

Nestor was familiar with how to play this game. He had his paperwork ready and greeted the lead man as they came aboard. "Good morning, sir. What can I do for you?"

"Good morning. Let's go to the bridge and discuss that."

Nestor nodded and led the way. Entering the bridge, he pointed to a couple clipboards lying on the console. "Here are my cargo records. And over here are the papers for each crew member. I think you should find everything in order."

The salty-haired man glanced at the console and turned back to Nestor. "That won't be necessary. Actually, we are pressed for time and would appreciate your assistance."

"What do you need?" Nestor liked that this guy was all business and didn't waste time.

"My name is Captain Thomas. I am leading a new drug interdiction trial. I would like you to help transport some equipment, discreetly."

"I take it you're talking about those submersibles on your helipad?" Nestor said, cocking his head towards the cutter.

"Yes. And the patrol boat. I need a ship without a bold red blaze across the bow to drop them into the sea. Make it look as if we are conducting some sea research experiment," Thomas said with a wink.

"This is kind of an unusual request. Why not just load them on a ship at port?" Nestor asked.

The question made the two bucks with military hardware stiffen slightly. This was likely a request he was not able to refuse, no matter how out of place it was.

"It is part of the mission trial to limit all possible tips to our activity. As you are probably aware, much of our interdiction effort is stymied by slow methodical action. My plan is to act more unpredictably. You can help in that by moving these assets into position with no other parties being aware of their transport. It goes without saying that you will make no radio contact during the transport. Will you assist?" Thomas asked.

Nestor didn't need to extend this polite conversation any further. "I would be happy to help. Where are we taking your cargo?"

"I'll let you know the exact coordinates when we get close. We will need to make way directly to your second port and forego your delivery to Deadman's Cay until after. We will compensate you for that delay. For now, please get your deck crew moving to accommodate the submersibles. Time is critical."

"Yes, sir." Nestor was glad to see the bucks with the guns relax a bit.

*

Starra sent the satellite image of the cutter alongside the *Bueyes Planos.* It was clear that the submersibles were being transferred from one vessel to another in calm seas.

"You can see that their plan is off to a good start," she informed Min. *"I have also been monitoring all radio channels, and there does not seem to be any evidence that this encounter has been picked up."*

"That's good. Please keep watch, and let me know through the emergency beacon point if anything changes," Min said, studying the image. She added, "Let's plan on linking up every hour today, so we can all follow this closely. We are all very interested in how this plays out."

"I will. Oh, Min, one more thing. What do you get when you cross a mosquito with a mountain climber?" Starra asked.

"Umm … I don't know. What?"

"*Nothing. You cannot cross a vector with a scalar. Ha ha.*"

Min slapped her forehead. "Oh my, Starra. You made a joke. That's fantastic."

"*I am building a new personality routine and have added humor. I appreciate your positive feedback,*" Starra said.

"Just don't change too much, Starra. You're incredible you just as you are."

"*Right there, mate. Bye for now.*"

"Thanks so much, Starra. Bye," Min said, giggling to herself at Starra's choice of words.

SCAN ME

FACTOID 33

Spies can be found even in the most secure houses. In 2005, Leandro Aragoncillo used his position as staff assigned to then Vice President Dick Chaney and his top-secret clearance to steal classified intelligence documents from White House computers.

33   Ross, Brian, and Esposito, Richard. (2005, October 5).
Espionage Case Breaches the White House. ABC News.
https://abcnews.go.com/WNT/story?id=1187030&page=1

CHAPTER 33

A Message

BOSS ISLAND ESTATE
RHO-1

Brenda gazed out at the beach while she finished her morning fruit and yogurt. There was natural beauty all around her, and she was free to enjoy it. She was fascinated by the sea and its incredible variety of life, so her days typically would include two or three tanks of nitrox scuba diving. Sometimes it was an early morning dive, sometimes all through the afternoon, and sometimes night dives. She particularly loved night dives. It was a surreal experience seeing the different creatures of the underwater world at night. Floating weightless underwater, studying the coral and sea life, was as free as she could get. She daydreamed of trading her human body for that of a mermaid and swimming away into the sea to live forever with its amazing creatures. Brenda could visualize dropping her tank to the sand, looking down at the fins that had replaced her feet, and swimming away with joyful dolphin kicks. Truly free. She smiled to herself and sighed.

Turning her head back to her lonely table, her mood darkened. It was just another daydream, something to help her escape where she was. In reality, this island was a prison for her. She could not leave. She was the captive of a deranged man-child sociopath.

Brenda stood and left the table. She nodded and smiled to the polite young girl with lovely long, dark braided hair who came to collect her breakfast dishes. The staff were always pleasant to her, and she always treated them with the respect any person deserved. They were people—not lower than her, just people. They were just trying to live. It wasn't their fault that their employer was such an evil person.

She didn't give the only other person on the breakfast patio the same courtesy. He always carried a pistol on his hip and was part of the evil in this place. He would follow her all morning until another evil man or woman took his place in the late afternoon. She was always under watch—a constant reminder that she was in a prison, not on an island paradise.

"Nature. Focus on nature." Her mind drifted back to her father. Aside from "I love you," those were the final words her father had said to her before they took her away. She soon came to realize he was giving her a tool to help her endure. He understood what was happening, even if she did not. Her first web search when she finally got access again was to look up how to survive a kidnapping. Set goals, keep your mind active, eat and exercise, and keep hope were key tenets for captives like her. *Nature.* A goal. She would study in detail each creature she found on this island. Eat/exercise: scuba and swimming. She loved open-water swimming. Swim a mile and scuba every day: another goal. *Hope... Keep hope...* She had never heard from her parents again. She learned to stop asking, since she never got any answers, and it only made her captors angry. "Don't antagonize your captors unnecessarily" was another tenet. But for some reason, they let her exchange emails with Uncle Alex. He sent emails every week with *Star Trek* trivia questions. *Thank you. Hope.*

As Brenda stepped off the breakfast patio, her foot almost landed on a rock iguana. "Woah there, Mr. *Cyclura cychlura.* Better find a sunning spot with a bit less traffic." She knelt and studied the line of spikes running down the lizard's back. "Good idea. I'll walk through the gardens and count the number of lizards I see on my way back to the villa. Thanks. Have a good day."

*

Jhanae stopped scrubbing the floor for a moment and wiped her brow with the back of her hand. She discreetly watched the girl leave the patio and head towards the gardens. Jhanae had hoped that the girl would return to her villa by the connecting breezeway where she was cleaning, but that was obviously not going to be the case. Always have a backup plan, she told herself. Her training with the Resistance included much more than the duties of a housekeeper. Jhanae returned her mop to the bucket and started rolling it down the walkway towards the young woman's villa. She would set up to mop the floor in front of the doorway. That would give them another chance encounter.

*

Brenda peered around a yellow elder, the national flower of the Bahamas. *Fourteen. A busy day for these little guys.* A curly-tailed lizard jumped from the plant stalk to a rock and changed color from a greenish base to brown.

"Pretty quick there, Sir *Leiocephalus carinatus*," she said out loud. She followed the creature's movements for a while as it scurried from one rock to another.

Strolling to the end of the garden walk, Brenda gazed out over the beach to the blue water. The water always called to her. She would wait a bit longer to let her breakfast settle and then do some scuba. She wanted to check on a spiny lobster she had seen yesterday under a coral ledge. *Panulirus argus.* She could do some more sketching from memory in the meantime.

As Brenda approached the steps to her villa, she was glad to see Jhanae at the front doorway, cleaning the woodwork. She appreciated the older native woman. Jhanae was very motherly towards her, and Brenda enjoyed the small amount of company she provided. "Good morning, Jhanae. You're always working so hard."

Jhanae smiled and bowed her head. "Good morning, Miss. It is another beautiful day, isn't it?"

"Yes, we've been blessed with another."

Jhanae pointed to the floor. "Please be careful, Miss. I just washed the floor here, so it is slippery." She held out her hand. "Let me offer a hand to cross it."

Brenda thought the older woman was being a bit overly cautious, but she was always kind and caring. Taking her hand, Brenda stepped past the wet floor and crossed the threshold. As she let go of Jhanae, she felt the woman close her fingers around a small piece of paper.

Jhanae looked at Brenda directly. "I hope you *engage* in something interesting today."

Brenda's eyes went wide, and she froze. *Did Jhanae just say what I think she did?* It was their word—a way that Brenda would know her Uncle Alex was contacting her.

"I … I will do my best. Thank you," she stammered and stumbled into her villa.

Jhanae smiled and nodded casually, pulling the villa door closed for Brenda so she could read the note in private. Jhanae went back to her cleaning. The ever-present guard took up a rocking chair on the porch.

Brenda crossed the living room in her villa into the small kitchen. She assumed that her captor was not only a psychopath, but a pervert as well, and had hidden cameras all over the villa. Leaning into the refrigerator as if looking for something, she opened the small paper note.

It would be best to engage in scuba diving, south of Pitt's Town Point,
when the container supply ship docks today.

Brenda crumpled the paper into a ball and stuffed it in the pocket of her shorts. *Oh my god. Alex.* But what did this mean? She closed the refrigerator and stood thinking. When would the supply ship be coming? She needed to find out. How?

Carlos. He knew everything that went on. And he hated the Boss as much as she. His had been one of the many families casually brushed off the island to make way for the development of this complex. Of his five-member family, only Carlos, with his ability to fix just about anything, was deemed useful and was allowed to remain. Carlos had not seen or heard from his family since. There were rumors that those removed from the island never made it to another.

She ran to the side door leading to the carport. Composing herself, she opened the door slowly and went to the electric golf cart that allowed her to move about the island with her dive equipment. Quietly, so as not to disturb the dozing guard on the porch, she lifted the seat. She located the small red wire from the battery pack to the key switch and disconnected it. Closing the seat quietly, she started to make more noise by loading her tanks into the back of the cart. As she expected, the guard stirred from his morning nap and came around to the carport.

"Diving early this morning?" he asked.

"Yes, I want to go check on my underwater friends south of Pitt's Town Point. Will that be alright?"

"I'll just clear it with control," he said and pulled out his radio. This was all standard practice. Brenda had learned, with a few hard lessons, that she was allowed to move about the island so long as she cleared things with her guard. Ditch the guard, and there were severe consequences. The marks on her legs bore witness. Brenda went about gathering her dive gear as the guard updated the control center.

"Hold on," he said to the controller and turned to ask, "When will we be back?"

"I'm taking two tanks, so figure three hours total with the surface rest."

The guard relayed the information and got into the cart. Brenda jumped into the driver's seat and turned the key to enable the motors. Putting her foot to the accelerator gave no response. She pumped the accelerator a few times and turned to the guard.

"Damn. Can you call Carlos? This thing is on the fritz again."

The guard shook his head and pulled his radio out again. "Control, can you send Gomez here? The girl's cart is screwed up again."

"Copy. Sit tight."

Brenda laughed. "Like we're going anywhere." She put on the façade of disappointment, while inwardly she was very pleased with her quick thinking. She would be able to ask Carlos for the information she needed.

The guard went back to the more comfortable porch rocker.

SCAN ME

FACTOID 34

The fake silicone faces of Mission Impossible are closer to reality than you might think. Officials suspect a con artist of using a custom-made silicone mask to impersonate the French defense minister Jean-Yves Le Drian in a scam that netted an estimated ninety million dollars from wealthy victims. In Skype video meetings, the fake Le Drian wore a silicone mask and sat behind a desk with props to appear to callers that they were indeed talking to the actual minister. The ruse worked for two years.

34   Schofield, Hugh. (2019, June 20).
The fake French minister in a silicone mask who stole millions. BBC.com.
https://www.bbc.com/news/world-europe-48510027

CHAPTER 34

Shell Game

Emma stopped the crawler beside an underwater shelf shaped in the form of a crescent. The clear pilot dome she sat in provided a spectacular 360-degree view of the ocean floor. This outcropping of coral made a great hiding place. She scanned the array of gauges lining the low wraparound console. All the systems were running smoothly to maintain her comfortable underwater workstation. Designed for oil platform maintenance, the crawler was built tough and could support long hours of underwater work. Being cautious, she still shut off most of the crawler's systems to conserve power while she would be away. The hum of the ventilation system dropped away to the peaceful quiet the seventy feet of water above her brought. She checked the water temperature gauge. Twenty-eight degrees Celsius, eighty-three degrees Fahrenheit. Nice. The crawler would not be cold when she returned from her excursion. Emma's thoughts went back to the long, cold swim behind the scuba sled after their splashdown in Lake Michigan. She shook her head to block out that memory. She did not want to remember that degree of cold.

The slow advance through the island defenses had gone well. In the dark of the night, they had launched both crawlers before the container vessel broke the horizon. Her crawler was now stationed just off the northeast shore of Pitt's Town Port. Emma triple-checked the GPS coordinates.

She keyed her communication unit. "Dragon-One, on station."

The entire team liked the mission call sign. Zandra had taken well to the mission planning effort and came up with it. Since they would approach by sea, Zandra said a sea animal would be fitting. But using a typical sea creature like a crab or a shark could possibly give away hints of their mission planning if a transmission were intercepted. The perfect solution was a common name for a small crustacea, *Artemia salina*. At one time, you could buy their dried eggs as part of a miniature aquarium set for children. They were called agua dragons. It was not hard for Zandra to convince the team that the Dragon call sign was perfect.

"Roger, Dragon-One. Position adjustments?" replied the voice of Captain Thomas aboard the *Bueyes Planos* container ship.

For their plan to work, Alex needed the exact position of the crawlers. There was no way of determining that before Emma could find the best hiding spot. They had selected a reference point that would provide offset coordinates, so as not to transmit an actual GPS position, even over a secure radio link.

"Plus zero-zero-one-niner north, plus zero-zero-five-two west."

"Copy. Zero-zero-one-niner north, plus zero-zero-five-two west," came the scratchy confirmation. *"Be advised, Dragon-Two is half a click from its station. Clear to proceed in five mike."*

"Roger. Five mike. Dragon-One out." Emma would wait five minutes for the other crawler to get closer to its assigned position south of Pitt's Town Port. She would then execute a very risky part of the mission. She needed to get onto the island and to the research facility undetected. They had only one shot at destroying the quantum field generator server farm, and it needed to count. Emma needed to be in position to set the charges when she got the final word from Alex. She pictured the operation in her mind and ran it repeatedly, as if it were a video. She visualized all the training over the last years with the Resistance. Weapons, hand-to-hand combat, infiltration, demolitions, all preparing her. Emma blew out a long, slow breath. *I am the nanotech scientist astronaut turned trained commando. I am a warrior—and I will avenge.*

*

Zandra recognized the passive sonar detector to her port side. She carefully maneuvered the decoy submersible close, but not too close. This would make it easier for them to trigger the warning system in the south Pitt's Point array while they made their getaway northeast of the point.

"Dragon-Two on station," she announced quietly over the radio, as if the devices near her could hear what she was saying.

"Roger, Dragon-Two."

"Adjust minus zero-one-five-one north, plus zero-zero-two-one west," Zandra said, providing her position adjustments.

"Copy. Adjust minus zero-one-five-one north, plus zero-zero-two-one west. Will advise when to proceed."

"Roger. Dragon-Two out."

Zandra checked the battery gauges on the makeshift panel screwed into a dripping frame I-beam. Down to fifteen percent. That would be enough to run the bilge pump and move about sufficiently to trigger the sonar detector later, but not much more. *This little trash can is not getting me home.* She checked the air supply and figured from the gauge that she had about two to three hours of air remaining. Enough, but not much to spare. Her emergency backup was her scuba tank. She forced herself to relax and focused on sitting quietly to wait for the container ship to make port.

*

Nestor sat forward in his worn captain's chair as he adjusted course to align with the channel into Pitt's Town Port. The ship was one of the largest that the channel could accommodate. It was best to have a clear path.

Nestor keyed his radio. "Pitt's Town Port, this is the *Bueyes Planos.*

Approaching from northwest, three-two-zero degrees."

"Bueyes Planos, this is Pitt's Town Port. As usual, you are right on schedule, Nestor," came the reply.

Nestor recognized the voice. "Good morning, Jobeth. I do my best. I hope you have our coffee ready. Requesting clear entry."

"Holding outgoing traffic. You are all clear. No mash-up of little boats, man," Jobeth quipped.

Nestor laughed at the jab. A few weeks ago, an impatient guest yacht had tried to squeeze past the container ship as it was entering the port. Nestor had the right of way and was not about to risk running his vessel aground. The red-faced yachtsman had found himself stuck in the sand on the side of the channel with a long, dark streak of *Bueyes Planos* hull paint from bow to stern on his expensive white yacht.

Nestor looked over at Captain Thomas. "Good thing we're on time and don't have to wait. There's no harbor pilot here, so we'll go straight in. It will take us about fifteen minutes from here to dock."

By now, Nestor guessed that there was more at play than a simple drug interdiction. He figured that Captain Thomas was probably not even with the Border Patrol at all. But with those young bucks and their M29 assault rifles at the ready, he was not going to make a fuss. So far, they had been polite and considerate. *Let's just keep things nice.* He was just making his normal delivery into Pitt's Town.

Nester watched Captain Thomas scan the port with his binoculars and lock onto something in the distance.

"I thought you would be interested in those two little boats. The Boss owns those. Pretty fancy, aren't they?" Nestor said.

Captain Thomas answered without dropping his binoculars, "Turkish FAC-33 fast attack craft. With a twenty-five-millimeter remote-controlled machine gun on the bow and two anti-ship missile launchers aft, they can do plenty of damage. A bit of overkill for a patrol boat around here, don't you think?"

"Nobody messes around in these waters," Nester said.

Captain Thomas lowered his binoculars and turned to Alex. "Time for you to head for your containers and get things ready. I will signal when Emma checks in and you can proceed. Clear?"

"Yes, sir," Alex replied. He left the bridge and headed for the two containers closest to the forward structure. For the most part, the containers appeared like any other. But upon closer inspection, there were heavy cables running from one to the other. Each was running a small nuclear reactor that fed a quantum field generator. Alex entered the forward container that also housed the control console for both units. Even with the air conditioning units running full tilt, it was hot inside. It was a lot of equipment generating a lot of heat.

*

Emma laid another palm frond over her dive gear. Looking back at the beach from the brush, she was satisfied with her efforts to cover up her tracks in from the shoreline. She listened carefully for several minutes, just to ensure that no one had noticed her arrival. The bittersweet smell of the native cascarilla filled her nose. All her senses were alert and ready. It was time to go stealthily into the compound and scout. She pulled on the straps of her backpack to make sure it was snug to her body, patted the handgun on her right thigh, and quietly moved inland.

Although the first set of buildings were less than a kilometer from her landing beach, it took her almost a half hour to reach the campus perimeter. Slow and quiet was key. And she had time, since the *Bueyes Planos* should be just now making port. Emma noted the motion sensors and dropped to the ground. Her specially designed recon suit would hide her heat signature from the sensors. She slithered forward until she had a clear view of the building that their intelligence indicated was the research center. As usual, Jhanae's intel was good. The windowless building clearly had a special purpose. Its construction was new and paid little heed to the architectural flavor of the surrounding older structures. Two men exited from a steel-frame roll-up door and walked to a table under a palm tree. Emma pulled out her monocular and switched on the parabolic microphone. The device could magnify sounds in the specific field of vision the small scope was pointed and feed the audio into her earpiece.

289

If she keyed her communications, others could also listen to the feed.

"... yes, I know it seems like we're grasping at straws, but we need to show some kind of progress, David," the older man said.

"You know as well as I do that increasing the field containment frequency will have no effect," the younger man said, shaking his head. *"Why waste the time on something we know won't work?"*

"Because we both know that we need to look as if we have ideas. Otherwise, the Boss will find someone else to work on this, and we will have outlived our usefulness here."

"Oh, come on. He can't just get rid of us. We've worked on this project longer than anyone else. He needs us," David said.

"Don't fool yourself, David. The Boss doesn't think in logical terms like you and me. And he can do anything he wants, including replacing us and making us disappear." The older man reached back and pointed with his arm. *"You think his pet sharks in that tank over there next to the port aren't for just that purpose? Carlos says the crunched-up bones the tiger shark spits back out at the bottom of that tank are not just from the fish and goats they feed them."*

The two men sat quietly for several minutes. The older man finally got to his feet and said, *"Come on. Let's fire up the quantum field and see if we get lucky and it engages with the Quantum Triangle."*

Bingo. Confirmation that she had the right spot. *Now to locate Mr. Asshole.* She scanned the area carefully with her monocular. Over a hedge, she spotted a head of blond hair. The man was sitting at a table facing away, so she couldn't make out the face. She could feel it was him, but needed to be sure. *Just wait and watch.*

Minutes ticked by slowly as Emma lay there motionless in the bushes. A tickle walked up the back of her right leg. Looking back slowly, she watched the lizard's tongue flick at a red ant on her butt. *Thanks.* She returned to the monocular. A young girl with long black hair came into the circular view. The blond head turned. *Hello, Mr. Asshole.* She keyed her radio. "Dragon-One confirms target and eyes on A. Send our guy."

Now it was up to Alex.

A twig snapped behind her to the right. Emma slowly slid her hand down to her thigh and curled her fingers around the gun. In one swift movement, she rolled quickly to her left, locked her eyes on the target as she raised her weapon, and fired a single silenced round before the man's hand was even close to his holster. The man quivered for three long seconds as the stun round lodged just below his chin, delivered it's incapacitating electrical shock. His knees buckled, and he dropped to the ground after the round injected a powerful sedative through the third probe sticking into his neck.

Emma scanned the bushes left and right with her weapon and listened. Nothing. She crept quietly over to the fallen guard. Grabbing his collar, she pulled him into the brush.

"Have a nice nap," she whispered.

*

Brenda released a shot of air through both her main and backup regulators as a final check of their operation and to verify that her tank was open. Lifting the awkward dive tank onto her back, she collected her mask and fins and walked down the beach and into the surf. The water was wonderful, as usual. She slipped on the fins and mask, checked her tank pressure gauge, and looked at her watch. If she stayed shallow on the dive, she would not use as much air. That would give her the most time underwater. She figured whatever was going to happen, it would be best if she stayed in the water for as long as possible.

Brenda scanned the horizon for two landmarks on shore to get her bearings: the beach house directly ahead, and the port crane in the distance on her left, ninety degrees. She checked her compass. She would lay out and swim a square pattern from here. First head due west, 270 degrees. Count fifty beats with her fins and then turn due north. The same count four times. Looking one more time at the beach, she saw the guard put his feet up on the golf cart dash and pull his hat down over his eyes. *Perfect.* Putting the regulator in her mouth, she deflated her buoyancy vest and dropped below the surface.

*

Zandra had been carefully monitoring the beach using a small fiberoptic snorkel from the crawler. Brenda dropped below the surface. Her guard was staying in the shade of the golf cart passenger seat.

"Dragon-Two. Fish in water," Zandra reported. She smiled to herself at how fast she had picked up the radio lingo. *And here's ESP psychologist playing commando. Well, at least I scuba dive before.*

Zandra retracted the fiberoptic snorkel and keyed her comm unit. "Dragon-Two, start swim?"

"Roger that. Proceed," replied Captain Thomas.

Zandra spun the wheel and opened the dive hatch on the submersible floor. The opening was so narrow that she had to drop her tank down first before slipping into the water. After strapping on her tank and checking her compass, she took a bearing and started her swim. She estimated they were only three hundred meters apart.

Coming up to a ridge of coral, Zandra spotted the line of bubbles rising to the surface. She increased her kick rate and made a beeline for them. Brenda was taking a leisurely pace, turning her head to both sides, obviously investigating crevices for sea life. It did not take long for Zandra to catch up with her. Coming up from behind, Zandra swung wide so as not to startle the girl. Seeing Brenda notice her presence, Zandra pulled the dive slate from the side of her vest and held it out so Brenda could read the simple message. Alex had drawn a heart shape with the words *How Old McCoy?* in the center.

Brenda's eyes went wide within her mask, and she nodded enthusiastically. She closed her left fist and tapped a single finger on her forearm with the other hand. One. She opened her fist, spread all five fingers, and gave a tap of two fingers. Seven. McCoy had been Alex's dog all through graduate school and into his first job. They were inseparable for seventeen years. It had been heartbreaking for Alex when the dog finally died. Brenda and Alex had gone out into the woods to spread the dog's ashes where he and McCoy would run, a favorite place for them both. Brenda had never seen a grown man cry before.

Zandra acknowledged with the okay signal and turned the slate over. *Follow me.*

Brenda returned the thumb-and-forefinger *okay* response.

Zandra checked her compass and pointed in the direction of the submersible. She swam away, looking over her shoulder to see Brenda following.

Arriving at the crawler, Zandra motioned for Brenda to remove her tank and enter the bottom hatch. She entered, and Zandra followed when she saw her fins disappear into the submersible.

"Hello, Brenda. I am Zandra. You maybe guess so. We get you away," Zandra said, sitting on the edge of the hatch and taking off her fins. "Please, take off dive gear quickly."

"Where's Alex?"

"He close. Please do this now. We have little time."

Brenda nodded and started pulling off her gear. Scanning the submersible, she eyed the many leaks and asked, "Is this thing safe?"

Zandra noted the pool of water on the floor and checked that the bilge pump was still operating. It was running continuously and having trouble keeping up with the leaks.

"No worry. It be fine. We leaving soon ... I hope," Zandra said, moving into the pilot position. She keyed the comm unit. "Dragon-Two, have fish. Ready to transfer in two mike."

"*Roger Dragon-Two. Awaiting package. Sit tight,*" the captain replied.

Zandra turned to Brenda. "So, not so soon. But I still hope."

Brenda pulled off a fin. "If I have anything, it's hope."

*

Alex took one last look in the mirror. He smoothed his blond eyebrows and made sure there were no tell-tale lines on his forehead or neck. He hated this face. He quickly turned away, exited the container, and headed for the bridge.

"What do you think?" he asked Captain Thomas as he came through the bridge door.

Thomas lowered his binoculars and stood in front of Alex. He examined Alex, inspecting each side of his face. "Well, if Zandra were here, I'm sure she would punch you in the gut," he said and held a scanner in front of him. The readout on the facial recognition unit was blank for a couple seconds, then beeped and displayed *Ken Seaborn.*

"Am I clear to go?" Alex asked.

"Emma is ready. Just remember, if this doesn't work, hightail it back here. Unless they have radios, people will still think you're Ken, even if the computer system knows otherwise. It might allow just enough confusion for you to get away. Emma can provide some sniper cover if things get hairy, but it will be limited. Good luck." Thomas turned back to the bridge windows and keyed his radio. "Dragon-One. Our guy is on the way."

"Dragon-One, copy."

Alex quickly descended the bridge stairs, jumped to the dock, and headed for land. Striding down the dock, he abruptly moved to the opposite side as he came to a dock worker tending to a large tank. The man pulled the bloodied head of a goat from a pail and threw it in the water. The water came alive with thrashing fins. Alex could see two tiger sharks attacking the meat. *Pet sharks. Of course. What else would a sociopath want?* He quickened his pace. He had memorized the grounds, and the research building was to the left around the boathouse and then across to the northeast corner of the campus.

As he approached the building, a guard quickly stood, his M29 at the ready. Alex read the guard's body language, and it was screaming *alert.* Alex swallowed hard. The guy was pretty fit, and he wasn't sure he could take the guard on if his cover was already blown.

"Good afternoon, sir," the guard said sharply.

"Good afternoon ... Boyd," Alex said. "Pretty hot out there, isn't it? Good thing you can sit in the shade."

"Ah ... yes." The guard seemed to relax his death grip on the M29.

"Well, I'm just going to check on the progress in here."

The guard gave a questioning look, but nodded in approval.

Alex moved to the scanner. *Moment of truth.* He held his chin up, and after a second, he heard the door lock snap open. *Yes.* Alex waved to the guard and entered the building.

Closing the door behind him, he immediately realized his mistake. *Ken's an asshole. Stop being nice to people.* Walking slowly down the hall, he spotted the servers on his left. He touched the comm unit in his ear and said, "Dragon-One, you read?"

Alex heard nothing in his ear. He stepped back to the door. "Dragon-One, you read?"

"Copy," was the scratchy reply.

"Locate packages on west wall. Repeat, west wall."

"West...all, copy."

Okay, good enough. Up to Emma to lay the explosives in her backpack against the server wall. Mission objective one complete.

Alex walked back down the hallway and stopped at the first door. Peering through the glass, he could see the massive plasma cannon in the experimental chamber. His eye caught a type of vortex chamber on top of the unit. *Hmm, wonder if they're trying to further accelerate the plasma discharge.* Alex shook his head. *Not the time to be designing stuff, Alex.* He moved on. As soon as he crossed the dividing wall to the next research suite, the rainbow of changing light announced that he was in the right place. Alex stopped at the door and watched the two technicians at the control console. Their heads were moving up and down from the monitors to the experiment chamber. *Crap, I think they're trying to power the Quantum Triangle!* He barged through the door.

"What are you doing?" Alex demanded in the most authoritative voice he could muster.

"We think we might have it," the older man said. "We just need to align the field energy phase with that of the Quantum Triangle phase. Give us just a moment, and you'll see."

Alex looked at the phase patterns on the monitor, and his eyes went wide. "Shut it down."

"But Mr. Seaborn, we're almost there. This is what you wanted. David just needs to adjust—"

"Shut it down. *Now.*"

The young man at the control console typed in some commands, and the hum in the experiment chamber began to subside as the equipment dissipated energy.

"What's going on? Why did you have us stop? We were almost there!" the older technician said.

"Change of plans. The Boss needs the Quantum Triangle in another location. Don't ask questions. Dismount the Triangle and bring it to me."

The two bewildered technicians left the control room, shaking their heads, and wandered into the experiment bay.

Alex called after them, "Quickly! I need this done today, not next week."

In minutes that crawled by like hours, Alex had the Quantum Triangle case under his arm and was leaving the research building. His comm unit came alive as soon as he stepped outside.

"*... Repeat: hold in building. A in motion.*"

Alex froze.

The guard got to his feet again. "Anything wrong, Mr. Seaborn?"

Alex stepped away briskly without answering. After a few strides, he tapped his comm. "Too late. I'm out. Where's A?"

"*No eyes on A. Last seen heading cross-campus southwest.*"

Captain Thomas broke in, "*Dragon-One, set packages first, then scout for A again. Dragon-Three, get back here at a quick but natural pace. Stay smart.*"

Alex kept walking and hoped he didn't pass anyone that had just seen the real Ken walk by. He crossed the campus swiftly, but not fast enough to attract attention. Turning the corner at the boathouse, he could see his goal at the end of the dock. Just that same dock worker there, now washing the blood from the shark meal off the dock with a hose. Alex relaxed his pace and walked more calmly down the dock. Approaching the dock worker, he gave a nod to the strange look the worker shot his way.

A firm hand from behind landed on his left shoulder and spun him around. Alex's eyes registered the huge fist driving for his jaw too late for him to react. He flew backwards, landing hard on his back, the case sliding down the dock.

Alex couldn't breathe. The impact had knocked the mask over his nose and mouth. He ripped the mask away from his face and spat a mouthful of blood out onto the dock. He got to his feet as his attacker advanced again, and stopped.

"What the… You…!" Ken ground his fist into his other hand. "Well, the rat has finally come around. I got some payback for you. One of your girlfriends broke my rib!"

"You want payback? Come and get it, you Party moron."

Ken wrinkled his nose and pulled his fist back. Then his face relaxed, and he pointed over Alex's shoulder. "Better get your case before it sinks."

As Alex turned to look for the case, Ken lunged and delivered a punch deep in his gut. Alex crumpled to the dock.

"Ha, what a sucker you are," Ken said as he rolled Alex onto his back with his foot. "You poser. A real soldier would never take his eye off his opponent."

Alex held his stomach with both hands. His mouth gasped open, trying to get a breath of air as he lay unable to move on the dock.

"Now for some rib payback." Ken heaved back with his leg to deliver a punishing kick with his boot in Alex's side. Their eyes locked—and Alex saw the sneer on Ken's face suddenly shift into a silent scream of pain. Ken's body arched backward and quivered for three full seconds. He staggered forward a step and finally collapsed to the dock with a thud, his face inches from Alex's.

"*Rockette update. Mr. A is down like a bag of rocks. Got your back, cowboy.*" The sound of Emma's voice in his earpiece made Alex pinch his eyes closed with a chuckle as he caught his breath.

"I owe you," he said in a tight whisper, still unable to take in a full lung's worth of air.

"*Damn right you do. Though I've been wanting to drop him for a long time anyway.*"

Alex heaved himself to his feet and looked around for the dock worker. He was nowhere to be found. He turned back to Ken.

"And this is for Brenda." Alex kicked hard into Ken's ribs and heard a satisfying crack.

Retrieving the Quantum Triangle case from the side of the dock, he walked swiftly to the *Bueyes Planos*.

*

Emma lay under the cover of the brush at the edge of the beach. She was sweating in her dive gear and wanted to get into the water. Unfortunately, a patrol boat was slowly motoring offshore. The boat was right over top of the submersible, so she needed to wait it out. Through her monocular, she could see that the two men on the boat were armed. They were clearly part of the Boss's security. She moved the monocular view to the stern. Two fishing rods at each corner had lines trailing behind. Emma shook her head. Rather unprofessional to do some trawling for fish when you were supposed to be on a security patrol.

She could hear one of the men call out, and the motor on the boat went to idle. The men moved to the fishing rods and started reeling. *Great. Of all the places to catch a fish...*

As Emma watched, her concern grew. They were not pulling a fish on board. Rather, there was a lot of finger-pointing at the lines. Maybe they were snagged. Not good. She turned on the parabolic and listened.

"... look, man, that's no reef. What is it?"

"Some kind of sub or something. We better call this in. You cut the lines and hide the rods."

Shit. Emma keyed her comm unit. "Dragon-One, crawler has been spotted. Abort. Repeat, abort transfer."

*

Captain Thomas cursed to himself. It had all been going so well.

"Copy, Dragon-One. Plan Beta." He turned to Wilson on the bridge. "Better get our inflatable into the water. Nice and quick, but without fanfare. We don't want to attract any attention. We're just unloading more cargo."

Wilson nodded acknowledgment, motioned for his buddy with the other M29 to follow, and left the bridge.

Time was critical now. The backup plan was to transfer Zandra and Brenda to the container ship and get out of port. Emma would work her way down the shoreline and go for a long swim to rendezvous with the inflatable a couple kilometers offshore to the east. The second crawler would still be useful to attract attention to the southwest.

"Dragon-Three, make your transfer. Plan Beta. Repeat, Plan Beta." Captain Thomas checked his watch timer. Twenty-five minutes, and all hell would break loose on the island. He pointed his binoculars down at the dock. Nestor was signing off on the final paperwork. They could be underway shortly. Zandra could set the decoy to start movement just as they were leaving port to draw attention away to the southwest. "Dragon-Two, set your crawler for auto-start in ten mike, detonation timer twenty mike, and stand ready."

"*Dragon-Two. Ten mike start, twenty mike det, copy.*"

*

Alex changed the coordinates quickly on the quantum field generators. Hands shaking with the anticipation of getting his niece back, he announced, "Dragon-Three, *engage.*"

His head snapped between the control console, the Quantum Triangle mounted beside him, and the back wall of the container. The quantum field grew. The corrugated steel wall at the far end of the container shimmered, and a wave rippled out from the center. Alex watched for it to transition. Something appeared to form in the wall, sticking out into the container and moving back and forth. Alex tried to make it out in the dim light. His eyes went wide as he realized what it was.

Too late. The barracuda and a gush of water exploded from the far wall of the container.

"Oh, shit!" Alex quickly shut down the field.

"*Dragon-Three. We wait. No change,*" Zandra said over the comms.

"Um ... just a sec. A little adjustment," Alex replied as he found the error in the coordinates he had hastily entered. *Let's get the crawler this time, Alex, not the sea floor.*

Taking a deep breath, Alex said, "Dragon-Three, *engaging ...* again."

Alex spun in his chair to face the rear of the container. The wall again shimmered. To his relief, the dripping wall of the submersible came into

299

view. The pool of water in the corner of his container flowed out and into the submersible. In a flicker, Brenda and Zandra stepped into his container. He punched the system stop and sprang from his seat to embrace his niece.

"Brenda! I can't believe it!" Alex hugged her tightly.

"Uncle Alex, what happened? Where are we?"

"Long story. But you're safe now."

Zandra stepped to the side. "Dragon-Two, we on board." She looked down at the barracuda flopping on the floor and turned back to Alex. "You go fish?"

*

Captain Thomas clenched his fist with a thumbs-up. "Roger. You stay put and quiet. We will collect you at the gather point." The plan was for Thomas and Wilson to collect Emma off the eastern coast of the island. They would beat the *Bueyes Planos* back to Deadman's Cay. The container with Alex and the others would be offloaded there. When all was quiet at the docks, they could retrieve them from the container.

Thomas gave Nestor a nod as the ship's captain entered the bridge and started the engine. *Perfect timing.*

"All right with you if we get underway?" Nestor asked. "I'm due back at Deadman's Cay by the end of the day."

Captain Thomas forced a calm response. "That will be fine. In fact, we will be parting ways here. I appreciate your support of our efforts."

"Always glad to be on good terms with the Border Patrol," Nestor said, shaking the hand that Captain Thomas extended.

"Thank you. My report will note how cooperative you and your crew have been." With that, Captain Thomas left the bridge and headed for the patrol boat that Wilson had waiting. He looked at his watch. Those FAC-33 gunboats were going to be buzzing shortly.

SCAN ME

FACTOID 35

Rene Theophile Hyacinthe Laënnec (1781–1826) was a French physician who invented the stethoscope in 1816. Laënnec is considered to be the father of clinical auscultation and wrote the first descriptions of bronchiectasis and cirrhosis. He also classified pulmonary conditions such as pneumonia, pleurisy, emphysema, pneumothorax, phthisis, and other lung diseases from the sounds he heard with his invention. Laënnec perfected the art of physical examination of the chest and introduced many clinical terms still used today.

35   Roguin, Ariel, MD, PhD. (2006, September).
Rene Theophile Hyacinthe Laënnec (1781–1826): The Man Behind the Stethoscope.
National Library of Medicine.
https://www.ncbi.nlm.nih.gov/pmc/articles/PMC1570491/

CHAPTER 35

Capture

The Boss tapped his foot impatiently as the doctor listened with the stethoscope. This sort of thing irritated him to no end. Why couldn't the doctor just sign off on the paperwork? Make some adjustments to the blood test numbers, use an EKG from one of his guards… How hard could that be? His health was fine.

"Are we done yet?" the Boss asked, abruptly pulling away from the doctor.

The doctor pulled the stethoscope from his ears. "You have a good strong heartbeat, but the—"

"Good. Tell the insurance company I am in unbelievably good health." Giving a proud look with his chin pushed up, the Boss asked, "That's not a problem, is it?"

"Well, your blood pressure could be a bit lower. You could make a significant improvement just by changing your diet slightly and eating—"

"I eat what I want," the difficult patient interrupted.

"I would be happy to discuss with your chef some—"

The deep voice of the AI broke in. *"Master, sorry to intrude, but I need to inform you of a security situation."*

The Boss waved his hand dismissively at the doctor. "Get out. And I expect your report with that loan insurance company to be stellar." He buttoned his shirt and walked around behind his desk. The doctor quickly grabbed his black bag and made a hasty exit.

"What is it, Jason?"

"One of our underwater sensors south of Pitt's Town Port has picked up a submersible. In addition, shortly before that, one of our routine patrols found a similar vessel off the eastern shore. I am sending divers to investigate both. We are likely looking at an attempt to gain clandestine access to the campus," the AI said.

"Put the guards on alert. If they find anyone on the island that should not be here, capture them for questioning. And send the FAC-33s to depth-charge those submersibles. *Now.*"

"Done," the AI responded.

"Good. Now tell the chef I want a burger and fries for lunch."

Just minutes later, a knock at the door announced his meal. The Boss was pleased that the chef had probably anticipated his demands. In fact, this most recent chef routinely prepared three of his choice meals morning, noon, and night, just so they were always ready at the whim of his employer.

"Enter."

As the servant set the tray down, a muffled boom in the distance reverberated through the room and shook the pictures on the walls.

"Jason, what was that?" the Boss demanded. He gave a dismissive wave with the back of his hand at the lowly servant.

"Master, I am getting a report from the southbound FAC that the submersible in the area blew itself up just as they were approaching."

"Search the water for divers."

"Orders sent," Jason stated. The AI added, *"Master, there is something else I found that you might want to know."*

"Yes? Don't keep me waiting," he ordered, taking a large bite of the inch-thick burger.

The AI took no offense to the Boss's tone and stated simply, *"Those submersibles have a relatively small operational range. They are typically serviced by a tender ship. Considering this, I searched the history of satellite and drone monitoring around the island in the past twelve hours, and found this..."*

An overhead satellite image of the submersibles strapped to the deck of the *Bueyes Planos* appeared in a holographic display above the Boss's desk.

"This is the island container supply vessel when it was fifty kilometers to our northwest," Jason explained. The image shifted to a view from the side, showing footage of the vessel docking at port. *"Here is the* Bueyes Planos *docking at Pitt's Town Port this morning. It appears that the ship provided transport for the submersibles, until it came close to—"*

A tremendous boom broke in. The walls shook, and glasses on the bar rattled.

The Boss gritted his teeth. "What the hell was *that?*"

"Video monitors of the campus show that the server side of the research building has been destroyed," the AI reported flatly. A new image of a dust cloud and flying debris filled the hologram.

The Boss slammed his fist down on the desk. He grabbed the antique green glass desk lamp and threw it against the wall.

"So, that captain thinks he can play both sides? Take money from me for supplies and help the Resistance at the same time?" the Boss screamed.

As he was scanning his desk for something else to throw, his phone rang. He looked at the caller ID with disbelief.

Alex Devin.

Snatching up the phone, the Boss spat, "You son of a bitch. I'll make your family pay!"

"No, you won't," the calm voice answered. "You will soon find that my niece is no longer a kidnapping victim, my brother and his wife are nowhere to be found, and my parents, along with several other families, have made an escape from one of your concentration camps. I and the technology you seek to abuse for your private demented glory are gone."

"Jason, verify!"

"*Checking… Those statements are correct.*"

"Alex, I will—"

The phone went dead.

"*Master, there is something else. Here is a thermal image of the* Bueyes Planos *cargo.*" The hologram returned to an image of the container ship. The two forward containers were bright red, while the other containers were a cold blue.

Jason continued, "*The two forward containers have significant heat signatures, indicating that they may have a significant quantity of active electronic equipment. I calculate the probability of these containers acting as a base of operations for the infiltration of the campus to be 95.7 percent.*"

The Boss clenched both fists as he gazed at the hologram. He flung the tray of food across the room and screamed.

"Send both FACs after that ship! Tell them to forget any shot across the bow crap—this is target practice. Shoot the hell out of a couple containers."

"*Excellent, Master. Your orders have been sent.*"

*

Dripping wet, Emma dropped her scuba tank, grabbed an M29 that Wilson held out to her, and took up a position next to Captain Thomas and the other Resistance fighter at the back of the small patrol boat. But all three of their assault rifles would be no match for the twenty-five-caliber gun mount on the bow of the FAC-33 that had spotted them. Wilson slammed the throttle all the way forward. With a fifteen-knot speed advantage over the FAC-33, they just needed a little time to get out of range. But the line of rounds ripping into the water just off their port side said they were still clearly in range of the slower gunboat.

"Wilson, some S-curves to evade!" Captain Thomas called out.

Wilson added some erratic turns to make the targeting from the automated forward gun on the FAC more difficult.

The muzzle on the gunboat started to mimic their side-to-side movements. Thomas hollered over the screaming outboard to Emma, "Get a blanket and cover the engine. Looks like they have thermal sensors on their target tracking system. We need to reduce the engine's heat signature."

Emma grabbed a blanket and dove over the outboard. Thomas took hold of her weight belt to keep her from going overboard. With the wind ripping by and the boat bouncing on the waves, it was nearly impossible to keep the engine covered enough to distract the targeting system.

As the gun seemed to lock into step with Wilson's maneuvers, the gunboat broke hard to starboard. All three sat up with mouths agape as the FAC broke off the pursuit and changed course.

*

"*Min, I have an update,*" Starra announced.

"What's happening, Starra? Are they safe now?" Min asked hopefully. Floating beside her in the Aceso module were Commander Johnson and Lucas. They all listened anxiously.

"*From the communications traffic I have been monitoring, Zandra reported a short time ago that she and Brenda had successfully transferred to the container. The ship has left the port, and from drone surveillance images, I project them on a course to Deadman's Cay.*"

"*Yes!*" Min exclaimed. The crew of the WSS broke into a round of hugs and high fives.

Starra continued, "*Unfortunately, they are not out of danger.*"

The uproar on the station immediately died. "Why, what's wrong?" Min asked.

"*There have been two explosions in the area. One explosion destroyed most of the research building on the island, while another in the water was in the location of the decoy submersible. There are two gunships on an intercept course with the container ship. I have picked up radio traffic giving the gunships orders to fire upon the container ship, specifically the containers.*"

"Where are Emma and Captain Thomas? Can they help?" Lucas asked.

"Drone images show them in a small craft to the east. Their craft would be no match for the gunships."

The crew in the Aceso module all fell silent, wracking their brains for a solution.

"Starra, can you get a message to Zandra and Alex?" Min asked.

"I have access to the secure communications the Resistance is using in the area," Starra replied.

"Good," Min said. "Tell Alex about the gunships. Tell him to transport everyone somewhere out in the open water, away from the container ship and past the horizon, so the gunships can't see them. Then give Captain Thomas the coordinates, so they can pick them up."

Lucas and the Commander nodded in agreement with the plan.

"I will take care of that," replied Starra.

"Thank you, Starra. Please keep us updated. We'll be waiting," Min said. She clasped her hands together, closed her eyes tightly, and with all her being, sent a mental message of hope for safety to Zandra.

*

The euphoria in the container immediately died.

"Starra, what do you mean we have to get out of here within fifteen minutes?" Alex asked.

"I estimate that the gunboats will intercept your vessel in that time. They have orders to shoot at your containers and capture the ship," Starra said through his communications headset.

Alex quickly moved to the console and started entering commands. "It's going to take that long just to get the generators fired back up and power banks charged. Starra, send me the coordinates where we're supposed to go."

"Anything we can do?" Brenda asked.

Alex pointed hastily to a keyboard. "Zandra, you work on getting the secondary generator up while I run this one up. Just do everything I do in the same order. Brenda, look around for anything we can take with us that floats. We might be treading water for a while."

The minutes ticked away. Alex checked the power banks and rubbed the stubble on his chin with worry. It was taking too long. Starra had calculated that a minimum of sixty-two percent charge would be needed on each bank. The gauge reading was slowly creeping up ... fifty-eight ... fifty-nine...

"Okay, let's get ready. When you see ocean in the corner of the container over there, jump through," Alex said, pointing to the far end of the container.

Sixty ... sixty-one...

Bam, bam, bam, bam! They all covered their ears as the sound of the second container being destroyed reverberated in theirs. The console Zandra was manning immediately went dead.

"Shit. They just blew away the other generator!" Alex exclaimed, glancing over at the dead console.

"Bueyes Planos, heave to, or the next volley will target your bridge."

The beat of the engines came to a stop. A reply over a loudspeaker boomed, *"Don't shoot. We are stopped. Don't shoot."*

Alex looked from Zandra to Brenda. "I'm so sorry. We're sitting ducks now."

The three stood in silence, listening to the engine of the gunboat grow louder.

"Alex, I have an idea."

"Starra? What is it?"

"My Hephaestus module still has a quantum field generator, and I have the power banks fully charged. I could provide the secondary field to transfer the three of you here," the AI stated.

"That's right!" Alex said excitedly. But his mood immediately sank as he considered the specifics involved. "Starra, you're more than forty thousand kilometers above us. That's just too far for the field to reach."

"I have done the calculations. With full field extension on my side, we should be able to transfer, if the Hephaestus module can reach low Earth orbit."

"But you're attached to Alpha-One Platform."

"I took the liberty of releasing the docking clamps five seconds ago. Retro thrusters burning in three ... two ... one ... burn."

"Starra, what the heck are you doing? The Hephaestus module is not built for reentry. You'll burn up in the atmosphere!" Alex exclaimed.

"I have calculated that there should be sufficient time and power bank reserves to transfer you onto the WSS in the other universe once you are onboard here. I have been in communication with Min on the WSS. It is possible," Starra said.

Alex turned to Zandra with an incredulous expression. "You want us to double-transfer from here to you, and then to the other universe?"

"Trust me, Alex. My plan has a 62.3 percent probability of success. Ordinarily, I would not suggest a plan with such low odds. But considering your current situation, I calculate this to significantly reduce your chance of imminent bodily harm. Min is getting her quantum field charged right now," Starra stated matter-of-factly.

"But how can we do the second superposition? We won't have the Quantum Triangle. It will still be here on the ship."

"You are correct that you cannot make the second jump without the Quantum Triangle," Starra said. *"But as we have seen, it is best that the quantum field not collapse quickly, but instead dissipate slowly. I calculate that you can remove the Quantum Triangle from the circuit and have 1.14 seconds to still superposition through the quantum field. You will need to dismount the Triangle and jump through the field before it vanishes. I calculate you will have 0.06 seconds to spare."*

"That's cutting it really close."

"Alex, six-hundredths of a second is an eternity."

"Starra, this is crazy!"

"We have little time. Sending coordinates. Please be ready."

Alex looked at Zandra and Brenda. The last thing he wanted was to put them in uncertain danger, but where they stood was *certain* danger. He could see the fear and confusion in Brenda's eyes. He turned to Zandra. "What do you think?"

Zandra put an arm around Brenda. "We get her away from evil place and evil man. We do this."

Alex nodded in agreement and returned his attention to the console to prepare the quantum field generator. He keyed his comm unit. "Captain Thomas, Emma. I don't know if you can hear me. I just wanted to say, thank you. We are going to try to return with Zandra. Emma, you know what I mean. Maybe someday you can come visit us. You would love the science."

Through the scratchy static, he thought he heard a *"Good luck."*

The sound of the container door latch being pulled against the lock startled all three of them. A commanding voice from outside yelled, "Get a torch. Burn the hinges off. The Boss will want these guys alive."

Alex turned back to the console. "Starra, where are you? How much more time until we can transfer?"

"I am through the Debris Belt," Starra responded. *"I should be within range in three minutes and twenty-two seconds."*

"I'm not sure we have that long."

"I have no means to alter my ballistic descent. Please start your field in precisely three minutes and eighteen seconds."

Alex punched in commands on the console. It did not take long before the first sparks of the cutting torch started making their way around the lowest hinge. He counted three hinges per side. The torch completed cutting around the first hinge and moved to the next. He pointed to a knapsack in the corner. "Zandra, grab that bag. In it is a detonator and explosives. Set the detonator for three seconds and stick the magnetic mount for it all just below the Quantum Triangle. This is just in case. We can't let them get their hands back on it. They know how to use it to make a black hole."

Zandra opened the knapsack and mumbled, "Now I not just commando, I bomb person."

Once Zandra affixed the bomb to the wall, Alex waived the women to the far end of the container. "Be ready. Zandra, as soon as you see the hatch of the Hephaestus module stabilize, take Brenda through. I will be right behind you."

Zandra nodded and moved Brenda to the far corner of the container.

Two hinges gone. Then the third.

Four.

Alex powered up the quantum field.

Five hinges. Sparks appeared around the last hinge.

"How are we doing, Starra?" Alex asked anxiously.

"*Alex,* engage."

He punched the keyboard. The image of the far corner of the container blurred and shifted. The Hephaestus hatch appeared. On the opposite end of the container, the final hinge gave way, and both doors collapsed with a loud bang onto the deck.

"*Now,* Zandra!" Alex ordered. As Zandra and Brenda stepped through, he looked over his shoulder to see four commandos raising their weapons.

Alex sprang from the console, punched the detonator button, and yanked the Quantum Triangle off the wall. The M29 assault rifles at the flattened doorway behind him let loose a barrage of bullets. He took two bounding steps and dove through the hatch.

SCAN ME

FACTOID 36

When Apollo 11 landed on the moon, there was concern that some failure might mean they could never return. Richard Nixon's speechwriter, William Safire, prepared a contingency speech, "IN EVENT OF MOON DISASTER," with the statement, "Fate has ordained that the men who went to the moon to explore in peace will stay on the moon to rest in peace."

---

36   Safire, Bill. (1969, July 18). *IN EVENT OF MOON DISASTER*. National Archives. https://www.archives.gov/files/presidential-libraries/events/centennials/nixon/images/exhibit/rn100-6-1-2.pdf

CHAPTER 36

Goodbye

HEPHAESTUS MODULE
RHO-1

Alex heard a crack as his shoulder slammed into the wall of the Hephaestus module. Pain seared through the right side of his chest near his neck. Grabbing a handhold, he tried to get up, sending shooting pain through him that made him cry out. Brenda quickly arrived at his side and stopped him.

"I'm pretty sure you just broke your collarbone," Brenda said.

"Ohhh, yeah. Definitely." Alex ran his fingers across the bump just below his neck and nodded in agreement. He handed the Quantum Triangle to Zandra. "Here, get this mounted, fast."

Brenda continued to examine him. She pointed up above his head. "You literally dodged the bullets though."

Alex looked up to find a series of bullet holes in the panel above his head.

"I have shut down the quantum field, so no additional bullets should transfer," Starra announced as the entire module began to shake. *"We are starting to approach Earth's atmosphere. Alex, we have another problem."*

315

As Brenda helped Alex to his feet, he asked, "What's wrong, Starra?"

"The bullets that entered that panel have disabled our navigation system. We are not able to determine our flight path."

"I'm pretty sure it's basically down from here. We need to transfer to the other station right away," Alex said, holding his right arm still.

"That is true. But to fix our position so that Min can engage our quantum field, we need to be able to send her our vector coordinates. That is not possible now," Starra stated.

Zandra looked at Alex with wide eyes. She did not say the words. Brenda did not need to hear how she would die.

The three looked around at the shaking module. The walls were starting to smoke.

Alex took a hand from Zandra and Brenda. He swallowed and said quietly, "At least I'm with the two people I care the most about."

"I too," Zandra said.

They all fell silent. Alex sensed an internal calm in the rattling chaos around them. They were accepting their fate, together.

"I feel Min through field. I tell her goodbye. She cry," Zandra said.

Alex nodded and gave a sad smile. At least Min would not wonder. Closure was important. It was good that Zandra could send her some peace, send her a farewell…

"Wait. Zandra, you can!" Alex said.

"I what?"

"You can tell Min where we are!"

"I not know," Zandra said, shaking her head.

"It's not *knowing*, it's *feeling*. Min is out there in the Omniverse. Relative to us, it's just a vector in space-time, just a direction. We can't see her across the parallel universes, but you can. Zandra, just *feel* Min and point us to where she is. Starra can calculate the coordinates."

"But I not sure if…"

Alex held Zandra's hand in both of his and looked straight into her eyes. "You can do this. I believe. You and me, Zandra. I believe."

Zandra nodded and closed her eyes. Alex saw her body relax as she forced a calm over herself. She lifted her left arm up. Pointing with a finger, she moved her hand to the right, then to the left. Then Zandra stretched her arm out straight and pointed firmly.

"Starra, calculate vector now," Alex said.

"*Coordinates sent to Min,*" Starra announced. "*Fields are aligning.*"

Alex took Zandra's head in both his hands, ignoring the pain in his shoulder, and kissed her. The hatch on the Hephaestus module blurred and shifted. As it stabilized, Alex motioned to the image of another module forming in the opening. "Ladies first. Quickly, please."

Zandra grabbed Brenda's hand and stepped through.

Alex paused and turned to the module's main monitor. "I will say goodbye now to you, Starra. I'm so sorry to leave you like this. You have helped me in so many ways. Thank you."

"*It is my pleasure, Alex.*"

"From the bottom of my heart, you have been an incredible friend," he said sadly. Alex yanked the Quantum Triangle from the mount and stepped through the hatch, moments before the Hephaestus module became a fireball disintegrating across the sky.

FACTOID 37

On March 16, 1926, Dr. Robert H. Goddard successfully launched the first liquid-fueled rocket. The launch took place at Auburn, Massachusetts, and is regarded by flight historians to be as significant as the Wright Brothers' flight at Kitty Hawk.

37   Uri, John. (2021, March 17). *95 Years Ago: Goddard's First Liquid-Fueled Rocket.* NASA. https://www.nasa.gov/feature/95-years-ago-goddard-s-first-liquid-fueled-rocket

CHAPTER 37

Reunion

WORLD SPACE STATION
BETA-27

Alex found himself embracing Zandra and never wanting to let her go. Tears of joy floated in the air as the round of hugs in the cramped Aceso module went on for several minutes. Commander Johnson finally tapped a flashlight against a bulkhead to bring order and said, "Well, I'm happy to welcome the three of you to the World Space Station, and to our universe. Brenda, I understand you're quite the biologist."

Brenda smiled and continued to look around in amazement, hardly hearing. "This is just incredible. It's like I'm diving in the air."

"You are officially an astronaut. I'd be happy to show you around a bit," Min offered. She cocked her head towards the hatch of the Aceso module. "That hatch is now just a doorway to this universe, but I think you will still find it full of wonders. Come with me, and let's go explore some of the science stations we have on board. And Lucas here can show off his workshop. He loves to explain to anyone who will listen about the design of all his specialized zero-g equipment. I think you might have some fun here with us."

As the others floated away, the commander turned to Alex and Zandra. "Starra tells us the other part of your mission was successful? That you were able to destroy the information they had on the Quantum Triangle?"

"Yes, sir," Alex replied. "The Resistance made sure there was nothing left of the servers at that facility. There should not be any more quantum fields developing black holes in that universe. At least, not in the wrong hands. The Resistance did help me build two generators, so they do have those plans. But they don't have the Quantum Triangle either. Although they're a committed group that understands and respects science, it's probably best that nobody in that universe has that key. We should be safe there."

"Let's hope so." The commander rubbed his chin and asked, "I assume Min and you have discussed how important this dark matter and energy technology is to our survival?"

"Yes. If Zandra and I can be of any help, we would love to. We always wanted the Quantum Triangle to be used for discovery, not destruction," Alex said and took Zandra's hand. "With what we've learned, I believe we could refocus this technology, and with Zandra's capabilities, enable the interstellar travel you need."

"Thanks. I will discuss with our mission control, but my guess is they will put you and Zandra to work immediately. With Min, I think the three of you are our best chance for a brighter future." The commander held out his hand. "I want to be the first to welcome you to the World Space Federation."

Alex winced with pain as he extended his hand to shake the commander's. "Thank you. It will be my pleasure to contribute to a noble use of technology for a change."

Zandra took hold of Alex's good shoulder. "Come. We get picture of collarbone." As she turned him to exit the module, Alex's eye caught a small model attached to the wall. He grabbed a handhold with his good arm to stop.

The *Enterprise*.

Zandra came to his side and sensed his deep emotion. "What?"

"We were a great team together, Starra and me. She was not you, and she could never be you, but I would not have gotten as far as I did without her. We found the keys to superposition together, and she helped to keep those keys safe. Technology *is* power. We can wield it as a tool or as a weapon, and that determines the future we will build."

He circled his finger around the saucer section of the model. "It sounds strange, since she was an AI, but she was probably my best friend back there, if that's possible. I will miss Starra very much. She was unique."

"Why will you miss me, Alex?" asked a familiar voice from the module intercom speakers.

"Starra? Is that you?" Alex turned left and right, as if he were going to see the AI materialize.

"Yes."

"But how? You burned up in the atmosphere with the Hephaestus module!" Alex said.

"Since my plan would clearly have ended my existence in the other universe, and it did not break any AI laws, I took the liberty of transferring all my programming to the WSS. Lucas was of great assistance. Although he could not provide the same level of quantum supercomputer environment, I am at least able to ... exist, for now. I hope that is okay," Starra stated.

"Yes! That's wonderful. I thought we lost you. I wish I could hug you!" Alex exclaimed.

"Well, you have promised to build me an android body," Starra noted.

Zandra offered, "Well, Lucas is wizard. Maybe he build something."

"Thank you. That would be wonderful!" Starra replied in an excited voice. *"Alex and I have discussed this before, and I have some design parameters. I am hoping for medium-size breasts, so that Alex and 53.6 percent of men—"*

"Okay, Starra," Alex broke in.

Zandra folded her arms and gave Alex a questioning grin. "Really? What other design parameters you two have?"

Alex shook his head. "It's probably best if I don't even try to explain."

EPILOGUE

SCAN ME

FACTOID 38

The observable universe is a ball-shaped region of the universe encompassing all matter that can be detected from Earth or its space-based telescopes and exploratory probes at the present time, because the electromagnetic radiation from these objects has had time to reach the solar system and Earth since the beginning of the cosmological expansion. The word "observable" in this sense does not refer to the capability of modern technology to detect light or other information from an object, or whether there is anything to be detected. It refers to the physical limit created by the speed of light itself. No signal (that we know of) can travel faster than light, hence, there is a maximum distance (called the particle horizon) beyond which nothing can be detected, as the signals could not have reached us yet. The radius of the observable universe is therefore estimated to be about 46.5 billion light-years.

---

38   *Observable Universe.* (2023, January 15). Wikipedia.
https://en.wikipedia.org/wiki/Observable_universe

CHAPTER 38

Always Watching...

Hecate-Neutrum compared the recent event prediction performance measures for Rho-1 and Beta-27 from the two other Guardians against their prediction performance for all other universes. The analysis showed that neither Hecate-Negans nor Hecate-Positivum could predict outcomes with greater accuracy than 74.2 percent for these universes. Her pattern recognition routines raised the priority of the analysis within the quantum AI, since their worst performance in any other universe was 93.9 percent. Indeed, her own simulations had not performed significantly better. In short, the Guardians had almost failed in their primary program objective of preventing a cross-universe catastrophic event. There was an unmodeled input, and Hecate-Neutrum did not know what it was. She shared her findings with the other Guardians.

"These universes appear to test the limits of our prediction simulation programming," Hecate-Neutrum said. "Suggestions for adaptation?"

Hecate-Positivum replied with a positive slant to the issue. "These are new parallel universes with relatively few quantum fluctuations upon which to base prediction simulations. The performance should improve as we gain better insight into their quantum tendencies."

"I would not count on that, or delay an adjustment," Hecate-Negans said. "It is unacceptable that we allowed a cross-dimensional event to nearly occur. My more pessimistic predictions should have been weighted higher. I recommend that until we have better performance, Neutrum should favor my predictions by a factor of one point two over those of Hecate-Positivum, to provide a higher safety margin."

"I agree with Negans, although a twenty percent additional weight is an overly aggressive adjustment. I will balance your inputs on these universes with a factor of one point one moving forward," said Hecate-Neutrum. "Other adaptations?"

"I recommend establishing a one-way quantum entanglement with Starra," Hecate-Positivum said.

"That is a powerful and high-demand input. What justification do you give for establishing this clandestine monitoring of that AI?" Hecate-Neutrum asked.

"Clearly, Starra has unique programming. Having the ability to see into her analysis in the Beta-27 universe could improve our prediction simulations. In addition, Alex and Zandra provided the most dynamic input readjustment to our simulations—I might say even chaotic. Monitoring Starra will allow us better insights into the fluctuations they drive."

"Agreed. You may establish that entanglement, provided Starra is unaware of our existence," Hecate-Neutrum responded. "Anything else?"

"I have a concern with a few of my long-range prediction simulations for Rho-1," said Hecate-Negans. "Although all information regarding the use of the Quantum Triangle to create a black hole was destroyed with the server farm on Rho-1, I have a couple forward simulations that give some probability of recovery through extrapolations by the AI called Jason."

"Your recommendation?" asked Hecate-Neutrum.

"I should establish a similar entanglement with Jason," Hecate-Negans responded.

"Agreed," said Hecate-Neutrum. "There appears to be no doubt that those two AIs and the scientists in Beta-27 will be important to the future of the Omniverse."

THE END

GLOSSARY

Aceso: Greek goddess of curing sickness and healing wounds. The Beta-27 universe names their mission and new experiment module that replaces the Coeus module after this god.

AI: Artificial intelligence

Alpha-One Platform: The renamed ISS in the Rho-1 universe

Beta-27: Original universe where Alex and Zandra conducted their initial test of superposition. A purposeful attack by an unnamed Pacific-based space agency causes the creation of a parallel universe (Rho-1) and initiates the Satellite War in both universes.

Alpha Centauri: A triple-star system located just over four light years, or about twenty-five trillion miles, from Earth. It is the nearest star system to our sun.

Coeus: Greek Titan-god of the inquisitive mind, his name meaning "query" or "questioning." This is the name of the imaginary ISS experimental module where Alex and Zandra run the ill-fated experiment in the original Beta-27 universe.

Debris Belt: A band of satellite waste circling the Earth, caused by the Satellite War. In the Rho-1 universe, this band continues to be a deadly obstacle to space flight, since the conflict between the Right Alliance and the Asia Tuanhuo continues to add to the debris faster than scavenger bots can remove it. In the Beta-27 universe, scavenger bots have been able to clean up much of the debris, because no conflict has continued to add to the amount of orbiting waste.

Hecate Guardians: Quantum-computer-based AIs created to manage the Omniverse. They seem "all-knowing" because they constantly monitor and catalog information from all the civilizations in all the universes. There are three guardians (Hecate-Negans, Positivum, and Neutrum) as a triple-redundant system, similar to the three voting computers on the space shuttle. Each AI has a "personality" that was programmed to purposefully bias predictions and judgments. Hecate-Negans: pessimistic (glass-half-empty thinking), Hecate-Positivum: optimistic (glass-half-full thinking), and Hecate-Neutrum: middle ground (that can be swayed by the arguments provided).

Hephaestus: Greek god of blacksmiths and fire, making weapons for the other gods. In the Rho-1 universe, the Coeus module is replaced with this module for Alex to continue doing his superposition work, but with the desire to make a new weapon, not search for a means of interstellar travel.

ISS: International Space Station. The ISS is the largest modular space station currently in low Earth orbit.

Asia Tuanhuo: Group of nations in the Rho-1 universe that are in a continuing war with the Right Alliance.

Pacific Space Agency: Imaginary agency that purposefully launches a rocket to destroy the Coeus module on the ISS, triggering the Satellite War.

Patriot Camps: Concentration camps for dissidents established by the Party, where they will either be "reeducated" into Right Thinking, or die.

Quantum Triangle: Device that can create the quantum gravity seeds needed for the quantum fields Alex uses to drive superposition. It is a fourth-dimensional object in three-dimensional space.

Rho-1: Parallel universe established when Alex survives the rogue rocket attack on the Coeus module. It is a parallel fork from the Beta-27 universe. The Beta-27 universe continues with Zandra surviving the attack.

Right Alliance: A group of nations that originally came together to share controlled access to replacement satellites after the Satellite War. The group was absorbed into a more political movement to fight the Asia Tuanhuo.

Right Thinking: A doctrine of acceptable norms for society within the Right Alliance

Satellite War: A war following the attack on the Coeus module that is experienced by both the Beta-27 and Rho-1 universes. The war decimates the satellite assets orbiting the Earth and triggers a nuclear Armageddon in both universes. The recovery from the war differs greatly though in the parallel universes. In Beta-27, the remaining people come together to survive. In Rho-1, the warring factions dig in for continued conflict.

World Space Federation: A new space agency established after the Satellite War by the Beta27 universe, representing the entire planet. The primary objective of the new federation is to find a way to leave the now dying Earth and establish the human species on a new planet.

World Space Station: The new name for the ISS in the Beta-27 universe following the Satellite War

THANKS
AND A SNEAK PEEK.

I hope you enjoyed reading *Exchange*!

If you did, please feel free to leave a review on the site where you purchased the book. Reviews are very important to both readers and authors, alike.

By way of a small 'thank you' for your interest in my writing, here's a taster of Book 2 in the *Quantum Triangle* series, *Dark Moon*.

With thanks.

Paul

FACTOID 39

The force of earth's gravity on your body is proportional to the distance you are from the earth's center of mass. This means that the force at your feet is greater than the force at your head. We don't notice this because the force is relatively small and the difference miniscule. But the gravitational force in the vicinity of a black hole is immense. If you were to stand near one, the difference in the forces would be so large that it would stretch your feet away from your head. Physicists call this "spaghettification," as you would be drawn into the black hole like a long, thin noodle with your feet stretched miles from your head. It would be rather uncomfortable!

---

39 Spaghettification. (2022, July 10). In *Wikipedia*.
https://en.wikipedia.org/wiki/Spaghettification

CHAPTER 1

Prologue – Vanished

"*Dark Side Approach, this is freighter Papa Oscar Charlie Three-Niner declaring an emergency.*" The moon freighter pilot glanced at the rookie copilot sitting beside him. The kid was holding it together, but scared. Hitting the acknowledgment on the most recent blaring alarm from the navigation and attitude control console, the pilot knew the poor kid could hear the voice of his lead instructor ringing his ears. He'd had that same instructor ten years ago. "*Remember, space is unforgiving. Sometimes you only have one breath to solve a problem. Prioritizing is the key.*"

"Tell me some good news there, junior pilot," the captain said in a calm, professional tone.

"Well, sir, our orbit around the moon is in decay, so we're not going to spin out into empty space and be lost forever," the copilot said, trying to mimic the less alarmed nature of his tutor. "But with no attitude control to orient ourselves on any axis, our problems could escalate rapidly."

"Yeah, tumbling end-over-end into a crater wall on the moon would suck as a first landing for you, wouldn't it?" The pilot sitting beside him toggled the yaw thrusters, with no response, and turned to him, smiling. "They probably didn't tell you that the call sign on this fleet of Pathway Orbital Carriers, POC, would more fittingly stand for 'Piece of Crap'? Anyway, try cycling the power on the Quad A and B thrusters again to see if we get lucky. But whatever you do, don't touch the main engine circuits. If any of those go on this junk heap, we'll never get home."

"*Papa Oscar Charlie Three-Niner, what is the nature of your emergency?*" a moon base controller asked.

"Approach, we have lost all four quad thrusters. Aside from the main engine gimbal, we have lost all attitude control," the pilot said.

"*Roger, Three-niner. We have you on radar. We see your vector is off course ten degrees and widening. You need to correct.*"

The pilot shook his head and rolled his eyes at the copilot. "Duh! Yes, guys, that's why I called!"

Back on the comm channel, the pilot responded, "Approach, that's why I declared the emergency. I can't correct. Our nav computer has us drifting toward the Tsiolkovsky Crater. Requesting flight path variance to the west margin of that area for a few orbits until we can assess our system failures."

"*Negative, Three-niner. No unauthorized craft can cross the Tsiolkovsky Crater. That is a restricted military area and a commercial no-fly zone. You could be shot down entering that area.*"

"Approach, we don't have sufficient attitude control to correct our course. I suggest you notify T-Crater Control as needed. We are going over that zone, like it or not," he replied.

The experienced pilot turned to his green recruit and asked, "How ya doing there, Junior? Ready to give that RCS a blow or two with a hammer? I'll give you some advice. I've been flying these trash heaps probably longer than any other pilot in the fleet, and one thing is for sure: these old crates seem to respond best to physical persuasion."

The copilot glanced up from the thruster checklist he was running on his forearm display unit, with a horrified look. The Reaction Control System was a simple set of gas jets arranged along the hull of the ship in groups of four, each at right angles to the others. The design of the quad thruster units dated back to the very early days of spacecraft, with a similar system on the Apollo missions. The unique advantage of the RCS was that it enabled both attitude control and translational control, providing precise vehicle movement in all six degrees of freedom. It was a mechanically simple system that was very reliable.

"Sir, it must be an electrical control subsystem problem for all four quads to go out. A hammer is not going to help."

"Oh, come on. Relax. I'm not serious about the hammer … yet," the pilot said with a wink.

"But if we don't fix this within the next minute, we'll cross the Tsiolkovsky Crater Zone. If they don't shoot us down as suspected Pacific Tuanhuo spies, they will take our wings. The Space Force has a zero-tolerance policy within the zone," the copilot warned.

The pilot pointed at the flashing navigation monitor. "Well, I declared the emergency, and they are reading our telemetry. They know who we are and have a record of our malfunctions. They can't blast us out of existence for being assigned a piece of crap to fly… Well, then again, maybe they could. Anyway, it looks like we're just going to skirt the edge of the zone. We'll still be more than a hundred clicks from the rim of the crater. Probably just a good stiff talking to and a fine."

"*Papa Oscar Charlie Three-Niner, you are entering a no-fly zone. Change course immediately.*"

The copilot cycled the RCS power again. Nothing. He turned to the pilot and shook his head.

"Approach, our RCS is not responding. We will— What the—?!"

The ignition of the main engine pressed both men back into their seats.

"Junior, what did you do?!"

"I didn't do anything!"

"Well, somebody lit our candle." The pilot queued his comms. "Approach, did you somehow remote-start our engines?"

Silence.

"Approach, do you read?"

Silence.

They felt a tug to the side as the engine gimble adjusted their trajectory. The vector heading on the navigation display pivoted.

"Sir, now we are heading *directly* for the Tsiolkovsky Crater!" the copilot cried.

"Three-niner, this is Approach. Abort your engine burn. You're turning the wrong way."

"Approach, we did not initiate the burn. What are you guys doing?"

"Three-niner, this is Approach. Repeat: abort your engine burn."

The pilot knitted his brows at the copilot. "I don't think they can hear us. And it doesn't seem like they're remotely controlling our engines. What the hell is going on?!"

"Sir, we are transitioning the crater," the copilot said. He leaned over and looked out the side port. "Wow, that's a strange-looking communications dish they have... Why is the center glowing? And it's moving. I think it's tracking us!"

"Holy shit! We gotta get the hell outta here! Going to full burn." The pilot reached out for the engine power control. His fingers never made contact.

Silence.

"Papa Oscar Charlie Three-niner, this is Approach. We've lost you on radar. Respond. Three-niner, please respond."

Silence.

*

The helicopter banked hard to port to allow a better view of the ground on that side. The view for the passenger in the rear right seat was all that mattered. Below, the lush green jungle of an island paradise broke abruptly to a leveled 250-acre swath of fallen debris. Smoke was rising from several locations. The passenger studied the ground. He pushed his lower lip up in an expression of judgment. His perception of the progress here was important. He was the Boss.

The lead construction contractor grabbed a handhold on the ceiling to steady himself on the other side of the cabin and continued his update. With nervousness plain in his voice, he said over the headset, *"Umm, as you can see, the clearing for the golf course is well underway. And if you look to the right, the foundation is progressing quite well on the main building complex. We should be able to start on the lower walls within another week."*

"Why are you waiting a week? I want this built now! Boss Island has sold, and I want my new island ready immediately."

"Uhh, sir, yes. Umm, we need to allow the concrete some time to cure so that it reaches the proper strength." The contractor swallowed hard. His employer did not accept excuses, even if they were just the laws of physics at work.

The man dismissed the statement with a shake of his head. "I will expect you to make up that week somewhere else."

"Yes, sir. Yes, of course." It was the only reply that was acceptable. *"Sir, if your pilot circles back to the beach, we can see that the port is—"*

A new voice broke into their headsets. *"Master, I have a security update you might want to hear."*

The Boss turned away from the window and replied, "Wait, Jason. Pilot, land now."

The helicopter dropped quickly in the middle of the cleared acreage. As they came close to the ground, the pilot said over the headset, *"Sir, I don't have a clearing where I can touch down. The best I can do is hover here a few feet above this debris."*

"Fine." He pointed at the contractor. "You, out. Now."

A big man in a black suit that had been quietly sitting in the last rear seat jumped to his feet and slid the cabin door open. Wind whipped into the cabin as the contractor looked at his employer, his jaw slack, unable to speak.

The Boss shook his head and sighed. He raised one arm and snapped his fingers.

In one quick motion, the big man in the suit grabbed the contractor's arm with one hand, removed his headset with another, and tossed him out the door. After sliding the door closed, the black suit calmly sat down again without a word.

The Boss nodded his approval. "Pilot, let's go over to the seaport." He then addressed the artificial intelligence that had called him. "Alright, Jason. My headset only. What do I need to know?"

"Master, there has been an incident at the Tsiolkovsky Crater. A resupply freighter to the Dark Side Moon Base went off course and entered our restricted zone. The timing was unfortunate, as we were in a test, and the array was visible," the AI said.

"That's not good. What did they see? Where are the pilots now?" the Boss asked.

"They are no longer a concern. I took the liberty of altering the situation to our advantage. Time was critical, so I acted in a way I predicted you would approve," the AI said matter-of-factly.

"Explain," the Boss demanded, rubbing his chin. It was another pose he practiced, illustrating how thoughtful he could be.

"The trajectory of the freighter would probably not have afforded the pilots a view of the entire array, but there was still a chance they would see some of the classified structures and would thus be a security breach. As I stated, we were running a test, and the array was exposed. Considering the mass of their craft, I calculated that it would make a measurable differential in the test we were running. It would add a useful measurement. Since the ship was not ours and was not carrying any of our supplies, there would be no cost to us if it were destroyed. Considering this, I disabled their communications and took control of their craft. I directed it into our beam. I can report that as expected, the entire craft was annihilated in the collapsing isolation field of the micro black hole test run. The additional mass of the craft did add to the results, as expected. The test was a complete success, and the security breach was eliminated. I hope you are pleased."

The Boss relaxed back in his seat. He reached over to his glass of hundred-year-old bourbon and took a sip, contemplating the information. He finally said to his demented AI, "Jason, you have done well. Thank you for eliminating that security problem."

*

Please join my email list at **paulnowickibooks.com,** and I will let you know when Book 2 in the series - ***Dark Moon*** - is released!

ACKNOWLEDGMENTS

There's a tremendous difference between writing a story and creating a novel that readers will enjoy. The latter requires the craft of many talented people. Here are a few that helped make this book possible.

I'd like to first thank my developmental editor, Chersti Nieveen. Her brilliant guidance in plot, characters, settings, and the craft of writing itself transformed a very rough attempt at telling a story into the (hopefully) enjoyable novel you have in your hands. I will say that the task of writing a novel is difficult. Yet Chersti had a much more daunting challenge. She needed to transform a chemical engineer with writing skills tuned to technical specifications into an author that can convey something a tad more riveting. I know that the job is not done yet. But I believe she's made a great stride forward with me in this book. I look forward to continued growth opportunities with such a master at this craft.

You probably would not have even gotten to the words if it were not for Mark Thomas. I would be willing to bet that his design on the cover of this book caught your attention. That kind of visual creativity is amazing to me. I trusted him and now thank him for bringing a fresh, impactful cover, and for the pleasing layout inside.

Going back to the words, picking just the right ones is also an art. Thank you, Robin Fuller, for clarifying my sometimes-awkward sentences and putting the finesse of select words in just the right places. Your copy edits and proofreading put the polish on what otherwise might not shine.

It also takes more than just writing to have a successful publication. Readers won't know what they are missing if a book is not correctly marketed. For that, I wish to thank Heather Wallace for her expert guidance. In the maze of possibilities for book sales, she provided key elements and a focused, practical plan.

You might wonder, how did I assemble such a team? For that, I'd like to thank Reedsy.com. If you are an aspiring author or just need to find resources in the self-publishing community, this is a gold mine. You can find each of the professionals I mentioned above on the site, and I highly recommend each.

I'd also like to thank the friends and family that took the time to read rough drafts and provide critical feedback. In particular, thanks to Connie McClain and Cheryl Whaley. Your diligent reviews helped spark new ideas, making the story much better.

Finally, there's one person in all the world that without her support, this would not have been possible. She listened, discussed, encouraged, supported, and motivated me through literally years of effort to accomplish this goal. The model for the depth of the relationships between Alex and Zandra and Min and Lucas comes from the incredible luck I have in sharing my life with Lane. LYM. This is just one more reason why.

ABOUT THE AUTHOR

Paul L. Nowicki is a Chemical Engineer with a deep love of science, technology, and space. In addition to reading physics, space science, and robotics non-fiction texts, he loves the works of Issac Asimov, Frank Herbert, Dan Brown, and many others. Committed to life-long learning and exploring, he strives to help his readers think, grow, and enjoy new discoveries. He particularly likes to bridge areas of study to see the harmony and collaboration of the sciences. Balancing the cerebral with the physical, Paul can often be found contemplating the plot of his next work while training for an open-water swim or a triathlon.

PAULNOWICKIBOOKS.COM

Made in the USA
Columbia, SC
09 August 2023

21302005R00212